Praise for #1 *New York Times* and *USA TODAY* bestselling author Linda Lael Miller

"Linda Lael Miller creates vibrant characters and stories I defy you to forget."
—#1 *New York Times* bestselling author Debbie Macomber

"Miller's return to Parable is a charming story of love in its many forms.... [A] sweetly entertaining and alluring tale."
—*RT Book Reviews* on *Big Sky River*

"Miller's down-home, easy-to-read style keeps the plot moving, and she includes...likable characters, picturesque descriptions and some very sweet pets."
—*Publishers Weekly* on *Big Sky Country*

"A delightful addition to Miller's Big Sky series. This author has a way with a phrase that is nigh-on poetic... This story [is] especially entertaining."
—*RT Book Reviews* on *Big Sky Mountain*

"Miller's name is synonymous with the finest in Western romance."
—*RT Book Reviews*

"A passionate love too long denied drives the action in this multifaceted, emotionally rich reunion story that overflows with breathtaking sexual chemistry."
—*Library Journal* on *McKettricks of Texas: Tate*

"Miller's prose is smart, and her tough Eastwoodian cowboy cuts a sharp, unexpectedly funny figure in a classroom full of rambunctious frontier kids."
—*Publishers Weekly* on *The Man from Stone Creek*

LINDA LAEL
MILLER

BIG SKY
Wedding

HQN™

ISBN-13: 978-1-335-99396-0

Big Sky Wedding

Recycling programs
for this product may
not exist in your area.

This edition published by arrangement with Harlequin Books S.A.

For questions and comments about the quality of this book,
please contact us at CustomerService@Harlequin.com.

® and TM are trademarks of Harlequin Enterprises Limited or its
corporate affiliates. Trademarks indicated with ® are registered in the
United States Patent and Trademark Office, the Canadian Intellectual
Property Office and in other countries.

www.HQNBooks.com

Printed in U.S.A.

Dear Reader,

We're back in Three Trees and Parable, Montana, where the wedding bells just keep ringing!

Big Sky Wedding brings you the story of Brylee Parish—a heroine who hasn't been so lucky in love. Only interested in running her multimillion-dollar business, she has no plans to hear those bells for herself anytime soon. Especially not with Zane Sutton—the A-list actor and playboy who's come back to his rodeo roots.

Brylee's not convinced of his charm, or that he's home to stay. But Zane's not giving up. This hardheaded cowboy is determined to make her see she's meant to be his bride. Love is in the air in Big Sky Country, and I think we're all ready for these two to take a big whiff.

Happy trails, and thanks for the listen.

With love,

Linda Lael Miller

For Bob Massi, of Fox News fame,
a generous soul to say the least, and to his lovely wife,
Lynn, a genuine cowgirl, inside and out.

Thanks so much for your help
setting up my scholarship foundation
and for hosting the Master Mind dinner in Vegas!

BIG SKY
Wedding

CHAPTER ONE

THERE WAS, AS it happened, considerably more timber in and around the town of Three Trees, Montana, than the name would lead a person to believe, and that was fine with Zane Sutton. He'd had enough urban crowds, concrete, steel and pavement to last him a good long while—say, forever.

Now? Bring on the trees, the blue-and-purple mountains, the wild rivers and the crystal-clear lakes and streams.

For most of his adult life, Zane had taken each day as it came, content with whatever those twenty-four fleeting hours had to offer, rarely planning anything beyond entering the next rodeo, in the next town over, the next county over, the next state over. Everything else—relationships, off-season jobs, mostly driving, loading or unloading trucks, and even his accidental career in the movies—wound behind him, basically meaningless, a long trail of things that had seemed like a good idea at the time.

It wasn't that Zane had a lot of regrets. Recently, though, he'd begun thinking that, at thirty-four, he ought to choose a direction, stop carousing and start acting more like a grown-up. He'd wanted to light somewhere and stay put, see if he couldn't rustle himself up a life with some substance to it.

Now, under a June sun bright as polished brass, with his boots firmly planted on land that belonged to him, mortgage-free, Zane took off his hat, ran the fingers of one hand through his light brown hair, drew a deep, smog-free breath and tilted his head back to admire the cloudless stretch of blue overhead, arching from horizon to horizon. As far as he was concerned, no ceiling in any cathedral anywhere, no matter how grand, could rival that particular patch of big Montana sky.

The sight stirred a certain reverence inside him, and he drank it in whenever he remembered to look up. He felt the tenuous beginnings of restoration in the rocky, parched terrain of his soul, a nurturing process, like a good, steady rain at the end of a long drought.

He'd finally found a home on these acres upon acres of land, and he intended to take root, like the venerable oaks and pines, cottonwoods and firs, all around him. He'd bought Hangman's Bend Ranch as an investment a few years before, in a what-the-hell-why-not kind of mood, going halves with his hotshot investment tycoon brother, Landry, who was a different brand of drifter than Zane, but a drifter just the same.

Neither one of them had bothered to visit the place; they'd just signed the papers and gone on with their lives.

Although Zane couldn't speak for his brother, he

himself had been restless for a long time, since boyhood, for sure, but just a few days before, he'd had an epiphany of sorts. Nothing mystical, no blinding light knocking him flat, no angels singing; he'd simply realized he was damn good and fed up with the status quo, glamorous though it was. Acting in movies was all right—mostly easy work, if deadly boring a lot of the time—but lately it had been getting harder and harder to tell the difference between playing a part and the real deal.

The offshoot of all this sudden clarity was that Zane had found himself on a car lot in LA, trading in his supercharged European ride for a shiny silver pickup truck with an extended cab. In a spate of nonverbal ad-libbing, he'd driven the new truck to the nearest animal shelter, gone inside and adopted a dog, an unprepossessing critter, big and black with floppy ears. He dubbed the animal Slim, mainly because its ribs showed, a consequence of missing a few meals along the way. Leaving pretty much everything else he owned behind, Zane, with Slim, had headed north by northeast, stopping only to grab a couple of drive-through burgers here and there, gas up the truck and snooze a little in rest-stop parking lots.

They'd reached Hangman's Bend late the previous night, camping out in the unfurnished ranch house. That morning, Slim had taken a liking to a certain shady spot on the porch, so he'd stayed behind when Zane set out to get a good look at the wooded section of his land. He was on foot because his horse,

Blackjack, was still in transit from the California stables where he'd been boarding the gelding since his move to LA several years earlier.

He followed the meandering creek for a bit, enjoying the way it stitched its path through the woods like a wide strand of silver thread, clear and sun-sparkled and almost musical as it rolled over worn stones that resembled jewels under the water, coursed around primordial boulders and tree stumps, some of them petrified, on its way to wherever it was going.

Zane made a mental note to check a map later, when he got back to the house, because he liked knowing the facts about things, liked knowing exactly where he was, both literally and figuratively, but at the moment, he was in no great hurry to turn homeward. He was out to find the southern corner of his property, supposedly staked out and flagged.

At least eight feet wide—probably ten or twelve in some places—the stream would be difficult to cross, but eventually he came to a natural bridge, a line of six flat stones, small and fairly far apart. Still fit, even after living fancy from the day he signed that first film contract till he left Hollywood behind him, he figured he could make it to the other side without getting his boots wet, let alone taking a header into that glacier-chilled creek water.

With his arms outstretched for balance, the way he and Landry used to do when they walked the top rail of a fence as kids, he moved with relative ease, never setting both feet down on the same rock, since there wasn't room. When he reached the opposite bank, no longer concentrating so hard, he stopped short, startled by what amounted to a vision.

A wood nymph, dressed in faded blue jeans, battered boots and a pale green Western shirt, stood in the center of the small clearing just ahead, both arms wrapped around the trunk of a lone cottonwood tree. Her hair was brown and shiny and thick, just brushing her shoulders, and it caught the leaf-filtered light, threw it around like colored beams in a prism. Her head was tilted back slightly, her eyes closed, and the expression on her fine-boned face was downright blissful.

What the hell?

Zane could have watched her for hours—just looking at the woman gave him the same belly-clenching thrill he'd gotten in his bronc-riding days, in that moment before the chute gate swung open and the official eight-second countdown began—but, suddenly off his game, he took an unintended half step in her direction, a twig snapped under the sole of his boot and the moment was over.

The nymph's eyes were wide, hazel or maybe green or pale gray, and at the moment, seeing him, they were shooting fire. She backed away from the tree, and Zane noticed that her shirt was open and she was wearing a tank top underneath. She had great breasts, neither too big nor too small, and bits of bark clung to her clothes. As she glared at him, she let her arms drop briefly to her sides, then fisted up both hands and pressed the knuckles hard against her well-made hips. He knew she recognized him when he saw her jawbones lock together, and that struck a wistful note somewhere in the vicinity of his heart. He'd have given a lot, in that moment, to be his pre-Hollywood self, just another cowboy with a cocky grin, an attitude and a line or two.

"What are you doing here?" the sprite demanded, finding her voice at last. She took a few marching steps toward him, evidently thought better of coming too close and stopped while there was still a safe distance between them. Her emphasis on the word *you,* though slight, chapped Zane's hide a little, since, after all, *he* wasn't the one trespassing on somebody else's land, now was he?

"I live here," he replied reasonably, in his own good time, standing with his feet planted slightly apart and his arms folded. The irritation he'd felt was short-lived, quickly replaced by a sort of amused delight. Whoever the lady was, the fact that she might have rescued those clean but otherwise shabby clothes of hers from somebody's ragbag notwithstanding, she was most definitely a looker.

She didn't come any closer, nor did she say anything, but it did seem that she'd lost some of her zip.

And Zane couldn't resist adding, "Were you just hugging that tree, or was I imagining things?"

She blushed then, her cheeks going a glorious, peachy shade of pink. Her mouth was wide and expressive—inherently kissable. And, now that they weren't standing so far apart, he could see that her eyes were hazel. The color probably changed, de-

pending on what she was wearing, her present mood
or even the weather.

"I was doing a personal-growth exercise," she informed him stiffly, as though any idiot would have
known that without asking, and Zane could tell she
resented telling him even that much. She was proud
and stubborn, he decided, and competent at everything she did.

But what the devil was a "personal-growth exercise," exactly? Something she'd picked up watching
the Oprah Winfrey Network?

He walked slowly toward her, put out his hand for
a friendly shake, hoping she'd get the message that he
wasn't fixing to pounce. "Zane Sutton," he said, by
way of introduction.

She looked at his hand, then at his face, then ran
both palms down the thighs of her jeans before shaking the offered hand for a full nanosecond. "Brylee
Parrish." She gave up the name grudgingly, like it
was a state secret. "And I *knew* who you were without being told, thanks."

Clearly, Brylee Parrish was not impressed by star-
dom, his or anyone else's.

And he liked that, liked it a lot, because he'd never
been all that dazzled by the phenomenon himself,
based as it was on appearances instead of reality.

"Then you had an advantage," Zane replied mildly.

Brylee cocked her head to one side, studying him
skeptically. "You actors," she finally said, not quite
scoffing, but coming real close.

Zane chuckled. "I like to consider myself a *recovering* actor," he said.

"Please," she said, and though there was mockery in her tone, she wasn't being sarcastic. Her hands were still on her hips, though, and her chin still jutted out, and everything about her warned, *Stay back.*

"You don't think we can recover?"

She sighed, considering the question. "I'd say it's unlikely," she decided, at some length. "Show business people are—show business people."

"Which means?"

"You come and go. You buy or build ridiculously big, elaborate houses, not just in Montana, but in Colorado and New Mexico and Arizona, too—all over the West, in fact, basically scarring the landscape and squandering natural resources. You get on your high horse and boycott things—beef, for instance—thereby putting good people out of business after generations of honest effort. You get involved in local politics just long enough to cause lasting problems, maybe start a few bitter feuds among the local yokels, and then you sell your property to some *other* famous so-called idealist know-it-all and move merrily on to ruin yet another community."

Zane gave a long, low whistle of amused exclamation. There was some truth to her words—maybe a *lot* of it—but he didn't like being lumped in with all those well-meaning, but too-often fickle celebrities. Hello? He was a rodeo cowboy at heart, raised country by a woman who waited on tables for a living—the movie stuff had been thrust upon him, greatness not included. "Why not just come right out and say what you mean, instead of sugarcoating your opinions so I'll feel all warm and toasty and welcome?" he gibed.

Brylee sagged a little at the shoulders, as though sighing with her whole body. "Most of us were hoping you wouldn't show up," she said. "That you'd just let the ranch sit there, instead of hitting Three Trees like some kind of consumer storm trooper, putting in media rooms, restaurant-style kitchens the Food Channel would envy, tennis courts and indoor swimming pools—Olympic-size, of course."

"Gee," Zane answered dryly. "Thanks for the generous assessment. Seems like you're assuming a lot, though."

"Am I?"

"Yes," he said. "I believe you are. You don't know a damn thing about me, Ms. Parrish, except that I used to live and work in Hollywood. And I happen to *like* the house I'm in now, pretty much the way it is. Except, of course, for the antiquated plumbing, the dry-rot in some of the walls, the missing floorboards and the sagging roof. Oh, and I'll be glad when they switch the electricity on later today, I admit. But you'd probably view *any* improvements as conspicuous consumption, unless I miss my guess."

"You won't stay," Brylee said flatly, after giving his words due consideration and then, obviously, dismissing them. And him.

"You'll see," he replied, every bit as nettled as he was intrigued.

And that was the end of their first conversation. She went one way, and he went the other.

Hardly an encouraging start, in Zane's opinion, but a *start,* nonetheless.

Something—God knew what, but *something*—had just begun, he knew that by the strange tightening in his gut, and whatever it was, there would be no stopping it.

By the time he'd crossed the creek again, he was grinning.

BRYLEE STORMED BACK to her office/warehouse, just beyond Zane Sutton's property line, her emotions veering wildly between fury and chagrin. Of all the people in the world who might have caught her in the middle of a sincere effort to ground herself, via a method she'd learned in a motivational seminar held for her salespeople, why did *he* have to be the one?

Snidely, her German shepherd, greeted her with a wagging tail and a wide dog grin as she entered her building by the back door. Since it was Saturday, the office and warehouse workers weren't around, so she and her faithful companion had the place to themselves.

Normally, Brylee enjoyed the peace and quiet, and got a lot done because the usual weekday interruptions weren't a factor, but that day, she'd have liked to vent to someone. *Anyone.*

For the time being, Snidely would have to do.

"We have a new neighbor," she told the dog, who, as usual, seemed fascinated by every word she said, however unintelligible to the canine brain. "He's a smart aleck and he's arrogant as all get-out and darned if he isn't *way* too good-looking for his own good or anybody else's. Mine, for instance."

Brylee locked the back door behind her and headed across the wide concrete floor of the warehouse, toward her nondescript cubicle of an office. Snidely, the most devoted of dogs, naturally followed, tail still swishing back and forth, eyes hopeful.

"Not that we have anything to worry about," she ranted on, chattily, in a singsong voice. "Because, like most of his breed, Zane Sutton will move on to greener pastures, sooner rather than later, if we're lucky."

Why did that prospect give her a swift, sudden pang?

She stepped behind her desk—army surplus, no frills, like the rest of the furniture—and booted up her computer. Her company, Décor Galore, was an international operation; all over the world, hostesses held parties in their living rooms, directed by one of her salespeople—aka independent contractors—in return for a carefully chosen gift and discounts based on total sales, and invited their friends and relatives to buy wall hangings and figurines, prints of classic paintings, bouquets of exquisite silk flowers and every conceivable kind of candle.

When Brylee started Décor Galore, less than six years back, she'd been a one-woman sales force, setting up home parties, lugging card tables and two-page catalogs around the county, selling items she'd either imported or purchased wholesale, at a gift show. Now, she had over a thousand people signed up to sell and, except for the local discount store and the Native American casino just over the Idaho border, she employed more people than any other business owner in the area.

She'd expected this kind of success to be a lot more satisfying than it was, though. Not that she'd ever admitted as much to anybody, especially after she'd been so driven, worked so hard. Now, she had money enough to last for three lifetimes, never mind one.

She had a closet full of beautiful, custom-made clothes—which she never wore unless she was conducting management meetings or leading sales seminars. She could live anywhere she wanted, go anywhere she wanted. Over the past few years, she'd traveled to every continent on earth, staying in the best hotels and dining in the finest restaurants.

Perhaps more important, at least to her way of thinking, she'd helped put Three Trees, Montana, on the map. Her sales conventions brought hordes of people to the town—people with money to spend. She'd set up scholarships for high school seniors in both Parable and Three Trees, and, damn it, she'd made a real difference.

So why wasn't she happier than she was?

Frowning, no nearer to answering that question than before, Brylee went online, scanned reports filed by her district and regional sales managers—

the movers and shakers who headed up teams, drove company cars, took exotic all-expenses-paid vacations and, to a woman, earned at least twice as much money as the President of the United States, even in the current white-water economy. As usual, the managers were outdoing themselves, and doing their level best to outdo one another, too.

The result of all this constructive competition, which she actively encouraged? More money. Another record quarter. Why, if she chose to, she could take Décor Galore public, walk away and do whatever she wanted to for the rest of her life.

Unfortunately, she wasn't entirely sure what that would look like. Would she still be herself, or some woman she didn't know?

Once upon a time, engaged to Hutch Carmody, a rancher from over near the town of Parable, Brylee had thought she had it all figured out. A sort of romantic slam-dunk. She'd love Hutch, have his babies, content to be a wife and mother, albeit a very *rich* wife and mother, and grow old alongside her undeniably sexy man—that was the plan.

Of course, things hadn't worked out that way. Hutch had called off their wedding, and not without fanfare, either. Not ahead of time, when she could have saved face, sent back the gifts, canceled the five-tier cake, uninvited the guests, talked to the photographer. No, she'd been standing in the church entryway in her wedding dress, her arm looped through her brother Walker's, about to step into the next phase of her life, when her devastatingly handsome bridegroom had suddenly broken rank with his best man and the preacher, walked halfway down the aisle and said, "Hold it."

Remembering, Brylee squeezed her eyes shut for a moment. Even now, the humiliation was vivid, visceral, an actual ache in her middle, like the aftermath of a hard punch.

Oh, but time heals most wounds, or at least desensitizes them a little. She'd eventually made peace with Hutch—he was now married to the former Kendra Shepherd, also of Parable, and they had two beautiful children, with another on the way. They were happy, and Brylee certainly didn't begrudge them that.

Just the same, there were still times, like now, when she flashed back to the whole scene, and when that happened, it seemed the proverbial rug had been yanked out from under her feet all over again, leaving her breathless, figuratively wheeling her arms in a hopeless attempt to maintain her balance.

Once the internal roller-coastering stopped, she logged out of the program on her computer and rested her elbows on the edge of her desk, her face pressed into her palms. She wasn't going to get any more work done today, might as well accept it.

Snidely gave a small, sympathetic whimper and rested his muzzle on her thigh, lending what comfort he could.

Brylee lifted her face, gave a broken chuckle and tousled the dog's ears. "If I ever meet a man who's *half* as loyal as you are," she told Snidely, "I'd marry him in a heartbeat. Even if I have to hog-tie him first and then *drag* him to the altar."

Snidely whined again, as if in agreement.

Brylee bent and planted a smacking kiss on the top of his sleek, hairy head and pushed back her desk chair carefully, so she wouldn't run over one of Snidely's paws. "Let's go home," she said, with gentle resignation.

Home was the family ranch, Timber Creek, and she and Walker owned it jointly, though Walker ran the place and did most of the work involved. Brylee and Snidely lived in a spacious apartment, an add-on behind the kitchen, and those quarters had always suited her just fine, since she spent most of her time at Décor Galore, anyway.

Now, though, Walker had married his singing-cowgirl sweetheart, Casey Elder, whom Brylee loved dearly, as she loved their two teenage children, Clare and Shane, and their new baby, three-month-old Preston. Casey and Walker were adding on to the house—they planned on having several more children—and happy chaos reigned.

As hard as her brother and sister-in-law tried to include her in things, though, Brylee felt like a third wheel, even an intruder. Walker and Casey were still on their honeymoon, even after a year of marriage, and the way those two loved each other, they'd probably be perpetual newlyweds.

They needed privacy, family time.

Besides, Brylee was beginning to feel like a spinster aunt, the legendary old maid hovering on the fringes of everybody else's lives.

Was it wrong to want a home, a husband and children of her own? Or was she asking too much? After all, she *had* a fabulous business, one she'd built with her own two hands, and barring global financial catastrophe, money would never be a problem. Maybe it was just greedy to want more, especially when so many people didn't have enough of anything, including the basic necessities of life.

She was still debating the subject when she arrived at the home-place, minutes later, in her trusty-dusty SUV. Casey sat in the porch swing, gently rocking the little bundle that was Preston in her arms.

Casey was a fiery redhead, beautiful and talented, but in that moment she resembled nothing so much as a Renaissance woman in a painting by one of the masters, a vision in shades of titian and green.

She smiled as Brylee and Snidely got out of Brylee's rig.

"Come sit a minute," she said, in her soft Texas drawl, patting the cushion beside her. "Preston is sleeping, and I'm just sitting here thinking about how I'm the luckiest woman in the world."

Something of what she was feeling must have shown in Brylee's face as she approached, because Casey's expression changed for an instant, and there was a flicker of sadness in her eyes. "You know," she said fretfully, "it's a wonder I can walk right, what with one foot in my mouth at all times."

Brylee smiled, climbed the porch steps, joined

Casey and her sleeping nephew on the ancient swing. It had been there for as long as she could remember, that swing, the place where, as a little girl, she'd cried every time her mother left again. The place where she'd dreamed big dreams, and talked herself out of the blues a thousand times, especially after the breakup with Hutch.

Would she ever rock her own sleeping baby there, as Casey was doing now?

For some reason, Zane Sutton popped into her mind just then, and she must have blushed, because Casey narrowed her green eyes and studied her closely, missing little or nothing.

"What's up?" Casey asked. "And don't say 'nothing,' Brylee Parrish, because I wasn't born yesterday, and you look as though you might be coming down with a fever, you're so flushed. Your eyes are bright, too. Do you feel okay?"

Brylee sighed, feeling pretty lucky herself, albeit in a melancholy way. Maybe she didn't have a husband and a baby, but she had Casey, and Walker. Clare and Shane, too, and a lot of friends who genuinely cared about her.

"I just ran into Zane Sutton," she confessed. "In the woods, between Décor Galore headquarters and his ranch house. Technically, I guess I was trespassing."

Casey's eyes twinkled with amused mischief. "Is he pressing charges?" she asked.

Brylee laughed, but it was a ragged sound, brief and harsh against the tender flesh of her throat. "No," she answered, "I don't think so. But I still feel extra stupid."

Casey frowned affectionately, and the joy didn't leave her eyes. Baby Preston, cosseted inside a lightweight blue blanket, stirred against his mother's chest. "Now, why on earth would *you,* of all people, feel stupid? You're one of the smartest women I know, Brylee, and that's saying something, because I know some sharp ladies."

Remembering, Brylee blushed again. "I thought I was alone," she confided. "I was…hugging a tree."

"Oh, horrors," Casey teased. "Not that."

"He thinks I'm a flake, Casey."

"Did he say that?"

"Not in so many words, but still. *I was hugging a tree.* And I feel like an idiot."

"Why? Trees are excellent company. What's wrong with hugging them?"

"You're being deliberately kind," Brylee accused, but with affection. Casey was the sister she'd always yearned for, and one of her closest friends in the bargain.

"Excuse *me.*" Casey grinned. "I happen to like trees myself—they're good people, so to speak. I like to hug them when I get a chance. Unless there's a reporter hiding up there in the branches, anyway."

Brylee laughed, and this time, there was more sincerity in the sound. "I probably looked foolish, that's all," she said, moments later, when she was more reflective.

"And you care what Zane Sutton thinks of you?"

Casey challenged mildly. "That's interesting. Also, encouraging. Walker will be thrilled to hear it."

"Don't you dare tell my brother," Brylee said, knowing the request was hopeless. Casey and Walker didn't have secrets, not from each other, anyway.

"Are you attracted to Zane, Brylee?" Casey pressed, still smiling mysteriously. "Because if you are, I can get you a date with him. We're friends, Zane and I—we did a movie together once."

Sometimes, like now, Brylee forgot that her sister-in-law was a major celebrity, a famous Country-Western singer and sometime actress. She'd sung for kings, queens and presidents, racked up dozens of prestigious awards. Still, Casey was so salt-of-the-earth that it was easy to forget how well-known she actually was.

"The last thing in the world I want is a date with Zane Sutton," Brylee said. "So forget the whole idea, please."

Casey grinned. "Whatever you say," she replied, with a note of slyness in her tone that unnerved Brylee a little. "But Zane *is* an old friend of mine, like I said. So don't be surprised if he turns up at our supper table one night real soon."

"Give me advance notice," Brylee responded, "and I'll make other plans."

Casey laughed. "You're as stubborn as your brother, you know that? Maybe even more so, if such a thing is possible. Do I really need to point out how many women there are in this world who would fall

all over themselves for a chance to spend just one evening with Zane?"

"Invite one of them," Brylee suggested briskly, as Snidely curled up at her feet.

Casey handed over the baby, a warm little armful that filled Brylee's heart with love and a bittersweet yearning. "Hold your nephew for a few minutes," she said. "I've had to pee for the past half hour."

With that pithy—and typical—announcement, Casey disappeared into the house, headed for the nearest bathroom.

Brylee gathered her nephew close, lightly kissed the downy top of the baby's head and whispered, "Your mama is right. She *is* the luckiest woman in the world."

ZANE STOOD AT the edge of the woods for a few moments, solemnly surveying his "new" home—the long one-story stone house, with its big porch and many chimneys. The windows were tall and set deeply into their casings, the inside sills wide enough to sit on, and the place had a quietness about it that had charmed him, even when he'd only seen pictures on a real estate website. In person, the effect was even stronger.

Those were the things he *liked* about the place.

The things he didn't like were more numerous: as he'd told Brylee out there in the woods, the structure needed a lot of work. The grass in the yard was seriously overgrown, of course, after being neglected for so long, and speckled with dandelions and other less comely weeds. As for the picket fence, weathered and falling over here and there, well, a coat of paint wasn't going to do the trick.

Slim, spotting him, rose and ambled on over to offer a greeting.

"We've got our work cut out for us, boy," Zane said, shifting his gaze to the barn. It was large and, like the house, made of stone. *Unlike* the house, it was in remarkably good shape. Maybe he and Slim ought to move into one of the stalls, or the tack room, while the renovations were going on.

Just then, he heard an engine, and turned to see a van pulling in down by the teetering mailbox, sides emblazoned with the electric company's logo.

"Let there be light," Zane said dryly, but his mind was still on Brylee Parrish, and her blatant belief that he'd change this ranch into some kind of flashy showplace.

Tennis courts? Indoor swimming pools? *Media rooms?*

He hadn't even had those things in Tinseltown.

A nice condo? Sure. An expensive car that could almost fly? You got it.

By Hollywood standards, though, he'd lived modestly, and all he really wanted, even now, was a place to keep his horse—he'd missed being able to ride Blackjack whenever the mood struck him, back there in California, gotten downright lonesome for the animal's company, in fact. The barn, four sturdy walls to keep out the wind and a solid roof over his head completed his current aspirations, as far as living arrangements went.

The van pulled to a stop in what passed for a driveway, dust billowing up around the vehicle in a cloud, and a balding man with a belly and a clipboard got out, grinning from ear to ear.

Zane drummed up a grin of his own. Put out his hand, because that was what people did in the country whenever they met up, and he'd missed the ritual.

The new arrival—the stitching on the pocket of his work shirt said his name was *Albie*—shook Zane's hand enthusiastically. "When I told my wife I'd be turning on the juice for none other than Zane Sutton himself today," Albie beamed, "she made me promise to get your autograph and tell you she loved all your movies."

Zane's expression, though friendly, might have seemed a touch forced, to anyone more observant than Albie. "Thanks," he said, and left it at that.

CHAPTER TWO

Alone in her apartment, except for Snidely, of course, Brylee did weekend things. She washed and dried her hair, gave herself a pedicure as well as a manicure, and then a facial to round out the routine. She chose a red-and-white polka dot sundress to wear to church in the morning, gave it a few quick licks with the iron and hung it carefully from the hook on the inside of her closet door. She selected white sandals and a red handbag to complete the ensemble, setting those on the cushioned window seat in her bedroom, where they would be in plain sight.

Brylee liked to make her preparations well in advance, wherever preparation was humanly possible, which was most of the time. In her considered opinion, there were enough surprises in life, careening out of nowhere, blindsiding her just when she thought she had everything covered, so she preferred not to leave herself open to the unexpected, if given the smallest option.

She would have described herself as "organized," but she knew there were other definitions that might apply, like "obsessive" or even "anal."

Okay, so she was something of a control freak, she

thought, leaving her shabby-chic bedroom, with its distinctly female decor, for the living room.

Here, she'd chosen pegged wood floors instead of carpeting, and the fireplace was a wonder of blue and white, burgundy and gold, pale green and soft pink tiles, each one hand-painted. She'd colored and fired them all herself, using the kiln at her friend Doreen's ceramics studio in Three Trees, and just looking at them made her feel good. Some had tiny stars, swirls or checks, while others were plain, at least to Brylee, and the result was a kind of quasi-Moroccan magic.

She'd hooked the big scatter rugs, too, mostly on lonely winter nights, while a blaze flickered on the hearth, managing to pick up many of the colors from the tiles. The couch, love seat and two big armchairs were clad for spring and summer in beige cotton slip-covers with just the faintest impression of a small floral print; when fall rolled around, she'd switch them out, for either chocolate-brown or burgundy corduroy. Most everything else in the room rotated with the seasons, too—the art on the walls, the vases and the few figurines, even the picture frames on the mantelpiece, though the photos inside remained the same: Casey and Walker, beaming on their wedding day, Clare and Shane goofing off up at the lake, Snidely sporting a stars-and-stripes bandana in honor of Independence Day. Now, of course, she'd added a few prized shots of little Preston, as well.

Brylee believed change was a good thing—as

long as it was carefully planned and coordinated, of course.

She was aware of the irony of this viewpoint, naturally, but she'd built a thriving business on the concept of fresh décor, geared to the seasons, to the prevailing mood or to some favorite period in history. Hadn't Marie Antoinette had her spectacular bedroom at Versailles redecorated from floor to ceiling in honor of spring, summer, fall and winter?

Yeah, but look how she *ended up,* Brylee thought, making a rueful face.

Snidely stood in the kitchen doorway, looking back at her, tail wagging, his mouth stretched into a doggy grin. Fluent in Snidelyese, Brylee understood that he wanted his food bowl filled, or a treat, or both, if all his lucky stars were in the right places.

Brylee chuckled and slipped past him, executing a slight bow in the process. "Your wish is my command," she said, her royal mood, no doubt spawned by the brief reflection on the French court, lingering.

The kitchen, like the living room, was big, especially for an apartment. The appliances were state of the art and there was an island in the center of the space, complete with marble top and two stainless-steel sinks. She'd picked up the dining set cheap, at one of those unfinished furniture places, stained the wood dark maple and tiled the surface of the round table in much the same style as she had the fireplace.

A bouquet of perfect pink peonies, cut from the garden her great-grandmother had planted years ago and placed in an old green-glass canning jar, made a lovely centerpiece. Brylee paused to lean over and draw in their vague, peppery scent. They would be gone soon, these favorites, and she meant to enjoy them while she could. The lilacs, which grew in profusion all over the ranch house's huge yard, had already reached their full, fragrant purple-and-white glory and quietly vanished, along with the daffodils and tulips of early spring. There were still roses aplenty, rollicking beds of zinnias, clouds of colorful gerbera daisies, too, but Brylee missed the ones that had gone before, even as she enjoyed every new wave of color.

She *needed* flowers, the way she needed air and water; to her, they were sacred, a form of visual prayer.

A knock sounded at her back door just as she was setting Snidely's bowl of kibble on the floor. Glancing up, she saw her teenage niece, Clare, grinning in at her through the oval glass window.

"In!" Brylee called, grinning back.

Sixteen-year-old Clare, a younger version of her mother, Casey, was blessed with copper-bright hair that tumbled to her shoulders in carefully casual curls, bright green eyes and a quick mind, inclined toward kindness but with a mischievous bent. If she looked closely enough, Brylee could see Walker in the girl, too, and even a few hints of herself.

Not for the first time, she marveled that Walker and Casey had been able to keep their secret—that Walker had fathered both Clare and Shane—for so long.

"I think I've got a date," Clare confided, in a conspiratorial whisper, tossing a bottle-green glance in the direction of the inside door that led into the main part of the ranch house. Maybe she thought Casey was on the other side, with a glass pressed to her ear, eavesdropping.

If anyone *was* listening in, Brylee reflected, amused, it was more likely to be Clare's brother, fifteen-year-old Shane, with whom the child shared a sort of testy alliance—with an emphasis on the *testy* part. She and Walker had been that way, too, growing up, though they'd had each other's backs when necessary.

Brylee lifted her eyebrows and quirked her mouth up at the corners, in a way that said, "Go on, I'm listening," and opened the refrigerator door to take out a diet cola for each of them. As she understood prevailing parental policy, Clare wasn't *allowed* to go on one-couple car dates or to go out with the same boy more than three times in a row, and her parents practically ran background checks on anybody new to her circle of friends. Now, her twinkly air of secrecy indicated that something was up and, at the same time, belied any possibility that an executive exception had been made.

Clad in jeans, boots and a long-sleeved yellow T-shirt that made her hair flame beautifully around her deceptively angelic face, Clare hauled back a chair at the table and said a quiet thank-you when Brylee set the can of soda in front of her, along with a glass nearly filled with ice.

Brylee sat down opposite Clare and poured cola into her own glass of ice. And she waited.

"It's not even an actual *date*," Clare confided, blushing a little, shifting her gaze in Snidely's direction and smiling at his exuberant kibble crunching.

"How is a date 'not actually' a date?" Brylee ventured, but only after she'd taken a few leisurely sips of soda.

Clare gave a comical little wince. She'd basically grown up on the road, accompanying her famous mother and an extensive entourage on concert tours, and, though sheltered, overly so in Walker's opinion, she was bound to be more sophisticated than the average kid. She'd been all over the world, after all, and met kings, queens, presidents and potentates. In Parable County—which had its share of troubled teens, like any other community—it was a good bet that Clare was considerably more savvy than most of her contemporaries.

"I guess a date isn't really a date when it's part of a youth group field trip," the girl said sweetly, showing her dimples. "Mrs. Beaumont—Opal—and the reverend are chartering a bus and taking a whole bunch of us to Helena. We get to tour the capital buildings and stay overnight."

Brylee smiled. She knew Opal and her husband, the Reverend Walter Beaumont, quite well, even though their church was in Parable and she attended one in Three Trees. They were beyond responsible, and both of them took a keen interest in the teen members of their congregation or any other.

"I see," she said. "And this *non*date *is* a date—how?"

Suddenly, Clare looked shy, and her lovely eyes turned dreamy.

Uh-oh, Brylee thought. Up to that moment, she'd been ready to dismiss a nagging sense that something was off. Now, she guessed she'd been right to worry, if only a little.

"Luke and I are going to sit together on the bus, that's all," Clare said. "And just sort of, well, *hang out* while we're in Helena. You know, hold hands and stuff, when nobody's looking. Spend a little time alone together, if we get the chance."

"You don't know Opal Beaumont very well if you think she won't be keeping an eagle eye on every last one of you the whole time," Brylee pointed out, with a little smile. She'd had a lecture or two from Opal herself—mostly on the subject of finding herself a good man and settling down—and she knew the woman didn't miss much, if anything at all. A matchmaker extraordinaire, she was credited, sometimes indirectly, with jump-starting at least four relationships, all of which had led to marriage.

By the same token, though, Opal was devout, with the corresponding firm morals, and she'd guard her younger charges, girls *and* boys, with the ferocity of a tigress on the prowl.

Clare moved her slender shoulders in a semblance of a shrug. "Mom and Dad already said I could go," she said, cheeks pink.

"And they know it's an overnighter?" Brylee pressed, but gently.

Clare nodded. Then, guiltily, she added, "It's the sitting together and the holding hands and the alone-time part I didn't tell them about."

Holding her palms up and opening and closing the fingers of both hands, Brylee imitated the sound the refrigerator made when she hadn't shut the door all the way. "Danger," she said, smiling again. "If you had a clear conscience about this, my girl, you wouldn't feel any need to keep secrets from your folks. There's something you're not telling me."

Clare sighed and looked at Brylee through low-ered eyelashes, thick ones, like her mother's. Like her *father's,* for that matter. "Honestly, Aunt Brylee, Luke and I aren't planning to *do* anything."

"Then why sneak around?" Brylee challenged, though carefully. She'd been a teenager herself once, after all, and she knew coming on too strong would only cause more problems.

Clare answered with an uncomfortable question. "Are you going to tell Mom and Dad?"

Until several months after her parents' long over-due marriage, Clare had persisted in referring to Walker by his first name, angry that he and Casey had kept the truth about their parentage from her and her brother, and, for that matter, the rest of the world. Both Clare and Shane were indeed Walker's biologi-cal children, but calling him "Dad" was a relatively recent development, at least for Clare. Shane, already full of admiration for the man he'd always believed was a close family friend but *wished* was his father instead, had been thrilled when Casey and Walker broke the news.

Not so Clare.

"No," Brylee said, after due consideration. "I'm not going to tell your mom and dad anything. *You* are."

"They'll just make a big deal out of it—maybe they'll even say I can't go on the trip at all," Clare protested, temper rising. "Especially if they find out Luke's a little older than I am."

"How much older?" Brylee asked. Clare tended to be adventurous and impulsive, and she'd been in trouble for shoplifting at one point, too, so if Walker and Casey kept a closer watch on her than they might have otherwise, Brylee couldn't blame them.

"Nineteen," Clare replied in a small voice.

Oh, Lordy, Brylee thought, but she wouldn't allow herself to overreact. After all, she didn't want her niece to stop running things like this by her older and, presumably, wiser aunt.

"You like this Luke person a lot?" Brylee ventured.

"He's awesome," Clare said, softening visibly.

"And you met him at youth group?" *Tread carefully here, Aunt Brylee. This is treacherous ground.*

"I met him at a basketball game last fall," Clare replied. "He was a senior then, and now he's got a full-time job at the pulp mill. He joined the youth group just last week."

"Isn't nineteen a little old for youth group?"

"They let him in, didn't they?" Clare reasoned, developing an edge. "It's not as though he's a pervert or something."

Silently, Brylee counted to ten before asking, "What's he like? Who are his parents?"

Clare looked fitful now, squirming in her chair, her glass of cola forgotten on the table in front of her. "Now you sound like *them*," she complained. "It's not like we're going to a drive-in movie in his car, or anything like that."

"Luke's out of school, and he's too old for you," Brylee stated reasonably. Then she arched one eyebrow and added, "He has a car?"

"He has a driver's license," Clare said, defensive now.

Brylee sighed wearily. Nineteen, a job at the pulp mill and a driver's license but, five will get you ten, no car. And what *was* this Luke yahoo doing in youth group? If he wanted to be part of the church community, there were certainly other options....

She paused, remembering how it felt to be very young, like Clare. Brylee's own mother hadn't been around much when she was growing up, but her dad had paid close attention to her activities, along with Walker's. He'd been a real drag at times, wanting all the whys and wherefores, insisting on knowing all her friends, and she'd been rebellious, resentful—and very, very safe.

Now, she was getting a glimmer of what she must have put the poor man through, all because he wanted to protect her. She'd gone on to college, built a business and a good life for herself, while some of her friends, notably those whose parents were less vigilant, had fallen into all sorts of traps—unwanted pregnancies resulting in early and ill-fated marriages, lost scholarships, dead-end jobs.

In that moment, Brylee missed Barclay Parrish with a keen sharpness radiating from behind her breastbone, wished she'd thought to thank him for caring so much about her and Walker both, *before* he'd died, over a decade before, of a heart attack, instead of now.

"What's the hurry, Clare?" she asked softly. "You're only sixteen, remember?"

Seeing a protest forming in Clare's stormy eyes, Brylee held up both hands in a bid for silence so she could go on.

"I know you think you're mature for your age, and you probably are, actually, but trust me, you don't know as much about the world as you think you do." *Who does?*

"You don't trust me," Clare accused quietly. "Or Luke, either."

"I *do* trust you," Brylee said. "You're a very smart young lady with a good heart. But this Luke person? Maybe he's nice and maybe he isn't—I don't claim to know."

"He goes to youth group," Clare reminded Brylee, her tone indicating that that one fact made him a saint. "At *church*."

"Then why not tell your folks about him?" Brylee argued. She had to say what she thought here, but she was worried about alienating Clare. The girl had come to her in confidence, after all—would she clam up after this? Start keeping secrets that might be a lot more dangerous than plans to sit together on a bus and hold hands "and stuff" with a nineteen-year-old, whenever they weren't being watched? Which, admittedly, with Opal on the job, would be never.

On the other hand, though, somebody had dropped the ball at *some* point. Was it possible that Opal and Walter didn't know Luke's age?

"Are you going to tell them?" Clare countered. "Mom and Dad, I mean?"

Brylee sighed. "No," she said, wanting to strike a balance of some kind, keep the door of communication open between her and her brother's child and do the right thing, too. What if something bad happened? She'd never be able to forget that she could have prevented whatever it was just by speaking up.

"You promise?" Clare was wheedling now. No doubt about it, the kid was a charmer and, besides, Brylee loved her.

She gave another sigh, this one heavier than the last. "I promise."

"Good. Then I'm not telling Mom and Dad, either," Clare said, pushing back her chair and standing up.

Snidely, finished with his kibble ration, sat nearby, watching the girl with concern.

Brylee felt a headache coming on. All her adult life she'd dreamed about being a mother, but she was learning pretty quickly that it was no job for wimps.

She remained at the table, stomach churning, for several minutes after Clare left by the back door without saying another word—not even goodbye.

Finally, Brylee left her chair, rummaged through her purse for her cell phone and scrolled through her contact list. Coming to a certain name, she thumbed the connect button and waited.

She'd given her word that she wouldn't mention Clare and Luke's plans for the youth group trip—which might be entirely innocent, on Clare's side, but probably *weren't* on the guy's end—not to Walker and Casey, that is.

But she hadn't promised not to tell Opal.

THE ELECTRICITY WAS ON—cause for celebration from Zane's point of view. He and Slim made a quick trip to town in the truck, loaded up on grub and sundries, along with an inflatable mattress and some sheets, blankets and pillows, and promptly headed home again.

After doing some scrubbing, mostly focused on the kitchen, Zane boiled up half a package of hot dogs on the temperamental flat-top stove, and shared the meal with Slim. No sense in dirtying up a plate—he used a paper towel instead.

Easy cleanup, that was Zane's modus operandi. He wasn't an untidy person, especially when it came to personal grooming, but he'd depended on his California housekeeper, Cleopatra, for so long that he was spoiled.

Thinking of Cleo, Zane felt a pang of guilt. He'd

given her a nice severance package—meaning he'd left her a hefty check and a note before he and Slim headed north—but otherwise, he'd basically left her high and dry. A cranky black woman with a gift for cooking that was positively cosmic in scope, she normally didn't get along with "Hollywood types" to use her term. She'd made an exception for Zane, and now he'd gone off and left her to fend for herself in a crappy economy, in a place where integrity, like beauty, was often skin-deep.

Even in Glitzville, folks were feeling the pinch of tough times, cutting back on the luxuries. What would happen to Cleo, once she'd used up that last check, sizable though it had been?

Engaged in grim reflection, Zane was startled when his cell phone rang in the pocket of his shirt. Frowning—he was not a phone man—he checked the caller ID screen, saw his brother's name there and grimaced even as he answered. "Hello, Landry."

Landry, a year younger than Zane, gave credence to the changeling theory, since the two of them were so different that it was hard to believe they shared the same genetic makeup.

"We have a problem," Landry announced.

Zane closed his eyes briefly, recovered enough to open them again and retort, "'We'? It just so happens things are going pretty well at the moment, out here."

"Congratulations," Landry all but growled. "But *we* still have a problem, and his name is Nash."

Nash. Their twelve-year-old half brother, the one neither of them really knew. Nash was the product of one of their feckless father's many romantic liaisons—the boy's mother, if Zane recalled correctly, was a former flight attendant named Barbara, who had a penchant for belly dancing, an overactive libido and a running start on a serious drinking problem. A creative baby-namer—"Zane," for instance, and "Landry"—Jess Sutton had never been much for hands-on parenting. He liked to *make* kids, give them names and then move on, leaving their moms to raise them however they saw fit.

"I'm listening," Zane said, after suppressing a sigh that seemed deeper than the well outside, the one rumbling up sluggish but clean supplies of water, now that the electricity was turned on and the pump actually worked.

"Dad just dropped him off here," Landry said, in an exaggerated whisper that led Zane to believe the boy was within earshot and, therefore, might overhear. "I can't take care of a kid, Zane. I've got a business meeting in Berlin tomorrow—get that? *tomorrow*—and Susan and I are on the outs. In fact, she's leaving." A pause. "Not that she'd be willing to help out, anyhow."

Landry's love life was only slightly less of a train wreck than Zane's own had been, an uncomfortable indication that they'd inherited more from their old daddy than good teeth, fast reflexes and a passion for risk-taking. "Again?" he asked, letting a note of sarcasm slip into his voice. Susan and Landry had been married—and divorced—twice, at last count.

Their marriage reminded Zane of a dizzying carnival ride; somebody was always getting on, or off.

Landry drew in a breath and let it out in a huff. Even though he was the younger of the two, he regarded himself as the responsible, reliable brother, considered Zane a loose cannon with more luck than sense. "I didn't call so we could discuss my personal life," Landry bit out. "The kid—Nash—needs somewhere to stay. Pronto. I was about to put him on the next flight to L.A. when it occurred to me that you might be on location someplace, pulling down ludicrous amounts of money for doing nothing special. Where are you?"

"I'm not in L.A.," Zane said evenly. "I'm on the ranch in Montana—you know, the one we bought together a few years back, pretty much just for the hell of it?"

"What the devil are you doing *there?*" Landry demanded. It didn't seem to bother him that he was pushing the envelope, given that he obviously planned on asking a favor.

A greenhorn through and through, Landry wore custom-made three-piece suits, lived in a massive penthouse condo in Chicago, employed a chauffeur and even a *butler,* which was just plain embarrassing, if you asked Zane, which, of course, nobody had. A complete stranger to horses and every other aspect of country life, Landry ponied up the money to pay for his half of the ranch as some kind of tax maneuver.

"I got tired of, well, just about everything," Zane admitted, suddenly weary. The inflatable bed hadn't held out much appeal earlier, especially since it was womanless, but by then, he'd started to think he could sleep for days, if not decades. "So I left."

"Whatever." Landry sighed. Dealing with Zane was an ordeal for him, what with his blatant superiority and all. "You have to take Nash," he said. "Dad dumped him on me—evidently our dear father has to lay low for a few months until his poker buddies calm down enough to change their minds about having his knees broken. It's you or foster care, and I think the poor kid's had his fill of that already."

"What about Barbara?" Zane asked moderately. "You remember her? Nash's mother?"

"She's out of the picture," Landry said. His tone was flat, matter-of-fact.

Their own mother, an early casualty of Jess Sutton's incomprehensible charm, had died a few years before of a lingering illness. Disagreements about how to care for Maddie Rose at the end remained a major sore spot between the two brothers.

"How so? Is Barbara sick? Dead?"

"She's somewhere in India or Pakistan—one of those third-world countries—on some kind of *spiritual quest*," Landry replied with disdain. "That's Dad's story, anyway. Suffice it to say, Barbara isn't exactly a contender for Mother of the Year."

"And this is my problem because…?" Zane asked, stalling. He couldn't turn his back on his own flesh and blood and Landry knew that, damn him. Still, it was an imposition, a responsibility he wasn't prepared to take on at this juncture, when his whole life was in transition.

"Because Nash is your brother," Landry said, with extreme patience.

"He's also yours," Zane pointed out. He was already wondering what a person *said* to a twelve-year-old kid who'd probably been shuffled between the homes of strangers, their dad's distant relations, the girlfriend du jour and then back through the whole cycle again. Repeatedly.

"If I don't make this meeting in Berlin," Landry replied, "I could lose one of my most important accounts."

"Sucks to be you," Zane responded mildly. "Who's been raising this child all this time, anyway?"

"My understanding," Landry supplied stiffly, "is that he's been knocking around the country with Dad. Recently, that is." His voice softened a little. "He's not a bad kid, Zane. And he didn't have the kind of mom who would go to bat for him, like ours did for us."

In that moment, Zane could see his late mother—an inveterate optimist, their Maddie Rose—in such vivid detail that she might as well have been standing right there in his kitchen. She'd waited tables for a living, and the three of them had lived out of her beat-up old station wagon more than once, when she was between waitressing gigs, but life had been good with her, despite all the Salvation Army Christmases and secondhand school clothes and food-bank vittles. She'd had a way of "reframing" a situation—

her word—so that moving on, when a job ended or a romance went sour, always seemed like an exciting adventure instead of the grinding hardship it usually was. Even when it involved considerable sacrifice on her part, Maddie Rose always made sure they stayed put when school was in session, come hell or high water, and she'd checked their homework and encouraged them to read library books and made them say grace, too.

As always, he wished Maddie Rose had lived to see her elder son become something more than a rodeo bum, wished he could have set her up in a good house and made sure she never lacked for anything again, but, too often, life didn't work that way.

She'd died in a hospital somewhere in rural South Dakota, a charity case, suffering from an advanced case of leukemia, before Zane could so much as cash his first Hollywood paycheck, let alone provide for her the way he would have done, given the chance.

Although he and Landry usually avoided the whole topic of Maddie Rose's death, it lay raw between them, all right, like a wound deep enough to rub the skin away, and, even now, it hurt.

"Send Nash to Missoula," Zane heard himself say. "Let me know when he's getting in, and I'll be there to pick him up."

"Good." Landry almost murmured the word. "Good."

It wasn't a thank-you, but it would have to do.

Zane didn't ring off with a goodbye. He simply hit the end call button and sent his phone skittering across the tabletop, causing Slim to perk up his mismatched ears and straighten his knobby spine.

Zane grinned, then ruffled the hide on the dog's back to reassure him. "You're not in any kind of trouble, boy," he told Slim. Then, with a philosophical sigh, he added, "And that makes one of us."

THE NEXT AFTERNOON, Zane was late getting to the airport in Missoula, and it was easy to spot Nash, since the kid was standing all by himself, next to the luggage carousel, a battered green duffel bag at his feet. Earbuds piped music into his head, and his blondish-brown hair stood up in spikes, as though he'd been accidentally electrified. Seeing Zane, he scowled in recognition and dispensed with whatever tunes he'd been listening to while he waited.

"Montana sucks," Nash said sullenly, and without preamble. "I thought I was going to Hollywood, and now I find out I'm stuck *here*."

"Life is hard," Zane replied, smoothly casual, "and then you die."

Nash rolled cornflower-blue eyes. His clothes were a sorry collection of too-big jeans, cut off at the knees and showing a good bit of his boxers, sneakers with no laces, a ragged T-shirt of indeterminate color and a pilled hoodie enlivened by a skull-and-crossbones pattern in neon green. "Thanks for the 411," he drawled, making it plain he'd already mastered contempt, even before hitting his teens. "I probably couldn't have figured that on my own."

Zane sighed inwardly and reminded himself to be

patient. Maddie Rose had seen that he and Landry had it good, in comparison with most poor kids, but Nash had been through the proverbial wringer.

"You hungry?" he asked the boy, stooping to pick up the duffel bag by its frayed and grubby handle.

"I'm *always* hungry," Nash replied, without a shred of humor. "Just ask Dad. I'm a royal pain in the ass, wanting to eat at least once a day, no matter what. Too bad the kind of motels he could afford didn't have room service." A beat passed. "I was lucky to get a bed."

Zane felt a clenching sensation—sympathy—but he didn't let it show. He remembered all too well how poverty ground away at a person's pride, how he'd hated it when people felt sorry for him and Landry. "Let's get out of here," he said. "We'll find you some food once we've left the airport."

Nash said nothing. He simply put his earbuds back in and rocked to some private serenade, ambling alongside Zane as they left the terminal and made their way to the outdoor parking area, where the truck waited.

Slim was there, pressing his nose against a partially lowered window as they approached. He gave a happy yelp of welcome and scrabbled to and fro across the backseat, unable to contain his excitement.

"You have a dog?" Nash asked, opening up his ears again and almost, but not quite, smiling.

"His name is Slim." Zane confirmed the obvious with a nod, as he opened the truck's tailgate and tossed the duffel bag inside. "Knows a thing or two about hard luck, I guess."

"Then we ought to get along," Nash replied, sounding far too world-weary for a twelve-year-old. "The dog and me, that is."

CHAPTER THREE

NASH LOOKED AROUND the ranch house kitchen with a discerning eye—surprisingly discerning, in fact, for somebody in a skull-and-crossbones hoodie, with six inches of underwear showing above his belt line.

"Man," he said, quickly evaluating the long-neglected space surrounding them. "This place is *seriously* underwhelming."

"Kind of like your manners," Zane retorted lightly, but without rancor. In the few hours he'd spent with this young half brother of his, he'd begun to understand the kid a little better. Nash probably thought he was doing a good job of hiding what he felt, but he was scared all right, jumpy as a cat in a room full of cleated boots. Ready to be shunted off at a moment's notice to the next place where he wouldn't fit in, and determined not to let anybody know he gave a damn when it happened. He'd consumed three cheeseburgers, a double order of curly fries and a milk shake when they stopped for lunch on the outskirts of Missoula, prompting Zane to wonder if Landry had fed him a meal or two before hustling him on board the first westbound plane with an available seat.

And then there were those god-awful clothes.

Going by appearances, his duds being rumpled, worn-out and not recently washed, the kid might have made the whole trip in the cargo hold instead of the main cabin. Landry, the multimillionaire investment whiz, couldn't have sprung for a few pairs of jeans and some T-shirts?

Most likely, Zane thought, with a stifled sigh, his brother hadn't wanted to be bothered with anything so mundane as taking the boy to the nearest mall and outfitting him with the basics. After all, he had to get to *Berlin,* where he had an Important Meeting.

The message in that was obvious: the *meeting* was important, but Nash wasn't. Susan, the soon-to-be ex-wife—again—had probably come to the same conclusion about her own place in Landry's high-octane life.

Zane seethed a little, feeling self-righteous—until he recalled that, up until Landry's phone call, he couldn't have said where Nash was, what he was doing, who he was with. He hadn't kept any better track of his kid brother than Landry had.

The boy was blood. How had he been able to ignore that fact for so long?

"Where do I put my stuff?" Nash asked, breaking into Zane's rueful thoughts, having reclaimed the duffel bag when they got out of the truck a few minutes before. "By the back door, maybe?"

"You plan on making a quick getaway?" Zane countered evenly, as he refilled Slim's water bowl and set it on the floor so the thirsty dog could drink.

Nash responded with a mocking grin. "You never

know," he said. He made a hitchhiking motion with one thumb. "I'm a travelin' man."

"You're a *kid,*" Zane pointed out, after taking a few seconds to rule out the snarky answers that came to mind ahead of that one. Leaning back against the sink, he folded his arms while Slim lapped loudly from the bowl of water. "And you ought to know, better than most, how mean the big world out there can really be."

Nash didn't bat an eyelash; he was already a hard case—at *twelve,* for God's sake. "But I'm safe now, right?" he drawled, dripping sarcasm. "No worries. You're going to *give me a home,* right here on the range."

A familiar desire to find Jess Sutton and throttle the man with his bare hands washed over Zane, but it was quickly displaced by a flash of admiration for Nash. The kid might be a smart-ass, but he had a quicksilver brain.

"Where, as it happens," Zane responded, playing along, "the buffalo don't roam."

Nash rolled his eyes, then his shoulders. He was on the small side, and skinny and raw-boned, but he'd match Zane's six-foot height one day in the not-too-distant future, maybe even exceed it.

"Can I take a look around?" the boy asked, sounding glum. Obviously, he wasn't expecting much.

"Be my guest," Zane answered. "Pick out a bedroom while you're at it. There are plenty to choose from."

Offering no comment, Nash wandered off to explore the premises. He was gone for a while, Slim trailing faithfully after him, which gave Zane a chance to assess the grub situation, peering into the fridge, opening and closing cupboard doors. Despite yesterday's shopping trip in Three Trees, it wasn't a pretty picture.

"Don't you have any furniture?" Nash asked, upon his return.

Zane shook his head. His household goods were still in L.A., in his condo, and he already knew there was no point in having all that expensive junk trucked to Montana. None of it would look right here—especially his bed. It was a gigantic, mirrored thing, a monument to unbridled hedonism, lacking only notches on one of the pillar-size posts to tally his conquests.

He *would* miss the water-filled mattress, though.

All the other pieces—chairs and couches, a dining room set, a TV so big it took up a whole wall— were decorator-approved and half again too fancy for a run-down stone ranch house. Like the bed, they'd be so ostentatious as to be an embarrassment.

Not that he'd be showing off his sleeping quarters anytime soon, of course.

When an image of Brylee Parrish seeped into his mind like smoke, he nearly laughed out loud. *As if,* he thought. She'd probably already written him off as a hedonistic, interfering *movie star,* but even if she hadn't, she *would* once she checked all the online gossip sites and found his name on practically every one of them.

"Just moved here myself," he finally replied, feeling a distinct lack of nostalgia for the old place back in L.A., and the fast-paced life that went with it. "I haven't had time to make a plan, let alone shop for a houseful of stuff." By then, he was sitting at the card table in the center of the kitchen, with his laptop open. It was time to do a little research on child-rearing. "Anyway, there's a lot to be done around the place, as you've probably noticed."

Nash dragged back the second folding chair, which completed the dining ensemble, and fell to the seat with a sigh. "It's not so bad," he said, taking Zane by surprise. Had the kid actually said something civil? "Anyway, beggars can't be choosers. That's what my mom always tells me. When I can find her, that is."

"You're not a beggar, Nash," Zane said, looking up from the computer screen, which indicated that he had a shitload of emails waiting for him. A daunting prospect, since at least eight of them were from his ex-wife, Tiffany. *Tiffany. What had he been thinking, marrying that woman-child?* Maybe he'd give her the monumental water bed; God knew, she'd get plenty of use out of it, and maybe even sleep once in a while. "You've had a run of hard luck, that's all. It happens to the best of us."

"With me, it's a lifestyle," Nash said, leaning back indolently, though his eyes were alert for any sign that trouble might be about to land on him like a cougar dropping out of a tree.

"You could look at it that way," Zane replied, "if

you were inclined to feel sorry for yourself. You've had it tough, but so have lots of other people. What matters is where you go from here, what you do next. When you get right down to it, it seems to me, almost everything hinges on what attitude you decide to take."

Nash widened his eyes, and his mouth had a scornful set to it. "What are you—some kind of rah-rah motivational speaker now?"

"I'm your brother. You can keep up the act for as long as you want, but it's basically a waste of energy, because, trust me, I can outlast you." Zane paused, letting his words sink in. "Also, I know a thing or two about having a no-account for a father myself, as it happens. And that means I understand you better than you think I do."

Nash's face, so like his own and, for that matter, like Landry's, too, hardened in all its planes and angles. Once the boy grew into himself, he'd be a man to be reckoned with.

"Dad's not a no-account," he retorted coldly.

"You have a right to your opinion," Zane answered. "And I have a right to mine."

Nash slammed one palm down hard on top of the rickety table, causing the dog to jump in alarm. "What's *that* supposed to mean?" he demanded.

"Exactly what it sounded like it meant—you have a right to your opinion. Mine happens to differ a little, it would seem. And don't scare the dog again— he's been through enough as it is."

"Dad's made a few mistakes, but he's not a bum,"

Nash said, but he lacked conviction. The sidelong look he gave Slim was genuinely remorseful. "Sorry, boy," he muttered, under his breath.

"He is what he is." Zane spoke in a moderate tone, but no power on earth could have gotten him to make Jess Sutton out to be more than he was. The man was good-looking, charming to the max and absolutely useless in the real world, an overage Peter Pan.

"You sound just like Landry," Nash accused, flaring up again. "Both of you are full of yourselves, the high and mighty *movie star* and Mr. Moneybags. I couldn't believe the things Landry said, right to Dad's face!"

"Guess that's better than saying them behind his back," Zane observed diplomatically. "Maybe you had a different experience with the old man than Landry and I did, growing up. We saw him every few years, when he needed a couch to sleep on between wives and girlfriends. When he did have a few bucks in his pocket, it was only because one of his scams had finally panned out, and he sure as hell never shared it with Mom."

Nash sat stony-faced and still. They were at a standoff, obviously, neither one of them willing to take back anything they'd said, though Zane, for his part, was beginning to wish that he'd kept his opinions to himself. If it comforted the kid to make-believe the old man had his best interests at heart, well, where was the harm in that?

Nash scowled on, two bright patches burning on

his otherwise pale cheeks. Zane didn't look away, nor did he speak.

"He could have changed," Nash finally said. "Dad, I mean."

"Yeah," Zane agreed, after unlocking his jaw-bones so he could open his mouth at all. "Or not."

Nash leaned forward, both hands flat on the ta-bletop now, fingers splayed. At least he didn't make a loud noise or a fast move and scare the dog again.

"Look," the kid ground out, eyes narrowed, breath quick and shallow, "I didn't *ask* to come here, to But-thole Creek or whatever this place is called, all right? I didn't ask to be dumped off on Landry's doorstep, either. So don't go thinking I'm some poor orphan who needs to be preached at, okay?"

"Far be it from me to preach," Zane said calmly.

Nash glared even harder. "In the movies, you al-ways play an easygoing cowboy with a slow grin and a fast draw. Now, all of a sudden, you're talking like some college professor or something."

"That first part," Zane responded, "is called 'act-ing.' It was my job."

"Did you go to college?" From Nash's tone, he might have been asking, *Did you rob a bank—mug an old lady—kick a helpless animal?*

"Now and then," Zane replied. "Mostly, though, I just read a lot."

There was another pause. Then, "You think you're better than Dad—better than me." Nash Sutton was obstinate to the core—just like both his older brothers.

"There's only one man I try to be better than, and

that's the one I was last week, last month or last year. It's a simple creed, but it serves me well, most of the time." Privately, Zane wondered where those lofty words had come from and, at the same time, realized they were true. He wanted to be himself, not the movie cowboy with the smooth lines, too much money and the steady supply of silicone-enhanced women, Tiffany included.

It was time to get real, damn it.

Another long silence stretched between them, broken when Nash finally asked, "Am I going to have to sleep on the floor?"

Zane grinned, aware that the tension had eased up a little and thus felt relieved. Although he could be pretty hardheaded—bull-stubborn, his mom would have said—he wasn't unreasonable. He liked people and preferred to get along with them when he could. Especially when they were kin—like Nash.

"No," he said. "You won't have to sleep on the floor. We'll head into town and buy a couple of decent beds in a little while—with luck, we'll be able to haul them home in the back of the truck and set them up right away. If that plan doesn't work out for some reason, you can use the air mattress in the meantime."

"Beds," Nash ruminated. He seemed wistful now, but that might be an act. "With sheets and blankets and pillows and everything?"

Where in hell had this kid been sleeping? Zane wondered that and many other things. "With sheets and blankets and everything," he confirmed, hoping the boy didn't notice the slight catch in his voice.

Nash's grin flashed, Landry-like. *Zane*-like.

There was certainly no question of his paternity. He was Jess Sutton's kid, all right, full of bravado and brains and smart-ass attitudes. Were there other siblings out there? Zane wondered, as he often did. Did he and Landry and Nash have sisters and brothers they knew nothing about?

It seemed more than possible.

"Let's go, then," Nash said. He actually seemed eager now.

Zane, not at all sure he wasn't being shined on, was unaccustomed to power-shopping—or any shopping at all, really, since Cleo or some assistant had done most of that for him.

Until now.

The furniture store in Three Trees agreed to deliver the beds, mattresses and box springs, dressers and bureaus later that same day, which was a good thing, because by the time he and Nash were done filling several carts at the big discount store out on the highway, there wasn't an inch of space left in the back of Zane's truck.

Even with the two of them working, it took twenty minutes just to carry all the bags and boxes inside and pile them in the far corner of the kitchen to be dispersed to other parts of the house later on.

Nash, evidently benefiting from the heavy dose of retail therapy, rustled through the loot until he found a towel, a bottle of liquid soap, new jeans, a long-sleeved gray sweatshirt, socks and underwear that actually fit him and, finally, boots.

He disappeared into a nearby bathroom—there were several in the house, but the others were in various states of rust and wreckage—and, soon after, Zane heard the shower running.

Nash was in there so long that Zane had time to log back on to his laptop and wade through his emails. He skipped over the ones from Tiffany, replied with regrets to half a dozen party invitations and deleted the obvious sales pitches. There were three missives from his agent, Sam Blake, each one more exasperated than the last. "Damn it," Sam had written, with a lot of caps and punctuation marks, he had "the role of a lifetime" lined up for Zane. All he had to do was get off this stupid hick-kick he was on, whatever it was, hustle back to L.A. and sign on the bottom line.

Zane sighed, decided to reply later and opened the last of the lineup, a virtual ear-boxing from Cleopatra Livingston, his former housekeeper. Where the dickens did he think she was going to find another job, she demanded, at her age, and in a tanked economy, no less. And what in *blazes* gave him the idea that he could get by without her? Who was going to cook his meals and wash and iron his shirts? When she wasn't around, she further declared, he tended to be careless about things like that.

Grinning slightly, Zane picked up his phone again. Keyed in Cleo's number. She didn't carry a cell, so he'd have to reach her at home. If she didn't answer—a possibility that had its merits, given the mood she'd been in when she wrote that email— he'd leave a message.

And say what? That he was sorry? That he'd send more money? That she could go on living in his condo until he got around to selling it? Only if he wanted to piss her off all over again by making her feel like a charity project.

"It's about damn time you called me!" Cleo boomed into her receiver, probably one of those bulky, old-fashioned ones, broad-jumping right over "howdy" and straight into giving him seven kinds of hell.

"I left a note," Zane said. Now *there* was a half-assed explanation.

"Big fat deal," Cleo scoffed furiously. "I work my fingers to the bone for you for almost four years, Zane Sutton, years I could have spent looking after somebody who *appreciated* me, mind you, and one fine day, you just go off on your merry way without a word of farewell?"

Reminding her about the note would be a mistake, so he didn't. While the gears clicked away in his head, he focused on Slim, visible through the arched doorway opening onto the hall, waiting for Nash to come out of the bathroom. The dog's patience was rewarded when the kid suddenly emerged, preceded by billows of steam.

Zane smiled. "Cleo," he said, "I have missed your sweet and gentle ways."

"I'll sweet-and-gentle you," Cleo shot back. "With a horsewhip!"

He laughed. "You know," he teased, "you sound a little like a woman scorned."

She made a disgruntled sound. "As if I'd ever

throw in with the likes of you, cowboy, even if I wasn't a good thirty years older than you are." A pause. "Darn it, I'm not *ready* to retire. I'm unlucky at bingo and I don't knit or crochet. And, anyways, I can't sleep nights, for worrying that you're living on fast food and wearing wrinkled shirts in public."

Nash came through the archway and headed for the fridge, looking like a different kid in his jeans, boots and sweatshirt. Except for the hair, of course—it looked as though he'd been cutting it himself lately, with nail scissors. Or maybe hedge clippers.

"Are you listening to me, Zane Sutton?" Cleo demanded, when he failed to reply to her previous diatribe.

"I'm listening," Zane said.

"Where are you?" Cleo wanted to know. *Would* know, by God, if she had to crawl through the telephone system and *drag* the answer out of him.

"I'm on my ranch," he said. "Outside Three Trees, Montana."

"Well, you get me a plane ticket for day after tomorrow," Cleo commanded. "I need some time to pack and say goodbye to folks. Make it one way, this ticket, and I had *better* be sitting in first class, too, after all you put me through. And don't you stick me in row one, neither. I need to be able to get to my purse when I want it, and in a bulkhead seat, they make you put it in the overhead." She made another huffy sound. "My blood pressure is through the roof," she added.

Importing Cleo wasn't a bad idea, Zane thought.

The lady might be prickly sometimes, but she could cook and clean, and she'd be the ideal person to oversee the forthcoming renovations, too.

Plus, he'd been telling the truth when he said he missed her.

"You'd do that?" he asked, moved. "Leave L.A. for Montana? It's real rural out here, Cleo. And we're roughing it—not much furniture to speak of and plenty of things in need of repair." *Or replacement.*

"Sure I would," Cleo answered briskly. "*You* might be used to living luxuriously, Mr. Movie Star, but I'm no stranger to doing without, let me tell you. Didn't I raise four kids by the sweat of my brow, with no man to help out? And didn't I do that in a part of the city a lot of folks would be afraid to set foot in, even in broad daylight?"

She was laying it on thick, Zane knew. The four kids she'd raised were all well-educated and prosperous professionals now, scattered all over the country and contributing generously to their mother's bank account. And Cleo had been living in staff quarters in his condo since she came to work for him, so it wasn't as though she took buses to and from the ghetto every day, dodging bullets as a matter of course.

"All right," Zane heard himself say. "I'll book your flight for the day after tomorrow and email you the itinerary."

"Good." Cleo huffed out the word. "Get me out of LAX bright and early. And there's one other thing, too."

"What's that?" Zane asked, a grin quirking at one

corner of his mouth. Nash, meanwhile, peeled a banana and stuck half of it into his mouth, so both cheeks bulged.

"Who's 'we'?" Cleo asked bluntly.

"Huh?"

"You said '*we're* roughing it.' Plural. Have you taken up with some pretty cowgirl? Is *that* what this is all about, you suddenly wanting your housekeeper back and all? Because there's somebody you want to impress?"

Zane laughed. He hadn't "taken up" with anybody, though he did want to get to know Brylee Parrish a little better. Okay, a *lot* better. "It's just me, my kid brother and my dog, Slim," he replied. "And I'm warning you, Cleo—we're a motley crew."

"You mean Landry's there with you? Did he split up with that crazy wife of his again?"

"No," Zane said, feeling no particular need to comment on Landry's marital situation. "I mean Nash."

"Who's that?"

"You're going to have to wait and find out for yourself," Zane answered. "The situation defies description—over the phone at least."

"You get me that ticket," Cleo blustered, letting the Nash question go, for the time being, anyhow. "I've got my computer turned on, and I'll be watching for new messages."

Again, Zane chuckled. "I'm on it, Cleo," he promised.

Nash gave the remaining half of his banana to Slim, who gobbled it up eagerly.

"First class," Cleo reminded him.

"It's as good as done," Zane said, glaring at Nash and shaking his head. As in, *don't do that again.* Human food wasn't good for a dog, and that meant Slim wasn't going to have it.

Fifteen minutes later, he'd gone online, purchased Cleo's one-way, first-class ticket, in seat 3B, and zapped a copy to her in L.A.

"Who was that?" Nash asked conversationally. By then, he and Slim had been outside and then returned.

"That," Zane answered, logging off and shutting the lid on his laptop, "was Super-Cleo. She can bend steel with her bare hands, leap over a tall building in a single bound—and she's faster than a speeding bullet, too."

No sense adding that she was as wide as she was tall, with ebony skin and gray hair that stood out around her head like a fright wig. A person had to meet Cleo to comprehend her, and even then, it took some time.

She yelled and flapped her apron when she wanted the kitchen to herself, and she had a tongue sharp enough to slice overripe tomatoes clean as the oft-mentioned whistle, but she also had a heart as expansive as the big Montana sky.

Nash's brow furrowed. Now that he'd showered and put on clothes that wouldn't get him beat up on the school grounds, he looked his age, which was an improvement over his former parody of a fortysomething homeless person in need of psychotropic drugs.

"This Cleo—is she your girlfriend?" he asked suspiciously, an indication that his previous experiences with girlfriends, probably his father's, had been memorable for all the wrong reasons.

Zane laughed again, partly because he was amused at the idea of Cleo as his main squeeze, and partly to hide the stab of sympathy he felt for Nash in that moment. "Nope," he said, with a shake of his head. "Cleo and I are definitely not romantically involved."

Nash looked relieved, and a bit sullen. "I guess we'll have to buy another bed, then," he said. "Because from what I gathered, she doesn't seem like somebody who'd want to sleep on an air mattress."

"You're right about that," Zane confirmed, with a chuckle. "If we know what's good for us, we'll have all new appliances, including a washer and dryer, before she gets here."

Something changed in Nash's face, an indefinable shift that might have meant he was beginning to trust this hairpin turn in his life and luck—or simply that he was mentally reviewing some felonious plan B, like burning down the house in the dead of night or committing murder with an ax.

Or both.

"Do I really get to stay here?" the boy asked, very quietly.

Zane had to swallow before he answered. "Yep," he said. "You really get to stay here."

"Zane?"

"What?"

"Thanks for not calling me 'Studebaker,'" Nash said. "Or Edsel."

"No problem," Zane replied, hiding a grin. "Do you run into a lot of that?"

"SOMEBODY TOLD MRS. BEAUMONT," Clare accused, on Monday morning, standing in Brylee's office at Décor Galore, hands on hips. "And *she* told my mom and dad, so now I not only don't get to go on the bus trip, but Luke's in trouble, too."

Brylee, sitting behind her computer, straightened her spine. "Really?" she asked, pretending innocence.

Fat lot of good that would do.

"I thought the top of my dad's head would blow off when he found out Luke was nineteen. He's already tracked him down and told him to stay away from me if he doesn't want to go to jail or become a candidate for reconstructive surgery. *Or both.*" She paused, but only to suck in a furious breath. "If that wasn't humiliating enough, Luke told Walker he'd written a song that would be a sure hit if Mom recorded it. He wasn't interested in me, he's just starstruck, that's all. He said straight out that he was just trying to meet Casey Elder and pitch his stupid ballad to her. All of which means, he was *using* me, the whole time!"

"I'm sorry, honey," Brylee commiserated. "But isn't it better to know the truth, painful though it may be?"

Tears sprang to Clare's eyes. She bit her lip and nodded in reluctant agreement. "But what if nobody ever likes me because I'm *me?* What if all that ever matters to anyone is that I'm Casey Elder's daughter?"

Brylee pushed back her desk chair, stood and went to put her arms around her niece's shoulders. "Oh, baby," she said, choked up. "*Lots* of guys will like you—even *love* you, I promise—and it will be because you're *you,* Clare Elder Parrish, *not* because your mom is a superstar."

Clare clung to her aunt, and a shuddering motion of her shoulders indicated that she was crying, even though she didn't make a single sound.

And that broke Brylee's heart, because Clare was so trusting. How long would that last, though?

"This *hurts,*" Clare said, face buried in Brylee's shoulder. "I thought Luke liked me for myself," she despaired. "I should have known this was really all about Mom, and what a legend she is, and not about me at all."

"Of course it hurts," Brylee responded, remembering how she'd felt after Hutch Carmody called off their wedding. She'd hurt plenty then, even knowing, on some level, that Hutch was right—they were all wrong for each other. She'd left that little church in Parable, a spurned bride in the wedding dress of her dreams, with her heart in pieces, her pride in tatters. "But things will get better, sweetheart. I promise."

Clare sniffled. "That's what Mom said," she admitted.

"Your mom is one smart lady," Brylee assured her niece. "When the right guy comes along, he won't care who your mother is, or your dad, either. He'll be interested in *you,* period. But don't try to hurry things along, Clare—take time to grow up, to become the woman you want to be, to pursue your own goals. That way, when the time to fall in love for real comes, you'll be ready."

Clare drew back, gazed earnestly into Brylee's eyes. "Do you really believe that?" she asked. Of course Clare knew about the Hutch disaster—everyone did.

Brylee was wounded, though she was fairly sure Clare hadn't intended that. With one broken engagement behind her, though, was she any kind of authority on love and marriage? Hardly. Still, she was intelligent, and not *entirely* dysfunctional. "Yes," she said honestly. "I believe there is someone for everybody—but we need to be open to the fact that this person might not be the one we've been expecting."

It was impossible not to think of Zane in that moment, although Brylee would have preferred not to, for sure. She'd believed that Hutch Carmody was the man for her and, since he'd fallen head over heels in love with Kendra Shepherd, she, Brylee, was just plain out of luck. She'd missed the last bus, so to speak.

Now, she'd begun to wonder if the whole heart-breaking experience of being dumped at the altar hadn't been a *good* thing. Hutch was happy with Kendra, and vice versa, and they were building a family together.

But was there a man out there for her—one she was *meant* to love with her whole heart, and share her life with?

Zane Sutton, perhaps?

Ridiculous. Of course not. She had nothing in common with the man. Nothing at all.

Except, of course, for an undeniable inclination to rip the man's clothes off his perfect and very masculine body and have her way with him on the spot.

"Am I going to feel better anytime soon?" Clare asked plaintively.

Brylee smiled and kissed her niece smartly on the forehead. "Trust me," she said. "You will *definitely* feel better, and sooner than you think."

"Did you tell Mrs. Beaumont about Luke and me?"

Brylee sighed. She played a mean game of dodge-ball, but she never lied. "Yes," she admitted.

Clare smiled a shaky, watery smile. "Thanks," she said.

Brylee laughed and hugged her niece again, hard. "You're welcome," she replied.

After Clare left the office, Brylee couldn't seem to get back on board her former train of thought. So she logged off the computer and woke a slumbering Snidely with a soft whistle.

"How about a walk, big guy?" she asked.

Snidely stretched and got to his feet, panting eagerly. Like *ride* and *car,* he knew the word *walk,* and he was all for the idea.

They moved through the busy warehouse, woman and dog, and out into the woodsy area behind the building.

Brylee gazed at the tree line. The adjoining property had been vacant for so long that she and Snidely had developed a habit of wandering there.

To trespass or not to trespass, that was the question.

Brylee came down on the side of bending the law just a little.

She headed straight for Zane Sutton's property line, her dog at her side, and made her way toward the creek.

CHAPTER FOUR

BRYLEE SAT ON the creek bank, with her bare feet dangling in the water, and soaked up the afternoon sunlight and the outrageously blue sky. Snidely was off in the woods somewhere, playing the great hunter, though in truth, that silly dog didn't have an aggressive bone in his body. He was most definitely the diplomatic type—a lover, not a fighter.

When the other dog appeared, floppy-eared and thin, Snidely returned to Brylee's side and sat vigilantly beside her, though he didn't make a sound— not even a warning growl. His tail switched back and forth, just briefly, and Brylee knew he was hoping for friendship, though he'd do battle in her defense if he had to.

She stroked his sleek head and murmured, "It's okay, buddy," and if Snidely didn't understand her words, he *did* comprehend her tone, because he relaxed.

The black dog, painfully skinny, with a dull coat, stood on the other side of the creek, watching Brylee and Snidely. He seemed calm and, at the same time, poised to flee if he sensed a threat of any kind.

Brylee was surprised when she spotted a collar

around the newcomer's neck, complete with tags. He looked like a stray, not somebody's pet.

Anger surged inside her. What was up with the symptoms of starvation and the timid manner? Whoever this dog belonged to— And it was no great stretch to figure *that* one out, since she knew every cat and dog and horse within a twenty-mile radius of Three Trees and she'd never so much as glimpsed this fellow before.

The poor creature had the misfortune to belong to none other than Zane Sutton, knee-meltingly handsome movie star. Major land owner.

Arrogant, self-indulgent, shallow *jerk*.

Brylee pulled her feet out of the creek, tugged on her socks and shoes and stood up. "Hey, boy," she said to the dog on the other side. "Are you lost?"

The dog eyed her, eyed Snidely and sat down in the tall grass to await his fate.

Brylee made her way to the line of flat rocks that bridged the creek—she'd been crossing that way for so long that she could have done it with her eyes closed—while Snidely plunged valiantly, if reluctantly, into the water and paddled across.

The black dog didn't move, though it gave a little whimper of fretful submission as she drew near.

"Let's get you home," Brylee said, after crouching in front of the dog and taking a casual glance at its tags.

Sure enough, he belonged to Zane. And his name was Slim. Was that some kind of cruel joke? On a surge of righteous indignation, Brylee shot like a geyser to her full height.

Snidely climbed gamely out of the creek and shook himself off, sprinkling both her and Slim with shimmering diamonds of sun-infused water, pure as crystal and freezing cold.

The march through the woods was familiar to Brylee, of course—she'd visited often, when her friend Karrie had lived on Hangman's Bend Ranch. Back then, of course, the place had been in good repair, a working cattle spread, with a larger house and barn than most of its neighbors boasted, to be sure, but Karrie and her family had been regular people, well-grounded country folks—not pearly teethed movie stars living out some weird fantasy of getting back to the land and all that other sentimental hogwash.

By the time she, Snidely and Slim emerged into the large clearing where the house, barn and corral stood, Brylee had worked up a powerful huff.

The illustrious Mr. Sutton was outside, shirtless, evidently repairing the corral fence. His jeans rode low on his lean hips, and his chest and back were muscular, probably honed by hours in some swanky gym. Seeing Brylee and the two dogs coming out of the trees, he paused, hammer in hand, a row of nails between his lips, and watched as they approached.

"Is this your dog?" Brylee demanded furiously, when she'd come within a dozen feet of the man and then suddenly stopped in her tracks. It was as though some kind of barrier or force field had slammed down between them.

"Yep," Zane said, after taking the nails out of his mouth and dropping them into the pocket of his beat-up jeans. They certainly didn't fit his image, those jeans—was he trying to look as if he *belonged* in Montana? "He's mine, all right."

Brylee sputtered for a few inglorious seconds. "Did it ever occur to you to *feed him* once in a while?"

Zane opened his mouth, closed it again. His grin was so insolent, and so damned sexy, that she would have slapped it right off his face, if her personal principles allowed—which, of course, they didn't.

A boy came out of the house just then, also shirtless, and sprinted toward them. "Slim!" he called jubilantly. "I wondered where you'd wandered off to."

Zane flicked a glance at the gangly child, a preteen actually, on the verge of a rapid growth spurt. "Brylee Parrish," he said quietly, "meet my kid brother, Nash."

Nash looked so pleased to make her acquaintance that what remained of Brylee's animal rights lecture died in her throat.

"Hello, Nash," she said, after swallowing.

The boy turned shy, blushing extravagantly. "Hello," he murmured.

Zane seemed to find the exchange mildly amusing. "Take old Slim into the house," he told Nash quietly, "and see if you can get him to chow down on some kibble."

Nash hesitated, glanced at Brylee again, from under the thickest eyelashes she'd ever seen on any guy—except maybe Zane himself—and whistled low to summon the dog.

The two of them vanished inside, Nash reluctantly, Slim going with the flow.

"He's a stray," Zane said presently. "I haven't had him long enough to fatten him up."

Brylee was flummoxed. She'd steamed over here on a mission of justice and mercy, and now, suddenly, she was becalmed, a ship with no wind in its sails.

"The boy or the dog?" she asked.

Zane's smile was affable, with a twinkle to it. "Both, I guess," he said.

By then, Brylee felt like a complete fool. She'd assumed the worst—movie stars, that disruptive, now-you-see-them, now-you-don't class of people, rarely proved her first impression of them wrong. This one had, though, and the realization left her tongue-tied and embarrassed, wishing she hadn't come on like the storied gangbusters, full of accusations and spitting fire.

"Oh," she said.

Zane's smile eased off into a sexy grin. "Is that all you have to say?" he asked, obviously enjoying her discomfort. "'Oh'?"

Heat burned her cheeks, and she knew her eyes were flashing again. "If you're waiting for an apology," she said, "don't hold your breath."

Zane leaned in a little—she hadn't realized how close together they were standing, though one of them *must* have moved—and she felt his substance, his energy, in every cell and nerve, like some kind of biochemical riot. "Now why would I expect an apology?" he drawled, though he seemed more amused than angry. "Just because you rolled onto my land like an armored tank and flat-out accused me of animal cruelty?"

Brylee blinked. Swallowed. "The dog's ribs show," she said lamely, after too many moments had passed. "Anyone would think—"

"He'd been going hungry for a while," Zane finished, when her words fell away in midstream. "As it happens, he wound up in a good shelter in L.A. just a few days before I adopted him. I've been giving old Slim as much kibble as he can handle, *Ms.* Parrish, but it's a slow process, requiring patience and understanding."

Brylee longed to melt into a puddle, like the Wicked Witch of the West in *The Wizard of Oz.* She wanted to say she was sorry, too, that she'd jumped to conclusions, but her throat had constricted like the top of a drawstring bag, pulled tight.

Damn her Parrish pride, anyway. It would be her downfall for sure.

Idly, Zane stepped back, collected his shirt from a nearby fence post and shrugged into it.

For Brylee, this was both a relief and a crying shame. All that spectacular man-muscle, covered up, hidden from view. Thank heaven. Or darn it. *Whichever.*

He turned his attention to Snidely then, bending to favor the dog with a few pats on the head and a grin that left no doubt of his love for four-legged furry people.

On that score, at least, Brylee had misjudged Zane Sutton, no doubt about it, but she still couldn't bring herself to apologize. It wasn't just her pride, either—she had a vague and very disturbing sense that she'd be opening a door to a whole slew of unpredictable developments if she dared let down her guard, even for a moment.

"Come inside," he finally said. "I can't offer you iced tea or a mint julep, but we do have sodas and ice, and I could probably rustle up some coffee, if you'd rather have that."

Oddly, it never occurred to Brylee to refuse the invitation. She simply followed Zane toward the house, shamelessly enjoying the rear view, while Snidely trotted along at her side, oblivious to the fact that the planet had just shifted off its axis and Ecuador could suddenly become the new north pole at any given moment.

By then, the boy, Nash, was in the kitchen, trying to look busy. He'd pulled on a T-shirt, and Slim, the slat-ribbed dog, was crunching away on a recently replenished supply of kibble.

Brylee looked around, remembering, and remembering eased some of her tension, made her smile.

Her friend Karrie's mom, Donna, had taught both her daughter and Brylee to cook in this kitchen, imparted simple sewing skills, listened benevolently to the ceaseless girl-chatter about boys and cheerleading tryouts and prom dresses, driven them to and from school events and the movies.

"You've been here before," Zane observed quietly, watching her.

His words startled Brylee out of her reverie. "Yes," she said. "My best friend, Karrie, used to live in this house." There was so much more to the story, of course—Donna, recognizing Brylee as what she was, basically a motherless child, had made room for her in this house, and in her heart. The Jacksons had been her second family.

Nash and Slim were both staring at Brylee now. Did she have something in her teeth? Stuck to the heel of her shoe?

Zane moved to the refrigerator—the same one that had always been in that spot, unless Brylee was mistaken—and opened the door. "What'll it be?" he asked. "Soda? Water?"

"Nothing for me, thanks," Brylee said, feeling a little like one of the birds who occasionally flew into her warehouse and got trapped there, wheeling and swooping in increasing desperation as it searched for a way out. "I really can't stay— I just—"

Nash moved to the card table in the center of the room, drew back a chair with a manly flourish. "You can't leave yet," he said with a grin, gesturing for her to have a seat. "You're the only person I know in this godforsaken place, except for my brother, and he's practically a stranger."

Brylee sat down, slightly mystified. Nash had charm, and he'd exhibited good manners by offering her a chair, but what was up with calling Montana—the place she loved best in all the earth, her soul's true home—"godforsaken"?

"Nash is used to finer digs than this old, neglected ranch," Zane explained dryly, when Brylee proved to be at a loss for a reply. With a weary sigh, he sat down opposite her at the rickety folding table. "You know—homeless shelters, juvenile detention centers, maybe a bunk in a rusted-out camper in somebody's backyard now and then."

Brylee's eyes widened. Where she came from—which was right there in Parable County, thank you very much—those were fighting words, yet Zane's tone wasn't unkind, merely matter-of-fact. And she'd thought *her* family relationships were complicated.

Nash, left to stand like the odd man out in a game of musical chairs, leaned casually back against a counter and folded his underdeveloped arms. There was something very reminiscent of Zane about the posture. The man-child smiled winningly and said, "As you can see by the way my brother treats me, I am in drastic need of a friend."

Brylee smiled back at the boy, amused and at the same time concerned. "You've come to the right place, then," she said. "Three Trees and Parable are both great towns, and I'd be glad to introduce you around, starting with my nephew, Shane—he's about your age—and my niece, Clare, too."

"Is your niece as beautiful as you are?" Nash asked smoothly.

Zane laughed and shook his head. "Next he'll ask

you what your sign is, or look puzzled and ask if you've met before."

Brylee liked Nash, even though he was half-again too smart-alecky for his own good or anybody else's, so she ignored Zane's remark. "And you're how old?" she countered lightly.

Nash reddened a little under her kindly scrutiny, and he seemed stuck for an answer. Brylee would have bet *that* didn't happen very often.

"He's twelve," Zane supplied graciously.

Nash glared at his brother.

Twelve? Impossible, Brylee thought. "Going on forty-five," she said.

A short silence followed, the air between the two brothers so charged that Brylee wouldn't have been surprised to see thunderclouds forming beneath the ceiling.

"I could show you around," Nash finally volunteered, effectively rendering his older brother invisible, at least as far as he was concerned. "I mean, since you haven't been here in a while and everything…"

Zane sighed at that, but raised no objection. Was he ashamed of the place? It *was* pretty dilapidated, an unlikely abode for an established movie star, certainly.

"That's a great idea," Brylee said, pushing back her chair to stand. "I'd love to have a look at the place." She glanced at Zane, who was standing now, too. "You don't mind?"

"I don't mind," he confirmed. The twinkle in his

eyes and the twitch at one corner of his mouth said he knew full well she didn't really care whether he minded or not.

"We're getting more furniture after the renovations are done," Nash hastened to explain. "Right now, we've got a couple of beds and an air mattress, and that's about it."

Following Nash, with Snidely right behind her, Brylee suppressed a smile. "Things take time," she said.

The house, though empty, was just as she remembered it—large and rambling, with spacious, raftered rooms and tall windows and a total of three natural rock fireplaces. There were four bedrooms and as many baths, along with a sizable dining area and a living room that not only ran the full width of the house, but offered a magnificent view of trees and mountains and that endless pageant of sky.

"Cleo gets here tomorrow," Nash announced, when they'd come full circle, after about fifteen minutes, and returned to the kitchen. Zane and Slim were both gone, and Brylee caught the rhythmic tap-tap-tap of a hammer somewhere nearby. "She was my brother's housekeeper, when he lived in L.A."

Brylee offered no comment. She was just glad she hadn't followed her first inclination and jumped in to ask who Cleo was before Nash got around to clarifying the matter for her.

So, Cleo wasn't a girlfriend or, worse yet, a wife. Brylee felt like a damn fool for caring either way, but care she did.

"I guess she can really cook," Nash went on conversationally, "but Zane says she's a stickler for neatness and order, and she'll raise hell when she gets a look at this place." He paused, sucked in a breath and went right on talking. "We ordered a washer and dryer and another bed, but we're holding off on all the other stuff because Cleo's the type to want a say-so in just about everything."

Brylee smiled, amused by this assessment of the unknown Cleo. She sounded like a SoCal version of Opal Dennison Beaumont, local force of nature. "That's probably wise," she said.

Suddenly, Nash looked wistful, and his gaze was fixed on something—or someone—very far away.

"You don't have to tell Zane or anything," he said, very quietly, "but I kind of like it here."

Brylee rested a hand on the boy's shoulder, touched to the core of her heart. "Why would you want to keep that from your brother?" she asked, searching his face. If she'd known Nash Sutton better, she'd have put her arms around him just then, the way Donna Jackson had so often done with her, and given him a squeeze, promised him everything would be all right. Since they'd just met, though, she knew that would be overstepping, and she'd done enough of that for one day, accusing Zane of neglecting, if not abusing, his dog.

A muscle bunched in Nash's jaw, and a fly buzzed against the torn and rusted mesh in the screen door, the sound of the hammer sifting through on a June breeze fragrant with pasture grass. "Because this is temporary," the boy finally replied, feigning non-chalance and deftly avoiding Brylee's gaze at the same time. "That's the way my life goes. Every-thing's temporary."

The backs of Brylee's eyes scalded, and she didn't speak for a moment, fearing her voice would catch if she did. Sure, she'd missed having a mother con-tinuously on the scene, both as a girl and sometimes even now, as a grown woman, but she'd always had her dad and Walker and a slew of good friends, in-cluding the Jacksons. From the sound of things, Nash was alone in the world, allowed to hang around until someone decided he was in the way and sent him packing.

Seeing Brylee's expression, and reading it all too accurately, Nash turned up the wattage on that killer grin of his, so like his brother's. He might have been only twelve, but he'd trained himself to act and talk like a man, and that saddened Brylee, sensing, as she did, that he'd missed out on much of his child-hood—skipped right over it.

"I wasn't trying to make you feel sorry for me," he said.

Too late, Brylee thought, but she smiled to hide her sympathy. Pride seemed to be about all Nash had to call his own. "I live on the next place over, with my brother, Walker, and his family," she said cheerfully. "We have lots of horses, and there's al-ways plenty of extra space at supper. Breakfast and lunch, too, for that matter. You're welcome to drop by anytime."

"You don't have a husband?" Nash asked, apparently having noticed the omission when she mentioned Walker and Company. He sounded somewhat surprised, which was a compliment, she supposed.

"Nope," Brylee said, rustling up another smile. This one was harder to come by than the last one, though. She *might* have had a husband by now, if she'd had the God-given good sense to pick anybody besides Hutch Carmody for a partner. "I'm single."

Nash frowned, as though he might be trying to work out an Einstein-worthy equation in his head. "And you live with your brother?"

The question gave her a pang, but it also amused her a little. "Like you," she confirmed. She leaned slightly to give her dog a pat on the head. "Snidely and I share an apartment on the premises, so don't picture me sitting in a rocking chair in the attic, knitting socks. I'm not exactly the maiden aunt."

Aren't you? taunted that inner voice, the one that never let her get away with a darn thing.

Nash actually laughed this time, with a boyish delight that made her think of Shane. "'Snidely'? That's your dog's name?"

Brylee grinned, already on her way toward the screen door. She'd stayed too long; it was time to make an exit. "Yes," she replied, glancing back over her shoulder. "For Snidely Whiplash."

Nash looked puzzled. "Who?"

Brylee sighed, opened the door to step out onto the porch, which, like the rest of the house, had seen better days. "Don't kids watch cartoons anymore?"

she countered, in pretend despair. "Look him up on the internet."

Nash made a salutelike motion with his right hand. "Yes, ma'am," he said, in a passable Western drawl. "I'll do that."

Outside, Zane had stopped working on the fence and turned to watch the road, where a truck was slowing down to swing in at his gate, hauling a horse trailer behind it. As Brylee looked on, oddly stricken—*again*—by the sight of him, a slow grin spread across his face, the kind of grin that put a person in mind of a brilliant sunrise following a long, dark night.

The driver of the truck got out, opened the gate, drove through, got out again and closed it behind him.

Slim, probably figuring he ought to earn his keep somehow, barked a couple of times, which got Snidely started.

"Shush," Brylee said, shielding her eyes from the sun-dazzle of the shiny silver trailer, and Snidely quieted and sat down obediently at her side.

Zane, meanwhile, waited, shirt open, teeth gleaming in his tanned face, his hands resting easy on his lean hips, making Brylee think of an old-time town marshal or a sheriff, there to welcome a wagon train full of trail-weary travelers yearning to settle down for good.

Brylee knew well enough that she ought to go on about her business instead of standing there staring the way she was, but she couldn't help it. She shifted her gaze from Zane to the truck and trailer and back again—several times.

Nash fairly shot from the house—apparently he hadn't seen or heard the arriving rig right away—and the smile on his face was downright transcendent.

"Blackjack's here?" he called to Zane.

Zane nodded, swallowed visibly. "Blackjack's here," he agreed, his voice just this side of raspy.

Blackjack, it turned out, was a magnificent gelding, his shiny coat dark as coal, and as Zane and the truck driver unloaded the animal, the creature tossed its gigantic head, mane flying, and looked around as if to say, *Home at last. Why did it take so long?*

Zane took the lead rope from the driver and spoke in a low, easy tone as he urged the horse the rest of the way down the ramp and onto the hard, rutted ground.

Brylee knew horses; she'd been raised around them, ridden with her dad when she was barely two years old and by herself or with Walker just about every day since then. And she'd never seen a finer animal than this gelding, with his ebony coat and silky mane. His conformation was nigh on perfect, and the sight of him brought an ache of admiration to her throat and a twinge of envy to her middle.

Unable to resist, she stepped forward.

"Stay back, now, ma'am," the truck driver said quickly. "This horse has been riding in that trailer for a long time, and he's likely to be a mite on the skittish side."

Zane didn't look at the man; his gaze was on

Brylee, and he didn't hesitate to speak up. "The lady knows what she's doing," he said, with a quiet conviction that caught Brylee totally off guard, caused things to tip over and spill inside her, warm and thick and sweet as honey fresh from a hive.

Oh, Lord.

She could dislike Zane Sutton when he was being obnoxious or arrogant, but his obvious respect for her expertise with horses was a game-changer.

She approached Blackjack slowly, let him sniff the back of her hand before stroking his long face and velvety nose. "Well, hello there, handsome," she said softly.

Blackjack nickered again, but he didn't sidestep or back up.

The truck driver, reassured, gave a low laugh and said, "I bet he gets that reaction from every woman he meets. Love at first sight." He paused, shook his head, resituated his worn-out straw hat. "Lucky critter."

Zane handed the lead rope to Brylee to take the clipboard the other man offered and sign for the delivery.

Still careful to move slowly, Brylee led Blackjack away from the trailer, walking him around in a wide circle so he could work some of the kinks out of his legs and get used to the feel of solid ground under his hooves.

Nash stood at a slight distance, clearly fascinated and probably a little scared, too, and silently, Brylee gave the boy credit for good sense. After all, Blackjack must have measured seventeen hands at least, and he had a giant, warrior's heart pumping away in that broad chest of his, sustaining well over a thousand pounds of sheer muscle—all of which meant he was a very powerful and very unpredictable animal. Even a well-trained and familiar horse could be spooked unexpectedly, and a frightened horse was a *dangerous* horse.

For all that, Blackjack clomped alongside Brylee, calm as a dog on a leash, and just being that close to the nearly mythic creature thrilled her ranch-kid heart through and through. She'd have given just about anything to mount that gelding, with or without a saddle, give him his head and let him fly like Pegasus, but it was too soon, of course. And even though Zane had gone up a notch in her estimation by trusting her around Blackjack, well, that didn't mean he'd let her ride.

Some people—especially men, being famously territorial—wouldn't share their horses, period. Furthermore, while Zane had somehow sensed her competence, he had no way of knowing that, like her older brother, she rode with the skill of a seasoned Apache on the warpath.

All these thoughts were going through Brylee's mind when the truck driver tucked his clipboard under one arm, shook Zane's hand in farewell and, after one last admiring glance at Blackjack, climbed into his truck, started the engine, made a broad turn and drove off, the now-empty trailer flashing aluminum-bright as it rattled down the rutted dirt driveway.

Zane appeared at Brylee's side, gently took the lead rope from her hand and gave Blackjack an affectionate pat on the neck. Nash didn't venture any closer, and both dogs trotted over to join the boy, evidently bored with the proceedings.

"Is it just me," Zane asked, his voice low and a little husky, "or did something change between you and me a few minutes ago?"

Brylee's heartbeat quickened, and so did her breathing—she actually thought she might hyperventilate—and she felt her cheeks heat up a little, too. She couldn't look directly at Zane, for fear of what she might see in his eyes, but she wasn't going to lie, either. "Maybe," she allowed cautiously. Then, with more certainty, she added, "Thanks for not assuming the little lady didn't know one end of a horse from the other."

Zane chuckled, inclined his head in the direction of the rapidly disappearing truck and trailer. "I think that guy's intentions were good," he remarked. "He didn't want you to get hurt, that's all."

"Nice of you to give *him* the benefit of the doubt," she said, miffed.

This time, Zane laughed outright. "Strange," he said, with a shake of his head. "I could have sworn you just thanked me for not writing you off as a greenhorn. And at what point, Ms. Parrish, did you give *me* said benefit? Did you or did you not accuse me of starving my dog?"

She was cornered, like a queen on a chessboard with no moves open. "I can sometimes be sort of contrary," she admitted, though it practically killed her to concede the point.

"*You?* Contrary?" Zane grinned down at Brylee, as at ease with her as he was with the horse, and waited for her to answer. The implication was clear enough: he could handle them both.

Brylee might have kicked him in the shins just then, if it hadn't been for her aversion to physical violence. The discouraging thing was, she was every bit as intrigued by this man as she was irritated by him. If Zane had tried to *kiss* her in that moment, for pity's sake, she'd probably have let him.

What was *wrong* with her?

"Go riding with me?" he asked next. "Tomorrow sometime, I mean? I presume you own a horse."

Brylee blinked. Of course she owned a horse—in fact, she owned several, since half of Timber Creek Ranch belonged to her.

"You could show me some of the countryside," he said, when she didn't speak right away. An impish grin danced in his eyes. "That would be the neighborly thing to do."

Suddenly, Brylee's palms began to sweat. She ran them down the thighs of her jeans, wishing she didn't like the idea quite as much as she did. "Okay," she said, turning to point toward home. "The ranch house and barn are a couple of miles that way. You can't miss them."

"Time?" Zane prompted.

"Late afternoon?" Brylee heard someone answer, using her voice. "I have to work."

"And I have to fetch Cleo from the airport," Zane said. "How about five o'clock or so? There'll still be plenty of light, and the heat might let up a little by then, too."

"Make it five-thirty," Brylee said matter-of-factly, feeling as though she'd just accepted a dare to bungee jump off a high bridge instead of a simple, harmless invitation to go horseback riding with a new neighbor, "and it's a date."

It's a date. She could have kicked herself for phrasing her reply that way, but there was nothing for it. The damage was done.

She blushed again.

Zane grinned that devastating grin, the one that fairly set Brylee back on her heels. "Five-thirty," he said. "See you then."

"Right," she said, somewhat awkwardly. She waved goodbye to Nash, turned away and started back toward the woods, Snidely keeping pace as always.

She was barely aware of the trees towering all around her, or of the creek when she crossed it, making her way from rock to rock. As before, Snidely chose to swim to the other side.

Reaching the opposite bank, where Brylee was waiting for him, he slogged up out of the stream and shook himself mightily, showering her with shining diamonds of ice-cold water, causing her to whoop in good-natured protest and then laugh right out loud.

It wasn't smart—or safe—to be this happy, she decided, even as her heart took wing and soared against the periwinkle sky.

CHAPTER FIVE

AFTER DOUBLE-CHECKING TO make sure the warehouse and offices were secured, Brylee grabbed her handbag and car keys, and she and Snidely got into her SUV to head for home.

She felt dazed and oddly reckless. More than once, she caught herself humming some nameless tune. "It's official," she told Snidely, as they came to a dust-raising stop near the barn. "I've lost my ever-lovin' mind."

She spotted Walker over by the corral fence, watching from under the brim of his battered hat as one of the ranch hands tried out a new bucking horse, probably fresh from the range. The cowboy pitched skyward well before the eight-second mark and landed on the ground in a graceful somersault, rolling right up onto his feet and grinning as he retrieved his hat.

As Brylee stepped up beside her brother, he smiled and jabbed an approving thumb in the air. Like any stock contractor, he appreciated a badass bronco or bull, mainly because he loved rodeo, and they were likely to perform well. The harder the critters were to ride, the better his reputation in the business.

"I remember a time when you would have ridden

that bronco yourself," Brylee commented. "You getting old, big brother?"

Walker laughed, adjusted his dusty hat, glanced down at her with a sparkle in his eyes. "If I am," he replied, "then you are, too."

She gave him a mock punch in the arm, narrowed her gaze to give him the once-over. "I'll bet Casey made you promise not to play cowboy," she surmised mischievously. "Why, Walker Parrish, some folks might even say you're henpecked."

"Not to my face, they won't," Walker replied, unruffled. Of all the men Brylee had ever known, her older brother was one of the most self-possessed *and* the most confident, and not without reason. He seemed to be good at everything he did. "And it just so happens, little sister," he continued mildly, "that my lovely wife didn't 'make me' promise any such thing. She merely *suggested* that, since I'm a husband and a father three times over now, I might want to be a bit more careful not to break every bone in my body."

This time, it was Brylee who laughed. "Oh, *well,*" she teased. "As long as it was only a *suggestion...*"

Walker ruffled her hair, the way he used to do when they were kids. "There's some color in your face," he commented. "Your eyes are sparkling, and you haven't stopped smiling since you got here. What's going on?"

Brylee thought of her rash agreement to go horseback riding with Zane the next afternoon, a little surprised to discover that she still didn't regret the decision. "Can't a woman smile around here with-out being asked what it's all about?" she threw out.

Walker grinned, adjusted his disreputable hat again. "Sure," he answered. "But you've got to admit, you've been pretty long in the face for the last while."

"The last while"? A classic understatement. What he'd really meant was, *Since Hutch Carmody left you at the altar,* but Brylee didn't get her back up. It was true enough that she'd taken her sweet time getting over the wedding-that-wasn't, and Walker, like ev-eryone else in her life, had been concerned about her.

She stood on tiptoe to plant a light kiss on her brother's beard-stubbly cheek. "That was then," she said mysteriously, "and this is now."

With that, she and Snidely made their way around the barn, toward the plot of land where the tamer horses were pastured during the day.

Reaching the fence, Brylee gave a low whistle, and her black-and-white pinto gelding, Toby, lifted his head at the sound, approached her at an eager trot.

She smiled and nuzzled his nose with her own, reaching up to rub his ears. "Hey, boy," she said, choked up because of the way he'd hurried toward her, with a gleeful whinny. It had been too long since she'd ridden Toby, or even paid much attention to him. "You up for a little spin around the pasture?"

Toby nickered and tossed his head, as if to say yes, making Brylee laugh and, though she quickly blinked back the tears, cry a little, too.

She climbed over the fence, while Snidely shin-nied underneath, agile as a trained soldier low-crawl-ing to avoid a barrage of bullets zipping by within inches of his hide.

Toby allowed her to check all four of his hooves; he was a patient horse, but young, and, as Walker liked to say, full of piss and vinegar.

When she found no stones or little sticks that might make him go lame or simply cause him discomfort, she looped her arms around Toby's thick neck and swung up onto his bare back, settled there and entwined the fingers of one hand in his gleaming black-and-white mane.

He sidestepped, tossed his head again, and when Brylee touched his sleek sides with the heels of her shoes, he took a few hesitant steps forward, looked back at her as if to confirm that she truly wanted to ride and then leaped straight into a gallop, which quickly became a run.

Brylee, leaning over his neck, holding on with her knees more than her hands, gave a shout of pure joy.

The other horses in the pasture watched with casual, grass-munching interest as Toby shot past like a spotted cannonball, soaring over the low barbed-wire fence on the far end of the five-acre pasture and landing with the grace of a private jet on automatic pilot. Without so much as a stumble, he raced onto the open range, while Snidely ran alongside, full-out, a furry blur.

Gradually, Brylee slowed Toby down, with just the lightest tug at his mane and a practiced motion of her knees, turning him around to head back toward the pasture at a leisurely walk. Breathless with the exhilaration of riding again, she pressed her face down into the sweaty hide of his neck and whispered, "I'm back, old buddy. I am finally *back*."

It was true, Brylee realized, with a wild rush of happy relief. She hadn't just come back to her horse, either—she'd returned to her life, to the person she'd been before she'd fallen for Hutch. She'd come home to *herself*.

"ARE YOU GOING to ride him?" Nash asked, indicating Blackjack. Though still cautious, the boy had ventured a little closer, no doubt reeled in by his fascination with the creature, like a fish on the line.

The delivery man had set Blackjack's saddle, bridle and blanket atop a nearby fence rail after the horse was out of the trailer, and as a reply to his brother's question, Zane inclined his head toward the gear. "Yep," he said. "A little, anyhow, just to get him used to having a rider on his back again."

Nash's eyes widened slightly, and he drew in an audible breath. "How long since Blackjack's been ridden?" he asked, looking wary and interested, both at the same time.

Zane patted the horse's neck, in part as a tacit apology for their lengthy separation. "The outfit where I boarded him was top-notch, and daily exercise was part of the deal, along with veterinary care and the rest. Most likely, somebody saddled him up and took him out the same day he left the stables."

"Still," Nash said, looking doubtful, "he's been

shut up in that trailer for what, two days? Three, maybe?"

Zane ran a light hand over Blackjack's side, his back, his flank, letting him get used to being touched. "Three, probably," he answered distractedly. "That's why we're going to take it real easy today. He needs time to get used to being free of that trailer, but he also needs to work the kinks out a little." He nodded toward the gear propped on the fence rail. "Get me that bridle, will you?"

"Sure," Nash replied eagerly, already on his way. "But don't you want the saddle and blanket, too?"

Zane shook his head. "That can wait until tomorrow," he said. Blackjack was anything but fragile, but he'd been cooped up in small quarters all the way from California, and just as the driver had said, he might be pretty jumpy for a while. No sense in asking more of the animal than necessary, after a long trip.

Nash brought the bridle over, handed it to Zane. "Will you teach me to ride?" he asked, with such hope in his voice that Zane hated to have to douse him with cold water.

"Not on this horse," he said, easing the bit into Blackjack's mouth and slipping the bridle over his head. After soothing the animal for another few moments, he swung up onto his back, waited to see how he'd react.

Nash had prudently moved back out of kicking range, but he was scowling and patches of red glowed in his cheeks. "I don't see any *other* horses around here," he said. "So that means I'm just shit out of luck, right?"

A quiver went through Blackjack's frame, from his shoulders to his flanks, but he didn't buck or go into a tight spin, one of his favorite ways to unseat a rider.

"Watch your language," Zane said mildly. "You're only twelve, remember?"

"How am I supposed to learn to ride a horse if you won't even let me try?" Nash demanded, ramming his hands into the pockets of his new jeans.

Zane sighed, eased Blackjack into a slow walk. "I didn't say you couldn't learn to ride," he pointed out reasonably. "I said you couldn't learn on Blackjack."

Nash was still testy. "Why not?"

Because I said so. Zane almost said it, but then he remembered how much it had rubbed him raw as a kid, hearing those words from any adult, and he bit them back. "He's high-strung," he said instead. "He's also big, in case you missed that, and it takes an experienced rider to handle him." He paused, relaxing into Blackjack and, by that strange and inexplicable synergy that had always existed between them, becoming a part of the animal.

"Which leaves me up sh—up the creek," Nash protested.

"We'll get you a horse," Zane assured the boy. "But that means you'll have to look after the critter. There's a lot of work—and a lot of responsibility—involved."

Nash stared up at him, practically gaping. "You'd

buy me a horse?" he asked, in a tone of stunned disbelief. "One that would be just mine?"

"Yes," Zane answered, as Blackjack moved along the rutted driveway.

Nash hurried alongside, as did Slim. "For *real?*" he quizzed, breathless. "I could name him myself, and have my own saddle and everything?"

"Your own saddle and everything," Zane confirmed, hiding a grin. "Don't be expecting Seabiscuit or Man o' War, though. We're talking about a kid-horse here, even-tempered and slow-moving."

Nash was frowning again. "Not a pony," he specified.

Zane chuckled. "Not a pony," he agreed, figuring the kid was probably picturing a Shetland. Even at twelve, Nash was too tall for one of those—his feet would drag the ground when he rode, and the experience wouldn't be all that good for the horse, either.

"I'll feed him and groom him and all the rest," Nash volunteered eagerly, mollified now that he knew he wouldn't be learning to ride on a four-legged refugee from some petting zoo or crummy kiddie carnival.

"You sure will," Zane answered, letting Blackjack have his head when the horse began to pull a little, making the reins go taut. "Keep that in mind when you figure you'd rather watch TV or play video games than muck out stalls and fill feeders."

Impatient now that he was no longer confined to a trailer or a stall, Blackjack broke into a trot, then a gallop, and they soon left the boy far behind, though the dog managed to keep up for a while.

There was a lot that was unsettled in Zane's mind and in his life—he had career and business decisions to make, a ranch house and barn to rebuild, a twelve-year-old brother to look after—but on the back of that horse, he felt the peculiar and perfect happiness of being an ordinary cowboy again. Just a man on a horse, nothing more and nothing less.

It was pure bliss.

Ten minutes later, back at the stone barn, Zane dismounted and led Blackjack into the largest stall. He'd picked up a few bales of grass hay and some feed on the shopping junket to town the day before, and had cleaned out the water trough and filled it from the garden hose.

He showed Nash, who was leaning against the stall gate and watching like a hawk, how to check the horse's hooves for rocks or other common problems, how much hay to put in the feeder, how to brush the animal down after a ride.

"How come you know so much about horses?" Nash asked presently. "You're an *actor*. Those guys just *pretend* they're good at stuff like that."

Zane chuckled as he gave Blackjack a farewell pat, slipped the bridle off over the horse's head and passed through the gate into the wide breezeway, forcing Nash to step back out of the way. "Before I was an actor," he said, "I followed the rodeo circuit."

Nash's blue eyes were practically popping out of his head. "No shit?"

Zane gave him a level look. He swore himself, on occasion, but then, he wasn't twelve years old.

The kid corrected himself. "For real, I mean?"

"For real," Zane said.

"Did you ride bulls?" Nash was double-stepping alongside as Zane strode out of the barn and into the sunlight.

"No," Zane answered. "Broncs."

"Were you any good?"

"I collected my share of prize money," Zane said, smiling again, thinking that maybe—just maybe—this whole crazy idea *might* work, after all, him and the boy living under the same roof on a permanent basis, forging some semblance of a family.

It was a nice thought, and Zane almost immediately shied away from it. This was the real world, he reminded himself, not some movie guaranteed to have a happy ending. Nash had problems. *He* had problems. Solving them wouldn't just take effort, it would require luck, too. And lots of it.

"And buckles?" Nash pressed. "Did you win any of those?" He didn't wait for Zane to answer, but rushed right on, carried away by his enthusiasm. "I watch rodeo on ESPN sometimes," he blurted, "and some of those buckles are so fancy you can't believe it."

Zane grinned, called to the dog as they drew nearer the house. "I might have a buckle or two," he said. In truth, he'd lost count of how many he'd won over the years, before he got suckered into the Hollywood scene. The only good thing that had come out of *that* was money. More money than he knew what to do with, actually.

"Can I see them? The buckles, I mean?"

"Sure," Zane said. "Right now, though, they're still at my place in California."

They'd reached the ramshackle porch and, instead of going inside, by some tacit agreement, they sat down on the steps. Slim nuzzled up close to Nash, and the boy stroked the dog's back, though his attention was still fixed on Zane. "I guess you must be planning to go back there," the kid speculated, with all the subtlety he could manage, which didn't amount to a whole lot. "If you didn't bring your stuff with you or anything."

Zane felt another twinge of sympathy for the boy, one he was careful to hide. "Stuff is stuff," he said. "I can live without most of it."

Nash frowned, thinking hard. "If you go back to California," he finally asked, "what happens to me?"

"I'm not planning to go back there—not to stay, anyhow," Zane answered gently. "If—when—I go to L.A. to tie up some loose ends, you can go with me. Unless it's during the school term, that is."

Skepticism and hope did battle in Nash's earnest face, and there was no telling which of them won, because an expression of studied disinterest fell like a mask over his features. "And if school is on, I have to stay here, all by myself?"

"Cleo will be around," Zane reminded his kid brother lightly. A silence took shape between them, both of them gazing toward the horizon. "You spend a lot of time by yourself, Nash?" Zane asked, at some length.

Nash shrugged his narrow shoulders. "Once in a while, Dad stashed me someplace where he figured I'd be all right on my own for a few days. It wasn't any big deal, though."

"What kind of 'someplace'?" Zane persisted quietly.

"You said it yourself, before," Nash said, with a note of defiance in his voice, indicating the house behind them with a nod of his head. "Shelters. Juvie, once or twice. One time, I spent a whole week in this really cruddy motel on the outskirts of St. Louis, but Dad left me money for the vending machine, so I didn't go hungry or anything."

Zane turned back to the horizon, not wanting the boy to see the look on his face. "Good old Pop," he murmured. "Always keeping his bases covered."

"To hear Dad tell it," Nash retorted defensively, "you and Landry didn't have it all that good living with your mom, so don't go acting all superior, okay?"

Zane felt a surge of rage, rage that had nothing to do with Nash and *everything* to do with Jess Sutton. "Things were tough when we were kids," he conceded, still keeping his face averted. "But Mom was always *there*. There weren't many extras, but she made sure we went to school, saw the dentist and the doctor when necessary—no small thing, since she never earned more than minimum wage and a few dollars in tips. Health insurance was an impossible dream for her."

"Dad *home*schooled me," Nash said, almost triumphantly.

"Oh, yeah?" Zane asked. "How? By parking you in front of the Discovery Channel once in a while?"

Nash reddened, and his fists, resting on his bony knees now that the dog had gone off to track something through the tall grass, tightened until the knuckles went white. *"No,"* he said furiously. "He bought those special books at Costco or somewhere, and I had to do all the lessons in them. I can read as well as anybody, and I'm good at math, too!"

Zane sighed. He hadn't meant to rile the kid up again, but when it came to their father, he had a hard time being tactful. "Have you ever gone to a real school?" he asked evenly.

"Lots of them," Nash said, in a so-there tone of voice.

"I'll just bet," Zane replied, with another sigh.

After that, things just kept right on rolling downhill. They heated up a frozen pizza for supper, when mealtime came around, and ate in stony silence at the card table in the kitchen.

Then Nash fed the dog while Zane disposed of their paper plates and plastic knives and forks, the bachelor equivalent of doing the dishes.

Cleo would have a cow when she got a look at this setup. Smiling a little at the thought, Zane opened his laptop and logged on, while Nash and Slim disappeared into Nash's room. They returned to the kitchen almost immediately, and Nash slammed a thick paperback down on the flimsy card table, next to Zane's computer.

"I read this," Nash said, shoving the words through his teeth. *"Twice."*

Zane glanced at the cover of the book. Saw that it was a four-in-one volume, containing *The Hobbit* and the *Lord of the Rings* trilogy. With a grin, he picked up the tattered tome in one hand, enjoying the heft of it—and the memory of consuming the Tolkien stories, one by one, courtesy of whatever library happened to be close enough to visit. Long past bedtime, he'd read the books voraciously, in the time-honored flashlight-under-the-blankets way of sneaky kids everywhere.

"All right," he said dryly, "you've convinced me. You can read. What grade are you supposed to be in, come fall?"

"I tested out of seventh," Nash answered, plunking down in the chair opposite Zane's and reclaiming the book, an obvious treasure. "So I guess I'm in eighth. Or even ninth."

"We'll see," Zane said.

"Not that I'll probably be here," Nash said. "Dad's bound to show up, soon as his luck takes a turn for the better." Then, with a stubborn set of his chin, "When he comes to get me, I'm leaving with him."

The hell you are, Zane thought, but what he said was, "Let's cross that bridge when we get to it."

That seemed to satisfy Nash, but just barely. He was definitely in a recalcitrant frame of mind. "I'm going to bed," he said, as though expecting an argument.

"You do that," Zane replied affably.

Nash left the room, taking the book along, but this time the dog didn't go with him. Instead, Slim gave a deep sigh and stretched out at Zane's feet for a snooze.

The rest of the evening dragged by, and Zane didn't sleep much that night, between thinking about Brylee Parrish and wondering how a person went about raising a twelve-year-old boy. The window-framed sky was still spangled with silvery stars when he gave up on getting anything like eight hours' sleep and rolled off the air mattress—he'd set the new bed up in the room Cleo would occupy—pulled on jeans, a shirt, socks and boots, and wandered outside. Slim went along.

Night sounds filled the air, a natural chorus of owls and crickets and critters scurrying through the grass. The three-quarter moon, along with all those stars, provided plenty of light.

Zane headed straight for the barn, made his way to Blackjack's stall, braced his forearms against the top of the gate and let his gaze range over the shadowy bulk of his horse.

On his feet, Blackjack gave a soft nicker of greeting, then went back to his midnight snack, the last of the hay Zane had given him earlier.

Zane felt a strange, swelling gladness in his chest, looking at that horse, but there was some sorrow, too. Or was it guilt? Before Hollywood, he'd taken Black-

jack with him wherever he went. *Afterward,* he'd
been lucky to get to the gelding once a month, what
with all the demands of making movies, promoting
movies, reading scripts for *more* movies.

His ex, Tiffany, had been after him to sell Blackjack, every hour on the hour, from the day of their
hasty Las Vegas wedding to the moment the ink
dried on the hefty settlement check he'd handed her
when their divorce became final. Now, hindsight
being twenty-twenty, Zane knew the marriage had
been doomed from the first, if only because Tiffany
had never been able to wrap her narcissistic little
brain around the fact that he *loved* this horse, that
getting rid of him wasn't an option because Blackjack was as much a part of him as his arms and legs.
Forced to make a choice, he'd probably have sacri-
ficed one of his limbs, if it meant he could keep the
gelding.

To Tiffany, all animals were mere nuisances,
shedding on her clothes, chewing up her shoes, in
constant need of some kind of care and attention—
God forbid. Not that Tiffany's antipathy to critters
was the only reason things didn't work out. There
were plenty of other problems.

Remembering their relatively brief but tempestu-
ous time together, Zane shoved a hand through his
hair, annoyed with himself, even now. Sleeping with
Tiffany had been one thing—he'd been a free man
at the time, after all—but *marrying* her? What had
possessed him to do a stupid thing like that? They'd
had nothing in common, outside the bedroom.

Tiffany, the daughter of a very successful Beverly Hills cosmetic surgeon, had never worn second-hand clothes in her life, unless they were "vintage," of course, with a pedigree to prove they'd been owned and worn by some famous actress like Vivian Leigh or Loretta Young or some other paragon from the golden age of motion pictures. She'd never had to wonder where she'd sleep that night, or whether there would be anything for supper. She liked to think of herself as an actress—they'd met when she was an extra in his first movie—but the truth was, Tiffany was basically a party girl, living on a generous allowance from Daddy until she and Zane were married. Once they were legal, she spent his money at warp speed, pouted when he said he wanted to get a dog, dragged him to black-tie shindigs where he found it easier to identify with the household help than the other guests.

She'd never loved him, he knew that now. If she had, she wouldn't have lobbied to get rid of Blackjack the way she had. To be fair, though, he hadn't loved her, either. He'd loved going to bed with her. He'd loved the *idea* of a wife and eventually a family, which was, like dogs and horses, definitely *not* on Tiffany's to-do list, as things turned out.

Kids? Was he serious? Pregnancy would ruin her admittedly remarkable figure, she'd informed him coldly, not to mention tying her down like some *housewife* and putting an end to her social life— though she'd been careful to avoid the subject of children until *after* his wedding band was on her finger.

One night, Tiffany had finally leveled with him. He'd been away on location, and they'd just had sex—even that had been more fizzle than fireworks by then. They'd been lying in their dark bedroom, with what seemed like an acre of icy sheets between them, and she'd told him, her voice dripping with contempt, that her friend Annette was expecting a baby. Four months in and she was already as big as a bus, Tiffany scoffed. Well, that wasn't for her, she went on, chattering away in the lonely gloom, while Zane silently resigned himself to a pile of broken dreams and the sad certainty that he and the missus would be calling it quits sooner rather than later.

A week later, the papers were filed, the tabloids were having the usual field day, with speculations of extramarital affairs on both sides, and Tiffany had gone directly home to Daddy. By then, Mommy was in her third or fourth stint at rehab—not that she'd ever taken an active role in her daughter's life.

Zane had bought that stupid mirrored water bed an hour after leaving the courthouse with his lawyer. Now, a little over a year later, here he was, in Montana. For the first time in recent memory, he had a sense of peace, of belonging somewhere.

He had a sexy neighbor named Brylee.

He had a young brother, who might be a good kid or not—the jury was still out on that.

And he had his horse with him again.

What was he supposed to do next? Zane didn't know, beyond getting the house and barn in decent shape, but he felt like the most fortunate man who'd ever drawn breath, just the same.

Finally, after a lifetime of rambling, he was home.

CLEO CAME BARRELING out through the security gate at the airport precisely at two o'clock the next afternoon, her round ebony face set in an ominous scowl. She wore ugly orthopedic shoes, thick stockings wrinkled at the ankles, a tweed coat that fairly swallowed her up and smelled of mothballs and a little round hat adorned by a red velvet rose the size of a man's fist. Her purse was patent leather and big enough to fend off a whole flock of angry crows bent on pecking out her eyeballs, if the need came up.

"Holy crap," Nash whispered, moving a little closer to Zane's side. "Is that her?"

Zane chuckled and let the buzzword pass, considering it to be relatively tame, all things considered. "That's her," he said.

Cleo stormed right over to them and stood practically toe-to-toe with Zane, her head tipped way back so she could glare up into his face. "Just as I thought," she sputtered. "I didn't get here any too soon—why just *look* at you. You need a haircut. There are dark circles under your eyes. And did you *sleep* in that shirt?"

"It's good to see you again, too, Cleo," Zane said, grinning. It really *was* good to see her, though he figured it would be a while before Nash came to the same conclusion. He looked scared stiff.

Cleo's dark eyes darted to the boy, and he seemed

to cower, just a little, under her hard scrutiny. "And I suppose you're the little brother I finally heard about in an email? Dash, wasn't it?"

"Yes, ma'am," Nash managed, then swallowed audibly and tried again. "I mean, I'm Zane's brother, all right. But I'm called *Nash,* not Dash." He seemed about to duck behind Zane, in an attempt to take cover, but he deserved some credit for correcting this daunting woman on the name issue. "Wh-what am I supposed to call you?"

"'Ma'am' will do just fine, for the time being," Cleo retorted crisply. "You behave yourself, and you can address me as 'Cleo.' You get on my bad side, though, and it'll be another matter entirely. Your life won't be worth a plug nickel."

"How was your flight?" Zane asked, in an affable effort to change the subject.

"We were delayed for an hour, and I had to show my boarding pass twice," Cleo blustered, spotting the baggage claim sign and trundling off toward it, leaving Zane and Nash to catch up. "Seems there are still some folks in this world numb-headed enough to wonder what an old black woman is doing in first class."

Zane's back teeth clamped together, and he was about to turn on one heel, head for the airline's customer service desk and proceed to raise hell, when Cleo read his mind, grabbed hold of his arm and gave her great, booming laugh.

"Let it go," she said. "I done told those people off already. But good."

"It might have been the hat," Nash suggested innocently.

Cleo's laugh changed everything but the weather and the all-around incompetence of Congress. Her smile was wide and bright, with teeth practically as big as piano keys. Her eyes shone with warmth and glee, and Nash, having never met her before, was thunderstruck by the transformation.

"I'm just glad to be off that airplane," she continued, in her rich, throaty voice. As a girl, she'd once told Zane, she'd been a torch singer, performing in smoky bars with jazz legends playing backup. Maybe that was why almost every word she said rolled off her tongue round-toned and mellow. "Can't wait to plunk my broad bottom down somewhere wide enough to accommodate it and put my feet up for a while, yes, siree."

Nash slanted a questioning glance at Zane, mouthed, *Yes, siree?*

Zane merely grinned. Nash didn't know it yet, any more than he had in the beginning, but Cleo was one of the best things that could ever happen to a guy.

At the baggage claim, they collected her luggage—two huge, beat-up suitcases and a plastic cooler sealed with duct tape—and Nash loaded everything onto a cart, clearly glad to help.

Being short of stature, to put it kindly, Cleo had a heck of a time getting into the pickup when they reached the parking lot. In fact, Zane finally had to give her a subtle boost from behind.

Nash stowed the bags and the cooler and climbed into the backseat.

"I'm gonna need a stepladder," Cleo observed, settling in and fastening her seat belt, "if I'm going to ride in *this* rig very often. Maybe even a forklift. You got any kind of regular *car,* Zane Sutton?"

Zane chuckled, started the truck, shifted it into gear. "No, ma'am," he teased, "but we do own a horse."

CHAPTER SIX

Two AND A half hours later, Cleo got her first look at the inside of the ranch house at Hangman's Bend, and it immediately became apparent that finding a place to park her "broad bottom" and put up her feet was no longer the number-one item on her agenda. After a sweeping glance of delighted horror that took in the whole kitchen, she commanded, "Fetch me a mop and a bucket, *now!*"

Zane tried to reason with her, get her to rest. After all, she'd traveled a long way and she was, to use her own unapologetically cliché-ridden terminology, no spring chicken, but she was having none of it.

"Hush yourself and show me where I can change my clothes," Cleo barked. The smile was gone, but the sparkle remained in her eyes, which was probably why Nash, openmouthed and a little pale, didn't bolt out the door and run for his life. The boy literally trembled when Cleo turned to him and thundered, "Let's see some action around here! I believe I just asked for a mop and a bucket!"

Zane bit the inside of his lip so he wouldn't laugh out loud at the beleaguered expression on Nash's face. They didn't own a mop, but there might be a few buckets knocking around out in the barn—rusty, mostly, and with holes in them.

He hoisted Cleo's suitcases, one in each hand, and, catching his kid brother's eye, inclined his head toward the duct-taped cooler. Nash scrambled to lift the thing in both arms, frowning at the effort. "Best get you settled in first, Miss Cleo," Zane said moderately. "There's plenty of time to whip this place into shape, remember."

Cleo looked around again, the picture of pleased scorn, and waved off Zane's remark. She definitely had her work cut out for her, and that suited her just fine. Cleo's world ran on attitude and elbow grease, and well-paid as she was, she was known to squeeze a nickel till the buffalo farted. Hence the shabby travel gear and a number of other strange economies. "Lord, have mercy on my poor bedraggled soul," she murmured, shaking her head from side to side, so the velvet rose on her hat bobbed comically. "Setting this place to rights ain't gonna be no job, it's gonna be a *career*."

Zane smiled at that statement—it was true enough, he supposed—and led the way toward the room he and Nash had chosen for Cleo. There was a genuine bed in evidence, made up with sheets and blankets fresh from their plastic wrappers, along with two nightstands and a chest of drawers, but that was it. No curtains on the windows, wallpaper so old that the pattern had blurred, vintage carpet in a weird and faded shade of gold that must have gone out of style around the time of the Watergate scandal.

"Land sakes," Cleo marveled, snatching off her hat with one-handed vigor. She swiped an index finger across the top of the bureau, in case of dust, before setting the headgear down.

Fortunately for the Sutton men, the woman loved a challenge. If she hadn't, Zane knew he and Nash would already be driving her back to the airport in Missoula, where she could catch the next flight back to La La Land.

Mop or no mop, Cleo wasn't going anywhere, and that was good news.

"Well, go on," she told Zane and Nash, making a shooing motion with her plump, short-nailed hands. "No need to stand there gaping all day like a pair of idiots at a freak show."

Somewhat feverishly, Nash looked around for a place to put the cooler, and finally chose the foot of the bed.

Cleo was clearly displeased by this decision, scowling as she did, but she didn't comment.

Knowing when to leave well enough alone, a lesson he'd learned the hard way over the rocky course of his life, Zane left the room, with Nash trailing hurriedly behind him, and the bedroom door closed with a snap the instant they were both over the threshold.

Slim sat patiently in the short corridor that led to the kitchen, his tail swishing a visible path through the dust on the floor.

Zane sighed and kept walking.

"She's the scariest person I've ever met!" Nash

confided, in a hoarse whisper, once they were in the kitchen.

Zane chuckled. Given the kid's history, that was saying something. "Cleo's all right," he said. "She's got a mean bark, but she almost never bites."

"Almost?" Nash echoed, after swallowing.

Grinning, Zane crossed the room, headed for the pantry, where they'd stashed what cleaning supplies they'd thought to buy on the last foray into Three Trees. There were various kinds of soap, sponges, paper towels, a broom and a dustpan—but, alas, no mop.

"Well, at least we managed to get the washer and dryer delivered before Cleo showed up," Nash said, hovering in the doorway. "Maybe she'll let us live."

"That's 'ma'am,' to you," Zane reminded the boy. "As for whether or not she'll let us live, I wouldn't count on it."

Taking an informal inventory of the stuff on the pantry shelves, he gave an inward sigh. Canned spaghetti and ravioli, chips of various kinds, coffee and a ten-pound bag of sugar, all adding up to nutritional disaster. It went without saying that Cleo would not approve.

A single low-wattage bulb dangled from a cord in the pantry ceiling, casting a gloomy light on the singularly inadequate array of goods.

"We're going to have to shop again, aren't we?" Nash asked, tone dismal, expression pained.

"Yep," Zane agreed, wondering what time it was. No matter how much Cleo fussed over the state of that ranch house, he wasn't missing the horseback ride with Brylee. The big discount store in town was open twenty-four hours, he reasoned, so they could go there after he got back from Timber Creek, get everything they needed. Maybe by then, Cleo would have toured the house, assessed the wreckage and drawn up an estimate.

Nash groaned. "We just *did* that," he reminded Zane. "I hate shopping!"

"Cheer up," Zane answered, and Nash stepped aside to let him pass through the pantry doorway and into the kitchen again. "We'll get you a TV or something." What did kids this age like to do, anyhow? Beyond watching TV and playing video games, he didn't really know.

The kid immediately brightened. "Can I have a flat-screen with a DVD player and keep it in my room?"

Before Zane could reply—he'd been about to say yes, but with certain stipulations—Cleo rolled into the room like an army tank. She was wearing colorful scrubs, her preferred garb when she was on duty, and canary-yellow sneakers, high-tops, probably. Cleo, somewhere on the far side of sixty, was the stylin' type—no doubt about it. She liked her colors in-your-face bright, and when she dressed up, she wore bling. Maybe that was where the money for new luggage went.

"I believe we ought to start with a bulldozer," Cleo announced, folding her stubby arms and exuding cheerful disapproval. "Taking a mop and bucket to this place would be like trying to put out a grease fire by spitting on it. I've got to make me a *plan*."

Oh, yes, Zane agreed silently, amused and, okay, relieved. A plan would be good. Why hadn't he thought of that?

Zane raised one eyebrow, doing his best to keep a straight face. "Whatever you want to do, Miss Cleo, will be just fine with me."

"Don't you *Miss Cleo* me, Zane Sutton. You in it up to your knees as it is, and talkin' pretty ain't gonna get you *noplace* with me," she scolded merrily.

Zane put up both hands, palms out, in a gesture of docile acquiescence.

"Your grammar needs work," Nash informed Cleo helpfully, prompting Zane to wonder if the kid was tired of living. "*Ain't* isn't even a word."

Cleo, always full of surprises, beamed like a lighthouse beacon shining a welcoming path of gold onto a dark and stormy sea. "Thank you for pointing that out, young man," she said. "Fact is, I like to say *ain't* sometimes, just for the effect. Same with droppin' my g's every so often. You might say it's my trademark." A pause. "Everybody ought to have a trademark."

"Oh," said Nash, baffled again.

Zane bumped his shoulder against Nash's. "Don't try to figure it out, professor," he advised, in a whisper meant to carry. "The ways of Miss Cleo are mysterious." In the next moment, he glanced at the grubby electric clock, which was shaped like a teapot, on the wall above the equally ancient stove. Its frayed cord dangled, ugly and dull with grime.

He concluded that he still had some time before he was due to meet Brylee at her place for the horseback ride, but he was already feeling jittery. The sensation reminded him of the old days, when he and Landry were kids, Christmas was coming up and his mom's tip jar was full—meaning there would be presents, new ones chosen just for them, not castoffs, like when times were hard.

Nash, evidently having followed Zane's gaze when he checked the time, smiled smugly and shifted emotional gears, going from Cleo-terror to smart-ass kid in the space of a heartbeat. "Thinking about your big date with the lovely Ms. Parrish?" he drawled, more obnoxious than your average twelve-year-old. Whatever that was.

Cleo leaped right on that one. "You've got a date?" she asked Zane, in a tone that said she couldn't quite believe it, even though she'd raised the possibility of a girlfriend in that first phone call. He might as well have said he'd seen a double rainbow on a sunny day, or bigfoot hanging out down by the mailbox. "With a real woman?"

"As always," Zane said mildly.

She laughed. "Is that so?" she countered, good-natured and obstinate, both at once. "Some of those females you went around with in L.A. had more plastic in them than ought to be legal."

Zane's mouth twitched at one corner. "Silicone," he corrected, having no clue why he needed to clarify the matter. "Not plastic."

Nash's eyes rounded, and his grin got wider—and

more annoying. "Tell me more about my big brother's love life," he said to Cleo. "Especially the babes with silicone implants."

But Cleo just swatted at the boy and laughed again, a deep ho-ho-ho sound, like a shopping-mall Santa Claus. "You just never mind," she scolded happily. "You're too young to be thinkin' 'bout such things."

Zane grinned to himself as he headed for his room, planning on a shower and a change of clothes, and as he walked away, he heard Nash ask a question, too low-pitched for Zane to catch, and Cleo's answer coming in her usual megadecibel volume, "*No,* I'm not telling you who your brother went out with and which ones were famous. It's none of your business, or mine, neither."

Zane's grin widened. As if Cleo had ever regarded his private life as none of her business. In his experience, nothing that even remotely concerned him was off-limits—she was mother-bear protective and hard to please when it came to his taste in women.

He could hardly wait to see how she reacted to Brylee Parrish.

No silicone filling out *those* curves.

BRYLEE LEFT DÉCOR Galore an hour early that day—something she *never* did—and drove straight home, Snidely riding shotgun in the front passenger seat. She parked her SUV behind the main ranch house, near her private entrance, and walked to the door at a deliberately casual pace, overriding the part of her that wanted to break into a skipping run like an excited five-year-old about to buy her first tutu.

She'd worn her usual jeans, long-sleeved T-shirt and sneakers to work and, since she hadn't done anything that would make her sweat, she reflected, she could have swapped out the tennis shoes for boots and gone riding in the clothes she had on. She always rode Western, after all, so it wasn't as if she needed to don jodhpurs and a fitted velvet jacket and one of those elegant little black hats with the strap under the chin, but she wanted to look, well, *good.* Okay, pretty. Maybe even a little fantastic.

Inside the apartment, she gave Snidely his afternoon ration of kibble and changed out the water in his bowl, then thumbed through what there was of the day's mail. Catalogs mostly, a bill or two, reminders to get her teeth cleaned and rotate her tires—at separate establishments, of course.

Brylee sighed, missing the good old days, when people actually wrote *letters* once in a while. Now, it seemed, human communication was limited to texts and emails and only the occasional brief conversation, usually in passing, always hurried. As often as not, even greeting cards were electronic, for pity's sake. Where would it end? With 3-D holograms replacing family and friends, the whole world gone virtual, like some gigantic video game?

God forbid, she thought, and shook off the whole idea.

While Snidely dined, Brylee put down the mail and proceeded to her bedroom, chose trim black jeans, a pink V-neck pullover and one of her more presentable pairs of boots, along with the requisite clean underwear.

After her shower, she toweled herself off, got dressed, then she blew her hair dry in front of the bathroom mirror, catching it up in a bulky twist at the back of her head, held in tenuous place by a faux-tortoiseshell clip. She applied minimal makeup—a swipe or two of mascara and some tinted lip gloss—and then stood back to examine her reflection. Was she too dressed up for a simple horseback ride? Overdoing it?

No, she decided, amused at her own girlie mood, sequins and a grand hat like the one Rose wore in *Titanic* would have been overdoing it. False lashes and glittery eye shadow would have been overdoing it. Jeans, an ordinary shirt and boots were just right.

Weren't they? She leaned closer to the mirror, smiled a nonsmile to make sure she didn't have lip gloss on her teeth.

Good to go. The bottle of costly perfume Casey had given her at Christmas caught her eye, but Brylee stepped away quickly, shaking her head. Perfume might send the wrong message, as in, *Hey, cowboy. Looking for a good time?*

A rap at the door leading to the main part of the house came as a welcome distraction.

"Come in!" Brylee called out, and when she reached the living room, she was pleased to see her sister-in-law standing there, looking more like a teenager in her stylish jeans and ruffled top than a wife and mother of three children.

Casey didn't miss much, and her green eyes twinkled as she took in Brylee's outfit and upswept hair. "Going somewhere?" she all but trilled. A singer by profession, Casey often put ordinary sentences to music. "If you're on the way out, I can come back later—"

"Stay," Brylee said, motioning for Casey to follow her into the kitchen. A glance at the digital clock on the microwave told her she had nearly an hour. "I'll make tea."

On most ranches, the kitchen table was the heart of the home, and Brylee's apartment was no exception to the rule.

Casey sat. "Okay," she said, "but I wouldn't want to make you late or anything."

Brylee blew out a breath as she strained to reach the bone china cups and saucers she kept on a high cupboard shelf. "Please," she said. "I'm going horseback riding with a neighbor, that's all. It's no big deal."

"Hmm," Casey responded, with lilting sweetness. "And which neighbor would that be? As if I couldn't guess without the slightest flutter of brain cells."

The cups and saucers rattled slightly as Brylee set them on the counter, and she was glad her back was turned to Casey, because she could feel a blush pounding in her cheeks. "It's no big deal," she hastened to repeat, busying herself with rinsing off the china and filling the electric kettle. "Zane Sutton isn't my type."

Casey chuckled. "Honey," she drawled, "Zane Sutton is *every* woman's type."

"He's new here," Brylee insisted, fitful. "I'm showing him around a little, that's all."

"Whatever you say, darlin'," Casey crooned.

Brylee tossed her sister-in-law a look over one shoulder, fumbling with the canister full of tea bags she kept near the kettle. "Can we talk about something else, please?" she asked pointedly.

"Sure," Casey agreed, smiling that knock-'em-dead smile of hers. "I came here to ask for your help. I got lassoed into heading up this year's rodeo-royalty committee, and I need some judges. Since you're a former rodeo queen yourself and know the ropes, so to speak, I figured you'd be a logical choice."

Brylee made a face. "That was a long time ago," she said, dropping a tea bag into each of their cups. "A *very* long time ago. Besides, I've already signed Décor Galore up as a sponsor, like I do every year. Why don't you ask Opal Beaumont—or maybe Joslyn Barlow? Or Tara Taylor? Kendra Carmody, perhaps?"

"I need three women and three men," Casey said matter-of-factly. "Slade, Hutch and Boone all volunteered, and their wives can't be on the panel, too, now can they? That would be nepotism or something. Opal's agreed to participate, along with Essie, from over at the Butter Biscuit Café, in Parable. That leaves one Brylee-shaped place to fill."

More responsibility. Just what she didn't need. "But—"

"Please?" Casey wheedled.

Brylee sighed heavily, splashed hot water into the cups and carried them over to the table, setting one down in front of Casey and the other at her usual place. She got out the sugar and milk, along with a pair of teaspoons, and finally sat down.

"You know I can't say no to you," she said, with a flimsy smile.

"I was counting on that," Casey agreed, adding milk and half a teaspoon of sugar to her tea. The delicate china tinkled, bell-like, as she stirred the concoction. "Come on, Brylee. You know how important this contest is to these girls—most of them have probably been dreaming about reigning as rodeo queen since they were knee-high to a Shetland pony."

Having been there, Brylee was well aware of what a big deal this was—there were scholarships, hefty ones, and a number of other desirable prizes, like new saddles and fancy boots and pink hats with sequined bands. Except for graduation, being queen of the rodeo had been the high point of her senior year in high school.

She bit her lower lip, remembering. "Somebody has to lose, though," she lamented quietly. She hadn't forgotten what a brave front the other girls had put on, back in the day, until they were out of the spotlight, that is. One or two of them had cried, they were so disappointed, and Cindy Johnson's mom had gone so far as to scold Cindy for not holding her stomach in. Another girl had refused to speak to Brylee all that summer.

Casey reached out, closed her hand over Brylee's and squeezed gently. "I know," she said, "but *everybody* loses sometimes, sugar, and that's good practice for life in the real world, don't you think?"

"True," Brylee conceded. *She* certainly hadn't come up a winner every time she went after some goal, no one did. And, looking back, she'd become convinced that her losses, painful as they were, had taught her far more than her victories. When Hutch suddenly torpedoed their wedding, for instance, in front of God and much of Parable County, she'd been devastated. Now that some time had passed, though, she could see what a mistake the marriage would have been.

Hutch had been right. Damn it.

"You'll do it?" Casey prodded.

Brylee sighed again. "I'll do it," she said, without a trace of enthusiasm.

"Good," Casey chirped, beaming again. "You're perfect for the job."

The *job* entailed one-on-one interviews with each of the contestants, sitting through a talent show that might well be excruciating and watching the girls ride, as well. Points would be awarded not just on the basis of looks, but personality, goals for the future, grade averages and extracurricular activities. The chosen one would compete in the state pageant and, if she won that, go on to the national event.

"You owe me for this, Casey Parrish," Brylee said.

Casey grinned and took a sip of her tea. "It'll be fun," she insisted. Casey thought just about everything was fun; she was one of those in-the-moment people who savored ordinary joys.

Fidgety, Brylee glanced at the clock again, unable to resist the urge.

Casey must have noticed, because she immediately got to her feet. She picked up her cup and saucer and carried them to the sink. "My work here is done," she said, going all twinkly with mischievous delight. "For now, anyway, I'm history."

She hummed one of her own hit songs, all about country lovin', as she hurried out. Just because she and Walker were crazy-nuts about each other, Casey probably thought that kind of special connection was possible, if not inevitable, for her famously jilted sister-in-law, as well.

Half an hour later, Brylee was outside, with good old Toby saddled up and ready to go, when Zane rode up on Blackjack. The man looked way better than just good, even in ordinary jeans, well-scuffed boots and a cotton shirt, and the horse wasn't hard on the eyes, either.

Brylee hoped her internal tizzy didn't show on the outside.

Zane ran his gaze over her, a swift and confident assessment, grinned with apparent appreciation as she stuck a foot into a stirrup and swung up onto Toby's back.

Next to Blackjack, poor, sweet Toby looked like an overgrown pony.

"Ready?" she asked, gathering her dignity around her like a cloak.

"Oh, yeah," Zane replied in an easy drawl. "Fact is, I think I've *been* ready for a good long while."

Brylee felt her pulse thumping in both cheeks. She had to bite down hard on her lower lip to keep from blurting out the obvious question—*ready for what?*—because she knew this yahoo was talking about more than an innocent horseback ride with a neighbor. He was teasing her, maybe even trying to throw her off a little, and she wasn't about to let that happen, though she was a beat or two late deciding that.

"Good," she said briskly, and led the way between the fences surrounding various pastures and corrals and forming a sort of maze behind the barn, skirting the river for the open range.

Zane rode beside her, both horses traveling at a relatively sedate pace. Blackjack, Brylee could see, wanted to move into the lead, but Zane restrained him with the kind of nonchalance that comes from years of skill-building.

With some difficulty, Brylee slid the cardboard movie-cowboy image she'd had of Zane Sutton off the main stage of her mind and fretted in silence, searching her brain for something to say. What had she and Hutch talked about, at times like this?

Not that there was any connection.

Zane sized up the bulls in their pens. "They look good and mean," he commented. Only in rodeo parlance, Brylee supposed, could these tornadoes on four legs be described in such contradictory terms.

"My brother, Walker, raises some of the best

rodeo stock in the Western states," she replied, with a note of pride. Then, for reasons she couldn't have explained, she added, "This is his place, really. Timber Creek, I mean. My name is on the deed, of course, but Walker practically runs the whole show."

Zane, standing briefly in the stirrups to stretch his legs, gave her a sidelong glance. "Does that bother you?" he asked.

It was a quiet question, direct and yet somehow nonintrusive.

Brylee relaxed a little, smiled and shook her head. "Nope. This ranch is home, and it always will be, but I'm content to share in the profits and do my own thing the rest of the time."

"And your thing is?"

Up ahead, the creek that joined the river sparkled in the golden glow of a summer day, and cattle, mostly Herefords, grazed contentedly in the wind-rippled grass.

Brylee took a moment to consider her reply. "Keeping my company in the black, I suppose," she finally answered. A vague sense of disquiet swept through her then, soft as an imagined breeze, and she stiffened her spine against it, jutted out her chin a little way.

Zane flashed a grin at her, and its impact was so palpable that, for the briefest moment, she thought it might actually jolt her out of the saddle.

No holograms here, she thought. This was pure reality.

One man, one woman.

Red alert.

"Confession time," Zane said, with another grin. "I read up on you—online, I mean. Décor Galore is something of a modern legend, it seems—the little start-up that could."

Brylee let Toby have his head then, and he went straight to the creek side, waded in ankle-deep and drank noisily. "I did a little research on you, too, as it happens," she replied, as Blackjack bent his gleaming neck to drink alongside Brylee's gelding. "The accidental movie star, thrust from the rodeo circuit to the big screen in no time at all."

That was glib, Brylee thought, with regret, a moment after the words were out of her mouth, and she saw by the brief tightening around Zane's mouth that she'd struck a nerve. She didn't know much about acting, but she'd certainly seen how hard Casey worked when she was recording, performing or making a video, and she guessed starring in films was at least that difficult, if not more so.

"There was a little more to it," Zane said mildly, and at the tag end of a rather uncomfortable silence. "But, yeah, I guess you could call it accidental. I sure didn't plan on any of it."

Brylee drew a deep breath, let it out slowly and forced herself to look Zane's way, to meet his gaze directly. His eyes had turned to a hot shade of blue, reminiscent of St. Elmo's fire, though his mouth had softened a bit.

"I didn't mean to minimize your accomplishments," she began lamely, and then, losing all momentum, fell miserably mute. The horses were restless, ready to move on, so, by tacit agreement, Brylee and Zane rode together up the gently sloping bank.

"Have you ever seen any of my movies?" Zane asked.

Inwardly, Brylee groaned. Outwardly, she smiled, albeit with rigid effort. "No," she admitted, wishing she could lie. "I mean—I don't go to the movies much...."

His grin practically blinded her. "That's okay, Brylee," he said, and he certainly looked and sounded sincere.

Then again, he *was* an actor. There was no telling what was *really* going on in that handsome head of his.

"I was just curious, that's all," he went on, now scanning the horizon. He was quiet for a while. "This is a beautiful place," he added presently, his tone almost reverent. "No wonder they call it God's country."

Brylee felt a strange sort of chagrin. She didn't pander to people, but she wasn't given to rudeness, either. And she hadn't given Zane Sutton a fair chance, not from the very first.

"I'd like to," she blurted, almost shyly, then, blushing again, hastened to clarify the statement. "See one of your movies sometime, I mean."

His smile was slow and way too understanding. "That could be arranged," he answered easily. "Join us for supper tonight and we'll watch the latest one online."

Brylee truly did want to see one of Zane's films, but she'd expected to have a little time to prepare herself. "You just moved in," she hedged. "I wouldn't want to impose."

Zane cocked his head a little to one side and regarded her from under the brim of his hat. "Are you this ambivalent about life in general," he queried moderately, "or just about me?"

Zap. The man had a *gift* for getting under her skin. Brylee felt her face heat up again, ever so slightly, but this time she was annoyed, not embarrassed. "Just about you," she answered, when she was darn good and ready.

That made him laugh, right out loud, a masculine sound, raspy and rich and wholly *un*selfconscious. "At least you're honest," he said, when the shout of amusement had waned to a grin. "That's a rare enough commodity these days, in my opinion."

They'd covered considerable distance by then and, unsettled as she was, Brylee didn't even think about turning back, calling it a day. "I'm definitely honest," she said, softening, and still dizzy with confusion, which wasn't the least bit like her. "To a fault, some people would say."

Zane adjusted his hat. He looked at home in the saddle, broad in the shoulders and lean through the waist and hips. The vibes he gave off were disturbingly fascinating, a sort of quiet, unshakable competence and an innate strength that had as much to do with character as muscle tone.

"Just what is it about me that scares you?" he asked.

There it was again, that no-holds-barred directness that always seemed to catch her off balance.

Brylee opened her mouth, closed it again. "Who says I'm scared of you?" she challenged, when she found her voice.

"I do," Zane said, in a low, matter-of-fact tone. "You take offense at about every other word that comes out of my mouth, for one thing. And this might just be my take on the situation, but I don't believe you're always so prickly. If you were, you couldn't have built an essentially people-based business from the ground up and turned it into a mega concern."

Just when she was prepared to be totally and irrevocably irritated, he *complimented* her, albeit in a backhanded way. She *was* proud of Décor Galore, justifiably so, and he was right about something else, too. She was, in general, a very nice person. "You think I'm prickly?"

Truth be told, she was a little hurt.

"Yeah," Zane answered, with another lethal grin. "I *do* think you're prickly—when you're around me, anyway. It's like you're expecting me to give you trouble, so you shoot quills like a cornered porcupine, as a preemptive strike of some kind. Why is that?"

Since she couldn't rightfully deny the porcupine theory, Brylee turned pensive, rolling the matter around in her mind for a few moments, trying to get a handle on the crux of it all. Normally, she knew her own mind, wasn't given to bouncing back and forth between thoughts like a pinball in an arcade machine. Did those even exist anymore, or were they obsolete? "I guess I'm wary of celebrities," she finally said. It wasn't much, but that was all the mental search produced.

"Including your very famous sister-in-law?" Zane asked.

"Casey's different."

"Maybe I am, too," he suggested.

"And maybe you're not," Brylee argued, though not with much spirit. "It probably isn't necessary to remind you that we get more than our share of movie stars out here, following some fantasy they picked up doing a guest spot on *Little House on the Prairie,* looking for peace and quiet and who knows what else."

Zane studied her, arching one eyebrow just slightly. "You object to the big houses, the landing strips—what?" He spoke reasonably. "I would imagine the Hollywood crowd pumps a respectable amount of money into the local economy."

A little of the wind went out of Brylee's sails. She sighed. "There's work for a while—carpentry and plumbing and that kind of thing," she conceded. "They move in and everything's great—until it isn't. Some of them even try to become part of the community."

"And then?" Zane prompted.

"And then they get bored and leave," Brylee said. "The party's over. The big house stands empty and forlorn, sometimes for years, and then another hotshot moves into the place, if they haven't decided to put up a brand-new monstrosity of their very own, and the whole process repeats itself."

"Ah," Zane said. That was all—just "ah." It was as though all the pieces of the puzzle that was Brylee had just fallen into place in his mind, and he'd come to some profound understanding of her deepest and most secret self.

Brylee was terribly afraid he was right.

CHAPTER SEVEN

HAD HE JUST stuck his damn fool neck right out, or what? Zane asked himself, shifting in the saddle, a place where he was seldom uneasy, and readjusting his hat for the umpteenth time as he awaited Brylee's response to the impromptu supper/movie invitation.

Now that it was too late, he could think of all kinds of good reasons why he should have kept his mouth shut.

To start with, it was too soon for even an innocent get-together like the one he'd suggested, and practiced instincts warned that he was moving too fast where Brylee was concerned. Practical, independent and in no way needy, she was nothing like Tiffany, or any of the other women he'd ever gotten tangled up with for that matter, and getting to know her, not just superficially but down deep, would be a slow process, requiring finesse, patience—and just about every other virtue he could think of.

He might as well just toss out all he supposedly knew about the fairer sex, too, he realized, because with Brylee, the ground rules were different.

Not that he'd figured out what in hell those rules *were,* exactly, because he hadn't.

Brylee was beautiful but earthy, and she had substance, a quality that went way beyond the physical. She was also skittish, and understandably so, if all that stuff posted on the internet about her and Hutch Carmody was even partly true. He'd seen the pictures, had to swallow hard when he thought of her standing there in that jam-packed church in Parable, looking like a storybook princess in her wedding dress, clutching her bouquet, confused and furious and, behind it all, very, very hurt.

Whoever this Carmody fool was, he had all the sensitivity of a grizzly bear with a toothache, and Zane had already made up his mind not to like him, should they ever cross paths in the first place. Which they almost certainly would, given that Parable and Three Trees—the thirty-mile distance between them notwithstanding—were basically one town, people-wise.

Hutch Carmody. What kind of low-down, yellow-bellied SOB waited until the wedding was in full swing before opting out on the marriage, anyhow?

Beleaguered, Zane finally set those particular thoughts aside, since they wouldn't lead him anywhere he wanted to go.

The reasons for *not* having company that night—especially *this* company—continued to rack up in his mind, like a passel of circus bumper cars all heading for the middle at once and crashing into one another.

To start with, the house was a shambles. *Worse* than a shambles. In his L.A. neighborhood, a place like that would have been condemned.

And as far as supper went, well, there wasn't any decent food to speak of—canned ravioli definitely wouldn't fill the bill—and since he hadn't bothered to bring along his TV when he left California, the only way to watch a movie, his or anybody else's, would be to hunch in front of his laptop like a pair of birds crowded together on a short stretch of wire.

Not that the idea of sitting close—the closer, the better, in fact—to Brylee Parrish, under just about any circumstances, didn't have its high points, but things had to be done right, damn it. Not okay, not passable, but *right*.

This get-together was important, though Zane didn't feel inclined to explore the reasons why he thought so, and he knew from experience that, sometimes, a man only gets one chance with a woman like Brylee. They didn't come along every day, after all.

Zane sensed that this was one of those times, dangerously pivotal, and he didn't intend to blow it.

Furthermore, he'd told Cleo they'd go to town for the stuff she needed to make the house at least semifit for human habitation, and Nash was expecting to score a TV, probably the first one he'd ever owned. Breaking a promise to the kid was no way to build trust, now was it? Furthermore, it was a Jess Sutton move for sure—get somebody's hopes up and then decide not to be bothered.

And if there was one person in the world Zane didn't want to emulate, it was his waste-of-skin father.

"Maybe another time," Brylee said almost gently, bringing him back from his mental meanderings. She looked so earnest, sitting there on that little gelding's back, even elegant, but, at the same time, mildly apologetic. Late-afternoon sunshine glowed in her glorious brown hair, like an aura woven directly into the strands, and he saw a certain reluctance in her eyes, along with something else that wasn't so easy to name. Never looking away from his face, she paused, bit her lower lip and finally went on, with a shaky effort at a smile. "You're still getting settled and all. How about coming to our place instead, you and Nash—and Cleo, of course—say, Saturday night? We could watch the movie then, all of us. And Casey says you two have met before, so she's been planning on asking you over anyhow...."

He'd wanted an out, Zane thought, and lo and behold, Brylee had given him one, along with an invitation for Saturday night. This was a *good* thing. So why did he feel deflated all of a sudden, as though she'd just shut him down, as though the main chance had already come and gone, with him barely noticing, never to come around again?

All these emotions were foreign to Zane, being a relatively uncomplicated person, and he shook them off. He'd known Brylee Parrish for a day, and she was already making him crazy, which was either the worst possible preview of coming attractions—or the best.

"I know Casey fairly well," he confirmed smoothly. "We did a made-for-TV movie together once. It would be good to see her again and meet the rest of the family."

Of course Brylee was using the kinfolk as a buffer, a way to establish a polite but safe distance between them when he ventured onto her turf, but that was okay.

Take things slow, cowboy, Zane told himself. *Real, real slow.*

Brylee's face lit up suddenly—was it the word *family?*—and knocked Zane back on his figurative heels a little. The woman actually *glowed,* like the figure of an angel in a stained-glass window flooded with sunlight, and the sight of her hit him where he lived.

"My niece and nephew will be thrilled to meet you in person," she went on, gathering momentum. "And Shane—that's my nephew, of course—is just a little older than Nash, so I think they might enjoy hanging out together."

She'd shifted her gelding's reins in the direction of home, a subtle clue that the ride was over and that, for the time being at least, Brylee preferred to go her way and let him go his.

"Sounds good," he said, by way of an acceptance, and tugged at the brim of his hat in the time-honored way of a cowboy bidding a lady "so long."

And Brylee Parrish was most definitely a lady.

"I'll get back to you with the details," Brylee said, fully at ease now, smiling. What had changed? "About all of us getting together for supper, I mean."

Zane grinned to himself. Given that she'd just issued an invitation on her sister-in-law's behalf, she probably had to clear the plan with Casey. "All right," he agreed, reining Blackjack toward his own place. "Thanks for showing me around, Brylee. I enjoyed it."

A soft, peachy-pink color blossomed in her cheeks. As though stuck for a reply, she swallowed visibly and nodded, but said nothing.

That would have to do for "You're welcome," Zane decided, amused and already looking forward to Saturday, which probably went to prove that he was a little shy of a truckload in the common sense department.

They parted cordially then and, recrossing the range land that bordered his own spread way off in the distance, Zane let Blackjack trot, then lope and finally gallop full-out, the way the critter had probably been wanting to do from the second he stepped down from that horse trailer. Once Zane was sure he was out of both Brylee's sight and her hearing, he whipped off his hat, swung it over his head in a wide loop and let out a hoarse shout of pure happiness.

By the time Zane's house and barn came into sight, Blackjack had slowed to an easy walk, his ebony hide glistening from the exercise.

Seeing Nash and Slim in what passed for a yard, Zane smiled to himself. They'd been playing a game of fetch, it appeared, but the dog was doing it his way. He sat still as a monument, there in the tall, weedy grass, watching Nash throw a stick, wait in vain for Slim to go after it and finally chase it himself.

Zane knew the boy had been waiting for him to

come back, though most likely a tow truck couldn't have dragged the admission out of Nash. The kid made a practice of not needing anybody—it was safer that way.

Not for the first time, Zane felt a sharp pang of regret. He and Landry were about all the boy had. Why hadn't either one of them stepped up and done something? On his part, he supposed, it had been plain old self-centered apathy. When you got right down to it, he hadn't wanted to be bothered, take time out of his busy life, and Landry's reasons were probably similar.

Riding nearer, Zane heard the echo of his mother's voice in his head. *If folks would just take care of their own,* Maddie Rose had often said, *there wouldn't be so many lonesome, hurting people in this old world.*

And Maddie Rose Sutton had *definitely* taken care of her own—him and Landry—even though it meant taking whatever work she could get and constantly moving from one place to another and never having two nickels to rub together.

Near the barn door, standing open as it did during the daylight hours, Zane swung down from the saddle, nodded to his younger brother and led Blackjack inside, to his stall. He was brushing the animal down, to help him cool off, when Nash sauntered nonchalantly along the breezeway and paused to watch the proceedings.

"Are we still going into town to buy stuff?" the boy asked, going for a casual tone and manner but not quite making the grade. "Miss Cleo's got a list, and she's already looking up local contractors on the internet."

"We're still going to town," Zane replied quietly. Finished grooming the horse, he put the brush away, patted Blackjack on one flank and opened the stall door to step out. A grin quirked one corner of his mouth as he regarded his little brother. "I thought you were fed up with shopping, the way you groused about it earlier."

Nash flashed a grin and, once again, Zane got a glimpse of the man the kid would grow up to be, given half a chance, a little love and a reasonable amount of guidance. "That was before you said you'd buy me my own TV," he replied.

Zane laughed and slapped Nash lightly on the back. Slim ambling alongside, they headed for the house.

The moment they stepped inside, it was clear to Zane that Hurricane Cleo had made landfall. Hardly a decorator's dream before, the kitchen strongly resembled a federal disaster area now, with the flooring rolled up in big, ragged curls and most of the cupboards torn from the wall as if by brute force.

The president would probably arrive with a boots-on-the-ground task force any minute now, accompanied by the Red Cross and various other relief agencies. Most likely, Oprah already had semis rolling, loaded with blankets, medicine, bottled water and brand-new issues of her magazine.

Zane sighed, shoved a hand through his hair. Good thing Brylee hadn't taken him up on that invite to supper, he reflected ruefully. One look at this place, and she'd have been scared off for sure—and maybe for good.

Cleo, still in her floral-print scrubs, her hair wild around her round face, now that it was no longer contained by the hat with the bobbing flower, rose and met Zane's stunned gaze with a fierce glower, clearly expecting a fight. Her jaw clamped down visibly, her eyes flashed and she folded her arms across her ample bosom. *"What?"* she challenged.

Zane laughed, looked around again and said, "Talk about shock-and-awe. Tell me you didn't do this all on your own."

"I helped," Nash put in proudly. "We found a sledgehammer in one of the sheds and, after that, it was easy."

"No chain saw?" Zane quipped.

Nobody got the joke.

"Just making things easier for the contractors," Cleo said, mellowing out a little now that she figured Zane wasn't fixing to hit the roof over the mess she and Nash had made. Given that he'd never so much as raised his voice to the woman in all the time she'd worked for him, he was amused that she'd braced herself for trouble the way she had. "They'll start putting in their bids first thing tomorrow morning. By the next day, this whole place will be swarming with construction people."

"Yeehaw," Zane murmured dryly, thinking of the noise and the sawdust and the general disruption.

Not that he'd planned anything for tomorrow that required concentration.

"You had a phone call," Cleo informed him as a brisk afterthought, indicating the cell Zane had left behind on the charger when he left to go riding with Brylee. "I don't know who it was, but they're persistent."

Zane shook his head and approached the counter, one of the few things in that kitchen that was still standing. He picked up the phone, touched the screen to bring the thing to life and frowned. Three messages, all from a Chicago number.

Landry? Wasn't he in Berlin or somewhere, wheeling and dealing?

Curious, he thumbed the voice-mail icon and put the device to his ear. "Call me," Landry said. No explanation, no "if you have time," not even a simple "Hello." Just a snapped answer and a hang-up.

He didn't bother with the other two messages. In fact, Zane's strongest impulse was to ignore the calls entirely, or return them whenever he got around to it, if that ever happened, but he couldn't do that. Landry rarely contacted him—the announcement that Nash was winging his way to Montana on a commercial jet was the first Zane had heard from his brother since a two-line email sometime around Christmas.

So he hit the callback button.

He wandered into the big, empty living room, waiting for Landry to pick up. Cleo hadn't gotten that far with her sledgehammer, but the space looked like the aftermath of a no-holds-barred demolition derby just the same.

"Zane?" Landry's voice was clipped, brusque. He sounded almost irritated, as though he'd been doing something vital to the future of the free world and Zane had interrupted him for a mundane chat.

"Just returning your call," Zane said, with an easy affability he didn't feel. There was a lot wrong between him and Landry, though they'd been close once, and he'd long since decided to steer clear.

"Good," Landry ground out. "That's good. Er—thanks."

"I'd say 'you're welcome,'" Zane drawled in reply, "but that would be stretching the truth, little brother. What's up?"

Landry huffed out an exasperated sigh. "I called to ask if the kid—Nash, I mean—got there okay."

"Nice of you to ask," Zane gibed, keeping his tone cordial. "He's here and he's fine. And how come you're not in Germany doing whatever it is you do?"

"There was a change of plans," Landry answered, after a beat or two. His tone was still grudging, but, though the change was nearly imperceptible, he'd backed off a little.

Something in the way his brother sounded made Zane uneasy. Landry didn't usually have any trouble speaking his mind, but he was choosing his words carefully now, and there was an air of awkwardness around them.

"You okay?" Zane asked, after a few moments of

silent debate with a part of himself that would rather leave this alone.

Landry gave a ragged sigh in response. "I'm just feeling kind of restless, I guess," he said. It was the closest he'd come to opening up, at least to Zane, since before their mother died. "You know that old bit about climbing the rungs to success and then finding out you had your ladder against the wrong wall?"

Zane let out his breath. "Been there, done that," he said, and waited.

Another pause followed, then Landry answered with a sort of deliberate cheer. "I thought I might come out there for a week or so—to Montana, that is—and have a look at that ranch of ours."

"All right," Zane said, mildly baffled. Landry had never shown an interest in Hangman's Bend, beyond plunking down a sizable amount of money for his half of nearly three thousand acres and signing the appropriate papers. Though he'd had no more intention of actually living out here in the boondocks than his brother had, Zane had paid extra for the existing house and barn, so on some level, he must have figured on winding up there at some point.

"What's the nearest town?" Landry asked, in a distracted tone, as though he might be taking notes but already chafing to get on to the next item on his agenda.

"Place called Three Trees," Zane answered.

"I thought it had some Bible name," Landry mused. Zane could picture his brother frowning.

"That's the next town over—Parable," he said.

"Right," Landry said. "Is there a hotel?"

Zane grinned. He hadn't done a whole lot of research on the area himself, but he knew Parable County boasted several run-down but respectable motels, the kind that used to be called "motor courts," along with a few bed-and-breakfast type establishments. Landry, the city boy, was probably picturing his usual accommodations—say, the Peninsula or the Ritz.

"You can stay here," he replied, expecting a refusal. "It's rustic, but we have plenty of room."

"Who's doing the cooking?" Landry wanted to know. "Not you, I hope."

Zane almost laughed. "Cleo is in charge of grub," he replied, picking up on his brother's indirect reference to an episode when they were probably nine and ten years old. One night, home alone in a motel room in some dusty Texas town clinging to the crumbling sides of a road all but obsolete now that the freeways were in, they'd been especially hungry, so Zane had decided to whip up a meal instead of waiting for their mom to bring home whatever was left of that day's special at the café. Since the room didn't have a kitchen, Zane had set the secondhand hot plate on the desk in front of the window, heated the burner to a red glow and proceeded to fry up a few slices of bologna in an empty aluminum pie tin.

Five minutes into this culinary endeavor, the cheap curtains had caught fire, and he and Landry had fled, panicked and coughing up their socks, into the weedy gravel parking lot. Black smoke billowed through the open door and the manager appeared, sweating and swearing, wielding a fire extinguisher that sprayed one shot of foam and then fizzled.

Fortunately, the volunteer fire department had arrived promptly to put out the blaze, and the whole place hadn't burned down, but the room was pretty much trashed—walls blackened, floor and furnishings swamped with water from the heavy canvas hoses.

When their mother got home from work, less than half an hour later, a boxed supper of leftover meat loaf and mashed potatoes in hand, she'd been greeted by the manager, who was, of course, raving by then. He'd reminded her loudly that the use of hot plates and other such appliances in the rooms was strictly forbidden, and now his insurance rates were going to go up, and then told her to load her brats in the car and hit the road.

Relieved that the kids were alive and unscathed and she wasn't being asked to pay for the damage, Maddie Rose Sutton hadn't said much at all; she'd simply listened to the old man's diatribe until he'd run out of steam, then loaded up what few personal belongings she could salvage, gestured to her wide-eyed boys to get into the battered station wagon, settled the motel bill with what was probably her last few dollars and driven away.

The backs of Zane's eyes burned, remembering how brave she'd been, and how patient, and how ridiculously young. Some mothers would have yelled—and not without justification—but she'd merely handed the box of food over the backseat, along with a couple of plastic forks from the stash in the glove compartment, and told them to eat before the food got any colder than it already was.

Realizing that Landry was still talking, Zane jerked himself out of the memory and back into the here and now. Whatever his brother had said, he'd missed it, and he was too hardheaded and proud to ask for an instant replay.

"So, anyway," Landry said, winding down now, "I'll see you when I see you."

"Great," Zane said, mystified. He had no clue when—or if—his brother would show up, or, if he did put in an appearance, whether he'd stay there at the ranch house or get himself a room in Three Trees or Parable.

Time would tell.

They said their goodbyes and the conversation was over.

When Zane got back to the demolished kitchen, Cleo and Nash were waiting impatiently. Cleo had changed into purple pants and a matching top with ruffles, but she still wore the yellow sneakers.

Zane, thankful for small favors, was glad she hadn't put her hat back on to complete the look. Leaving Slim to snooze contentedly in his favorite corner, apparently heedless of the ruin surrounding him on all sides, Zane, Cleo and Nash climbed into the truck and left for town.

The process took a couple of hours, and by the

time they got back to the ranch, after supper at the Bluebell Café, it was getting dark. Zane sent Cleo on into the house while he and Nash began unloading a dizzying array of purchases from the back of the pickup.

"How did your hot date go, anyhow?" Nash asked companionably with no preamble whatsoever as he lugged his newly acquired TV, still in its box, across the yard, following a path of light spilling from the open door Cleo had just passed through.

Zane hadn't been thinking about Brylee, but about the old days, and Maddie Rose, and how he and Landry had been thick as thieves when they were younger. He took a moment to register his brother's question, and then answered, not unkindly, "That, boy, is none of your damn business."

Nash accepted the reply with equanimity—most likely, being out of the loop was nothing new to him, given that Jess had always been long on doing what came naturally and short on explaining why—hesitated, then posed a question of his own. "Do you think Dad knows where I am?"

Zane was glad it was fairly dark in the yard, and his face was in shadow beneath the brim of his hat, because he wouldn't have wanted the boy to see the expression on his face, a combination of pity for Nash and cold anger at the man who'd gone off and left him on Landry's doorstep. Sure, Landry was family, but, like Zane, he was still a virtual stranger to the kid.

"He'll be in touch," Zane heard himself say, his voice husky. *Or not.*

He should have been straight with him, told the boy what he surely already knew, that Jess Sutton was about as dependable as a cheap flashlight with low batteries, but it was no use. People mostly believed what they *wanted* to believe, especially when the alternative was a hard truth. Why should Nash be the exception?

"You think so?" Nash asked, sounding hopeful and worried, both at once.

Lugging half the contents of the supermarket in Three Trees, Zane didn't have a free hand, or he would have given the kid a brief pat on the shoulder, in an effort to reassure him a little. "What's his pattern?" he asked, as they climbed the porch steps, Nash in the lead with his TV.

"His pattern?" Nash asked, glancing back over one shoulder and nearly tripping over the dog awaiting him just inside the kitchen door.

"When he takes off," Zane replied, with no inflection, "how long does he usually stay away?"

Over Nash's head, Zane locked gazes with Cleo, who frowned.

Nash set the box down with obvious relief, ruffling Slim's ears and laughing a little as the dog jumped, and circled and finally sat. His eyes were serious, though, when he looked at Zane, and one of his skinny shoulders moved in a halfhearted shrug. "It depends," he admitted. But then the glum expression slacked off just slightly, and he added, "He always comes back, though. Sooner or later. When he does, we have a good time, going to movies and eating in restaurants and stuff."

By then, Zane was avoiding Cleo's eyes, but he knew that she was thinking pretty much the same thing he was. Jess Sutton wasn't worth the space he took up or the air he breathed, and all the wishing and hoping in the universe wasn't going to change him.

"Let's get this stuff inside and put away as best we can," Zane managed, still sounding rusty. "I don't know about the two of you, but I'm looking forward to a shower and eight hours of sleep."

"You just carry in the rest of what we bought," Cleo interjected. "We're going to have to live out of bags and boxes for a while, anyhow, since there's no place to put everything, once the refrigerator is filled up."

Zane nodded. Cleo hadn't said anything particularly profound, but she'd made the situation easier, just the same.

He and Nash unloaded the truck, then Nash went off to his room, Slim at his heels, to try out his new TV.

Zane said a quiet good-night to Cleo, who looked like she expected him to say something and was going to be nonplussed if he didn't, and retreated into his own space, such as it was.

The shower was soothing—for once, there was plenty of hot water.

The air mattress was tolerable, even bordering on comfortable.

Still, Zane didn't fall asleep right away, tired as he was. He lay in the darkness, with his hands cupped behind his head, thinking about the way Brylee Parrish looked in a pair of jeans and grinning like an idiot.

CHAPTER EIGHT

BRYLEE BIT HER lower lip as she studied Casey's face, there in the kitchen of the main ranch house. "Really?" she asked anxiously. "You don't mind?"

Casey, who was peering at a page in an old cookbook, an apron tied around her tiny waist, scratched away a splatter mark with one fingernail and chuckled. "Of *course* I don't," she said, giving the words a musical lilt, as she often did. Sometimes, it was hard to decide if Casey was talking or singing—she had music in her at the cellular level, it seemed, and she exuded it. "I told you I wanted to invite Zane over for supper one day soon, since he and I are acquainted. Besides, this is still your home, too. You don't need my permission to have guests, Brylee." Earnest tears glistened in those famously green eyes for the briefest of moments, then she added huskily, "You're not feeling shut out, like you're not part of the family, are you? Because you *are*."

Brylee gave her sister-in-law a quick, impulsive hug, touched by the pained expression on the woman's face. Casey was deliriously happy, now that she and Walker were finally married, no doubt about that, but it didn't stop her from fretting that she and the kids had somehow swept Brylee aside.

"No," Brylee protested. "Casey, I'm thrilled that you and Walker finally got your acts together and tied the knot, and you know I love Clare and Shane and Preston as if they were mine." She folded her arms, tilted her head to one side and studied her brother's wife with mock solemnity. "I've been living in that apartment since I came home from college, you know, and that was long before you came on the scene. I like it. In other words, I'm *fine.*"

Okay, so it was a good thing Brylee didn't happen to have her hand resting on a Bible just then, but what she'd said was *mostly* true. She *was* glad Casey and Walker were married, and she *did* adore all three of the children, too. But if she admitted that she sometimes felt like the proverbial fifth wheel, no longer comfortable having free run of the main part of the house the way she used to, Casey wouldn't understand that it had nothing to do with her and the kids being there. She'd stew and worry, because that's how she was—she cared about other people, cared a lot.

"You'd say something if you were unhappy, wouldn't you?" Casey pressed, very softly. Her eyes were dry now, but her lower lip quivered just slightly.

Brylee was forced to tell another white lie. "Yes," she replied, shifting her focus to the well-used cookbook Casey had been perusing. Passed down from Walker and Brylee's great-grandmother, the volume was dog-eared, marked up and positively bristling with slips of paper bearing notes in faded handwriting. "What are you planning on whipping up, Mrs. Parrish?" she asked, to change the subject.

Casey twinkled. "Biscuits," she replied. "Walker loves the things—he'd eat them at breakfast, lunch and dinner—and I thought I'd take a stab at making a batch the old-fashioned way. He never complains about the ones that come from the supermarket in a cardboard tube, but I know he misses the homemade kind."

Brylee rested a hand on Casey's shoulder, gave it a light squeeze. "You know what?" she said gently. "Walker's one lucky cowboy, getting you for a wife." This time, she was being completely truthful.

Casey gave a chortling laugh, along with an involuntary sniffle. "I'd say *I'm* the lucky one," she countered, holding the heavy cookbook up in front of her face and squinting comically at the printed recipe, even though there was nothing wrong with her eyesight. "It looks so simple—flour, some shortening and buttermilk, a little salt—but…"

Brylee moved to the sink, washed her hands with soap and hot water. "You can do this, Casey," she lectured, grinning. "But if it would make you feel better, I'd be glad to give you a few pointers."

Casey beamed. "That would be *excellent!*" she said.

Soon, both of them were up to their elbows in sifted flour—standing side by side at one of the long counters and chatting away as they built a double batch of country biscuits.

"How are Shane and Clare doing?" Brylee asked, leaving Preston out of the inquiry only because he was lying in his portable crib nearby, sleeping soundly and obviously thriving.

Casey made a face. "Shane's behaving himself, though he's still hectoring both Walker and me something fierce about letting him enter the rodeo next month," she answered. "Clare's been a little quiet, since she found out that boy she liked was just using her to get to me, but having Zane Sutton here for supper will probably cheer her right up. She's a huge fan."

The reminder of Zane gave Brylee pause—she always felt better when she forgot to think about him, since whenever he came to mind a jolt of sweet electricity went through her—but it didn't break her conversational stride. She dropped her voice to a mischievous whisper and went on to confide, "He's a looker, all right. If I wasn't afraid he'd find out about it and get the wrong idea, I'd rent all his movies and watch them one right after the other."

Casey giggled. "I knew it," she said, with a note of soft triumph in her voice. "You're *smitten* with the man, Brylee Parrish."

"I'm not *smitten*," Brylee insisted. *Heck, no,* chided her inner critic, the one who always had an argument ready, *you just want to rip his clothes off and roll around with him in the tall grass naked as the day you were born, that's all.*

Brylee blushed at the inevitable—and X-rated— image that had taken shape in her brain.

Watching her, Casey gave a bubbly burst of amusement. "If you could see your face!"

Thank heaven the woman wasn't psychic, Brylee thought. But Casey *was* perceptive—more so than most people, anyhow—and she was whip-smart, too. With that agile mind of hers, it wasn't any big leap for her to guess what Brylee was thinking. In fact, Shane and Clare swore up and down their mom had eyes in the back of her head.

"It's time to roll out this dough and cut some biscuits," Brylee said decisively, all business now. "Set the oven temperature at 375 and I'll get out a couple of glasses and some cookie sheets."

Casey frowned and squinted at the cookbook again. "The recipe says 350," she told Brylee seriously.

Brylee waved a hand to dismiss that. "This oven has been twenty-five degrees off for as long as I can remember," she answered. "So 375 will do it."

Casey sighed and moved to the stove, while Brylee scrounged through the cupboards under the counter for a pair of cookie sheets, found the rolling pin in a drawer and finally reached overhead for a pair of drinking glasses. They'd use the rims to cut perfect circles in the dough, once they'd rolled it out on a floury surface.

By the time Walker, Shane and some of the ranch hands came in for supper a short while later, the air in that kitchen was downright redolent with the smell of perfectly baked biscuits.

Brylee snatched a couple for herself, placed them on

a paper towel and stood on tiptoe to kiss her brother's beard-stubbled cheek. "See you around," she told him, smiling at the sheer delight in his face as he breathed in the aroma and gave Casey an exuberant hug.

"Biscuits?" he said, almost as though he might be afraid to hope.

"Yep," Brylee replied, summoning Snidely, who had been sleeping under the table since she got back from the ride with Zane Sutton, and heading for the apartment. At the door, she paused, looked back over one shoulder and said, "That wife of yours is definitely a keeper, Walker Parrish. I hope you're thanking your lucky stars for her, and often."

Walker chuckled, his eyes glowing, and planted a smacking kiss on Casey's upturned, flour-splotched face. "Believe me," he replied gruffly, as his bride smiled back at him, "I say thank you with about every breath I draw."

The words touched Brylee in parts of her heart that were still bruised, and she wondered if she'd ever know that kind of love.

Determined not to let her feelings show, she exchanged a glance with Shane, raised her eyebrows and slipped out, with Snidely right behind her, his toenails clicking on the tile floor.

No more than two minutes could have passed when someone knocked at the door between Brylee's apartment and Casey and Walker's kitchen. It opened, and Shane stuck his head inside.

"Can I come in?"

Brylee had just buttered both the biscuits she'd

helped herself to and was on the verge of devouring the first one. She hadn't realized how hungry she was. "Don't let me stop you," she teased, with a small grin. "Want a biscuit?"

Shane shook his head. "No, thanks," he said, stepping into the corridor. "Mom's got about a million of them stacked on a platter, and we'll be having supper in a few minutes. You were out of there so fast, Dad didn't get the chance to ask you to join us, so he sent me to do it."

Brylee might have said she wasn't hungry, if she hadn't had a growling stomach and a mouth full of fresh, flaky, delicious biscuit at the moment. She chewed, swallowed and reached for the second one, still resting on its paper towel nearby, oozing butter where she'd sliced it in half. "Not tonight," she said pleasantly. "I've got things to do."

"Like what?" Shane asked. He'd had a growth spurt since school let out in the spring, and he was nearly as tall as Walker. It was scary how fast kids grew up—why, in no time at all, she might be having a similar conversation with Preston.

An honest reply—she planned to wash her hair, check her personal emails and possibly set the DVR to record one of Zane's movies—was out of the question. On the other hand, she didn't want to fib again, as she had earlier, to Casey, in case it got to be a habit. Taking the easy way out was tempting, but it was also a slippery slope. Therefore, she was stuck for an answer.

Shane didn't miss her hesitation, of course—that would have made things too easy and, besides, like his sister, he was a sharp kid. His expression was sort of wistful, and he was watching her closely. "You mad at us or something?" he asked.

Brylee was horrified. "No," she responded quickly. "Of course I'm not."

"You always say no when we invite you to come over," Shane reminded her. He actually looked a little hurt, and sounded that way, too. Still pretty grubby from herding cattle all day with his dad and some of the ranch hands, he shifted his weight slightly, from one leg to the other. "It's weird."

Brylee realized she *had* been making a lot of excuses lately, keeping to herself when she wasn't at the office, and there was no point in denying the fact. "I'm just trying to give you guys some space over there," she said lamely, forgetting all about the second biscuit she'd been planning to gobble up. "Let you be a family, just the five of you."

"*You're* part of our family, too," Shane said, as a Walker-like smile crept to his lips and then rose to flicker in his eyes. He spread his hands in a got-you-there kind of gesture. "Come on, Brylee," he urged. "If I go back and tell Mom and Dad you think you're in the way or something, they'll bring out the big guns. You'll get no peace at all, ever."

He was right, of course.

"Can we make a deal?" Brylee asked, attempting a smile and wringing her hands a little.

"Depends," Shane said. He was barely a teenager, yet already his voice was changing. And he was gaining confidence as well as lean muscle.

"I'll come and have supper with the rest of you if you promise not to tell your folks what I said. About why I haven't been over that much lately, I mean."

Shane considered the bargain, pursing his lips and narrowing his eyes mischievously as he worked the matter through in his head.

"Okay," the boy finally agreed, with one of those sun-parting-the-rain-clouds smiles that always reminded her of her big brother. Soon enough, Shane would be irresistible to the female gender. Too bad there was no way to warn girls and women everywhere. "Maybe you can get Clare to talk. I always wished she'd shut up, but now, all of a sudden, she's got nothing to say, and it's creepy. She's been pouting for days over that stupid guy who was going to romance her on the bus trip to the capital, and it's a total bummer just to be around her."

This time, Brylee smiled without effort, nodded. "I'll do my best to draw your sister into the conversation," she promised. "Give me five minutes to wash up and feed Snidely, and I'll join you."

Shane, having accomplished his mission, grinned again and went out the same way he'd come in.

Once the door closed behind him, Brylee sighed and rolled her eyes heavenward, but she wasn't really exasperated. In fact, a part of her rejoiced at the prospect of sharing a meal with the rest of the Parrish clan.

She'd been lonely lately—she could admit that now.

Not out loud, of course. Just to herself. But that was progress, wasn't it?

THE FIRST CROP of contractors showed up at Hangman's Bend bright and early the next morning, clipboards in hand, retractable tape measures at the ready, expressions serious and businesslike as Cleo shepherded them from room to room, explaining what she wanted done—which was amazingly specific, in Zane's opinion. She had it figured out right down to the style of fixtures for the bathrooms and the color of each and every wall.

Looking on in amused silence, Zane marveled at her energy and the quick certainty in her voice. He'd figured out that the floors ought to be replaced, and the kitchen brought into the twenty-first century—the room had skipped the twentieth entirely—but that was as far as it went. He hadn't thought about furniture at all, except to acknowledge that they'd need some, but Cleo seemed to have her mind made up about couches and chairs, tables and lamps and the like.

He was more than willing to let the woman have her way.

Nash, meanwhile, sat at the rickety card table in the center of the bomb-zone kitchen, spooning cereal from his bowl and then putting it back before it got to his mouth.

"What's the problem?" Zane asked mildly, watching his younger brother and sipping coffee from one of the six mugs they'd bought the night before, on the shopping expedition to Three Trees.

"It's boring around here," Nash complained. He glanced down at Slim, who was waiting for him to finish breakfast, and idly stroked the animal's head. When he went on, his voice was quiet. "I can't even get a game of fetch going with this dumb old dog. I throw the stick and throw the stick, and he won't chase it. He just sits there until I go get it myself."

Zane hid a grin behind the rim of his mug. He guessed the charm of the new TV must have worn off already—not that he would have suggested, let alone allowed, the boy to hole up in his room and watch the tube on a fine day like that one.

"I was thinking we could drive around a little," Zane said. "Maybe make a run over to check Parable out, or scout up some good places to go fishing."

Nash looked cautiously hopeful. "You and me and Cleo?" he asked.

Zane chuckled. "Cleo is busy becoming America's Next Top Decorator, and I'd as soon poke at a rattlesnake with a short stick as interrupt her now, with her in her element and all. Nope, it'll just be you and me." The dog looked back at him then, as if to make it known that he wanted to go along. "And Slim," he finished.

Nash's grin was sudden and somehow surprising, a dramatic switch, given the sullen mood he'd been in since he got out of bed. Twenty minutes before, he'd wandered into the kitchen wearing nothing but the oversize flannel boxers he'd slept in, started riffling through bags and boxes looking for food and grumbled under his breath when Cleo told him to go back to his room and get himself dressed like a civilized human being with a place in polite company.

He'd followed orders, all right, but he'd been sour as last week's cottage cheese when he got back, wearing jeans, a T-shirt, socks and sneakers.

Now, though, Nash practically broke his neck to carry his bowl and spoon over to the one remaining counter, next to the sink, with its exposed pipes and rusty faucet handles, setting them down with a thump.

"Can I feed Blackjack?" he asked eagerly, already on his way to the door.

"I already did that," Zane said, leaving his mug beside Nash's breakfast bowl. "First rule of ranching, little brother—no sleeping in half the day while the livestock waits for hay and fresh water."

Nash executed a crisp salute. "Yes, *sir!*" he said, grinning.

Zane resisted an urge to muss up the kid's hair, just for the heck of it. "Go tell Cleo we'll be out for a while," he told the boy. "I'll start up the truck."

For once, Nash didn't offer a comeback—he just followed the sound of Cleo's voice into the next room.

Zane and Slim went outside, and Zane hoisted the dog into the backseat of the rig.

Maybe they'd stop at the courthouse over in Parable and get old Slim licensed, he decided, make sure the mutt was legal.

He'd barely climbed behind the wheel when Nash burst out of the house, leaped right over the porch steps without touching down on any of them and sprinted across the yard toward the truck.

Cleo's voice rang out behind him. "Didn't I *tell* you not to slam that screen door, Nash Sutton?"

Nash ducked slightly, as though he expected her to hurl something at the back of his head, and then scrambled, grinning, into the passenger seat. While he was fastening his seat belt, Slim leaned forward and licked the kid's face in welcome.

Nash laughed, turning just far enough to give one of Slim's floppy ears a gentle tug. "Stupid dog," he said, with obvious affection.

Slim panted, happy that the gang was all there, and sat back to take in the scenery.

"I never had a dog," Nash remarked as they passed the mailbox at the bottom of the dirt driveway. "We moved around too much, but Dad promised I could have one someday."

Zane's throat tightened. *Someday* was Jess Sutton's favorite word. Not that "someday" ever actually rolled around.

"That so," he said, watching the boy out of the corner of his eye. No cars had gone by since he'd gotten up soon after sunrise, but he looked in both directions, then looked again, before pulling out onto the county road.

"How come you don't like him?" Nash asked. There was no challenge in his tone, no petulance— just curiosity. Slim made a scrabbling sound as he rebalanced himself on the backseat after the turn. "Dad, I mean?"

Zane hesitated. "I don't know him well enough to have an opinion, one way or the other," he finally replied. He couldn't avoid the subject of their father forever, he knew, and the kid wasn't going to stop asking until he got answers and made sense of them.

"How can that be?" Nash wanted to know. A glance in his direction showed he was genuinely confused.

Ask him, Zane might have said, but he didn't. "Landry and I didn't see much of the old man, growing up," he said, shifting from first gear to second and choosing his words carefully. Keeping his gaze fixed straight ahead on the winding, rutted road that wouldn't turn to blacktop until less than a mile outside Three Trees. He cherished a brief and futile hope that the kid would let the topic drop, but, naturally, he didn't.

"Dad told me that your mom left him in the middle of the night and took you and Landry with her," Nash said matter-of-factly. "He looked everywhere for you, but it was a couple of years before he caught up."

Zane suppressed a ragged sigh, and it swelled inside him, hurting like a gulp of beer that had gone down the wrong pipe. It probably didn't help that he'd swallowed what he wanted almost desperately to say in reply—*Did Dad happen to mention that he'd been gone for three days when Mom finally loaded us into her old car, along with most of our clothes, some of our toys and every edible scrap left in the refrigerator? Did he tell you he was shacked up the whole time with some woman he met in a bar, and that wasn't the first time he'd cheated?*

"That's his story, huh?" he asked instead. Admittedly, the remark was a mite on the snarky side, but it was also the best he could do right then, remembering, as he was, how many times that rusted-out wreck of a station wagon had broken down on some lonely highway, how the food, which didn't amount to much in the first place, ran out the second day.

In the backseat, Slim gave a whimper that sounded strangely cautionary.

"Are you saying Dad lied?" Nash asked, but he still didn't fly mad or even raise his voice. His tone was conversational, if a touch on the sad side.

Zane cleared his throat, spared his brother a glance, turned his attention back to the road ahead. "He did catch up with us," he said, after a few moments of grim self-control. *Eventually,* he clarified, in the privacy of his own head. Then he went on, because he had to give Nash something, didn't he? "We were staying with Mom's dad and stepmother back then, on the outskirts of Tucson—Mom was between jobs, and she hadn't had much luck finding work—and one morning, as if out of nowhere, Dad turned up at the front door." Zane paused again, chafing at the way his father had grinned and spread his arms in a sweeping here-I-am kind of gesture, evidently expecting a warm welcome, even though better than two years had gone by without so much as a letter, let alone a check for child support. As it turned out, he'd hitch-hiked all the way from New Mexico, where they'd all lived before the breakup, to Arizona. He didn't have a car, even the dimmest prospect of a job or a plug nickel in his pocket.

"What happened?" Nash pressed. "I'll bet you were glad to see him."

They were approaching Three Trees now, and Zane was relieved to swap the hard-dirt roadway for solid asphalt.

Glad to see him? Not really.

Zane might have cut loose with a chuckle, raw as his throat felt, but even after all these years, it hurt to look back on that day. They'd loved their father, he and Landry, but young as they were, they'd long since shed any illusion that the man would change. In fact, Zane suspected their mom had held out hope that Jess *would* come looking for his family, gather them up and, well, do all the things he hadn't done before.

"My grandfather gave him some money, bought him a bus ticket and said he'd be wise not to come back." Zane's voice sounded hollow in his own ears when he finally spoke.

"Did Dad try to talk to you and Landry or anything? Where was your mom at the time?"

Zane slowed way down as they cruised along the main street of Three Trees. "She was out looking for work that day," he allowed. "Got herself hired on at a burger joint. The job didn't pay much, but she was all excited when she got home."

He recalled the look of hope that had overtaken Maddie Rose's face and then her whole countenance when she learned that Jess had been at the house.

That was when Grandpa thundered that he'd sent the bastard packing, and Maddie Rose was instantly weary again, and sadder than she'd been in a long time. Just recently, she'd even stopped crying herself to sleep at night.

"Where were you?" Nash's question startled Zane. "That day when Dad came, I mean?"

Damn, the kid was like a hungry dog with a soup bone.

"We were hiding in the basement," Zane said, well aware of how that must sound and not really caring. "Waiting for Dad to go away."

Nash's eyes rounded. "You didn't want to see him?"

"We were scared," Zane said. The truth was the truth and, hell, he and Landry had been little boys at the time. Still, they'd known even then that they were better off with their mother.

"Of Dad?" Nash was still keeping his cool, but his forehead was wrinkled up and his eyebrows almost met in the middle. "He wouldn't have hit you or anything."

Zane shook his head. "No," he said. "And that's a point in his favor, I guess. He never laid a hand on us or on Mom, as far as I can recall, though they had some pretty spectacular fights back in the day."

"Then why were you scared?" Nash wasn't letting this one go and, in a way, Zane respected him for it, even if he *was* borderline pissed off by then. His anger wasn't directed at the boy—that was the thing that helped him keep a lid on his temper. But he would have liked to throttle dear old Dad with his bare hands, and that was bad enough.

"We figured he might steal us from Mom if he got the chance," Zane said, very quietly. Of course he wouldn't have—having two small boys in tow would have cramped Jess Sutton's style. He'd have had to feed them, and that took money, and a man couldn't get money without effort.

Ergo, he'd never had any.

"Didn't you even love him a little bit?" The question was plaintive, and the bewilderment in Nash's tone made the backs of Zane's eyes scald for a second or two.

"Yes," he answered, his voice dry and rough. "We loved him." Storefronts and gas stations and a post office with a flag flying from a tall pole out front rolled past the window before he continued. "He was our dad, after all. But we loved Mom, too. And we knew she'd never go off and leave us, no matter how tough things got."

Things had gotten tougher after Jess's visit, all right, and fast.

Grandpa might have stood up to Jess that day, and hustled him out of town, pronto, but he hadn't approved of his daughter's choice of a husband in the first place, and he just couldn't let that go. He took to reminding Maddie Rose how she'd wrecked her life, marrying a no-account loser like Sutton, and now she had two kids to show for it and precious little else, and if she thought he and the wife were going to support her and her boys, she had another think coming.

Maddie Rose's stepmother, a kindly woman named Sharon, had tried to smooth things over, but Grandpa got mad all over again every time he even thought of Jess Sutton, and he didn't try to hide it.

Less than two weeks later, Maddie Rose had quit her job at the fast-food joint out on Highway 10, and used her last paycheck to fill the car with gas and buy some cold cuts and fruit for the trip. Then the three of them left Tucson behind, this time, for good.

"Wow," Nash said, breathing the word. "That's bleak."

They'd passed the town limits by then, and hit the open road that wound toward Parable, rich grasslands sprawling on either side, the sky so big and so blue that if Zane looked at it too long, he figured it might just break his heart.

"You wanted to know," he replied. "So I told you."

Of course, there was a whole lot Zane *hadn't* told Nash, too. There was always the possibility that Jess had matured in the years since he'd tracked down his runaway family again. By then, Maddie Rose had found herself a good man, Hal Banks, a farmer she'd met in the café where she worked, down in Colorado, and she was starting to make noises about settling down. Zane and Landry had liked Hal, and they'd liked his small but prosperous farm, too. Then, around Christmas, Jess came back like a bad penny, driving a secondhand car and bearing gifts.

Maddie Rose didn't welcome him, but she let him sleep on the couch in the front room of their rented trailer for a few nights, and Hal, convinced she was still in love with her ex-husband, had quietly pulled out of the relationship.

Jess stuck around just long enough to mess everything up for all of them, as it happened, and then, to no one's surprise, he was gone again.

Same song, second verse.

They'd packed up and moved again, a few days later, and Zane and Landry said silent goodbyes to regular meals, a roof over their heads and riding the bus to and from the same school instead of finding themselves in a new one every fall.

The muscles in Zane's forearm corded as he shifted the truck into a higher gear, picking up speed, and Nash settled back in his seat, sighed and stared out the window, asking no more questions.

CHAPTER NINE

PARABLE, ZANE AND Nash soon discovered, was a bit smaller than Three Trees and a whole lot quainter. Where Three Trees boasted a couple of mega discount stores, a few strip malls and at least half a dozen franchised burger joints, Parable had small shops on Main Street, along with a café or two, and there was a well-kept park in the middle of town, too. Kids and dogs played rough-and-tumble in the neatly trimmed grass, climbed monkey bars and zipped down a curving metal slide while young mothers looked on benevolently, chatting among themselves but with an undercurrent of vigilance.

Being the county seat, Parable had a modest courthouse, a library and one beauty shop out on the highway—they'd passed it coming into town—with an honest-to-God mom-and-pop grocery store directly across the way. For some reason, the sight of that old-fashioned business, clearly thriving, cheered Zane up considerably.

"Not much to this place," Nash commented, breaking the silence that had stretched between them after the conversation about Jess. It hadn't been awkward or uneasy, that silence—they'd just run out of things to say. That was easy to do, Zane supposed, since he and his youngest brother were not all that well-acquainted.

"I kind of like it," Zane answered, with a slight smile. Three Trees wasn't exactly a bustling metropolis, with a population of just under ten thousand, but Parable, with half as many people, seemed sleepy by comparison. Most of the houses were freshly painted in tasteful pastel colors, with shutters at the windows and inviting porches, and the yards neatly mowed and surrounded, almost without exception, by tidy white picket fences.

They cruised on, taking their time, riding up one street and down the next.

"There sure are a lot of churches," Nash observed, after some time had passed.

"Sure are," Zane agreed. He wasn't a churchgoer; he and God had a you-mind-your-business-and-I'll-mind-mine pact going.

They continued to explore for a while, then headed for the courthouse, tree-shaded and quite august, for such a small community. There, Zane found a cubicle marked Animal Control, paid a license fee and showed the clerk a card the people at the shelter had given him, official proof that Slim was current on his shots and therefore no threat to society. He was putting the card back in his wallet as they reached the sidewalk again, Nash eager to attach the shiny new tag they'd been given to the dog's collar.

They'd spotted the Butter Biscuit Café earlier, over on the other side of the street, and even from that distance, the smells of good country-style cooking reached their noses, wafting out every time the door opened to someone going in or out.

"You hungry?" Zane asked Nash, waiting beside the truck while the boy conferred the tag on Slim with all the ceremony of royalty bestowing knighthood.

"I guess," Nash said doubtfully. He'd hoisted Slim down from the backseat and clipped on his leash, by then. "But I don't have any money."

Zane held in yet another sigh. "I didn't ask if you had money," he pointed out, with affable reason. "I asked if you were hungry. Very different questions."

Slim was tugging at the other end of the leash, wanting a walk and, most likely, a place to lift his hind leg against something.

"I could eat," Nash admitted, in that offhand way he had, which was probably supposed to indicate a lack of concern one way or the other. "I was about to let Slim stretch his legs a little, though. He's been cooped up in the truck for a while and—"

"I'll wait," Zane said, when the boy fell silent. He leaned back against the side of his dusty truck and folded his arms to show he was in no hurry.

Nash brightened, just briefly, then looked troubled again, but all he said was, "Okay."

Zane watched, full of emotions he wasn't eager to name, as the boy and the dog headed down the sidewalk, away from the truck. Away from him.

He was no mind reader, but he'd have sworn Nash was worried that Zane might ditch him and Slim,

simply drive off and leave the two of them to stay
afloat or go under.

The thought ached in his mind like a bruise, then
settled into his heart like silt stirred up in a shallow
pond. He watched as the boy and the dog passed
under dappled shadows cast by venerable oak and
maple trees, rounded a corner and disappeared behind the courthouse.

Love, Zane thought. This tangle of feeling in his
chest and his gut was love, for his little brother, and
for that cast-off dog, too. Slim was settling into his
new life nicely, but the kid had a longer memory. He
expected to wear out his welcome at any time and
find himself alone in the world.

Zane's throat screwed shut again, and he rubbed
his eyes hard with a thumb and forefinger, once again
remembering Maddie Rose. She'd never had a pot
to piss in, as Grandpa had reminded her at every
opportunity, but there was never any doubt that she
cherished her children. She'd been proud of them,
scraped the money together for school pictures every
fall and tucked the new likenesses into dime-store
frames, prominently displayed no matter where they
happened to be living. The shots from the previous
term wound up in a photo album that was always the
first thing Maddie Rose packed when it was time to
move on again.

He straightened, waited out the strange rush of
sentimentality and thought about other things, carefully avoiding the past, until Slim and Nash reap-
peared, several minutes later.

Nash loaded the dog into the backseat of the truck and made sure the windows were rolled down a little way, so the air could circulate.

Slim, content to stay behind, settled on the seat, sighed and immediately fell asleep. Zane locked the truck and he and Nash crossed the street—there were lots of cars in the lot next to the Butter Biscuit, and parked out front, too—but a plump lady with a name tag that read "Essie" seated them right away.

Nash held down the fort while Zane went to wash his hands, passing three men gathered around a table near the jukebox, one of them wearing a sheriff's badge. They seemed comfortable together, as if they'd known each other a long time—maybe their whole lives. Once, Zane had been at ease with Landry in the same way, but that time was over, and the brief realization stung. He nodded as he passed, and they nodded back, cordial enough.

When he got back to the booth he and Nash were sharing, the menus had been delivered and there were glasses of ice water waiting.

"I'll have—" Nash began, having already perused the menu, evidently.

"You'll wash your hands before you have anything," Zane interceded, quietly but firmly.

"I'm not dirty," Nash argued. "And besides, I'm *starved*."

"Go," Zane said, cocking a thumb in the direction of the men's room. He didn't smile until the boy had turned his back. Nash dragged his feet as he went, looking put-upon.

Meanwhile, Zane reached for a menu and studied it, deciding immediately on the meat loaf special, only to look up and find the sheriff standing next to the table. A dark-haired man with a solemn face, albeit a face women probably found attractive enough, put out a hand and smiled in greeting.

"Howdy," he said. "I'm Boone Taylor."

Zane nodded, shook the offered hand. "Hello, Sheriff," he replied.

"Boone," the sheriff said. "Call me Boone." Then, after a beat. "And you are...?"

Zane felt a surge of relief. The man didn't recognize him; he was just meeting and sizing up a newcomer to his county. Most likely, it was routine for him.

"Zane Sutton," he answered mildly. "Glad to meet you, Boone."

Boone nodded, indicated his two companions with a slight motion of his head. "That's Slade Barlow over there, in the blue shirt, and the other yahoo is Hutch Carmody."

Overhearing, both men nodded a silent hello.

Hutch Carmody. The name struck Zane like a shock from a cattle prod. Sure enough, this was the same guy he'd seen on the internet, a few years older now than in the pictures and videos, the very one who'd run out on Brylee on her wedding day.

Zane's back molars locked together, a reflexive response, and he forcibly eased up on his jaw muscles, returned the other men's unspoken hello with a nod of his own.

Nash came back from the restroom, clean-handed and no longer visibly perturbed, looking the sheriff over with good-humored interest. "I guess the law finally caught up with you, big brother," he said, grinning at his own cleverness. "It was only a matter of time, I suppose."

At the periphery of his vision, Zane noticed several waitresses huddled together behind the lunch counter, staring at him and giggling as they whispered to one another. He swore silently and told Boone, "This is Nash. He's twelve and he thinks he's a wit."

Boone chuckled. "Howdy, Nash," he said, and repeated his name for the boy's benefit. The sheriff seemed to be in no hurry to go on about his business, and that made Zane strangely uneasy, like the gaggle of blushing waitresses on the other side of the room. Not to mention the sudden and pulsing silence that had fallen over the previously noisy café as everybody in the place looked their way.

"We live over by Three Trees," Nash announced, though nobody had asked. "At Hangman's Bend Ranch."

Boone nodded, taking in that information and a whole lot more, it seemed to Zane, who was, by the way, a law-abiding citizen, though he *had* gotten into a scrape or two back in high school. Nothing serious enough to count against him now, though.

The sheriff's friendly attitude never wavered, but it was obvious that he took his job seriously. He probably made a point of introducing himself to every stranger he met up with, just on general principle.

"Well," Boone finally drawled, "welcome to Parable County, both of you." He paused, and his service belt creaked as he shifted slightly. "I see you haven't had a chance to order yet—the BLT is real good, and the hot beef sandwich is even better."

"Thanks," Zane said, deciding he liked Sheriff Boone Taylor.

Boone nodded again and walked away, but he didn't go back to his friends. Instead, he ambled over to the cash register to pay his share of the check before leaving, a man who knew he had plenty of time to do what needed doing.

One of the waitresses, shooed forward by the others, approached Zane and Nash's table, order pad in hand.

"My name's Lucy," she said. Her narrow face was mottled with red patches of sheer embarrassment, but her gaze was avid, as if she was taking an inventory and mentally recording the results.

"Hello, Lucy," Zane replied, checking the menu again. Maybe he didn't want the meat loaf special, after all—a good BLT was hard to beat, and it usually stuck to a man's ribs without making him feel as if he'd just gorged himself at Thanksgiving dinner.

"And you're Zane Sutton," Lucy trilled.

Nash tried not to laugh, but the sound came sputtering past his lips, and his eyes were dancing. *And you're Zane Sutton,* he mouthed, gleefully mimicking the waitress.

"Yes," Zane said smoothly, though he felt the heat of temper rise up his neck and tingle behind his ears.

"At least, that's who I was when I got up this morning."

"I've seen all your movies!" Lucy blurted out.

The other waitresses, still behind the counter, were giggling again by then, but the other customers had, mercifully, lost interest. Or maybe they were just being polite.

Essie, the woman who had greeted Zane and Nash when they came into the café, must have been the boss, because she looked mighty impatient as she marched over and snatched the order pad from Lucy's hand.

"Lucy," she said summarily, serious as a heart attack, "get your silly self in back and don't come out until you've pulled yourself together." Essie turned her head to shoot a look at the apron-clad crew behind the counter, and though she didn't speak, they all got busy real fast. Lucy scuttled away, blushing magnificently, and Essie turned back to the matter at hand. "I sincerely apologize, Mr. Sutton. We get famous people in here now and again, we surely do, but my people never seem to get used to it. Fall all over themselves every time, like a bunch of gum-popping junior highers."

Zane didn't let his amusement show. It wasn't as if things like this didn't happen to him right along, so he'd long since gotten used to effusive fans. Plus, he didn't want Lucy to get into trouble on his account.

"That's all right," he said kindly, waving off the woman's earnest apology, and ordered the BLT on wheat, with a side of fries and a strawberry milk shake.

Nash asked for a cheeseburger deluxe, onion rings and what sounded like a five-gallon drum of cola.

Essie wrote everything down, turned on the crepe-soled heel of one sensible shoe and trundled away, waitresses scattering before her like a flock of startled chickens.

"I bet you get that a lot," Nash said. He was trying not to grin, but not very hard.

By then, Zane was thinking about Hutch Carmody again, and what he'd done to Brylee on their wedding day. Carmody seemed like an okay guy, on the surface, anyhow, not somebody who made a habit of breaking women's hearts as publicly as possible—but then, what did that kind of man look like?

Like you, Tiffany might have said, if she'd been there and heard the question. Zane rarely thought about his ex-wife, especially since he'd made Brylee Parrish's acquaintance, and he dismissed her from his mind immediately.

"Yo, Hollywood," Nash said, waving a hand in front of Zane's face. "You in there?"

Zane gave the boy a look fit to strip paint from a wall and said nothing.

"Okay, okay," Nash said, leaning back in the vinyl seat, palms out in a bid for peace. "So I guess you don't like to be called 'Hollywood.' No problem, that's cool."

Before Zane could answer, Carmody and the other cowboy-type—Barlow?—scraped back their chairs and stood up, ready to leave.

Barlow, clearly a man of few words, settled up

with Essie and went out, putting his hat on as he passed through the doorway onto the sidewalk.

Carmody, on the other hand, walked over and stood in the same spot Boone had occupied earlier. "Hutch Carmody," he said, putting out a hand, a slight grin quirking up the corner of his mouth. "My wife, Kendra, and I are throwing a barbecue this Sunday afternoon, out at our place. We'd be pleased if you could join us." He paused, blue eyes twinkling, and lowered his voice a notch. "Never mind those gals back of the counter. Most folks around here are country, through and through, and they won't crowd you or anything."

Zane was a little taken aback. He'd been prepared to dislike Carmody, but it was proving difficult, even at this early stage of the game. The last thing he'd expected from him was an invitation to a barbecue.

"That would be great!" Nash piped up, instantly enthused. "Can we bring our housekeeper? Her name is Cleo and she dresses wild and talks loud, but, down deep, she's okay."

Carmody grinned at that. "Sure," he said, before shifting his gaze away from the boy and back to Zane. "Well, then," he added, "I guess it's decided. We'll start things rolling around one in the afternoon, and there's no need to bring anything, because my wife and all her friends will be building potato salads and stuff all week."

Lunch arrived just then, delivered by a chagrined and speechless Lucy, who barely managed to set the plates down on the table without spilling the contents to hell and gone.

Hutch chuckled as she rushed back for the milk shake and the cola. "We live at Whisper Creek," he told Zane, in parting. "The ranch is easy to find. Name's on the mailbox, number's in the book."

With that, he walked away. Like Barlow and Sheriff Boone Taylor before him, he paid his bill, took his hat from a peg on the wall and settled it on his head as he went out.

"Thanks for jumping right in there and accepting for both of us," Zane told Nash with a frown, after the drinks had arrived and Lucy had left them to eat in relative peace. "I really appreciate it." *Not.*

"Don't you want to be sociable, big brother? Get to know the locals?" Nash asked, that impish glint back in his eyes, as he swabbed a french fry through a pool of ketchup on his plate.

The truth was, Zane wanted to be part of the community, and that meant getting acquainted with the folks who lived in Parable County. Still, he liked to make decisions like whether to attend a barbecue or not himself. "In the future," he said, casting an appreciative glance over the good old-fashioned bacon, lettuce and tomato sandwich on his plate, along with a pile of fries and a few slices of pickle, "I'd prefer to speak for myself."

"I bet it'll be cool," Nash speculated thoughtfully, reaching for a second french fry. "Visiting a real ranch, I mean."

"As opposed to one like ours?" Zane countered,

arching an eyebrow slightly and picking up half his sandwich. His mouth was already watering, but he remembered his mother's advice on etiquette—*Keep one foot on the floor while you eat, boys. That's all I ask.*

"You know what I mean. Whisker Creek probably has lots of horses and some cattle—"

"I believe the name is *Whisper* Creek," Zane commented. For the next few seconds, he was busy eating, and so was Nash.

"Well, *excuse* me," Nash said, after chewing and swallowing what appeared to be a full one-quarter of his cheeseburger in one bite. "*Whisper* Creek, then."

Zane chuckled, then shook his head. "Sometimes," he observed, "you're a real pain in the ass, you know that?"

Nash looked righteously affronted. *"Language,"* he said.

Zane laughed.

"I'm just a kid," Nash hastened to remind him. "You have to set a good example or God knows how I might turn out."

"God and Cleo," Zane clarified. "She's reason enough to behave yourself, because if you don't, she'll have your hide."

Nash absorbed that information and they both went on eating, enjoying their lunch and keeping the chatter to a minimum.

CLARE BURST INTO Brylee's office right after lunch and shut the door hard behind her. She looked fran-

tic, rather than angry, and more childlike than she'd
probably intended in sandals and an airy sundress,
pink, with ruffles and touches of white eyelet.

Brylee, who had been going over an inventory
list with her employee and best friend, Amy Dupree, frowned slightly, concerned. Was something
wrong at home? Were Walker and Casey and Shane
and little Preston all right?

Amy, a petite blonde, hurried out of the room,
rolling her eyes at Brylee before closing the door
in her wake.

"Clare, what on earth—" Brylee began, pushing
back her chair, about to leap to her feet and take appropriate measures against, well, whatever.

"I'm going to be an old maid!" Clare burst out.
"A spinster! I will never, *never* have a social life!"

Relieved, Brylee hid a smile and gripped her niece
gently by the shoulders. "Sit down," she counseled
gently. Last night at supper, with the rest of the family, Brylee had engaged Clare in conversation, just
as Shane had asked her to do. The girl had opened
right up, prattling about something her friend had
said in a text about a boy they both knew, the pair
of shoes she was certain she couldn't live without
and the book she was reading for her school's summer extra-credit program. Now, she was in tizzy
mode—big-time.

"People still use the word *spinster?*" Brylee
teased, buying time, perching on the edge of her
ugly desk. Clare was slumped in the extra chair by

then, shoulders hunched, head down, hands twisted together in her lap.

Clare looked up at Brylee in that moment, and her eyes, the same incredible shade of green as Casey's, brimmed with tears. "I'm *serious,* Brylee," she said, in a wail-like whisper. "My life is *over.*"

Do not smile, Brylee instructed herself silently. Having been a teenager herself once, she knew that whatever was going on in her niece's young life—or *not* going on—seemed earth-shattering, apocalyptic and very, very final to her.

"Okay," Brylee said carefully. "Talk to me, kiddo. What's going on?"

"It's *awful,*" Clare sputtered, wiping furiously at one eye, then the other, with the back of her right hand. Her slender body rippled with a visible shudder.

"Sweetheart," Brylee persisted, "*what* is awful?"

"Mom and Dad are having another baby," Clare replied. "I heard them talking about it in the kitchen this morning. They were all moony and it was—*gross.* I mean, Preston is so little and already—I mean, don't they do anything but *have sex?*"

Brylee felt several emotions at once—joy, excitement and, alas, envy. "First of all, Clare, you shouldn't eavesdrop when people are having private conversations. Second, your parents are adults, they're still young, they're legally married and they are very much in love. Furthermore, they've been up front about wanting a big family from the beginning." She folded her arms then, watching her niece's face, huffed out a sigh and went on. "*Third,* I fail to see how getting a new brother or sister will condemn you to spinsterhood. What's the connection?"

Clare looked exasperated. Her hands gripped the arms of the spare office chair. "They won't let me date, even when I'm old enough," she said. "I'll have to *babysit.* By the time Preston and Little Whoever can take care of themselves, all the good guys will already be taken—and there'll be nobody left but *fortune hunters!* Jerks who only like me because I have a famous mother!"

Adolescent hormones, Brylee thought pragmatically, were a force to be reckoned with. She'd forgotten how crucial it was for a young girl to be like the others in her social circle, how easily molehills could be ratcheted up to mountain status. Still, Clare *did* face special challenges, being the child of a celebrity.

"So, you think your folks are just going to turn this baby over to you and expect you to raise him or her single-handedly while they waltz off to do other things?" Brylee asked, letting a touch of humor creep into her voice and her expression—but *just* a touch. "Is that what's happened since Preston came along?"

"No," Clare admitted, with another sniffle. "But I'll be older when the new baby comes—old enough to *babysit.*"

"Clare," Brylee reasoned, "I'm having a hard time believing you're really this upset about something that hasn't even happened yet. What's *really* going on here?"

Clare was silent for a long time, then she started to cry again. "Shane gets to go on the rodeo circuit with Dad," she said miserably. "I wanted to go along and Dad said no, I'd better stay home in case Mom or Preston needed me. Obviously, it's because I'm a *girl*."

"Oh," Brylee said, frowning a little. Her brother, Walker, wasn't a chauvinist, but he *was* a classic alpha male, so he tended to be overprotective, especially where his daughter was involved.

"It's not fair," Clare insisted, calming down a little but still riled.

There was no way Brylee was going to offer an opinion, since how Walker and Casey raised their children was their own business and certainly none of hers, but she did see Clare's point. As a little girl, Brylee had accompanied her own father and big brother when they hauled bucking stock to various rodeos, but once she'd sprouted breasts and most of her sharp angles had turned to curves, her dad had started leaving her behind. Shaking his head sadly at her tearful protests, making lame excuses.

They'd have to share cramped motel rooms along the way, the three of them, her father had pointed out, albeit somewhat apologetically, which meant there would be zero privacy. And a young woman needed privacy. Plus, he and Walker would be busy all day and probably half the night, too, unable to keep an eye on her the way they should, and they'd be in rough company some of the time, etc, etc, etc.

The problem with that logic was, they'd always

bunked in together when she was younger and, rough company or none, between the two of them, her dad and brother had kept an eye on her just fine, thank you very much.

Looking back, Brylee understood her father's concerns, but her heart had been broken, just the same. She'd stood in the dusty driveway, watching a virtual convoy of trucks and trailers full of livestock pull out as her dad, brother and half the ranch hands on the place lit out for other towns, near and far, headed for the rodeo, and she'd wondered what she'd done wrong.

Now, Brylee brought herself back to the present moment and focused on her niece. "Did you talk this over with your mother?" she asked. A simple question, right? That wouldn't qualify as meddling—would it?

Clare bit her lower lip. "She's on *his* side. Just because I got into a little trouble that time, at the Parable rodeo—it was, like, *forever* ago—Mom doesn't trust me."

"Hmm," Brylee said, remembering that particular incident. Clare, feeling rebellious, had swiped something from one of the vendors' booths on the rodeo grounds and subsequently gotten herself arrested, hauled away in a police car. Casey and Walker had dealt with the situation admirably, and the charges were dismissed, but the tabloid press had a field day, running pictures of Clare in handcuffs, Clare being marched into Parable's tiny police station, Clare leaving said station, subdued and ashamed, with a grim-faced Walker at her side. The headlines had petered out pretty quickly, but they'd been humiliating, not only for Clare herself, but for Walker and Casey as well and, by extension, even for Shane.

"I know what you're thinking," Clare accused, though she seemed to be running out of emotional steam. "That I blew it and now I have to take the consequences. But that was *a long time ago,* and what? I'm supposed to stay grounded until I'm fifty?"

Finally, Brylee smiled. "There was that thing about the boy you met at youth group, and the bus trip to Helena," she said.

Clare sighed, sagging back in her chair. She was, as Shane often claimed, the original drama queen. Even without a rose between her teeth and a limp hand against her forehead, she was the very embodiment of hopeless martyrdom.

"One *more* reason I'll be an old maid," the child lamented forlornly. "Because, through no fault of my own, I happen to have *Casey Elder* for a mother, and if some guy likes me, it's only because he's trying to get to *her.*"

Brylee chuckled then, drew her niece to her feet and gathered her in her arms for a brief but heartfelt hug. "Trust me," she said, holding Clare by the shoulders again and leaning back just far enough to study the girl's tearstained face. "When you're ready, as in grown up—" she paused, sighed, went on "—and, alas, you'll probably have to kiss your share of frogs along the way, like most of us do—you'll definitely find Mr. Right. Most likely, you'll have your choice of *several* Mr. Rights, and the lucky man you fall in love with won't care *whose* daughter you are. He'll love you for your smart, beautiful, funny self, I promise."

Clare's angst gave way to curious concern, and her brow wrinkled with a slight frown as she looked back at Brylee. "*Your* Mr. Right turned out to be a frog," she said, not unkindly.

Innocent though it was, the remark struck Brylee like a blow, the kind that leaves bruises but doesn't show. She managed a small laugh. "Hutch Carmody *wasn't* Mr. Right, but he wasn't a frog, either. He's a very nice man, actually—with the good sense to see what a mistake we were about to make."

"Why didn't *you* see it?" Clare asked, her eyes liquid with sympathy. The poor child was a hopeless romantic, that was obvious. No doubt there would be other tear storms and hissy fits as she traveled the difficult road to womanhood.

Brylee thought a few moments before she answered. "I guess because I didn't want to see the truth," she admitted, not only to Clare, but to herself. "I was in love with love, and I had stars in my eyes. I wanted a husband and a home and babies and I was out to make it all happen, by hook or by crook." She touched Clare's cheek gently. "Don't be in such a hurry to grow up, honey. Just trust that everything will work out in the long run, because it will."

Clare hesitated, then accepted the advice with a little sigh and another sniffle.

"If you say so," she finally murmured.

Now, Brylee thought, hugging her brother's child once more for good measure, if she could just convince *herself* that Hutch Carmody hadn't represented her very last chance at happiness…

CHAPTER TEN

ZANE SMILED TO himself as he saddled Blackjack early the next morning, when the sky was still more peach and gold than blue and he was feeling a sudden and specific need for lots of wide-open spaces around him. Dinner with Brylee and her family Saturday night, a barbecue at Whisper Creek Ranch on Sunday—and he'd thought the *Hollywood* scene was a social whirl. What was next? A barn dance? A hayride, maybe, followed by hot dogs and beans spiced with tall tales swapped around a campfire?

Grinning at his own whimsical turn of mind, he led the gelding out of the barn and mounted up, leaning forward slightly in the saddle to pat the animal's neck and speak a few words to him. Slim, losing interest in the whole project by that point, though he'd supervised the goings-on in the barn, ambled over to the porch, curled up near the kitchen door and dozed.

Since Landry's part of the ranch, beyond a line of trees at the far end of the pasture, with its fallen fences and weedy ground, seemed as good a destination as any, Zane headed that way. Nothing helped him think like riding alone, way out in the countryside, choosing his course as the spirit moved him.

And Zane *needed* to think. He felt swamped by choices and options—not that either was a bad thing; it was just the way his mind worked. Despite his accidental career in the movies, he was a planner at heart and he was always happier if his ducks were in a row.

The first leg of the ride took fifteen minutes or so, the air pleasantly chilly and the sky so big and sprawling and blue that he ached to look at it. When he emerged from the stand of pines and cottonwoods and scrub brush that served as an informal boundary line between the two properties, Zane found himself at the edge of acres and acres of wind-rippled, sun-washed meadow grass. A wide creek cut through the area to the east, shining like mercury in the daylight. He'd been here before, of course, in the truck, but taking it all in on horseback was a different experience altogether.

All that grass and domed sky, edged with green foothills and, in the distance, framed by snow-capped mountains that couldn't adequately be described even by the word *majestic,* lassoed his breath somewhere around his gizzard and hog-tied it.

Zane simply waited, letting all that peace and quiet settle over him, a balm to his spirit and his usually busy brain.

Presently, Zane stood in the stirrups for a few seconds, stretching his legs and recalling how he and Landry had divided Hangman's Bend Ranch in the first place—by swapping plat maps via the internet, drawing property lines, dickering by email and *re*drawing said lines until they were both satisfied.

Zane didn't regret any of the choices he'd made where the joint purchase was concerned—he saw potential in both the old house and the stone barn, and the scenery on his part of the spread still caught him by surprise now and then, pumping a little jolt of adrenaline through him at unexpected moments, kicking his heartbeat up a notch. Now, surveying Landry's share of the land, he knew the deal he'd made with his brother was a fair one, on both sides.

Which wasn't to say that Landry was likely to lay eyes on the place, anytime soon. Oh, sure, he'd made noises about coming out for a look around when they talked on the phone before, but Zane knew the man preferred bright lights, big cities and a ready supply of sexy, sophisticated women. They'd both grown up ragtag, he and Landry, living in cheap motels and run-down trailer parks and, back then, neither of them had felt particularly deprived, despite the things they did without.

Zane still had a pretty clear idea of what he genuinely needed—not much more than food, freedom, shelter and the regular company of dogs and horses, even now—but Landry had changed, and changed a lot. Sometimes it was hard to believe he'd ever been that eager kid with freckles and a buzz cut, wearing secondhand clothes and ratty sneakers with the laces always broken off, and always ready for the next adventure.

If Landry even *owned* a pair of jeans these days—and it wasn't a sure bet by any stretch of the imagination—they were probably the custom-made kind that cost as much as a decent used car. And that kind of getup was bound to be an embarrassment in a place where all the men and many of the women wore one particular brand of denims, the known favorite of country people everywhere, readily available at any discount store for a price regular folks could manage when the mortgage was paid and the kids didn't need shoes.

Zane shifted in the saddle, loosened the reins when Blackjack tossed his head, letting it be known that he'd stood still long enough and wanted to get on with whatever it was they'd headed out to do.

So they proceeded, man and horse, the grass, rich and fragrant, actually *smelling* green, reaching almost to Blackjack's breast in places. They came to the creek and splashed across it, raising jewel-bright sprays to sparkle on all sides. Reaching the other shore, Blackjack hauled himself up the steep bank and then paused to shake off the water like a dog after a hosing down.

Zane's boots were soaked, and so were his jeans, right to his knees, but he not only didn't care, he barely noticed. He could have stayed out there on the range for days on end, he reckoned, sleeping under a black-velvet canopy dappled with stars at night, following that bright, twisting creek wherever it led, letting the song it sang ease his parched soul, wash away every memory save the good ones.

He sighed at the thought—he really *was* getting fanciful in his old age—and crested a rise, letting the horse choose his own path now, and that was when he saw the fields of flowers on the next place, more colorful than any rainbow. He didn't know the names of a single one of those blossoms—well, except for the roses and the lilacs, anyway—but just looking at the tidy rows of orange and yellow, blue and red and pink and white, stretching almost to the horizon, was somehow inspiring.

A small, slender woman, clad in worn jeans, a long-sleeved flannel shirt and sneakers, carrying a box from the back of an old truck toward the modest wooden house, spotted him and Blackjack approaching right away, hesitated visibly and finally waved. As Zane rode nearer, she set the box on the edge of a rickety porch, pressed both hands to the small of her back and stretched, clearly weary even though the sun hadn't been up all that long.

She had a short cap of dark hair, round blue eyes and an expressive mouth. Smiling, she crossed the yard, shading her face with one hand as she looked up at him.

"Zane Sutton," he said, by way of introduction, and tugged at the brim of his hat.

The woman stretched out one hand, so he leaned from the saddle to clasp it briefly in greeting. "I know," she responded, with a little twinkle and a lot of reserve. "I'm Ria Manning, and I'm new here, as you've probably guessed."

"Me, too," Zane said, wishing he hadn't gone and made himself famous, because it was so often a barrier that made the prudent and practical types hold back. Hell, even his own name had been hijacked, belonging more to his big-screen persona than to him. "This is quite a layout."

The house and the outbuildings weren't much, but Zane wasn't inclined to share that opinion. After all, considering the shape Hangman's Bend was in, he didn't have room to talk.

Ria drew a deep breath, hugged herself with both arms as she looked around at the acres of flowers and, finally, sighed happily. "It sure is," she agreed. "Lots of work to be done, since the owner died a few years ago, and except for a few kindly neighbors stopping by to water and do a little weeding, nobody's turned a hand since then. Still, I'd say the place is in pretty good shape, all in all."

A shapely gamine type with an air of tired mischief about her, Ria Manning was the type—read: unHollywood—who would surely have caught Zane's eye, before he'd met Brylee, that is. His interest in her now was cordial, in a neighborly way, period. And that was a little unsettling, given all the years he'd spent chasing women. He wondered distractedly if it was some kind of curse, this sudden feeling that there was only one woman in the world he could hope to share a life with, and that woman seemed to think he was—what?

He didn't rightly know what Brylee thought of him, that was the problem. One moment, she treated him with benign disdain, as if he'd been molded from plastic, like some toy action figure instead of a flesh-and-blood man, knitted together in his mother's womb like everybody else on the planet. The next, she was cautiously friendly, going so far as to invite him to supper—with Nash and Cleo and a full contingent of family around to run interference, of course.

Ria watched him, arms akimbo, head tilted to one side, probably waiting for him to leave so she could get on with her day, polite though her expression was. "I'd better get back to work," she finally said, and that was when he reined in his wandering thoughts and noticed the gold band on the ring finger of her left hand. Married, then. Odd that the husband didn't seem to be around, helping out with the lifting and carrying, but maybe he was working or something.

Zane nodded in response to her statement, shifting the pressure of the reins from one side of Blackjack's neck to the other. He'd have offered to lug boxes for her, but he figured that might make her uneasy, since she was evidently alone. She'd recognized his face and his name, but that didn't mean she trusted him. He was still a stranger, after all.

He cocked a thumb over one shoulder, indicating Hangman's Bend. "I live on the next place over," he told her. "Old house, stone barn. If you need anything, don't hesitate to let me know."

"Thanks," Ria said, after another hesitation, brief but thoughtful.

Then she raised a hand slightly in farewell, summoned up a semblance of a smile, picked up the box she'd set on the edge of the porch a few minutes back and got on with it.

Zane, wondering about Ria Manning—there was

a brave fragility about her that gave him pause—
reined Blackjack around and headed for home.

BRYLEE SAT AT her office desk, studying the same
columns of figures over and over again and making
no sense of them whatsoever.

She gave a groaning sigh and Snidely, napping
under the desk, muzzle resting on her left foot, crept
out of his dented metal burrow to look up at her with
concern.

Brylee chuckled ruefully and patted his head. "No
worries, buddy," she said gently. "I do seem to have
misplaced my handy-dandy Protestant work ethic,
though. Seen it around anywhere?"

Just then, a shadow figure—Amy-shaped—tapped
at the frosted glass set into the door, opened it a crack
and stuck her blond head around it. "We shipped off
the last of the orders for the week," she said. "I sent
the warehouse crew and the office people home an
hour ago—no sense in running up a big overtime
tab."

Startled, Brylee checked the digits in the lower
right-hand corner of her monitor and grimaced. *Six
o'clock? Already?*

How was that possible? One moment, she'd been
clocking in at 8:30 a.m., as usual, primed for an ordinary Friday; the next, the warehouse and offices
were dark and empty.

A lonely feeling swept over her in that moment
of realization.

Lingering, Amy bit her lower lip, and Brylee registered a hint of concern in her friend's eyes. "Some of us are meeting up over at the Boot Scoot, in Parable, in an hour or so, for some cold beer, greasy junk food and music guaranteed not to improve our minds." Another pause, another faltering smile. "Wanna meet us there?"

Brylee, still barely tracking what was going on in the real world outside her computer, took one last look at her on-screen ledger, gave up on untangling the numbers and logged off, all with the few seconds it took to decide on her reply. "Not tonight, thanks," she said, with false good cheer. "Snidely's been stuck inside all day, and he needs some exercise before it gets dark. Plus, I have a million things to do at home."

Amy looked disappointed. "You *always* have a million things to do, Bry. When are you planning to start having some *fun* again?"

Again. As in, *since Hutch Carmody cut you loose at the altar and you crawled into a hole and pulled it right in after you.*

Brylee sighed. Girls' night out was a long-standing tradition in her circle of friends—half a dozen of them had been meeting over at the Boot Scoot at least two Friday nights out of any given month, since forever, just to hang out and stay current on one another's lives. They'd been friends for most of their lives, and they were tight, partly because they were the ones who'd stayed on in Parable County after high school or, in Brylee's case, college.

They'd been there for her before, during and

after the wedding-that-wasn't, coming up with an estimated eight million ways for Hutch Carmody to die while they drank too much wine and beer and lamented the sad state of good old-fashioned romance in today's society. Some were married, some divorced, and one was widowed. Brylee was the only certified old maid in the bunch.

"Hello?" Amy prompted, ducking her head a little way to peer into Brylee's face.

"Next time," Brylee said. "I promise."

Amy's slender shoulders sagged visibly under her T-shirt, and she frowned at Brylee, narrowing her eyes. "You always say that," she countered. "Do you realize that you've been ducking out on us—your *best* friends—a *lot,* since you and Hutch broke up?"

Brylee waited for the pang of sorrow that usually struck her, somewhere in the region of her heart, whenever the Great Debacle was mentioned.

But it didn't happen. Now that she'd ventured out of her head and started to reenter reality, leaving the accounting snarl behind in her brain to be dealt with later, it was Zane Sutton who'd invaded her thoughts, not Hutch.

She promptly shook him off, and a long to-do list scrolled through her brain. Snidely *did* need some time to run and, well, just behave like a dog in general. It wasn't normal for him to be confined in an office for so many hours at a stretch—they usually took regular breaks, outdoors when the weather was good.

Furthermore, she needed to scour her favorite

cookbooks and online recipe files, throw together a menu for tomorrow night, when Zane and Nash and the mysterious Cleo were coming over for supper, *and* shop for whatever ingredients she didn't have on hand.

She made another attempt to put girls' night out off for another week. "Honestly, Ames, I can't," she said, but she totally lacked conviction. It *would* be nice to spend some time with her friends, and she *had* been neglecting them. She knew that.

So, obviously, did Amy. "Two hours," she cajoled, holding up the appropriate number of fingers. "That's all I'm asking, just two paltry hours with your pals. A mug of beer or a glass of wine, a couple of tacos, a little twangy pathos from the jukebox, and you're good. Back in the game."

If only it were that easy, Brylee thought. "I'd need to take Snidely home first, feed him and change clothes," she said reluctantly. One problem with hiring people you'd known since finger-painting days— they weren't afraid to pester you to death when they wanted something.

Amy's pretty, still-girlish face flared with a sudden, sunny grin. "Great!" she said, looking down at her jeans and T-shirt, grubby from a day in the warehouse, packing orders. "You didn't think I'd be seen in public wearing *this* getup, did you? I'm stopping off at home to get myself all spiffed up—hair spray, makeup, the works—and I'll have to wait for Bobby to pick up the kids for the weekend, too." She paused. "He'd *better* not be late, either."

Bobby was Amy's ex-husband and the father of her two children, three-year-old Mandy and six-year-old Sara Jane. Bobby might have been a lousy spouse, but he was a good father, and both girls adored him.

"Oh, all right," Brylee said. Then, still ambivalent, she took her purse out of the bottom drawer of her desk and rummaged through it for her car keys as she rose from her chair. By then, Amy had given a satisfied nod, waggled her fingers in a so-long-for-now wave and hurried out, probably afraid Brylee would change her mind if she got half a chance.

Snidely strolling amiably along beside her, she set the alarm, locked up for the night and shed a little guilt by deciding to stop off at the supermarket on the way home from the Boot Scoot for necessary supplies. In the meantime, she'd take her patient dog back to the ranch house, throw a stick or a tennis ball for him to fetch in the yard till he tired of the game and give him his ration of kibble after that. While Snidely was munching, she'd pick out a few recipes, take a quick inventory of her refrigerator and pantry shelves, dash off a grocery list and, finally, do what she could with her work-bedraggled appearance.

Or, she reflected, as she drove through the summer twilight toward home, she could call or text Amy and say something had come up and, darn it all, she wasn't going to make it to the Boot Scoot that night, after all.

Except that would be lying. On the few occasions in her entire life when Brylee had stretched the truth, even in a small way, it had always snapped back on her like a rubber band, stinging on impact.

She sighed, looked over at Snidely, who was sitting contentedly in the front passenger seat, wearing his special harness and buckled in for the short ride back to Timber Creek, and gave a wan smile.

"Do I look pale to you?" she asked. "Like I might be coming down with something? No?" Brylee gave a rueful chuckle. "I was afraid that was going to be your answer."

AFTER THE PEACEFUL ride on Blackjack, Zane's day descended into a state of continuous and frazzled chaos.

Cleo, probably operating on the theory that she who hesitates is lost, had already hired on three of the contracting companies she'd called in to bid on the renovations—an outfit to tear out old flooring and put down new, a passel of electricians and, of course, plumbers.

She was in her element, ordering people around and spending somebody else's money. Namely, *his*. Not that it mattered, because when Cleo was happy, everybody was happy, and the opposite was just as true.

Nash hid out in his room, with Slim for companionship, watching TV, and though Zane didn't entirely approve of wasting hours on end in front of the tube, especially when the sun was shining, he left the kid alone. After all, the screech of electric saws and the constant pounding of hammers were driving *him* a little bat-shit crazy, and Nash wasn't enjoying it, either.

Zane stayed outside as long as possible, working on the fence repairs he'd begun before the onslaught of home improvement, tending to Blackjack, assessing what needed to be done to bring the barn up to par.

After lunch, served buffet-style from the card table in the kitchen, right there in the midst of the wreckage, prepared and overseen by the relentlessly efficient Cleo, fence-mending lost its charm, and Zane found himself fresh out of distractions. With one horse on the whole place, the chores were minimal, and he'd done them all in fifteen minutes or so. There was firewood to cut—one of the previous occupants had left a pile of deadfall timber and scrap lumber out behind the barn—but he didn't own an ax, let alone a chain saw.

Therefore, the obvious next move was to head for town and buy out half the local hardware store. He invited Nash to go along, but the boy was binging on old episodes of *Law & Order* and noshing on potato chips, and wasn't inclined to move. The dog, stretched comfortably beside Nash on the unmade bed, didn't appear to be up for a trip to the big city of Three Trees, either.

It was just as well, Zane figured, since Slim would have had to stay in the truck most of the time, so he backtracked to the kitchen, where Cleo was explaining to a man with a clipboard which floors ought to be torn out entirely and which were made of good, solid hardwood, and ought to be sanded down and varnished instead of ripped up.

"Want anything from town?" Pausing at the door, ready to make his escape, Zane queried the housekeeper casually.

"It would take too long to tell you," Cleo answered, done explaining and now so busy scouring brochures of modern cabinets and fixtures to replace the junky ones in the bathrooms that she barely looked up.

"Right," Zane answered, hiding his relief. Shopping for hardware was a testosterone-friendly undertaking, but Cleo might have asked for sheets and towels and the like, and he wouldn't have had a clue about kinds or colors. He tapped his shirt pocket to indicate that he had his cell phone and used his other hand to reach for his hat and put it on. By then, clipboard man was long gone. "Call me if necessary," he finished.

Cleo lifted her gaze from the array of tubs, toilets and vanity cabinets, a smile tugging at one side of her mouth. "And what do you consider 'necessary,' Zane Sutton?" she asked dryly. Of course she knew full well that there was no pressing business in Three Trees; he was bailing on all the sawing and hammering and the clouds of dust everywhere.

Zane quirked a little grin and tugged at his hat brim, just the way he had when he was leaving Ria Manning's place that morning. "Bloodshed," he answered. "Fire, flood, armed invasion or any earthquake above seven-point-two."

Cleo laughed and rolled her eyes. "Get a gallon of milk while you're out," she said. "We'll need it in the morning to wet down young Nash's usual three or four bowls of cereal."

Zane nodded and left, before the grocery list could get any longer.

Outside, he fired up the truck and pointed the grill toward Three Trees, taking the route that led past Brylee's headquarters, on the off chance he might catch a glimpse of her, but no luck. The place was bustling, deliveries arriving, shipments going out, but the boss lady was nowhere in sight.

Once he got to town, Zane decided he wouldn't head straight for the hardware store, since, if he finished too quickly, he'd have no good reason to stay away from home until he was sure the construction people had called it quits for the day.

He visited the library, a trim brick building with shutters at the windows, and signed up for a card. That done, he passed over an hour browsing through the stacks, though, in the end, he didn't check out a book.

After that, he scoped out the junior high Nash would probably attend, come fall. If Jess didn't show up feeling all fatherly before then and take the kid with him when he inevitably left again, that is. The mere thought of their dad putting in an appearance just in time to create the usual havoc made the hinges of Zane's jawbones ache from the strain of biting down.

He forced himself to relax. Breathe.

And he drove.

The school, like the library, was a redbrick affair, with lots of windows, skylights on the roof, well-maintained lawns. The building looked good-sized and relatively modern, and there was a separate gym on the property, along with a baseball diamond and a flagpole flying Old Glory, wind-snapping against the azure sky.

Zane made a mental note to stop in one day soon— surely, if the flag was up, there were some staffers putting in summer hours—and ask a few questions. Nash had been homeschooled, by his own admission, and while he could obviously read, that was no guar- antee that he was up to speed on all the other subjects, like math and science, for instance.

No surprise that Jess had encouraged the boy to read—that, after all, would keep him occupied at least part of the time, leaving dear old Dad free to do pretty much whatever he wanted.

Zane felt another surge of resentment, took off his hat and flung it onto the passenger seat, plowed the splayed fingers of his left hand through his hair to diffuse the burst of unwanted energy.

Finally, killing time being a challenge in a place the size of Three Trees, Montana, he gave up on procras- tinating and headed for the hardware store, a family- owned establishment that must have been holding its own against the big chains and the discount store, since the parking lot was fairly crowded.

While he wasn't exactly handy with tools, Zane knew how to use a hammer and a handsaw, and as

soon as he stepped inside that cluttered and somewhat dusty store, he started to feel better.

He liked the aluminum ladders of various lengths,
leaning against a far wall. He liked the bright reds
and greens of the lawn mowers and other landscap-
ing equipment, the bins of nails and screws and bolts,
the electric sanders and the power drills, the rows of
paint cans and all the rest.

A hardware store was man-territory, he reflected,
a kind of sanctuary. Not two seconds after he had
that thought, he rounded a tall pyramid of motor oil
and all but collided with Ria Manning. She was pushing a cart full of DIY gear: a toilet plunger, a couple
of flashlights, a coil of green garden hose, a hoe and
a shovel and a long-handled spade.

Clearly, the lady meant business.

"Hello, again," she said, with a little smile.

Zane nodded. "Howdy," he replied, with a slight
grin, eyeing the stuff she'd chosen and thinking it
was going to take a lot more than a little digging and
watering to set things right out there on the flower
farm. The house, for instance, looked like it might
blow over if somebody sneezed, and the various
sheds leaned at comical angles, their boards weathered to gray. On the other hand, a person had to start
somewhere, and the yard and flower beds were as
good a place as any. Was she depending on a pay-
ing crop?

None of his business, he promptly decided, fixing
to move on and examine the chain saws and other
manly man stuff he might need. "Good to see you

again," he said, reaching for the brim of his hat before he remembered he'd left it in the truck.

Ria nodded, politely disinterested now, and consulted the tattered list in her hand. Zane noticed the wedding band again, and the way her fingernails were bitten back. She must have had a story—everyone did—and he wondered what it was as he walked away.

The chain saw selection was surprisingly broad, and it took Zane a while to settle on the right one. He'd have to study the instructions later—hopefully, they were in English—to figure out how to run the thing, but he wasn't inclined to explain to the balding, portly clerk that he'd never used that particular species of machinery before and could have used a few pointers.

After that, one thing seemed to lead to another. He'd need a couple of gas cans, wouldn't he, and safety goggles, and heavy work gloves, too. Maybe he even needed to spring for some steel-toed boots, since sawing off a toe wasn't part of the plan.

By the time he'd paid up at the lone cash register and loaded all his loot in the truck, twilight was coming on, and he was hungry.

His phone jangled the moment he'd climbed into the driver's seat and stuck the key in the ignition.

Inwardly, he sighed. Most likely, Cleo had come up with a list of urgent purchases, after all, in addition to the requested gallon of milk, so he didn't bother to check the caller ID panel before he thumbed a virtual button and said, "Let's hear it."

There was a pause on the other end.

"Cleo?" Zane prompted.

The response was a bitter and wholly masculine laugh. "Nope," Landry responded, and there was a certain tightness in his voice, even though he was trying to sound amiable, "it's your brother. The good-looking one."

Zane frowned, lingering in the lot while other cars and pickups started up around his rig, driving away. "Is everything all right?" he asked, a moment or two later.

"I guess that's debatable," Landry answered, his tone dry now. "My rental car turned out to be a lemon, and I'm stuck in some dive called the Boot Scoot Tavern…in—" He paused, audibly consulting someone for the name of the town he was in. "Parable," he said. "Now, that's quaint."

Zane closed his eyes for a moment. Forewarned wasn't necessarily forearmed, and since he hadn't expected Landry to follow through and actually come to Montana, he was at a loss.

Holy crap, now what?

"Okay," he said, and waited, still grappling with the knowledge that Landry was only thirty miles away.

"The car's been towed," Landry went on presently, and that was when Zane noticed that his brother was slurring his words a little. "Even if it was running, I've had a few beers, so—"

"You've had a few beers," Zane repeated woodenly.

"That's what I said," Landry confirmed, and the

words had a fine edge to them, like a steel blade, freshly sharpened. Then he laughed, sounding more like the kid he'd been way back when than the man he'd become since. "Actually," he went on, sounding drunker by the second, "I've probably had slightly more than a few."

Zane swore under his breath. As far as he knew, Landry didn't have a drinking problem, but he supposed he'd had plenty of time to develop one since they'd last seen each other in person.

Anything was possible.

"Hello?" Landry prodded, waxing impatient now. When he talked, he expected people to pay attention.

"I'll be there in half an hour," Zane replied briskly. "Do yourself a favor and order up a cup of strong coffee, will you? In fact, why don't you make it a double?"

CHAPTER ELEVEN

EVEN AFTER SEVERAL purposeful delays, Brylee arrived at the Boot Scoot Tavern before any of her friends did. She was chronically punctual, it seemed.

When she drove into the gravel parking lot, with its patches of weeds, there were several vehicles taking up space. None of them were familiar and, though she'd been to the Boot Scoot about a million times before, she was strangely hesitant to go inside, at least by herself.

Sighing in resignation, she reached over and lifted her shoulder bag from its place on the passenger seat, set it in her lap and then sat there for a few moments longer, biting her lower lip and wishing she'd stayed home.

She was strongly tempted to give in to previous temptation, ditch Amy and the others, do her shopping for tomorrow night's dinner, then head back to Three Trees, where she could hide out at the library or take in a movie.

Except that it would be cowardly to skip out now, and anyway, to Brylee, a promise was a promise— and besides, she was vastly overdressed for a night of browsing through the stacks at the library or munching popcorn in a theater. Bad enough that she'd have to enter a supermarket in this outfit, later in the evening. She'd look flat-out ridiculous—or worse, as if she was out to find herself some action.

Inviting as the prospect was, turning back wasn't an option. After mulling all that over and feeling no less confused than before, Brylee paused before opening the door of her SUV, checking her hair and lipstick in the rearview mirror, and felt a jolt of chagrined alarm at her own reflection—hair pinned up in a saucy do, with tendrils curling at her nape and cheeks, sprayed into helmetlike submission. She was wearing not only eye shadow and mascara, but liner, too—along with foundation and powder and blush.

She'd even plucked her brows and shaved her legs, for pity's sake, and then there was the dress—the *dress*. It was a "heads up, handsome, I'm back on the market" kind of getup, for sure, flirty and red, with a clingy fit through the bodice and hips, where it flared out subtly into three tiers of flapperlike ruffles.

Had she bought the darned thing for a costume party or what? She'd found it hanging at the back of her closet, tried it on to see if it would still fit and had decided the slip of silk would do as well as anything else she owned. She couldn't remember buying it *or* wearing it, which was just as well, because the occasion had probably had something to do with Hutch Carmody.

Some things—and some men—were better forgotten.

"Who are you?" she asked the image looking back

at her in irritated amazement. "Nobody *I* recognize, that's for sure."

What, she wondered now, long past the point where she could have done anything differently, had she been thinking? She was having tacos and beer with the girls at the Boot Scoot, not going out for a glamorous night on the town in Manhattan or L.A. with Prince Charming.

Exasperated, having just come to her senses with a hard slam, Brylee thought about fleeing yet again, just turning right around and heading back home to the ranch—forget the grocery list she'd keyed into her smartphone. Yes, it would be a yellow-bellied thing to do, but wasn't discretion the better part of valor, at least *some* of the time? Would it be so *very* wrong to beat a retreat without even setting foot inside that seedy cowboy bar at all?

She might have given in and split the scene in spite of earlier misgivings—if Amy hadn't pulled in next to her, with a jaunty honk of her car horn and a wave of one hand. The woman was beaming when she got out from behind the wheel; she locked up, and came around to stand next to Brylee's driver's side door.

Forcing a smile—after all, it was *herself* she was put out with, not Amy—Brylee rolled down her window.

"Well, I'll be," Amy marveled, cheerleader-cute in her rhinestone-studded jeans and striped, off-one-shoulder shirt. Her blond hair, like Brylee's, was pinned up and sprayed within an inch of its life. It was a good thing neither one of them smoked,

Brylee decided fitfully, because they might have become human fireballs just by trying to light up. "I really thought you were going to come up with some lame but extremely inventive excuse and cancel on us again. But here you are."

"Thanks for the vote of confidence," Brylee replied, shoving aside the fact that she'd been about to boogie for the hills, but now she had no choice but to serve out the two-hour sentence ahead of her. But she wasn't going to stay a *minute* longer than that. So she drew a deep breath and asked, with a flimsy smile, "Are we going in, or shall we wait out here for the others?"

Amy dismissed the idea of marking time in the parking lot with a wave of one manicured hand, shook her head and stepped back so Brylee could climb out of the SUV.

The other woman's eyes gleamed with appreciative mischief as she took Brylee in with a sweeping visual inspection, taking pointed notice of the red dress, the makeup and sexy hairdo, the F-me opentoed high heels. Her perusal was so thorough, in fact, that Brylee felt like squirming. Was Amy taking an inventory, or what?

"You clean up real nice, Boss Lady," she finally said, grinning. Then, in an impish whisper, she added, "It'll probably just be the usual Friday-night-in-Parable crowd in there tonight, you know. Unless you've got a steamy date afterward and didn't bother to share the information with your BFF."

Brylee quickly turned away and made a major

project of rolling up her window and locking the SUV, hoping she'd moved fast enough to hide the blush warming her cheeks. "I guess I just got carried away," she said offhandedly, when she was facing her friend again.

How long had it been since she'd had any reason at all—even a flimsy one, like tacos and beer—to dress like this? Heck, she was even wearing perfume.

Inwardly, Brylee continued to fret. Was she possessed? Did she have an alternate personality she hadn't known about prior to tonight? None of this was like her—including the hesitation.

As if divining her friend's thoughts, Amy took a firm grip on Brylee's arm and hustled her toward the entrance to the Boot Scoot, music and laughter and the heady aroma of fried food rolling out into the cool dusk to greet them.

Unaccountably, in the instant it took for her eyes to adjust to the dim interior of the bar, Brylee's heart began to pound, and she wanted once again, but more fiercely than ever this time, to spin around on one spiked heel and bolt.

And then her vision acclimated itself to the scene before her. Zane Sutton was ambling in her direction, and he gave her a slow, approving once-over as he drew nearer.

"Oh, hell," Brylee muttered, stiffening. What was *he* doing in the Boot Scoot, a good thirty miles from home? If he wanted to party, well, Three Trees had a run-down tavern or two of its own.

"Is that Zane Sutton?" Amy asked, in a stage

whisper, after closing her gaping mouth. *"The movie star?"*

"Yep," Brylee answered wearily. "That's him, all right."

She worked up a neighborly smile, despite her many misgivings, because it was a free country and if the man wanted to hang out at the Boot Scoot Tavern, of all places, tonight of all nights, then she'd just have to accept it.

Zane, looking cowboy-good in perfectly ordinary clothes—clothes that were better suited to the location than her own, in fact—came to a stop within touching distance and grinned down into Brylee's face. Amusement, along with something else, sparked in his eyes.

"Hello, Brylee," he said easily, letting his gaze slide over her again, leaving invisible fire in its wake, instantly followed by a rash of goose bumps.

Amy elbowed Brylee hard and cleared her throat, which meant, in girlfriend vernacular, *Introduce us, damn it.*

Brylee remembered her manners, smiled even more determinedly than before and told herself to suck it up and deal. Sometimes, when there was no way over, under or around a situation, a person simply had to go *through* it. "Amy Dupree," she chirped brightly, "this is Zane Sutton, my new neighbor. Zane, my good friend Amy."

"Amy," Zane said, with a nod of acknowledgment.

"H-hello," Amy stammered out. She wasn't usually shy, but then again, she didn't meet movie stars every day, either. Those who graced Parable County with their presence generally kept to themselves, for the most part, anyway—except, of course, when they felt called upon to interfere in local politics or to boycott products that were the lifeblood of the year-round inhabitants, like beef.

Zane's grin rose to his eyes, lingered there, with whatever it was he thought was so damn funny. "Join us?" he asked smoothly.

Us? Brylee thought, barely resisting an embarrassing urge to peer around his shoulder to see who made up the other component of "us."

"Sure!" Amy said quickly, her smile as blinding as a prison-yard searchlight. "That would be great!"

"Good," Zane said smoothly, watching Brylee's face and acting as if he knew every last one of her deepest secrets and a few she herself had yet to discover in the bargain. With a sweep of one arm, he gestured toward the tables lining the far wall, but the Friday night crowd was thick, and Brylee still couldn't see where he was directing her and Amy to go.

Amy, on the other hand, seemed to come equipped with her own personal GPS. The rhinestones on her hip pockets caught colored lights from the jukebox as she sashayed confidently across the room and headed straight for the table with the ratty old moose head hanging on the wall just above it.

A man stood, smiling, as they approached, weaving a path between line dancers and waitresses and people just trying to elbow their way to the restroom. He was breathtakingly handsome, whoever he was, and he obviously knew it, which didn't endear him to Brylee.

In fact, she bristled a little.

"My brother," Zane explained mildly, and with a touch of what might have been irony. "Landry Sutton."

Landry beamed, showing teeth as white and straight and perfect as Zane's. Were they *born* that way, or was cosmetic dentistry a factor? The brother's hair was the same toasty shade of dark blond, too, his eyes the same intense blue. And yet, Brylee thought, he was very different from his sibling. His clothes— jeans and a crisp white shirt, regulation dress-up garb for a cowboy—were too, well, *tailored,* fitting him like a layer of spray paint. They were not just expensive, those duds, they were out-and-out flashy, and his boots, with their pointed toes and elaborate embroidery, must have been custom-made.

On an oil baron or a trick-rider in an Old West show, circa Buffalo Bill Cody's heyday, they might have worked. In Parable County, Montana, they were the unmistakable marks of a wannabe, a greenhorn.

Amy, apparently unconcerned by all this, or just failing to make the same observations Brylee had, gushed all over Landry Sutton, welcoming him to the community and all that, but Brylee could manage only a wooden smile and a stiff "How do you do?" as she put her hand out for Landry to shake. In a sidelong glance at Zane, she saw that his mouth had taken on a slightly smug curve at one side.

Zane's once-over had at least been subtle—sort of—but when Landry measured Brylee from the crown of her head to the soles of her scandalous shoes, she felt, well, not trashy, exactly, but on display, like a ripe peach at a roadside produce stand.

She might have made excuses then, said she and Amy were expecting a few friends any minute now and promptly chosen a table as far away from Zane and Landry's as possible, but her BFF was already batting her glue-on eyelashes at the new guy in town, and he suavely pulled back her chair.

Once Amy sat down, Brylee was stuck. Zane, looking strangely sympathetic but still amused, offered her the chair beside his and waited until she took it before sitting down himself.

"Things are looking up," Landry said in a low drawl, his gaze fixed somewhere in the vicinity of Brylee's cleavage.

Damn that stupid push-up bra, anyway, she thought. She should never have *ordered* the thing, let alone put it on, but the woman on the shopping channel had promised the earth, plus lasting peace and global prosperity, all for $29.99 plus shipping.

Sucker, Brylee castigated herself silently, remembering. Had she bought the red dress at the same time, on the same recklessly romantic impulse? Who knew?

"Landry," Zane said coolly, "quit while you're ahead, okay?"

It wasn't a suggestion, Brylee realized, but an order, or even a warning, however politely delivered.

An invisible charge flashed, white-hot, between the two men.

"We really should get a table of our own," Brylee interjected, with desperate goodwill. "Before the place gets too crowded." She paused, blushed because she could feel Zane's sidelong glance stinging tiny hair follicles on every inch of her skin—and not just the visible parts, either. "W-we're meeting friends."

"They're late, anyhow," Amy said quickly. "Who knows? They might not show up at all. You know how they can be."

Brylee glared at her friend, contentedly seated beside Landry on the opposite side of the scratched tabletop.

Amy, undaunted, made a face at her.

An unfamiliar waitress came over, harried but, at first, friendly. Whip-thin in her narrow jeans and boob-hugging tube top, she sported big hair, pink boots and a plastic name tag that read "Sharlene." The finishing touch was a tattoo of a small, grinning skull, its bony head crowned with pink flowers, nestled on the upper curve of her right breast.

If that top shrunk a mere fraction of an inch in the dryer next time Sharlene did her laundry, Brylee thought uncharitably, it would be Nipple-o-rama at the Boot Scoot—forget taco night.

"What'll it be, Mr. Movie Star?" the waitress asked in a near-croon, eyes twinkling. Evidently, she'd noticed Zane and no one else—even Landry, an unusually attractive man in his own right, might have been part of the wall, for all the attention she gave him.

Amy and Brylee, well, they were just plain transparent, it seemed.

Ms. Tattooed Boob, Brylee reflected, seemed to be the predatory type, one of those felinelike females who not only discounted other women as people but wrote off much of the male gender, too. Only the man caught directly in her crosshairs mattered to Sharlene and her ilk.

Harsh, Brylee scolded herself silently. *You don't even know this woman.* Reasoning didn't help, though. The dislike remained, a thing of instinct rather than logic.

Brylee would have chosen to ignore the bimbo altogether, thus returning the favor, but, unfortunately, her stomach gave a long, rumbling growl, audible even over the throb of the jukebox and the shuffling of feet out on the minuscule dance floor.

Mercifully, Amy, Landry and the waitress-in-a-tube didn't seem to hear, but Zane immediately turned to Brylee, grinned conspiratorially and said, addressing Sharlene, "I think my lady friend here is hungry."

His *lady friend?* Now *there* was a term straight out of yesteryear.

Catching the way Landry's brows knitted together in an instant frown, though, Brylee had to wonder

if the remark had actually been directed at him, and
not at her at all.

The prospect, though insufferably territorial, was
unnervingly pleasant, too.

"Okay," the waitress said, annoyed, her glance
slicing to Brylee's face. "What can I get you, honey?"
*A side order of cyanide? A one-way ticket to Tali-
ban headquarters?*

Brylee decided she was definitely being bitchy
and forced herself to smile as she requested a diet
cola—normally, she would have had a beer, but she
intended to split at the first opportunity and that
might not give the alcohol enough time to wear off—
along with two tacos.

"Shredded beef or chicken?" Sharlene snapped.
Clearly, doing her job was an imposition now that
it appeared Zane wasn't fixing to ask for her phone
number anytime soon.

"Chicken, please," Brylee said sweetly. *Oh, and
you might want to watch it, "honey." Two can play
your game, and cowgirls fight to win.*

Zane chuckled under his breath, but Landry was
still watching him, and by then the frown had turned
to a glare.

Tattoo Girl, aka Sharlene, switched her scowl to
Amy and raised one eyebrow in impatient query.
Amy, nobody's pushover, scowled right back. "Same
thing," she said tartly. "Chicken tacos and a diet
cola." A pause, during which Amy's mouth tightened to a straight line and then softened into a saucy
smirk. "And make it snappy, will you—*darlin'?* My

friend and I have a big night ahead, and we're starving."

Zane smiled again, pretended to peruse the limited menu, a laminated photocopy stained with last week's chili sauce and something that might have been cheese at one time, and asked for a deluxe burger, a double order of fries and a chocolate milk shake.

The waitress beamed on him like sunshine, as if she'd never in her livelong *life* taken such a brilliantly unique order as that one.

Landry, obviously not happy to be persona non grata, as Brylee and Amy were, said he'd have a draft beer and it would be a marvelous thing if Sharlene refilled the peanut bowl, because they were down to shells and salt grains.

Marvelous? Brylee was struck by the term. There probably wasn't another man in the entire county—not a straight one, anyhow—who would have used that word, especially in a place like the Boot Scoot.

Sharlene flounced away, taking her tattoo and her snippy attitude with her, ostensibly to put in their orders at the fry cook's window, and another look passed between Zane and Landry, cryptic and not all that brotherly, when you thought about it.

Brylee stole a surreptitious glance at her watch, under the table, and suppressed a sigh. Where on earth were her friends, Margie and Francesca and Susie and the others? If only they'd make an appearance, she'd have ample reason to take her tacos and her diet cola, once they were served, that is, and make her escape.

She tried to reason with herself, silently, of course. What *was* the big deal? She'd already been horseback riding with Zane, and he'd be coming to the ranch for supper the very next night. It wasn't as though their paths hadn't crossed, and would *continue* to cross, in the foreseeable future.

Brylee was uncharacteristically jittery, sitting so close to Zane, fit to jump right out of her skin, in fact. And the worst thing about that was, she was starting to *enjoy* the vague sense of danger, the intangible force pulsing between his body and hers.

Oddly, the sensations reminded her of her first barrel race, in her first real rodeo, albeit the junior variety, when she was no older than ten. She'd been scared to death and thrilled to the marrow of her bones at one and the same time, anxious in a way that, ironically, made her want to shout for joy, certain she'd burst wide-open if she tried to hold it in.

The food and drinks came, but there was still no sign of her and Amy's pals.

Brylee began to wonder, as paranoia set in, if this was a setup. Had Margie and the others ever even *intended* to gather at the Boot Scoot for beer, gossip and the best tacos in Montana? Or had Amy pulled off some kind of BFF maneuver aimed at getting Brylee back on the figurative horse that had thrown her?

It was a crazy thought, of course, because Amy couldn't have known Zane and Landry would be there, for one thing. Still, she *was* acting as though everything was going according to some plan Brylee had never been privy to. She chatted with Landry and he finally quit trying to burn a hole in Zane with his eyeballs, picked up the conversational ball and ran with it. The man could charm the socks off a department store mannequin, Brylee observed to herself. Odd that he did less than zip for her, drop-dead gorgeous as he was, but the needle on her bring-it meter wasn't even twitching.

She and Zane, neither of them able to get a word in edgewise, began to eat. Then, midway through the meal, Landry asked Amy if she wanted to dance, and she almost tipped over her chair, she was in such a rush to get to her feet.

In seconds, she and Landry were out there on the floor, their food abandoned.

Brylee watched them for a few moments, realizing only when Zane laughed and nudged her upper arm gently that she'd narrowed her eyes to suspicious slits.

"Is he safe?" she asked, completely serious. She was protective of Amy—had been since school-bus days, when her undersize friend had had braces and a lisp and some of the bigger kids had taken to picking on her during the rides to and from town.

"Safe?" Zane echoed, looking mystified.

"Amy's still half in love with her ex-husband," Brylee explained earnestly, in a rapid undertone, one word tumbling over the next. "She's especially vulnerable right now, that's all, because Bobby is dating a flight attendant from Missoula."

Zane grinned, setting his burger back in its plastic basket, where it nestled among fries and a few pickle slices. "Landry and I aren't close," he said, in that mild, irritatingly sexy way he had, "but I can honestly swear to you that he's not an ax murderer."

Brylee picked up her second taco, unwilling to dignify Zane's remark with a response. She hadn't *said* his brother was an ax murderer, hadn't even suggested as much.

Still, stranger things had happened. All a person had to do was watch the ID network on TV for a half hour to get a new insight into deviant behavior.

Zane chuckled again, unwilling, it would seem, to let her off the old hook. "Lady," he said, in a drawl that raised her body temperature, "you are *something else* in that red dress. Are you planning on wearing it again tomorrow night, when I drop in at your place for supper?"

He just *had* to remind her that they'd be thrown into close proximity again within twenty-four hours, didn't he?

Brylee was thrilled, *and* infuriated, by the way he'd gotten under her skin, and she did her level best to hide all of that. "Of course I'm not," she snapped. "I shouldn't have worn it *tonight,* either."

"I'm glad you did," Zane said, in a honeyed, sleepy murmur.

Brylee's face heated up in an instant, and her heart

raced like an overenthusiastic Thoroughbred busting through the starting gate ahead of the gun.

Zane saw his advantage and pressed it; he leaned in a little, dropped his voice to a rumbling, throaty whisper. "That's your cue to say thank you."

Brylee pushed her plate away, dizzied by the speed of her thoughts, never mind her heartbeat. Everything inside her seemed to be careening wildly, with no particular destination. This was totally *embarrassing*.

"I need some air," she blurted suddenly, no longer able to keep her cool.

Before Zane could answer, she pushed back her chair, shot to her feet and fled, squeezing between the dancers and the serious drinkers lining the vintage bar, a relic from an old saloon, the Broken Boot, that had burned to the ground sometime around 1910. Her shoes hurt and she kicked them off the moment she was outside, in the parking lot.

The gravel would probably ruin her panty hose but, *oh, well*. She had another pair at home and, anyway, she only wore them at church and the national sales conferences she held for her Décor Galore people once a year.

Brylee breathed deeply for a few moments, drawing in the night air and the sky full of stars. At first, she was afraid she might hyperventilate, with no paper bag in sight, but after a minute or so, she began to calm down.

She did this just in time to see Zane standing beside her, arms folded, head tilted to one side, expression curious—and still amused.

"Are you all right?" he asked, and his tone indicated that he expected her to answer no, if not ask him to call 9-1-1 for an ambulance, though the look on his face belied any such urgency.

He *knew*. He knew she was attracted to him, and fighting against the feeling every inch of the way. Brylee was mortified, and she didn't know the answer to his question any more than he did. *Was* she all right?

"I don't know," she finally admitted, and then—and this was *really* unlike her—she started to cry.

"Hey," Zane said, his voice husky. He moved closer then, took her in his arms and held her. He smelled of grass and rivers and sunshine, and his chest was warm and hard against the side of Brylee's face. A flash of pure wanting slashed through her, sundering bone and muscle, lodging in her very soul. His raspy chuckle echoed to her core and melted something there, something hard and chilly and very, very old. "Whatever it is, it can't be *that* bad."

Brylee struggled valiantly to regain her self-control—this wasn't her, she *must* be possessed, or suffering from multiple personality disorder.

"I didn't expect to see you here!" she sobbed, probably staining his shirt, as well as her face, with liquefied mascara.

Zane hooked a curved index finger under her chin and lifted gently, so she had to look him in the eyes.

That impossibly sexy grin played at the corners of his mouth.

"Obviously," he said. "I must admit, though, that it's something of a disappointment, given the way you look in that dress. I'd hate to think of you wearing something that hot for anybody else."

"Don't say that!" she commanded, after a few inelegant sniffles.

"Why not?" Zane asked reasonably. Here she was, falling apart at the seams, and he seemed to be *enjoying* her meltdown. Adding fuel to the flames, as a matter of fact.

"Because I'm not some *Hollywood* woman, that's why!" she burst out.

"That's for sure," he said, eyes twinkling even more than before.

Brylee stiffened, indignant. "And what is *that* supposed to mean?"

Zane laughed. "It means *this,*" he said, his voice low and gruff.

And then he kissed her.

Thunder clapped and the earth moved and Brylee went from stunned to stun-*gunned,* in two seconds flat. When she should have pushed Zane away, she slid her arms around his neck instead and stood on her tiptoes to kiss him right back.

When she did those things, Zane held her even closer and kissed her even more deeply.

The gears of Brylee's private universe ground to a stop, then lurched into sudden motion again, and all the stars in that big Montana sky overhead seemed to coalesce into billions of silvery particles, drifting down all around them, but *only* them, like some kind of baptism of angels.

Just when Brylee thought she might actually *drown* in this man—this impossible, unsuitable, infuriating man—he lifted his mouth from hers and made a hoarse sound low in his throat. If he hadn't been holding Brylee up, one hand on either side of her waist, she was sure her knees would have buckled.

Zane averted his eyes then, apparently fascinated by the beat-up propane tank on the other side of the lot, and his breathing was fast and shallow.

"Okay," he said, as though something vital had been decided and there would be no turning back.

Brylee was irritated, not so much because he'd kissed her—*twice*—but because she'd let him do it, even *encouraged* him. He was an *actor,* she reminded herself, with belated and bitter practicality, and she, despite her education and her successful business, was still a country girl at heart. Compared to Zane, she was utterly naive.

The sexy Mr. Sutton was not only out of her league, he was a threat to her emotional well-being. He'd already breached barriers even *Hutch* hadn't been able to get past, hadn't he?

Brylee remembered her shoes—discarded in the rough gravel—and jammed a foot into one, then the other. "Okay, *what?*" she demanded.

Incredibly, he smiled. Granted, it was a sad smile, not his usual obnoxious and slightly arrogant grin, but that didn't make her feel one bit better—or *worse,* for that matter.

Unsettled as she was, some part of Brylee was soaring, and there were wings beating inside her heart and in the back of her throat.

Before Zane could say anything more—a blessing in disguise, no doubt—Amy and Landry wandered out of the Boot Scoot and into the coolness of the evening, both of them looking concerned.

"Bry," Amy said gently. "Are you sick or something?"

"No," Brylee said, too quickly. Then, "Yes."

Zane wasn't gripping her waist now, but he'd looped one arm around her shoulders, and she knew it was because he wasn't entirely sure she could remain upright under her own power. She both resented and appreciated the gesture, and she felt drunk, even though she hadn't had a drop of beer or wine the whole night.

"Shall I drive you home?" Amy asked, searching Brylee's face anxiously. The worry in her friend's eyes was genuine.

Brylee shook her head and limped off toward her SUV, rummaging in her purse for the keys as she went.

Amy hurried after her, caught hold of her arm. "Bry? What's going on?"

Brylee paused, shook her head again, unable to explain since she didn't entirely understand what was happening herself, and forged on toward her vehicle.

Amy let her go this time, but Zane wasn't so accommodating.

The whole way back to Timber Creek Ranch, he was right behind her, he and his big truck and his brother. Only when she'd pulled off the road and started up the long, winding driveway leading to the house she'd lived in all her life did he go on his way, the headlights of his truck beaming bright in the darkness.

CHAPTER TWELVE

IT WASN'T ZANE'S style to back out on a commitment, *any* commitment—which was probably the main reason he so rarely made one to begin with—but for Saturday night supper at Timber Creek Ranch, with Brylee and her whole clan, he knew he'd better make an exception. He'd lost his head back there at the Boot Scoot Tavern, testosterone levels ratcheted way up by the sight and scent and feel of Brylee Parrish in that damnable, sex-on-wheels red dress of hers, and he'd just hauled off and *kissed* her—definitely a tactical error, in hindsight. She'd gone all wide-eyed afterward, like a doe startled in the woods, and practically *loped* to her car, she was in such a hurry to get away.

From him.

Seeing Brylee again so soon might make her feel cornered, and he didn't want that. Still, he wished he didn't have to cancel, and not just for selfish reasons. Nash's chance to meet Brylee's nephew, Shane, a boy about his age and thus a potential friend, would be postponed. Even Cleo, the human dynamo, could have used a night out of that old house and a taste of someone's cooking in place of her own.

Damn, Zane thought. When had his life gotten so complicated? He'd come to Montana partly to simplify his existence, but in retrospect, L.A. seemed peaceful by comparison. Probably an illusion.

All too aware of Landry, slumped sullenly in the passenger seat of Zane's truck, he suppressed an audible groan. His brother had witnessed most of the debacle at the Boot Scoot, and what he hadn't seen for himself, he'd probably guessed, because whatever Landry's other shortcomings might be, he wasn't stupid.

Zane swore again, silently. He'd kissed a lot of women in his day, and some of those women were beyond hot, no denying it, but he'd never felt anything more than normal, if pleasant, heat with any of them, not even Tiffany, and he'd truly believed he *loved* her. Once upon a time, that is.

The warm and receptive sweetness of Brylee's mouth under his, by contrast, had caused a seismic shift inside him, a sort of violent connection—or, more accurately, a *collision*—of their two souls, and the aftermath felt alarmingly permanent. Oh, the shock had let up a little, all right, but the echo of that was tattooed on every cell in his body and branded on his heart and mind.

Was this love? Damn, he hoped not, because it was too soon for that, too. Seemed like it was too soon for just about *everything,* and he wasn't a patient man.

Landry, having been on the peck since Zane had practically shirt-collared him away from the

Boot Scoot and into the truck, determined to make damn sure Brylee got home without incident, given how upset she'd been. Leaning forward on the seat, Landry twiddled with the sound system on the dashboard, producing fragments of songs and newscasts, but mainly ear-splitting static, before giving an exasperated growl, low in his throat, and, mercifully, shutting the noise off again.

Something ventured, nothing gained, Zane thought. They'd just made the U-turn at Timber Creek's front gate, and Zane was heading for home. Nights at Hangman's Bend were relatively quiet, but the days were pure chaos, with Cleo and Nash and the dog and the contractors all vying to see who could raise the most dust and clatter and all-around annoyance in general.

Now, damn it, *Landry* would be tossed into the mix, nasty-assed attitude, drugstore-cowboy getup, and all.

Frustrated, Zane shoved a hand through his hair, reminded himself that the man riding with him wasn't some troublesome hitchhiker but his own blood, his *brother*. He didn't see where he had any choice except to suck it up, concentrate on finding the man a place to sleep for the night and try hard not to go for his throat. Landry, being Landry, would inevitably decide to go back to Chicago, where he belonged. If he wanted a change of scene, why not New York? Boston? Or L.A.?

In the meantime, the situation simply had to be endured.

"I never figured you for a knight in shining

armor," Landry said dryly, in the dimness of the rig's fancy interior, breaking the uncomfortable silence that had prevailed, for the most part, since they left Parable. Out of the corner of his eye, Zane saw his brother cock a thumb over one shoulder, presumably indicating Brylee's turn onto her driveway. "Guess you missed it, big brother, but the lady clearly did not want you to escort her home. Following her the way you just did is called stalking, where I come from."

Zane's back molars locked together, and he purposefully relaxed the muscles in his aching jaws. He *had* crossed at least one line with Brylee that night, but he wouldn't have put the indiscretions into that particular category. *Stalking?* "Thanks for that observation," he finally ground out on a raspy breath, keeping his eye on the dark and winding country road ahead because, when this edgy and all-too-familiar energy arced between him and Landry, it generally led to a fistfight, the bare-knuckle, no-rules kind. "I really appreciate your expertise. Not to mention the benefit of a doubt."

Landry's laugh was raw and a little ragged around the edges. "What? You think you're the only one around here who knows a thing or three about women?"

Zane made a conscious effort to go all Zen on the inside, but it didn't work, possibly because he didn't know spit about the process. Nobody—not even Tiffany—had ever been able to get under his hide the way Landry did, always with a minimum of effort, too. Like he was born for it.

"Look," he said, with a quiet but unmistakable warning in his voice as well as his manner, "I'd just as soon not discuss Brylee, if it's all the same to you."

"The woman is seriously hot," Landry went on, undaunted. "If you're not planning to go after the delectable Ms. Parrish in earnest, kindly step aside and let *me* give it a shot."

That did it. Zane slammed on the brakes and brought the truck to a dust-roiling, tire-screeching stop alongside the road. "Make a move on Brylee," he said, sounding deadly calm, which he damn well wasn't, "just one move, and you're going to need a brand-new set of teeth, *little* brother."

Landry pretended to cower slightly against the truck door, putting both hands up, palms out in a gesture of mocking capitulation, but the glint in his eyes told the real story. He'd have enjoyed a good row himself, Landry would have, right then and right there, in the ditch or even on the road, and avoiding a potential melee wasn't on his priority list.

"All right, all right," he said, with notable irony, "I *get* it. Brylee is off-limits." He paused while Zane, white-knuckling the steering wheel with both hands, tried to defuse the ticking bomb in his middle. Landry, of course, chatted merrily on. "Of course, there is the matter of the lady's obvious reluctance to have anything whatsoever to do with you, so that might mean I'll get my chance, after all, at some point. I trust you noticed how jumpy Brylee was, from the moment she came through the door and caught sight of you? I was watching her—who could *help* watching her, with looks like that?—and she would have done a disappearing act, pronto, if her friend hadn't grabbed her arm and forced her to stay."

All that was true, of course—except maybe for the part about Landry having a snowball's chance in hell with Brylee, *ever*—and that was why Zane planned on calling Casey Elder as soon as he got home and asking for a raincheck on the home-cooked dinner. If he crowded Brylee now, Zane figured, he wouldn't just miss when he tried to catch the brass ring, he'd fall clear off the merry-go-round, and getting back on would be a bitch, if it was possible at all.

"Let it go, Landry," he said, very quietly. He started the truck up again, grinding the ignition, checked the mirrors, and pulled back out onto the road. "We'll be at Hangman's Bend in a couple of minutes. You can sleep off all that beer and whatever else you've been swilling since you got to Parable. There might even be some hope that you'll come to your senses by morning."

But Landry was shaking his head. "I'm not bunking in at your place, cowboy," he said. "There's an establishment in Three Trees called the Somerset Inn. Place looked halfway decent on the internet. Anyway, I have a reservation, and the rental company is dropping off a replacement car there first thing tomorrow."

Zane hoped his relief wasn't too obvious, intense as it was. "Okay," he agreed casually. "But you might have mentioned this when we drove *through* Three Trees fifteen minutes ago. I could have dropped you off then."

"You were busy tailing the Lady in Red," Landry reminded him airily. "Far be it from me to interfere with your love life, bro."

"Right," Zane said skeptically. "Far be it from you."

"That woman I was dancing with," Landry mused aloud, as they passed the mailbox at the bottom of Zane's driveway and headed on toward town. "You happen to recall what her name is?"

Zane's grip tightened on the wheel again momentarily, and conversely, he felt a weird impulse to laugh. He'd just been congratulating himself on not getting into a knock-down-drag-out, in the middle of nowhere, with his obnoxious brother. Now, what little self-control he'd been able to hold on to gave way to another rush of hostility.

"You don't remember her name?" he asked, when he figured he could trust himself not to yell, or pull over again, haul Landry out of the truck and beat the hell out of him on the spot. "You were all over her, man. She's probably expecting a phone call at any minute, followed up with a major date, if not a proposal, and you *didn't catch her name?*"

Landry sighed, long-suffering. "I see you're still the same judgmental bastard you always were," he remarked, feigning great sadness at the discovery.

"Amy," Zane bit out, determined not to acknowledge the gibe. "Her name is Amy."

"Right," Landry said. "It would have come back to me eventually, but thanks, anyway."

"She's Brylee's friend," Zane pointed out, remembering what Brylee had said about how Amy was still in love with her ex-husband—against the dictates of common sense, evidently, since the man was busy romancing a flight attendant—and kept his tone as even as he could. Landry was goading him, and he needed to put on the brakes, get a grip before "bad" morphed itself into "worse." "Amy's a nice person, a small-town girl." A pause. "So suppose you summon up the decency to leave her the hell alone? You're not even divorced from what's-her-name, are you?"

"Susan." Landry let out a long breath. "We never got around to getting married again, after that last divorce," he said, dismissing the most recent wife/girlfriend/whatever, as if she'd been hired from an escort service for a night. "Is Amy the first runner-up or something?" he went on, all innocence and phony concern now. "I mean, if things don't work out between you and Brylee—and from my viewpoint it looks like they won't, sorry to say—you want to keep her friend in reserve for a replacement?"

Zane simmered in silence for a long time, refusing to give in to his baser instincts, which called for immediate brother-blood by the bucket load. The flash flood of adrenaline rushing through his system took a while to subside.

When the outskirts of Three Trees finally came into view, though, Zane was ready to talk again, and he went straight to the point. "What are you doing here, Landry?" he asked, without any inflection at all. "In Montana, I mean. It definitely isn't your kind of place."

"I told you," Landry said, the soul of patience. "I want to get a good look at my half of the ranch. I need a change of perspective, a chance to get off the hamster wheel for a few days and figure some things out." Attitude aside, this was probably the first true thing to come out of Landry's mouth all night.

"That must be why you bought yourself those road-show jeans and circus boots," Zane speculated flatly.

Now Landry was genuinely offended; Zane could tell that by the freeze in the formerly heated atmosphere. And he not only didn't give a rat's ass what Landry's response was, he was jazzed.

"These clothes," Landry said stiffly, "are *custom-made*. The best Chicago-land has to offer."

Zane chuckled, crossing the town limits and trying to remember exactly where the Somerset Inn was located. He might have seen it on one of his trips to town; he wasn't sure. "Exactly," he answered idly. "Around here, people buy their pants at Wal-Mart or Target or over at the Western-wear store—wherever they can get the best price—and no man who called himself a cowboy would be caught dead wearing duds like yours, especially those sissified boots."

That remark shut Landry up for a moment or two. He lifted one of his feet and gave his boot a cursory once-over. *"Sissified?"* he echoed, unconvinced but wavering a little, too.

Up ahead, Zane spotted the sign for the Somerset Inn, behind the Denny's and a convenience store/gas station surrounded by semitrucks.

He grinned to himself. *Score,* he thought. "Down-right girlie," he confirmed, pulling into the lot next to the motel. It was a good-sized outfit, though modest, well-maintained and with a lot of welcoming light spilling out through the lobby doors and windows.

Still, it was surely no match for the digs Landry was probably accustomed to gracing with his presence. Here, there might be a free breakfast, a pool and a few exercise machines, but room service, private wet bars, high-thread-count sheets, retractable TVs and spacious showers with multiple sprayers were unlikely prospects indeed. So much for personal concierges and complimentary champagne and rose stems on the pillows at night instead of a square of cheap chocolate, too.

And yet, Zane thought, slightly deflated by his own observations, unassuming as it was, the Somerset Inn was in a lot better shape than *his* place. Once Landry got a look at the ranch house—and there was no getting out of that—he would have plenty to say about the new setup, and none of it would be favorable.

Landry was still scowling over Zane's comments on his duds, and he shoved open the truck door before Zane even came to a full stop under the fake-stucco portico outside the lobby. He got out, slammed the passenger door behind him, wrenched open the one in back to get his traveling gear and then slammed that door, too, hard enough to dent the framework. Without a goodbye or even a backward glance, let alone a thanks-for-the-ride, Landry walked away and disappeared into the inn.

Zane was at once relieved and stricken by the seemingly unbridgeable chasm that had yawned between him and his brother, once his closest friend, from around the time their mother died.

He let out a breath, drove away into the dark country night and headed for home. The lights were out in the house when he got there, except for one dim bulb glowing above the kitchen sink, which might mean he could avoid Cleo and Nash until morning. That would be *some* consolation at least.

He parked the truck, jammed the keys into his pocket and made his way to the barn, where he spent a few soothing minutes leaning against Blackjack's stall door, communing with the sleepy gelding. Horse-energy almost always restored Zane's equanimity, and that night was no different.

Later, walking toward the darkened porch, he scrolled through the lengthy contact list on his cell phone and came to a number for Casey. Since the area code covered that part of Montana, he figured it must be current. Keying it into his phone must have been his agent's doing—Marcella was big on building and maintaining networks.

Zane touched the green Call icon and waited. Inside the kitchen, Slim scratched at the other side of the door and gave a plaintive whimper, so Zane let him out and waited, the phone pressed between his shoulder and his ear, as the dog darted into the yard and ran around in a big circle, wild with the joy of being on the loose.

Zane had to smile then, and it made him feel better.

"Hello? Zane?" The voice was Casey's; she'd picked up just as he was about to disconnect, realizing he hadn't checked the time before dialing, and everybody over at Timber Creek might have already been asleep—until he roused them, that is.

Zane bit the figurative bullet, grateful for caller ID because he didn't feel like explaining who he was or even talking on the phone at all in the first place, and besides, he felt like a first-class heel for lying his way out of a perfectly good supper invitation. "Hi, Casey, I'm sorry if I woke you up or anything—I didn't—"

She laughed. "Heck, Zane," she replied, "the baby and I are both night owls, anyway. Besides, it's only about ten-thirty or so. How've you been since I saw you last, anyhow?"

"Good," Zane said, his tone giving the lie to the response. "You?" he took a breath, not waiting for the answer. "It was big news when you got married, and even *bigger* news when you came up pregnant."

Casey grinned; he heard it in that famously musical voice of hers. "Why, old buddy, I'm as happy as a pig in a puddle of molasses," she told him, deliberately thickening that honeyed Texas drawl of hers. "It's been too long, Zane. I can't wait to catch up over supper tomorrow night, have you meet Walker and the kids—"

Zane wedged in a sigh, stopping the flow of Casey's words. "That's the thing," he said glumly. And then he lost his momentum, lapsing into an awkward silence.

Casey hazarded a guess. "You can't make it," she said, making no effort to hide the drop in her level of enthusiasm.

"Not tomorrow night," he managed. "Maybe another time, but—"

"Sure," Casey replied, quick to let him off the hook. She was an easygoing type, as he recalled, and he'd liked her from the first. On the set of their TV movie, they'd been pals, skipping the usual hanky-panky to have fun instead of set-trailer sex. "Another time."

"Thanks," Zane said, feeling like three kinds of an SOB. At least Casey hadn't pushed for the reason he was begging off, which spared him the necessity of lying to her outright.

Zane straightened his spine, glanced up at the stars and reminded himself that he was doing this for Brylee. He was giving her space, that's all.

"I'll give you a call in a few days," Casey told him.

Would a few days be long enough for some of the dangerous heat smoldering between him and Brylee to die down? He sure hoped so, because he couldn't keep on like this for much longer. Real life was no place for honing his acting skills, and besides, blowing people off was *Landry's* usual M.O., not his. "That would be good," he finally replied, feeling even more like a shithead in the face of Casey's kindness.

Goodbyes were exchanged and they both hung up.

"Crap," Zane told the dog, who'd finished his celebratory dash through the overgrown grass and stood looking up at him now, watchful and adoring, tongue lolling as he panted in happy exhaustion.

Slim, of course, had no answer for that. He simply wagged his tail and followed Zane inside the pile of junk lumber they called home.

Time to call it a night.

CHAPTER THIRTEEN

BRYLEE'S DAD HAD always told her and Walker that no matter how bad something seemed at night, it would look better in the morning light, and her present good mood certainly bore the theory out.

The night before, she'd been in a classic dither, beelining for home after fleeing the Boot Scoot parking lot, seeking the sanctuary of her small apartment like a rabbit bolting for its hole with a pack of hungry coyotes closing in fast.

She'd blown in like a hurricane, heart pounding, breathing fast and shallow, kicked off those bad-news shoes right away and then tossed them decisively into the trash bin for good measure. Snidely, baffled by this unusual behavior but happy to be reunited with his beloved mistress just the same, had followed her to her bedroom, where she'd immediately peeled off the red dress, dropped it in a silky heap at her feet and then kicked it into the dim recesses of her closet, from whence it came. This time, she didn't bother with a hanger.

Awash in furious satisfaction, next she'd stomped into the bathroom, scrubbed off the layers of makeup, disposed of her ruined panty hose and let down her hair, brushing and brushing until it was no longer stiff with spray, took her nightshirt from the hook on the back of the door and squirmed into it. She had trouble finding the armholes, and for a moment or so, she felt as though she'd been slapped into a straitjacket—a strangely appropriate image, taking her mental state into consideration.

Even after swilling two cups of herbal tea like a drunk downing whiskey after a lengthy dry spell, followed by a much calmer and wholly genuine attempt to mellow the heck out by slowing down her brain, sleep had still eluded her. Mindful of Snidely's patient confusion—the way she'd been carrying on, for pity's sake, the poor dog must have thought the world was ending, at that very moment—she finally flung herself into bed, wriggled around a bit in a vain effort to settle in, then shot bolt upright again, muttering, because she'd forgotten to switch off the lamp on her nightstand.

For all that ruckus, Snidely, seemingly reassured that civilization would continue on its usual hurly-burly course, for the time being, anyway, curled up in his customary place on the hooked rug beside Brylee's bed, gave a sigh of profound relief and drifted off to doggy dreamland with enviable ease.

Brylee, by contrast, lay stewing in her own juices, her face hot with self-recrimination as she relived every wretched detail of her over-the-top, silly-schoolgirl reaction to Zane Sutton's mere *presence* at the Boot Scoot. As if he'd broken some cosmic law by showing up in a place she hadn't expected to run into him, and therefore hadn't had a chance to prepare in advance for the encounter.

And what was *that* about, this need to gird her figurative loins, like a female gladiator about to go into battle, before having the briefest contact with her sexy new neighbor?

Brylee had always prided herself on her cool head and good manners—the only real exception to the rule having occurred at the wedding-that-wasn't, after Hutch dumped her without even letting her get as far as the altar. On that infamous day, she'd thrown down her bouquet, stomped on it a couple of times and then marched outside in her fairy-tale bridal gown to snatch the Just Married sign, with its wacky shoe-polish letters, right off the back of the waiting limo. She'd ripped the strip of cardboard into shreds and thrown the remains in the gutter.

On top of making a fool of herself in front of people *with cameras,* she'd gone and *littered.* While she wasn't proud of acting like a character in a bad soap opera, she did wonder who could really blame her. Her *wedding* had been ruined, after all, and no red-blooded woman would have smiled sweetly and said, "Oh, well," now would they? But last night, in Parable—well, that was a different matter entirely. She'd behaved like an idiot, especially after the kiss.

The kiss.

And holy crapola, *what* a kiss. She'd never experienced one like it before, not even with Hutch, and she'd been crazy about the man—crazy enough to want to *marry* him, for Pete's sake.

Thank God for unanswered prayers, she'd thought, lying there in her lonely bed. And soon after that, she'd begun to feel like herself—her *true* self—again. Anyone with eyes could see that Hutch belonged with Kendra, not with her. And she belonged with—well, who the hell *knew* who she belonged with?

Maybe nobody, the way things were shaping up.

Okay, so she might have to soldier on alone— lots of women did—but she'd do it with class and aplomb, by God. She'd dress to kill and speak her mind and go for the things she wanted. Why, she'd be the Katharine Hepburn of Parable County, Montana.

Finally, after much angst and a few vain efforts to figure things out—again—she'd tumbled into an awkward slumberlike state, shallow as a mud puddle and anything but restful.

But now it was morning, and the world was a whole different place. Zippity-do-dah!

The sun was shining fit to bring up next spring's grass right along with what was there already, the famous big sky was bluer than blue had any business being, without a permit from God, and she could ramble around her place in sweats all morning, if she wanted to, except for brief forays outside with Snidely, of course, and a quick trip to the supermarket in town. She could indulge her not-so-secret passion—cooking.

Why, she probably wouldn't even set foot in the warehouse all weekend, and for her, that was a major shift.

Yes, sir, Brylee had a plan, and she followed it,

awash in that crazy mixture of anticipation and wary dread no man had ever made her feel before.

Until Zane Sutton.

Tonight, he would be coming over for supper, bringing Cleo and Nash with him, and she'd be fully restored by then, batteries charged, ready for anything. Well, maybe not *anything,* but she had regained most of her composure, and she might at least be able to get through the evening without making a spectacle of herself.

She was humming cheerfully when a soft knock sounded at the inside door and Casey opened it to call out, "Anybody home?" The phrase was part of the vernacular in that household, had been for as long as Brylee could remember.

"Come in!" Brylee practically sang, from the kitchen, where she was running cold water over the frozen game hens she'd bought at the supermarket on her brief grocery run into Three Trees. Hastily, dressed like a gym rat and hoping to go unnoticed, Snidely waiting in the car, she'd selected four bottles of the best wine one could expect to find on supermarket shelves, taken her time choosing prime brussels sprouts and premium baby potatoes and all the stuff for a whiz-bang salad.

Maybe she couldn't hold on to a man, but damn it, nobody made a better salad.

Casey wandered on in, Preston nestled against her right shoulder, patting the baby's tiny back distractedly. When she focused on the array of food and cooking accoutrements set out on Brylee's center island, a tiny frown creased the porcelain-perfect skin between her eyebrows.

"What?" Brylee prodded good-naturedly, though Casey's troubled expression had her a little worried.

Casey scanned the produce and the frozen game hens once more, and then sighed a big, shoulder-moving sigh. Her beautiful necklace, a gift from Walker, specially designed, with a heart and two tiny, dangling Western hats, one representing her, the other, her husband, gleamed between the lapels of her faded cotton shirt. Somewhat nervously, she ran her free hand down the side of her respectably worn jeans.

"Something came up," Casey said, at long last, and her effort to overrule her reluctance and say what she'd come to say was painfully obvious.

Preston stirred a little, made baby sounds and Casey soothed him with another back pat and a gentle, "Shush now, sweet pea. Everything's fine."

The infant settled down right away.

"Something came up," Brylee repeated. "Such as?"

Not that she didn't have a sneaking suspicion what the answer was going to be. She'd made such a scene the night before, at the Boot Scoot, that Zane must have decided to back off, keep a prudent distance.

Funny how that realization, which should have provided a modicum of relief, opened a trap door in the pit of Brylee's stomach instead, one she thought she might just fall right through, end over end, forever, never quite hitting bottom.

Casey's reply confirmed everything Brylee had

already guessed. "Zane isn't coming to supper," she said sadly, and Brylee knew her sister-in-law wasn't sad for herself, or for Walker and the kids, much as they'd all been looking forward to entertaining a genuine movie star. Oh, no. Casey was sad for *her,* Brylee, the spinster—the woman who had made a lifestyle of being kicked to the curb by every man she found attractive.

"Oh," Brylee said, because that was all that came to her and because hiding things from the ultraperceptive Casey had proven impossible from the very beginning.

Casey looked pained, and though she tried to smile, the effort faltered on her mouth and failed to stick. "Something must have come up," she hastened to add. Again, she checked out the baby potatoes, the perfect brussels sprouts, the game hens just beginning to thaw in the island sink. "He said they'd come over some other time, he and the rest of his outfit. Sometime soon."

Sometime. Soon. In a pig's eye. Zane Sutton was on the run, thanks to her. He probably wouldn't come within a country mile of Timber Creek, ever.

Brylee was definitely *not* going to cry, she decided, even though, for some inexplicable reason, she wanted very much to do exactly that. Maybe the alternate personality, she of the red dress and the sexy shoes and the hey-sailor hairstyle, was trying to reassert herself, take over again and cause even *more* trouble.

She, the crazy fringe persona, might feel bad that

Zane would be a no-show for supper, but the authentic Brylee, the person she truly was and wanted to remain, thank you very much, was *glad* to be spared an unavoidably awkward evening.

Really glad, damn it.

"Whatever," she said, with a breeziness that, of course, didn't deceive Casey for a second. She gestured toward all that carefully chosen food laid out on the island. "I'll cook this stuff up, anyway—no sense trying to jam it into the fridge. We'll have a nice family dinner, just you and Walker, Shane and Clare, and me."

The look in Casey's expressive green eyes wasn't one of pity, but she was trying too hard to project good cheer and optimism for Brylee's comfort. Obviously, Casey knew the truth: that her sister-in-law's already-tattered pride had just been rubbed raw. "You're sure?" she asked hesitantly, gently. "I mean, really, that seems like a lot of work to go to, just for us."

"'Just for you'?" Brylee asked, summoning up another smile, though this one felt as though it had been cemented to her mouth and was already beginning to crumble because there was nothing to hold on to. "'Just,' nothing, Casey Parrish. Nobody is more important to me than all of you. *Nobody.*"

Casey couldn't seem to make herself leave, though she did turn slightly, angling one shoulder toward the door she'd come through just minutes before. "There's probably a good reason," she reiterated lamely. "After working sixteen hours a day with Zane on the set of that TV movie we did a few years ago,

I *know* he's not the type to change his mind on a whim…."

What Casey *didn't* know, of course, was that Zane had kissed Brylee, just the night before, kissed her like she'd never been kissed before, at the edge of a gravel parking lot, beneath a sparkling spill of stars, and she'd not only *liked* it, she'd wanted a whole lot more. She'd let him know it, too. *Then,* as if that wasn't bad enough, she'd flipped some emotional switch and gone from a red-dress, spiked-heel-wearing buckle bunny on the make to a sniveling, half-hysterical child—in a matter of a few heartbeats, no less.

The man had probably thought she was screwed up enough to qualify for a whole slew of twelve-step programs, and who could blame him? He'd probably encountered obsessed *fans* who were more rational, and those poor souls at least had the excuse of needing medication.

Worst of all, he'd never even *met* the real Brylee.

"Don't worry, please," she told Casey, smiling so hard now that she thought her face might actually crack. *Fake it till you make it.* Wasn't that one of the stand-by slogans in the recovery movement? "I'm fine. Really. I don't even *like* Zane all that much."

Oh, no, not much. *She'd merely have gone home with him, and straight to his bed, if he'd kissed her even once more, that was all.*

Casey wasn't buying any of it, of course, but she nodded compliantly and retreated into the other part of the house, humming under her breath to the baby as she went.

"Well, *hell*," Brylee told Snidely, who, as usual, was stuck to her like a postage stamp with too much glue on the back.

Snidely gave a philosophical-sounding sigh and meandered to the back door, wanting to be let out.

Brylee crossed the room, opened the door for him and watched as he zipped through the space, as if anxious to be shut of her for a while and find himself some better company to hang out with.

There seemed to be a lot of that going around lately.

Zane had gone to bed feeling like a damn peckerhead the night before, and he woke up with the same low opinion of himself. Rolling off his crumpled air mattress, he stood, rooted through dresser drawers until he found clean shorts and some socks. He put them on, then snatched yesterday's jeans from the floor and got into those, following up with a colorless T-shirt and his shit-kicking boots.

After brushing his teeth, splashing water on his face and neck and deciding categorically not to shave, even though he already had a pretty good stubble going, he made his way to the war-torn kitchen in search of coffee.

Cleo, frying up bacon and eggs on a double-burner hot plate, the stove having been junked right away, gave him a wry glance. "Bad night?" she asked, looking like a ride at Disneyland in the bright primary colors she was wearing.

Zane ignored the question, figuring the answer

was obvious enough to go unspoken, found a mug and filled it with black coffee. "Where's Slim?" he asked, looking around for his faithful dog. The critter had been right there last night, when it came time to bed down, but he'd been gone when Zane opened his eyes.

Cleo chuckled. "He's outside, with Nash," she replied.

"Why is it so quiet around here, anyhow?" Zane quizzed, after a few restorative sips of Cleo's excellent java.

"It's Saturday," the housekeeper reminded him. "Everybody needs time off, now don't they? Especially construction crews, since they work so hard during the week and all."

Zane sighed. "Good," he said. "Maybe I can have two thoughts in a row without a handsaw screeching or a rain of plaster dust falling on my head."

Cleo puckered her lips and frowned, but her eyes were dancing with kindly disdain. "Poor you," she said. She lobbed some of the food she'd just cooked onto a throwaway plate and held it out to him. "What, may I ask, has gotten under *your* hide so early in the morning, Boss Man?"

"How much time do you have?" Zane retorted grimly, taking the plate she offered, his mouth already watering and his stomach rumbling. He would have sworn he had no appetite at all, and damned if it wouldn't have been perjury. "It's a long freakin' list."

WALKER CASUALLY DROPPED in at Brylee's apartment for coffee and a visit in the early afternoon, trying to act as though the idea had been his own. Just a brotherly whim, not a rescue mission.

Of course, Casey must have been behind this sudden decision, because Walker was always busy around the ranch, even on Saturdays, tending to the surprisingly constant needs of bulls and broncos, the lifeblood of his stock-contracting business. On top of that, rodeo season was well under way, and he'd be heading for Colorado soon, with half a dozen loaded trucks and a good share of his crew. And that meant even more work than usual, with all the preparation such trips required.

"Coffee on?" he asked, nodding a greeting to Brylee before drawing back a chair and sitting down at her table. She was already pouring him a cup, black, the way he liked it.

She smiled, welcoming the interruption, because for hours now, she'd been marinating poultry, cleaning and slicing each little brussels sprout into neat halves, to be seasoned and roasted with the hens, peeling just a stripe around what seemed like jillions of baby potatoes and leaving the rest of the skin intact, just to make them showy. Except for a couple of runs outside with Snidely, the supermarket foray and a visit to the barn to groom her horse, Toby, in his stall, she hadn't taken a break.

"I'm fine," she said, preempting the inevitable how-are-you. She filled a coffee mug for herself and joined her brother at the table, trying to shift her sisterly viewpoint to a more objective one and see what Casey saw when she looked at him.

Walker was undeniably handsome, the rugged, outdoorsy type, at home on horseback or mending fences, inseminating cows with bull semen, or loading and unloading rambunctious rodeo stock in a din of bawling and neighing and kicking and clouds of throat-parching dust. His brown hair was attractively shaggy, his greenish-gray gaze was piercing and he had the classically square jaw of a movie cowboy.

Oops, Brylee thought, with an inner wince. *Stay off the movie-cowboy trail, girl, because it leads straight to Zane Sutton, and you* don't *want to go there.*

"Did I say you weren't fine?" Walker challenged, leaning forward in his chair a little, a grin flickering in his eyes and doing an almost imperceptible jig at one corner of his mouth. He needed a shave, but he must have showered recently, because his tanned skin looked scrubbed and his hair was still a bit damp. His clothes were clean, too.

Busted.

Brylee sat back, folded her arms, tilted her head to one side. "Casey sent you," she asserted mildly. "Big brother rushes to smooth his spinster sister's ruffled feathers."

Walker gave a mild snort and shook his head, as though marveling at the range of her wild imagination. "That's not true," he said, after a thoughtful sip of his coffee.

"You just dropped everything to stop in and have coffee?" Brylee chided. "I think you even took a shower and changed clothes for the occasion. Come *on,* Walker. I might not be a rocket scientist but, please, give me *some* credit."

He cleared his throat, looked serious for a moment, then recovered his usual low-key but cocky attitude. "Actually," he said, pleased to contradict her, "Casey *didn't* send me. Clare did."

"Clare?" Brylee frowned, puzzled. Surely Clare didn't know enough about the situation with Zane, if it could be *called* a situation, to be worried about her aunt, but if she *had* been, the girl would surely have paid a visit herself instead of sending her dad as an emissary.

Walker sighed as though the weight of the world had just settled onto his broad shoulders and was fixing to stay there a while. "She wants to tag along to Colorado with Shane and me," he said. "She's managed to get her mother to come over to her way of thinking, but I'm still holding out. The road isn't a place for a teenage girl, Brylee. You ought to know that better than anybody, but for some reason, my lovely daughter thinks you might be able to change my mind."

So that was it. A soft, sweet sadness swept through Brylee as she sat there, remembering how searingly lonely it felt to be left behind when her dad and Walker and some of the ranch hands hauled stock to some rodeo, near or far. They—the men— stayed in motels and took all their meals in restaurants, and there were always new things to see and do, as well as the deliciously familiar ones, old friends you never ran into anyplace else, and new people to get acquainted with, as well. It was hard to believe those same wonders would appeal to Clare, who'd grown up aboard her mother's tour bus and had been literally everywhere, including the White House and Buckingham Palace. But to that younger Brylee, a country girl looking at the very same scenery every day of her life, it had been an amazing adventure. A gift.

Until it abruptly stopped, that is. She sat up a little straighter and ran her hands down the thighs of her sweatpants, choosing her words carefully. "Walker," she said, "you know I don't interfere in these things. You and Casey set the rules for your family, and that's the way it should be—"

"But?" Walker asked, arching one eyebrow.

Brylee expelled a long breath. Well, hell, if he was going to *force* her to meddle, she'd do it. "But," she said, picking up where her brother left off, "it's a real bitch of a thing to be part of something for a long time and then suddenly find yourself shut out of the action, left behind at home like an extra saddle, just because you're growing up."

Tears formed in her eyes, an unexpected development to be sure, and she blinked and looked away in an effort to hide them, even though she knew it was already too late for that.

Walker reached across the table, squeezed her fingers together briefly with a steely strong, calloused hand. "Is that how you felt way back when, Brylee?" he asked, with a gentle gruffness that was very nearly her complete undoing. She was already on emotional overload, after all, barely keeping it together, and stuff just kept on coming at her, right and left. "Left behind?" he added. "Shut out?"

She sniffled and squared her shoulders, determined to hold on to what was left of her dignity. "Yes," she said. "That's how I felt. I know Dad meant well—he probably thought I'd get in trouble with a boy when he wasn't looking or come down with cramps and need Midol and a hot water bottle, or do some *other* girlie thing he wasn't prepared to handle, but it *hurt,* Walker. Mom was gone most of the time as it was, and then you and Dad bailed on me, too—seemingly without reason and *definitely* without any solid explanations." She paused. "What would *you* have thought, in my place?"

Walker sighed heavily. "About what you did, I reckon," he admitted solemnly. "But Dad *was* trying to protect you, honey, not break your heart—I can promise you that much. And bad things *do* happen on the road—trucks break down in the worst possible places at the worst possible times, stock gets loose and has to be rounded up and sometimes somebody gets trampled in the effort. Most cowboys are good men, I grant you, but they're *people,* just the same, and there are always a few bottom-feeders hanging around."

Brylee breathed deeply and slowly for a few moments, stunned at how deep the bruises went, even after all these years. She hadn't even been *conscious* of them, in fact, until the other day, when Clare had expressed the same desire to be included and the same confusion because that clearly wasn't going to happen.

"I know all that, Walker," she managed, after a long time, her voice rickety and a little thick. Afraid another crying jag might be coming on, she dragged herself back from the emotional brink, sat up straighter in her chair and closed her hands around her coffee mug. "I was young, but I wasn't stupid. I grew up on this ranch, just like you did, and I was a pretty fair wrangler, if I do say so myself. But I still got thrown into the penalty box, when push came to shove, for the crime of being a girl."

Walker swallowed hard, visibly moved. This was one of the many things Brylee loved about her brother, as Casey surely did, though obviously in a very different way—for all his rock-hard muscle, cowboy know-how and bone-deep self-assurance, he could put himself in another person's place, and not only see things from their point of view, but empathize.

"I'm sorry, sweetheart. I know Dad would be, too, if he were here to listen to your side of things." A sheen brightened Walker's eyes, promptly disappeared. He gave another sigh, so heavy it raised and lowered that powerful set of shoulders. "Damned if the kid wasn't right," he added, dryly rueful.

"What kid?" Brylee asked, having temporarily forgotten the genesis of this conversation.

"Your niece? My daughter?" Walker teased, rapidly becoming his ordinary self again. "Clare and Casey both said I was being bullheaded about this, and they were right. You made me see that."

Brylee smiled a genuine smile, and her spirits

rose measurably. "So you'll let Clare join you on the rodeo circuit?"

Walker grinned, but he held up an index finger to indicate that a stipulation was forthcoming. "Once," he said, with conviction. "If she behaves herself, then fine, she can be a regular part of the crew, until she gets tired of the hard work and the impossible schedule, anyhow. On the other hand, if that little girl gives me any cause at all to be concerned for her safety and her well-being, she'll find herself right back here on the ranch, before she can say jack—anything about it. And for the duration, too."

Brylee chuckled, holding up both hands in humorous surrender. "Fair enough," she said. Then, archly, she added, "What if *Shane* got into some kind of trouble, somewhere along the line? What would happen then?"

"Shane's a boy," Walker pointed out. He was turning a little grumpy now, forgetting his coffee, shoving an irritated hand through his hair, leaving furrows behind each finger.

"Precisely," Brylee said. "Does that mean the rules are different for him?"

"Damn it, Brylee, you're not being fair here," Walker complained. "Boys do get themselves in Dutch once in a while—of course they do—it's part of growing up. But whether you like it or not, there are some important differences here—boys don't get pregnant, for one thing."

"That's about the *only* thing," Brylee reasoned. "They do their share of mischief and then some, and you know it, Walker. And how do you think these theoretical females you've been yammering about *get* pregnant, anyhow? By osmosis? A *boy* is required."

Walker grinned wryly, shook his head again. "Cut me a little slack here, will you, sis? Clare can go along on one trip and she'd better mind her *p*'s and *q*'s, if she wants to go again. Right now, that's all the concession *this* nervous daddy is willing to make."

Brylee laughed and stuck out her hand in tacit agreement, and they shook on it, as though sealing a bargain.

Walker finished his coffee, said goodbye and left the apartment.

Five minutes later, Clare burst in, face glowing, eyes bright, without bothering to knock. She hurled herself into Brylee's arms, saying, "Thank you, thank you, *thank you!*"

Brylee hugged her niece back, then assumed an expression of solemn warning. "Don't blow this, Clare," she said quietly, but with a smile. "If you act up—as, let's be perfectly honest here, you've been known to do before—your dad will send you home in a heartbeat, and that will be it. You'll probably never get another chance to go on one of these road trips before you're a grown woman—if then."

Clare nodded eagerly. "I will be *so* good," she vowed.

Brylee chuckled and hugged the girl again, as pleased by Walker's decision as Clare was. "On behalf of girls and women everywhere," she reminded the child, with mock sternness, "*behave yourself,*

Clare Parrish. Prove to your dad that he's right to trust you."

Clare, smiling now, wiped at her cheeks with the back of one hand. "You're the absolute *best,*" she bubbled. A pause, another sniffle. "How did you manage to get Dad to give me a shot at this? He's been stonewalling me *and* Mom, right along."

Brylee smoothed a lock of coppery hair back from Clare's slightly flushed cheek. "I just told him how *I* felt, when *my* dad stopped letting me go out on the circuit with him and Walker and the others. Your father isn't trying to spoil your fun, Clare—he loves you, and he's trying to look out for you, keep you from getting hurt."

Even as she said those words, Brylee felt old wounds healing over, at long last, in the deepest regions of her own heart. Her dad *had* loved her, just as Walker loved Clare, and he'd honestly believed he was doing the right thing by sheltering her from a dangerous world.

Now might be a good time to pick some flowers in the yard, she thought, and pay a visit to Barclay Parrish's grave, in the small, shady cemetery just outside Three Trees.

It couldn't hurt to say, *Thank you, I understand,* even so long after the fact.

FOR WHATEVER REASONS, Landry didn't show up on Hangman's Bend Ranch all day on Saturday—at least, if he did, he didn't stop by the house—and Zane was both glad about and troubled by the fact.

Cleo and Nash were disappointed and peevish that he'd canceled the visit to Timber Creek as it was, and Landry's prickly presence wouldn't have improved the emotional climate any.

There might have been a full-scale insurrection, in fact, if Zane hadn't reminded the disgruntled natives that they'd all be attending a barbecue over at Hutch and Kendra Carmody's place the next afternoon, thus ending their social isolation. He'd even volunteered to drive into town and fetch pizza for supper, though he was getting sick of the stuff, and would have preferred a home-cooked meal. Still, dining on takeout for the ten millionth time was a small price to pay, he supposed, for keeping the peace.

After supper, Zane retreated to the barn, saddled Blackjack and led the animal out into the cool of the gathering twilight.

Nash, evidently burned out on reruns of vintage TV dramas, was standing almost directly in his path when he emerged, and Slim was right there beside him, sizing up the proceedings. In the little time he'd had that dog, Zane thought, with distracted satisfaction, the critter had filled out a bit through the middle, and gained a little confidence, too. His coat gleamed, even in the rapidly fading daylight, and his eyes were bright with eager interest.

Nash, on the other hand, was clearly in poor humor again, now that he'd finished off the last of the pizzas. He stood still, with his hands in his pockets and his head slanted slightly to one side, watching as Zane swung up into the saddle.

"You *said* I could get a horse of my own," the boy said, with just a touch of accusation underlying the reminder.

"Give me a break, buddy," Zane replied, hoping to jolly the kid out of his prepubescent mood. Were there going to be a lot of these? "You've only been here a few days, and a lot's been going on."

Nash shifted from one foot to the other, but his hands remained in his pockets and his shoulders were still rigid under his T-shirt. "There's *always* going to be a lot going on," he said, and Zane couldn't rightly deny that, ranch life being what it was. "But that's okay. Just promise the kid stuff and then ignore him—I'm used to that."

Not for the first time, the boy's words pierced something in Zane, something tender and already bruised. Nash was admitting, if in a roundabout way, that Jess Sutton wasn't the paragon he'd made him out to be.

Big surprise there.

"I don't plan on ignoring you, Nash," Zane said, leaning one arm against the saddle horn and holding the reins loosely in the opposite hand while Blackjack fidgeted, prancing sideways, eager to cover some ground. "And when I make a promise, I keep it."

Nash's expression remained skeptical, but there was a chink in his armor, Zane could see that—a glint of hope in the kid's eyes.

"Landry's in town," Nash went on, his voice still dull. "I heard you telling Cleo all about how he's a train wreck—Landry, I mean—and you wish he'd just go back to Chicago and stay put."

Guilt flashed through Zane, but he knew there was more the boy meant to say, so he braced himself for it and waited while Blackjack became increasingly impatient, tossing his head now, dancing backward a few steps.

"Is that what you say about me?" Nash asked. "When I'm not around—or you think I'm not? That you wish I'd get out of your hair?"

Damn, Zane thought. "No," he said, after a beat or two, "it isn't. It's just that things are a little complicated between Landry and me, that's all."

"Why?" Nash persisted.

"They just are," Zane said, not really having an explanation.

"I would have liked to have a brother, somebody to grow up with. Even a sister would have been okay, I guess. Just *somebody* to hang with when Dad went away all those times."

The backs of Zane's eyes throbbed, and he had to clear his throat before he answered. "Look," he ground out, hoarse despite those efforts, "if you want to, climb up on the fence over there and get on behind me. We'll ride double."

Nash's whole face brightened. "Really?"

"I don't say things I don't mean, boy," Zane told him. *Unlike some people I could name.*

Quick as mercury escaping from an old-fashioned thermometer snapped in half, Nash was up on the fence. Zane rode over and made the horse stand still until the kid was on behind him.

Cleo, meanwhile, materialized on the porch, glowering with disapproval. "Nash Sutton," she called, "you get down offa that big ole beast of a thing this minute!"

Zane grinned and ignored the woman. "Put your arms around my middle," he told Nash, "and hold on to Blackjack with your knees."

"Have you both lost your minds?" Cleo ranted on, for all the world like a hellfire-and-brimstone preacher warning of certain doom, pacing and gesturing and finally flapping her apron at them as if to shoo them right out of her sight if they couldn't behave like decent human beings.

"Yes, ma'am, I guess we *are* a little crazy," Nash replied cheerfully. Then, to Zane, in an eager whisper, he said, "Make him run."

Zane chuckled. "No possible way," he answered. "You probably wouldn't get hurt, but Cleo might just have a heart attack right before our eyes." He headed Blackjack down the rutted driveway, toward the road.

Nash bounced behind him. "This is great!" he yelled, loudly enough to split Zane's eardrum. "I knew it! I'm a natural!"

Zane laughed and eased Blackjack into a trot, once they reached the dirt road below the house. The gate, in sore need of repair like just about everything else on the place, stood open, the hinges long since rusted solid.

The ride had to be short, since it was getting dark,

but it lasted long enough to let Blackjack burn off some energy and satisfy Nash's thirst for adventure, for the time being at least.

Back at the barn, Zane dismounted by swinging one leg over Blackjack's neck and jumping to the ground, and Nash immediately scooted forward into the saddle, grabbing the reins. "I *told* you I could do this," the boy crowed, face beaming as bright as the moon overhead.

"Be careful getting down," Zane counseled, gripping Blackjack's bridle strap just in case Nash got any ideas. He was pleased that his kid brother was happy for once, though, and that he'd had a part in it.

By then, Cleo had retreated into the house in headshaking disgust, and Slim, for whatever reason, had gone along with her.

Heedless of his older brother's advice to dismount slowly, Nash leaped to the ground, limber as an Apache warrior, and winced comically when the balls of his feet made contact. The inevitable jolt of pain made him howl.

Zane shook his head slowly from side to side. "I tried to warn you," he said.

Nash had straightened, but he was still making faces. "Oww," he repeated.

"Next time, when I tell you something, listen."

With that, he led the horse back into the barn, made sure he had food and water and showed Nash how to undo the cinch and slide the saddle and blanket off Blackjack's back, how to remove the bridle, positioning his hand to catch hold of the bit so it wouldn't knock against the animal's teeth. After that, they checked the gelding's hooves for stones and other debris and gave him a thorough brushing down. Nash had a lot to learn, naturally, since he'd never been around horses before now, but he did seem to have a knack handling them, and that was a very good sign—wasn't it?

RATHER THAN CARRY plates and platters across the house to the other kitchen, Brylee served supper at her table, instead of Casey and Walker's. It was a squeeze, the space being considerably smaller, but that just made the occasion cozier.

Shane and Walker ate like wolves at the tail end of a starvation winter, while Clare was so ebullient at the prospect of traveling to Colorado with her dad and brother that she hardly touched her food. Instead, she chattered, her pretty face flushed, her eyes bright with excitement.

Only Casey seemed to see through Brylee's cheery facade, and she alternated between stabbing at a brussels sprout or a baby potato or a bite of game hen with her fork and shifting the blanket-bundle that was Preston from one shoulder to the other.

She was careful not to watch Brylee too closely, of course, but there was no mistaking her concern.

Brylee simply smiled a lot, listened and consumed just enough supper to avoid attracting attention, profoundly grateful that there was no real point in trying to make conversation. Clare prattled blissfully on about what clothes she wanted to take along on the trip to Colorado, and Shane, a typical kid brother, interjected a scoffing grunt once in a while. Mostly, though, he shoveled in food, stoking the fire of growth raging inside him, multiplying cells, stretching bones and filling out muscles.

Walker complimented Brylee on the meal, to which he had done a respectable amount of justice, and took baby Preston from Casey so his wife could finish her supper.

In the midst of all this, Brylee watched, and silently counted herself lucky to be part of this lively gathering of kinfolk and, at the same time, wondering if she'd ever have a family of her own.

CHAPTER FOURTEEN

THE NEXT DAY, cars and pickups filled the driveway and much of the barnyard at Whisper Creek Ranch, Hutch and Kendra Carmody's place outside Parable, and still more rigs lined the road below. There were a few motorcycles in evidence, too, Zane noticed, and probably an extra horse or two in the barn and corrals.

Cleo, all dolled up in a bright green polyester pantsuit, her best outfit, she claimed, and brand-spanking new in the bargain, sat stalwartly in the passenger seat of Zane's truck, one hand gripping the extra handle just above her window as though she expected the vehicle to go pitching over a steep cliff any second now. And never mind that there *wasn't* one within miles.

Nash, riding in the backseat, wasn't saying much—probably because he was too busy gawking at the Carmodys' fine ranch house, first-rate barn, miles of painted fences and the many horses and cattle grazing in the surrounding pastures. Once he'd looked his fill, Zane suspected, amused, the boy would most likely busy himself trying not to look overly impressed by it all.

They'd left Slim at home, where he'd be safe and no bother to anyone, but as Zane pulled up in front of a makeshift valet station near the mouth of the driveway, manned by a pair of grinning teenage boys, he reflected that there were probably almost as many canine guests at the party as there were people.

One of the young men hired to park cars opened Cleo's door for her and suavely helped her down after she'd swung her legs around and taken a teetering perch on the running board. Zane couldn't tell for sure, since her back was turned to him, but he'd have bet she was blushing that plum color she turned when she felt flattered. Nash scrambled out right away and headed for the action without a moment's hesitation.

Apparently, the kid wasn't shy, Zane thought, pleased. He would have pulled away then, found a place to park, but the other boy already had his door open and was holding out one hand for the keys.

Zane placed the jingling tangle of metal in the kid's palm, and the next thing he knew, his truck was pulling away at a good clip, leaving him to breathe dust.

With a chuckle, he followed Cleo and Nash toward the noise and the good-cooking smells, but they were well ahead of him by then and soon disappeared, swallowed up in the busy, noisy merriment of a good old-fashioned, down-on-the-ranch, eat-till-your-belly-busts barbecue. Smoke rising from somewhere in back of the large, rambling house flavored the air with the tempting aromas of beef and chicken and pork crisping on the grill.

Stepping through a wide, trellised gate in the back fence, Zane estimated the happy crowd at somewhere around a hundred head or so, not counting kids and dogs, and noticed the large brick barbecue, with its concrete base and shingled roof, obviously a permanent fixture designed to feed a cast of thousands with no problem. The structure was surrounded by men drinking beer, swapping yarns and offering unsolicited advice on when to turn the meat over, so it wouldn't burn.

A stranger and an outsider, Zane nonetheless felt immediately at home in this bunch; he'd grown up mostly in the country, after all, and rural ways had always made more sense to him than cloverleaf freeways and folks who'd never met even a single one of their neighbors, no matter how long they'd lived at the same address.

Carmody, sporting a cobbler's apron over the usual jeans and cotton shirt and wielding a long-handled cooking fork, looked up, spotted him and waved him over with a grin. Boone, the sheriff, was there, too, in civilian clothes like before, at the Butter Biscuit Café, and Zane recognized Slade Barlow, as well.

Somebody handed him a beer, still slippery from the ice-filled cooler nearby, and Hutch made casual introductions, at the same time keeping an eye on all that beef, chicken and pork. There were hot dogs and hamburgers, too, and a nearby table fairly groaned under the load of homemade potato salad and pies and all kinds of other such delicacies, along with the usual buns, pickles and condiments.

Folks laughed and yammered all around, the women clustered at picnic tables under shade trees, the kids and dogs weaving in and out, chasing one another, dogs barking and kids shrieking with glee.

Sipping his beer, Zane privately wished he'd brought Landry along, greenhorn clothes, sorry attitude and all, but he hadn't been able to raise his brother, either by calling his cell or his room at the Somerset Inn. He'd done his sibling duty by trying, he figured, and he'd expected to be glad he hadn't made contact but, instead, he felt a lonely ache taking shape in the pit of his stomach.

Landry loved a good party and, whatever was gnawing at him, joining in the celebration might have cheered him up a little.

Overhead, thunder grumbled, but nobody seemed to care, or even notice. And why *should* they? Things like bad weather wouldn't spoil the day for these hardy folks, used to hard winters and sizzling summer heat and about a million other shifts of climate— they'd just laugh about a little rain, and maybe take refuge inside if the stuff started coming down hard.

To Zane, Whisper Creek's main ranch house looked spacious enough to accommodate this crowd and another one just like it, and he felt a mild pinch of something like envy at the thought. Would *his* place ever be bursting at the seams with friends and relations, like this one?

He finally looked up, when he felt a single drop

of rain land on his shoulder, and he saw the formerly blue sky filling with gunmetal-gray clouds, but like the other guests, he was soon drawn into the conversation around him, and forgot all about the weather.

Once, he caught a brief glimpse of Cleo, in that traffic-light-green outfit of hers, sipping punch and getting to know the group of smiling women who'd drawn her into their circle.

Another glance around the big yard proved that Nash, too, had found his niche—he was already playing horseshoes with a flock of older kids, a mixture of boys and girls.

Zane reckoned they'd been at the party, he and Cleo and Nash, for almost an hour when an influx of new arrivals showed up, laughing and calling out greetings to friends, bringing more kids and more dogs and more *food* right along with them. The women, wearing either cotton dresses or jeans and short-sleeve shirts, kissed cheeks and squeezed hands, genuinely glad to see one another, while the men gravitated toward either the barbecue grill or the open bar sheltered beneath the patio roof. The food was already being served, on a buffet-style, help-yourself basis, and Zane had worked his way to the front of the chow line, and was filling a paper plate, when everything inside him went suddenly still.

It was as if every clock in the universe stopped ticking for a nanosecond, every heart stopped beating, every sound went still.

He turned his head and immediately saw the reason: Brylee was there, along with Casey. A baby nestled in a fleecy slinglike arrangement draped across Casey's chest but, otherwise, they seemed to be traveling alone. Casey spotted Zane right away, beamed that searchlight smile of hers and came in his direction. Brylee, walking behind her, looked disconcerted and dragged her feet a bit as she followed in her sister-in-law's wake.

"I was *hoping* you'd be here," Casey said, when they were nearly toe-to-toe, poking Zane playfully in the chest with one finger to emphasize her point. "I didn't reckon you could hide out forever."

Zane chuckled, though he was jittery inside, and not just because of the oblique reference to the invitation he'd ducked the night before. He kept his attention focused on Casey, but he was keenly aware of Brylee standing at a small distance, clearly caught by surprise and uncomfortable, too.

"Hey," he said, and kissed the crown of Casey's head. Even though she'd raised herself on tiptoe, he had to bend a little. "How've you been since I saw you last, Mrs. Parrish?"

The woman literally glowed, as though she'd swallowed a whole swarm of live fireflies in a single gulp, and tipped back the baby's blanket to show a downy head resting against her chest. "If I were any better," she chimed in response, "I'd probably be breaking some law. This is Preston, by the way. He's getting too big to carry, but I haven't had the heart to break the news to him yet."

Zane smiled and admired the little guy, who slept contentedly on, despite the jostling and the noise.

When he risked another glance at Brylee, she was looking studiously away, toward the gaggles of women at the picnic tables.

"I'm happy for you," he told Casey, and he meant it. She was one of a kind, with a legendary talent and a voice that caressed her listeners from the front row to the nosebleed seats whenever she performed. On top of that, she was a truly nice person. "Where's the rest of the family?"

"Well," Casey said, "Walker—that's my husband— is off chasing the rodeo, and the other kids, Shane and Clare, are with him. So Brylee and I are on our own for a while."

Zane nodded to Brylee, and she nodded back in a reserved way, and she still seemed poised to bolt for parts unknown as soon as a path opened through the crowd so she could get away.

"Step up here and be neighborly," Casey told her husband's hesitant sister, her tone good-natured enough, but not to be ignored, either. Casey might have been little, but she was used to running the show. "We can't have this man thinking folks in Parable County are standoffish."

Brylee looked miserable then, and a little annoyed, as well, even though she made an effort to smile. "No," she said, in a voice that was smooth on top and serrated like a steak knife underneath. "We can't have that."

"I'd better say howdy to Hutch and Kendra," Casey put in. Like a spirit, she vanished into the mob.

Brylee folded her arms and regarded Zane with a

chilly challenge lurking in her eyes. She wasn't going to make this easy, he could tell. He'd ticked her off, and she wanted him to know it.

Zane, rarely at a loss for words, especially with women, found himself struggling for something to say. "Hungry?" he finally asked, remembering the plate in his hands and lifting it slightly, as though for her inspection.

She shook her head. And she waited.

Zane, realizing that he was damming the flow past the buffet table, stepped out of line. And then he said something even more unimaginative. "Looks like it's going to rain."

Brylee's mouth twitched at one corner, ever so slightly, but the freeze was still on. "Looks like it," she agreed.

He gestured for her to precede him and, somewhat to his surprise, she did. She led the way to one of the few unoccupied places in the yard, a corner flower bed with a wide, knee-high brick wall edging it.

She sat.

Zane sat. He didn't remember being this nervous since he was in high school and made a move on a rodeo queen who happened to be two years older than he was, and that confounded him more than a little bit. What *was* it about this woman that turned him into a tongue-tied rube?

"I'm sorry about last night," he said, when nothing better came to mind, letting the plate rest on his lap, untouched. "I just—well, I thought maybe you'd need some space, after..."

After the kiss of the century.

Brylee's shoulders, left bare by her green sundress except for tiny straps holding the garment up, moved in a very slight, shruglike way, then fell back into graceful alignment again. "I guess you didn't expect to see me here," she surmised, and a mischievous twinkle sparked in her hazel eyes now.

Zane didn't know what to say to that, so he just sat there like, to use his mother's favorite cliché, a bump on a log.

"You're probably not the only one, considering what happened between Hutch and me, I mean," she went on, her tone almost breezy now. "Or, to put it more accurately, what *didn't* happen."

High above, thunder boomed again, loud but still distant, and a cloud briefly blocked the sun, spilling shadows over the amiable gathering for a few moments.

"You mean the…non-wedding?" Zane asked stupidly.

She nodded. "So you already knew about that," she said.

"Yeah," Zane admitted, picking up the plastic fork that had burrowed into the baked beans on his plate and immediately putting it down again. He'd been ravenously hungry fifteen minutes ago; now his throat was as dry as an empty creek bed in a drought, and he didn't figure he could manage so much as a bite of food.

"It *was* all over the internet," Brylee mused

lightly, smoothing the gossamer skirt of her sundress over slender thighs.

Where, Zane wondered, a little frantic, was this conversation headed? "Things happen," he said. Eloquence on the hoof, that was him.

"Yes," she agreed, with a philosophical sigh. She smiled a wisp of a smile that tugged at an especially tender place in Zane's heart and, taking in the milling guests, the brightly colored paper lanterns dangling from tree branches, the astounding spread on the buffet table with a sweep of her beautiful eyes, went on. "Things worked out for the best," she added softly, watching as an obviously pregnant Grace Kelly–blonde moved through the gathering, accentuated by a shaft of sunlight that seemed to shine only on her. "She's beautiful, isn't she?" Brylee asked, very softly. Then, with more spirit, she finished with, "Rats. I don't even know why I'm telling you all this. I apologize."

Zane followed the blonde's progress for a second or two, saw her draw up alongside Hutch, who was still officiating at the barbecue grill, and slip an arm around his waist. He grinned down at her with a love so plain it could have been seen from outer space, like the Great Wall of China and the lights of New York City, and gave her a gentle squeeze and a peck on the forehead.

This would be the woman Carmody had chosen over Brylee, back in the day, Zane reflected. "Yes" was all he said, in the end, because Brylee was right—the lady was a looker, though for his money, their hostess was no match for the vision sitting right beside him in a floaty green dress.

"I guess I'd better circulate a little," Brylee said, sounding resigned but not unhappy. "Otherwise, Casey will never let me hear the end of it. She *made* me come with her, but being here is probably better than sitting home alone."

The reference to her sister-in-law was made softly, with a note of wry humor to show she felt no resentment at being dragged along.

Brylee rose to her feet then, and Zane automatically stood, too, nearly spilling the contents of his plate into the grass because he'd forgotten, at least for a moment, practically everything but his own name. All along, on a subliminal level, he'd been reliving last night's mind-blowing kiss, outside the Boot Scoot Tavern. Now, the recollection slammed into him like a body blow.

He opened his mouth, ready to ask Brylee not to go, but she swept away in a flurry of soft green fabric, trailing a flowery but utterly unique scent—*her* scent—behind her. He didn't even get a chance to say goodbye before she vanished like thin smoke caught in a sudden breeze.

With a sigh of his own, Zane sat down on the brick wall again and silently listed all the reasons he ought to tackle the grub piled on his plate, starting with starving children in China, another of his late mom's old standbys, invariably trotted out when he and Landry were kids, prone to balk like mules when anything set before them at mealtime happened to be green. His improved understanding of good nutrition notwithstanding, even now he couldn't quite work out how a bunch of kids on the other side of the world would benefit if *he* ate his broccoli, or spinach, or string beans.

He took a few bites—in an effort at good manners—but it was a lost cause. All he could think about was Brylee Parrish, how it felt to kiss her, how much he wanted to do that again—and a lot more. Finally, he carried the meal to the nearest trash receptacle, tossed it and decided he ought to do a little more circulating himself.

After fifteen minutes or so, during which Zane caught intermittent glimpses of Brylee, smiling that killer smile of hers and chatting with people she'd obviously known all her life, he began to get restless. Well, *more* restless. Maybe it was the weather, which was turning more ominous by the minute, now that the wind had picked up, ruffling the hems of tablecloths and women's skirts, tossing the paper lanterns and sending empty paper cups and plastic glasses skittering across the yard.

He was trying to make heads or tails of an indepth discussion of local politics, spearheaded by two elderly ranchers, when Cleo edged up alongside him, holding down her flying hairstyle with one hand and grinning as broadly as if she'd just won first prize in a church raffle.

"When you get ready to leave," she told him, raising her voice a little to be heard over the wind and another crack of thunder, "don't you trouble yourself about me. I'm making friends right and left, and it's bingo night in Parable, so a bunch of us are going to try our luck. Mabel Evans goes right past your place on her way home, and she'll drop me off after."

"Okay," Zane said. Hadn't Cleo claimed to be a bust at bingo, somewhere along the line?

Cleo had barely trundled off to rejoin the gambling contingent when Nash materialized at his elbow. "There'll be fireworks after it gets good and dark," he announced. "Can we stay?"

Zane wasn't keen on the idea; nightfall was still several hours away, and he had a horse and a dog that would need to be fed eventually, and he was still thrown by the unexpected encounter with Brylee—not that he'd have missed it. "Well—"

"Those kids over there on the patio, by the soda cooler..." Nash interrupted, pausing to point out the adolescents in question. "A couple of them are from Three Trees, and Jack Carlson—he's the one in the Che Guevara T-shirt—said I could catch a ride home with them later, if you didn't feel like sticking around."

Zane frowned slightly. First Cleo had seemed to assume he was waiting for a chance to bail, and now Nash had apparently come to the same conclusion.

Was it that obvious?

"Who's driving?" he asked his kid brother.

"Jack's dad," Nash answered, in the tone of one deigning to react respectfully to a really lamebrain question. He scanned the yard again, found the man he was looking for. "That's him," he went on. "The guy by the wheelbarrow full of—whatever those yellow flowers are called."

Zane chuckled. "We'll see," he said, knowing his own desire to head for home was exceeded only by Nash's excitement over the upcoming fireworks display and a chance to spend more time with kids his own age. God knew when he'd enjoyed that simple pleasure—maybe never.

He crossed the yard, approached the man, put out a hand and introduced himself as Nash's brother. Andy Carlson replied with his name and a friendly grin and shook Zane's hand.

Carlson, it turned out, was a high school math teacher who spent his summers fighting forest fires and working part-time as a paramedic. He definitely seemed like a solid citizen, Zane reasoned. Probably wouldn't have been invited to this shindig in the first place if he hadn't been.

Andy said he'd be more than happy to bring Nash home after the fireworks. It was likely to be around midnight when they got there, though.

Zane nodded and thanked Jack's dad. Each man keyed the other's cell number into his phone, and then Zane turned to go in search of Nash, only to practically stumble over the kid, he'd been hovering so close behind him.

Grinning, Zane broke the good news, though he was sure the boy had overheard his conversation with Andy Carlson.

Nash gave a whoop of triumph, just the same, and rushed off to blend in with the other kids.

There was another game of horseshoes in the off-
ing. Horseshoes. Probably another new experience
for the self-proclaimed travelin' man.

Zane watched his little brother for a few moments,
then made the rounds, finding Kendra Carmody and
thanking her for the hospitality. She smiled warmly,
even prettier up close than she was at a distance,
prominent baby bump and all, and said the party
wouldn't be over for a long time yet. Dessert hadn't
even been served, and then there were the fireworks
to cap off the evening. Was he sure he wanted to leave
so quickly?

He *was* sure, he realized. The sky was angry,
the color of slate, threatening to bust the sky wide-
open and dump torrents of rain through the cracks,
but that wasn't what made Zane so jittery—no, that
had begun when his and Brylee's gazes connected,
right after she and Casey and the baby had arrived
at the party.

He looked around for Brylee once more, after saying goodbye to the lovely Mrs. Carmody, but she
was nowhere in sight. Casey, however, was nearby,
beaming with pride while a bevy of grandmotherly
types admired her baby boy.

Since Hutch had finally stopped playing chef,
filled a plate for himself and sat down at one of the
picnic tables to eat, surrounded by jocular friends
and neighbors as before, Zane decided not to interrupt the man's meal to say his farewells, and headed
for the spot where he'd surrendered his truck.

As soon as he was out in the open, the downpour

started in earnest—no preliminary sprinkle, no gentle mist—just a hard, sudden fall of rain, warm as bathwater and roaring like a forest fire.

The kids parking cars had on yellow slickers now. They'd taken refuge under a nearby tree, but one of them sprinted off after Zane's rig, evidently stashed somewhere down on the road.

He waited, idly wondering if the storm would let up before the fireworks were scheduled to start, heedless of the moisture plastering his shirt to his torso and his back, dripping off his hair and soaking his jeans through.

He'd have laughed at himself, and his all-fired hurry to get back to Hangman's Bend, if it hadn't been for the light tug at his right shirtsleeve.

He turned, and there, to his surprise, was Brylee, nearly transparent dress clinging to every perfect curve, hair hanging in wet clumps around her face, smile brighter than the flashes of lightning that split the sky every few moments.

"Casey wants to stay and show off the baby for a while," she said, over the pounding din. "After that, everybody will want her to sing, so—"

Mud splashed around them as drops the size of quarters pummeled the ground and formed puddles. The downpour went from loud to deafening.

Zane stared down into Brylee's wet, smiling face, confounded by everything he felt. He knew he ought to say something—anything—but he didn't have a damn clue what. Meanwhile, his truck sped through the ranch gate and fishtailed up the driveway toward them.

"Can I catch a ride with you?" Brylee asked, after waiting in vain for Zane to stop gawking at her and speak.

He nodded, a strange, wild joy coursing through him, and took her hand. They both ran through the rain, toward the waiting truck, and she scrambled inside, holding her white sandals in one hand.

Zane tipped the kid-valet, wrenched open his own door and climbed behind the wheel. Rain sheeted the windshield, all but swamping the wipers.

Brylee wriggled her muddy feet, grinned at him and, holding up one calf to show him a long run in her stockings, said, "I'm hell on a pair of panty hose."

He laughed then, a deep letting-go that cleared his muddled brain and soothed his soul, and she laughed with him.

SHE'D KNOWN IT was going to happen; Brylee could admit that now, to herself at least. What she wasn't so sure about was why—why she'd made the rash decision that it was time to stop living in limbo and *find out,* once and for all, what—if anything—was actually going on between her and Zane. All she knew for certain was that she was bone-tired of hovering on the sidelines, waiting for her turn at—whatever. *Life,* maybe.

The *when* wasn't all that clear, either—she'd agreed to attend the barbecue only because Casey wheedled her into it, and anyway, Zane Sutton had been the *last* person she'd expected to run into at Hutch and Kendra's barbecue, if only because he was new in the area. Duh. She hadn't expected to see him at the Boot Scoot the other night, either, but she'd been thunderstruck at the sight of him, back there in the Carmodys' yard, with friendly chatter and the delicious scent of food being cooked in the open air all around, and a certain sweet sorrow had overtaken her, too.

There were so many couples—newlyweds and long-time marrieds and every sort of pair in between. Even Casey, temporarily on her own, was secure in the knowledge that Walker, on the road at the moment, would be home soon, and once again enfold her in his love, as well as his arms.

Zane seemed to be concentrating on the road, the windshield wipers barely adequate against the driving summer rain as they drove toward Three Trees, lightning splintering the world around them at regular intervals, thunder crashing in the big sky far above. He'd turned the heater on as they left Whisper Creek, but the warmth had promptly fogged up the windows, so he'd switched it off again, in favor of the defroster.

They didn't talk much as they passed through Parable and then covered the thirty-odd miles between there and Three Trees, but there didn't seem to be a need for words, anyhow.

The air inside that truck was so charged with electricity that Brylee figured she'd get a shock if she touched anything.

Zane didn't ask her what was going on in her mind, though he must surely have wondered, nor did he inquire whether or not Casey knew she'd left early.

It was slow-going, because of slick roads and low visibility, but they reached Three Trees soon enough; it was a blur of neon and asphalt and Main Street businesses as they passed through.

Zane drove on, without saying a word except to ask if she was cold—she wasn't—and turned in at the Timber Creek gate without any prompting from his passenger.

"Around back," she directed, when he would have turned onto the concrete skirting in front of Casey and Walker's garage.

Rounding the big house, he spotted Brylee's SUV, pulled up beside it, looked over at her with an uncertainty she suspected was foreign to him and waited for a cue. Walk her to the door? Wait in the truck until she was safely inside before driving away?

"Come in," Brylee heard herself say. "You're soaked. You can grab a shower, and I'll get you some of Walker's clothes to wear. You're probably not the same size, but close enough."

Zane opened his mouth. Closed it again.

Brylee suppressed an urge to giggle hysterically, at Zane's bewilderment, at her own impetuous actions, at the rain and her wet hair dangling around her face in soggy ropes and the globs of mud coating her feet. *Gumbo,* that was what Montanans called the incomprehensibly sticky slop, and the name suited it perfectly.

She pushed the passenger's-side door open and climbed down, holding her sandals in one hand and draping her purse strap over the opposite shoulder, and then dashed for the door that led into her apartment, Zane beside her.

Snidely met them in the kitchen, curious and probably relieved not to be alone anymore. Snidely, though Rin-Tin-Tin fierce in some ways, quailed whenever a loud storm broke. Thunder could send him scrabbling under her bed for shelter, and lightning made him whimper so pitifully that it broke her heart.

Brylee paused long enough to reassure the dog, then headed through the apartment and crossed into Casey and Walker's territory, leaving a trail of muddy footprints that would just have to be dealt with later. She greeted their dogs, three chocolate Labs and a sweet mutt called Doolittle, and went straight on to the laundry room.

Sure enough, there was a basket full of clean clothes on the folding table across from the washer and dryer, and Brylee flipped through the various garments until she found a pair of Walker's work jeans, a lightweight sweatshirt and a pair of socks.

She drew the line at borrowing underwear, and figured Zane would be on the same page where that was concerned, so he'd just have to make do without. Delicious thought.

The family dogs—there were a couple of cats around somewhere, too, but they'd made themselves scarce—trooped after her when she returned to her own apartment, still on a mission, and though she couldn't have said precisely what that mission was, she had her suspicions.

Zane waited in the kitchen, carrying on a one-sided conversation with Snidely, who lost interest as he greeted the other dogs with sniffs and some tail-wagging.

"Here," Brylee said, handing Zane the clothes she'd just purloined from Casey's laundry room. "Put these on before you catch your death of...something. The shower is that way." She pointed.

He grinned then, and she saw a fire kindle in his eyes, warming her through and through, which was unsettling, considering she hadn't been cold in the first place.

Zane didn't head for the shower right away, though. Instead, he took Brylee's hand. A white-hot charge jolted through her, and he asked the question without saying a single word.

She bit her lower lip and nodded yes.

Which was how the two of them wound up in her bathroom, kissing desperately and repeatedly, all the while peeling off each other's clothes.

CHAPTER FIFTEEN

"It's too soon for this," Zane gasped, as they stood under the steady spray of Brylee's shower, clinging together, bare-ass naked and reveling in it. Kissing again and again, finding it impossible to stop, except to draw in brief, ragged breaths.

"I know," Brylee agreed, and she slid her arms around his neck, loving the hard smoothness of his skin, the magnificent contour of his chest and shoulders, the lean power of his hips and thighs.

"And I don't have a—" Zane managed, between yet another kiss and the one that would inevitably follow.

Brylee, figuring there would be plenty of time for regrets later, had planted herself squarely in the present moment; she felt fully alive and one thousand percent female. Her left brain was on hiatus, leaving her imagination and her body at the controls. "Condom?" she finished for him, when their mouths broke apart again.

Zane nodded. Water poured down over his head, beading in his eyelashes, flowing in rivulets between well-defined chest and arm muscles. "And our first time together *isn't* going to be in the shower."

So there *would* be a first time, then. And that implied that there would be *other* times, didn't it? Glory be.

Brylee had been intimate with very few men, and not one of them had offered her an out, the way Zane just had. Nope, it had been full-throttle, zero-to-sixty in seconds, a two-body free-for-all.

"What's wrong with making love in the shower?" she teased, wanting to prolong the moment, to prolong *everything,* running the tip of one finger lightly along the line of Zane's breastbone. The hair on his chest was golden, lighter than his hair, and surprisingly fine, almost silky.

He groaned and drew her against him, his fingers interlaced behind her bottom, even as he continued to argue. "Nothing," he said, in a rasp, "it's just that—"

Brylee laughed, exultant, fully herself in a way she'd never dared to be before, ever, at any point, in any situation of any kind, in the whole of her life. "Fine," she said. "We'll use the bed."

She turned off the shower spigot then and slipped past Zane, making sure to brush against him so that all relevant points of contact touched, generated sparks in the process. She grabbed a towel for herself and then tossed a second one to him.

He caught it with slightly unsteady hands and began to dry himself off while Brylee wrapped her towel around her upper body, toga-style, tucking it beneath her armpits. The bottom of the swath of terry cloth barely reached the tops of her thighs.

Even then, Zane wasn't through making his case,

which seemed to be promoting celibacy. "There's still the problem of—"

Brylee rolled her eyes, laughed again. "I happen to have a few on hand," she said, opening a cabinet where she stored various articles one might expect to find in any ordinary bathroom. She ferreted through tubes of various sorts of pastes and creams and ointments, over-the-counter cold remedies, most of which were probably past their expiration dates, though this certainly wasn't the time to find out, the usual hair-care products and a carton of tampons. In the way back, she found it, a small box tucked away behind all the other stuff. She handed it to him.

Zane eyed the supply of condoms with an expression of mingled relief and concern. Whatever misgivings his mind might be entertaining, his *body* said, *Go for it.*

Brylee hoped he wouldn't raise any awkward questions, especially the kind beginning with words like *who* and *when.*

"Don't ask," Brylee advised pertly, turning to head for her bedroom.

Zane could follow or not—his choice.

They'd reached a crossroads, she supposed. Go or stay, put up or shut up.

He chose to follow.

Zane wore his towel wrapped around his waist now, and he set the condoms on the nightstand and then reached for Brylee, pulling her close again, a low growl-like sound rising from his diaphragm.

Passion surged through her, along with a strange

and crazy joy, and a whole tangle of other emotions, all of them jubilant and fiery and—okay—*brazen*.

"Fresh out of excuses?" she asked, with a little smile. Lordy, he was a wonder, a cowboy with the body of a classic Greek statue, come to life.

Zane chuckled. "Fresh out," he conceded.

And then he kissed her, not feverishly like before, but deeply, thoroughly, with just the right combination of gentleness and strength. She loved that his muscles were chiseled and lean, rather than bulky, but that observation soon vanished, along with every other coherent thought in her head.

If the kiss outside the Boot Scoot had been jarringly, fiercely, damnably good, this one raised the bar, well into the realm of the transformative, the impossibly perfect, the predestined. It was a bold claiming, it was reverent homage; it was as all-consuming as a wildfire racing out of control, gobbling up everything in its path.

Brylee knew it for sure then, that there would be no second-guessing this time around, no retreat. She'd fled from the last kiss, dashed home from Parable in a tizzy of confused desire, berating herself the whole way. Now, no power on earth could have made her turn tail and run.

She *wanted* this dangerous thing, wanted Zane Sutton, the way a drowning person fights for air, and consequences be damned. She was a grown-up, not a child, and she was tired of shunting aside perfectly normal human needs, tired of denying herself the pleasures her body and even her soul were wired to crave. Tired of pretending that what she had—money, independence, a well-earned confidence in her own abilities—was enough.

Because it wasn't. Not for her.

The kissing went on for a long time, slower now, generating sensations so profound, so poignant, that tears of amazement stung Brylee's eyes at intervals, fell like rain into the broken canyons and dry meadows of her heart, each one a seed of wholeness and healing, certain to take root and then thrive.

They soon wound up on the bed—she didn't recall the mechanics—and she grasped at Zane as he laid her down, poised himself above her, nibbling at an earlobe, stroking her from breast to thigh, again and again, ever so slowly and ever so gently, until she thought she might implode with the need to be joined with him, have him inside her, make him part of her.

But the man refused to let her set a faster pace; every move he made was separate and distinct from any other, a miniature eternity in its own right. He savored one of her breasts, then the other, at his leisure, and he made no secret of the fact that he was enjoying her far too much to be rushed.

His attention to each luscious detail of loving her made her feel beautiful, desirable, even cherished. It also made her that much more desperate.

Brylee whimpered and tossed her head from side to side on the pillow as the pleasure built inside her, rising to impossible heights, surpassing even those, and then subsiding, like an ebbing tide. Just far enough, though, to drive her even *closer* to the brink of dissolving in a huge burst of fire and light.

"Soon," she choked out, at long last, "Zane, please, *soon*—"

But Zane only chuckled and made his meandering way down the hills and hollows of her body, already quivering as every nerve came alive under his mouth, his hands, his tongue.

And then he was at her very core, the apex of her femininity, easing her legs apart, preparing her.

Only an instant after she realized what he was about to do, and gave a long, guttural and completely involuntary groan of surrender and false protest, she was in his mouth.

He nibbled, he teased, he feasted. The feeling was exquisite, unrelenting.

A ball of fire rolled up from Brylee's very center, split itself into separate blazes to shoot down her legs and along her arms, wringing a low, lusty shout from her that came from somewhere deep, deep within her. Her toes *and* her fingers curled with the effort to hold on, to keep from hurtling skyward in ecstasy.

The release, when Zane finally allowed her to have it, shattered Brylee into sweet, tremulous fragments, each one aflame and trailing sparks. For a few moments, she couldn't see or hear or think— only feel.

It was glorious.

Afterward, he took his time kissing his way back up to her mouth, pausing to tease her navel, to taste the hard peak of each breast, to arouse her all over again, so that she gave a soblike croon of hungry welcome when, at last, his lips found hers again.

"You have to be sure about this, Brylee," Zane said, very quietly. "We can still stop, if you say the word, but if this goes much further—"

She opened her eyes, her hands still trailing up and down his back, dreamily now, instead of the frantic haste of before, each finger tracing a path from Zane's strong shoulders to his firm buttocks, following the same course, over and over. Instinctively, she entwined her fingers in his still-damp hair, as she'd done while he was pleasuring her moments before, and she murmured, "No more talk, cowboy. Just make love to me—right *now*."

Zane grinned, reaching for the box on the nightstand, taking out a packet and tearing it open, and finally putting on the condom, his every motion smooth, practiced, unhurried.

No doubt about it. This wasn't *his* first rodeo.

He studied her face once more, his eyes solemn and searching, alert to any sign of reluctance on her part, and then he eased himself inside her, just far enough to give her one last shimmering mirage of a chance to say no.

And to make her want him even more.

When Brylee bit her lower lip and arched her back instead of putting an end to their lovemaking, wordlessly offering herself, he took her in a single, deep-driving stroke, filling her with his hardness and power and heat in ways that were more than physical, pausing in her depths, letting her body seize around him in spasms so delicious she wasn't sure she could bear them.

Slowly, Zane began to move on top of Brylee, *inside* Brylee, conquering her and yet surrendering to her, and she matched his rhythm with her own, thinking she might die of the wanting and the need if he didn't bring her to an almost immediate climax and, at one and the same time, praying these sensations would never, ever end.

She'd enjoyed sex, whenever she'd felt close enough to a man to make herself vulnerable, which hadn't been that often, but this—*this*—was so much more than she'd even guessed was possible.

Their pace increased slowly, their bodies grew slick, and both of them moaned as the friction intensified, Zane's cries torn from him, low and ragged and hoarse, Brylee's responses eager and greedy for more of him, all of him, body *and* soul.

When their restraint finally snapped, it happened simultaneously, causing them to flex in unison, straining wildly, taking and giving and, most of all, *sharing*.

Brylee soared, breathless and dazed, long after Zane had recovered his control, and he murmured gently, senselessly, in her ear, while she came apart in his arms.

Nonetheless, his meaning was as clear as if he'd spoken every word in plain English: *It's okay, let it happen, let go—you're so beautiful—I knew it would be like this. I knew.*

By the time Brylee crashed back into her everyday

self, with the virtual impact of a skydiver sans parachute striking hard ground from a very great height, Zane had already begun to kindle new desires in her.

He succeeded admirably.

And the lovemaking, this lovely communion of two bodies, went on—and on. Brylee couldn't have said for how long, but she was pretty sure the condom supply was destined to give out soon.

Time shifted; the past and the future blended seamlessly into one magical *now.* The rain stopped hammering at the roof. The light changed.

An hour might have passed, or a day, or a decade—Brylee had no way of knowing, didn't care. She'd been lost in Zane Sutton's touch, his words, his kisses, for what seemed like always.

"I have to go," he said presently, his head resting beside hers on the pillow, his breath warm in her hair and soft against her ear, one leg sprawled over both of hers, a welcome, steely weight against her skin.

Brylee didn't object to Zane's leaving; she had too much self-respect for that. Nor did she ask when she'd see him again, or if he'd call soon, or what he was feeling—physical satisfaction, certainly, but was there some regret, too?

She didn't dare explore *his* feelings, since her own were confounding enough. She was happy and, somehow, sad, too. She was at once mended and broken, restored and ruined. She was completely, deliciously sated, but she knew Zane could stir her, make her need him again, turn her right back into the she-wolf she'd been only minutes before, clawing at his back, pleading with him for more and then still more, making plaintive, howl-like sounds when another release overtook her.

If he'd chosen to do that, anyway. Which he didn't.

She couldn't say anything at all. Doubted, in fact, that she would have the strength even to whisper his name, let alone make any speeches.

Zane kissed her once more, briefly and gently, and then he was sitting up, getting out of bed, finding the clothes she'd lent him after they came in out of the rain, putting them on. He paused in the bedroom doorway, a figure framed in faint light, coming from where Brylee didn't exactly know, and she heard him sigh, a heavy sound that settled over her chest like a chilly blanket and made it hard to breathe.

"Brylee," he said. That was all.

It wasn't a question or a statement, it wasn't a reprimand, and it wasn't a promise, either. He said it again, in a husky voice, and then he turned away, and the doorway was dark and empty with his absence.

Brylee pulled the rumpled covers up over her head and snuggled down into the soft, tangled, still-moist sheets. She waited to feel something—rage or grief, joy or sorrow, but there was only the sweet aftermath of being loved the way she'd yearned to be loved, and blessed exhaustion overtook her in the next moment

She slept.

ZANE RECKONED HE must have driven home to Hangman's Bend by rote, because he had no conscious recollection of actually making the journey, not then and not years and years later, whenever that particular night, the one that changed everything, came to mind.

He hadn't noticed whether it was raining or not, recognized a single landmark or even sustained one clear, cohesive train of thought. No, for him, what had happened with Brylee was all about feelings, emotions, concepts—not words. The flesh-and-blood woman he'd just left was all he knew or wanted to know. The awareness of her, her image, her voice and her scent, the silken smoothness of her skin against his own—all of those things pulsed inside him, like a new heart, strong and steady but definitely prone to breakage.

Reaching his place, though, Zane began to come home to himself, as well, noted that all the lights in the house were off, except for one burning in the window above the kitchen sink. Cleo and Nash were home—or they weren't.

Did it matter? Probably, he decided distractedly, but right then he couldn't seem to drum up even a ghost of a preference, one way or the other. He shut off the truck, got out and walked into the darkened barn to check on Blackjack, as he did every night, and the gelding greeted him with a sleepy and faintly quizzical nicker.

Zane grinned, relieved the universe as he knew it seemed to be reassembling itself around him, bit by bit, falling back into place like the scattered pieces of some cosmic puzzle, and left the animal to settle back into horse-slumber and whatever equine dreams might await him there. Slim was at the kitchen door, as usual, when Zane turned the knob and stepped inside.

"Yo, dog," he said gruffly, bending to pat the mutt's head.

Slim squirmed past him and headed for the yard, intent on night business, and Zane waited until he came back a few minutes later before closing the door again.

"You here all alone?" he asked Slim, who wagged his scruffy tail in good-natured reply.

"No," said a familiar and definitely human voice from the arched doorway opening onto the shadowy dining room beyond. "He's not."

With that, Landry flipped a nearby light switch, and the sudden illumination from the new fixtures, with their tubelike, megabright fluorescent bulbs, made Zane blink.

"Well," he said, after letting a beat or two go by, making his way to the new refrigerator and extracting a bottle of water. "I'm glad you made yourself at home, anyway."

Landry, barefoot, clad only in a pair of gray sweatpants and his usual surly outlook, ran a hand through his hair and proceeded into the kitchen, offering no reply. Instead, he stepped around Slim, opened the pantry door and rummaged around inside for a while, eventually emerging with a box of cereal.

"You already wear out your welcome at the Somerset Inn or what?" Zane asked, after a long swig from the water bottle. At the moment, he would have preferred whiskey, but there wasn't any on hand and, just now, that was probably a good thing.

"Something like that," Landry said, helping himself to a bowl, a spoon and a jug of milk from the fridge. "I won't be around here for long—at least, not under *your* roof—so don't get your skivvies in a twist, okay?"

Skivvies? Zane had to chuckle at this verbal vestige of days gone by. "If you're hungry," he said, with affable irony, taking a seat at the card table and settling as best he could into one of the metal folding chairs, "just dig right in."

Landry gave a grumpy snort, probably meant to pass for a laugh. A derisive one, of course. He took the chair across from Zane's, poured cereal into the bowl, sloshed a few dollops of milk over it and began to crunch away.

"Are Cleo and Nash around?" Zane asked presently. It seemed like a nonincendiary question. Those were in relatively short supply, right now.

"I assumed they were with you," Landry responded, with a shake of his head, talking with his mouth full. "Wherever *that* might have been."

Zane suppressed a sigh. "Where were you today, Landry?" he asked evenly. "I tried to call you a couple of times."

"I was buying a truck," Landry said, as though this interesting fact should have been out-and-out obvious to anybody with enough brains to walk and chew gum at the same time. "Guess you didn't notice it, parked out there by the barn."

"Guess I didn't," Zane answered, emptying the water bottle and setting it down in front of him with a slight clunk.

"I bought a buffalo, too," Landry went on, looking up from his cereal now, still not smiling, though there was a faint gleam of—of what, mischief?—in his eyes.

"You bought a *what?*"

Landry looked mighty pleased with himself while he chewed industriously on his late-night snack. "A buffalo," he repeated, eventually. "I'm starting a herd."

"Hold it," Zane said. "One buffalo doesn't make a herd—and what the hell do you know about them, anyhow?"

Landry raised one bare shoulder in a desultory half shrug, spooned up the last of his cereal, then unceremoniously raised the bowl to his mouth and downed the remaining milk in three noisy gulps.

"This," he said, raising his voice slightly, the way some people did when they addressed the hard-of-hearing, or foreigners who might or might not speak the language, "is a *pregnant* buffalo. The foundation of a dynasty. Once I'm a little better situated, I plan to send for a bull, too. That'll get things rolling."

"This is cattle country," Zane pointed out, though the remark was a lame one and he knew it. He hadn't been surprised that Landry had purchased a truck—

that was a statement that had more to do with machismo than reliable transportation—but a *buffalo?* He was a suit-and-tie man from a big city—had he ever even *seen* one of those critters, except on *Animal Planet* or maybe at the zoo?

Landry put down the empty bowl, licked away his milk-mustache with one swipe of his tongue and grinned like the certifiable fool he was. "Did you know that bison meat is leaner than beef?" he countered, letting Zane's words hang in the air, unacknowledged. "Get with the program, big brother. Today's consumer is more health conscious than ever before. The market is just beginning to take off."

Zane closed his eyes for a moment, opened them again. He guessed that must be because obesity was at an all-time high all over the developed world and rising steadily, but he wasn't out to start an argument, so he kept the factoid to himself. "And you'll be rich in no time."

Landry looked cocky. "I'm *already* rich," he retorted, "but that's beside the point."

Zane held on to his perspective, such as it was. "And you found this pregnant buffalo, where? It's not as if they're readily available, even out here in the golden West, like sheep and cattle and goats."

"I ran an internet search, of course," Landry answered expansively. He stood, carried his bowl to the sink. Cleo wasn't even around to see the gesture, Zane thought grudgingly, and his little brother was already trying to score points with her. Landry glanced back over one shoulder, grinned at Zane, and for the first time since he'd arrived in Montana, there was no chill in the expression. "Bessie's on her way out here from North Dakota by train right now, bun in the oven, a classic two-for-one deal."

Zane wanted to roll his eyes, but he didn't. The peace between him and Landry was still too fragile and, damn it, he did love the maniac, and that was a fact, inexorable as death and taxes. "It's a little late in the year for a calf, don't you think?" he ventured carefully.

"There's a timetable?" Landry countered airily, returning to the table.

Outside, a vehicle pulled up, quickly followed by a second rig, both with their high beams on. The lights blazed across the kitchen wall like twin comets, causing Zane to squint against the dazzle. Doors closed, goodbyes were exchanged and both cars drove away again.

"Never mind," Zane told his brother wearily. Hell, he was no expert on livestock, he reminded himself. For all he knew, bison mamas gave birth year-round, like the human variety.

A moment later, Nash burst into the house, just ahead of Cleo, and the kid seemed only slightly taken aback when he saw Landry.

He immediately shifted his focus to Zane. "You should have stayed for the fireworks," the boy crowed, laughing and mussing up Slim's ears as the dog jumped on him in delighted welcome, practically knocking him to the floor. "It was *awesome!*"

Of course, Zane wasn't inclined to mention that he'd experienced a few fireworks himself earlier that night, in Brylee Parrish's bed; the experience was obviously too personal, and too private, to discuss with anybody but Brylee herself. In addition, he still needed to sort through a lot of raw emotions, most of them entirely new to him, try to make some kind of sense of what had happened, figure out where he and Brylee ought to go from there.

If, indeed, they went anywhere at all. Their love-making had changed him in profound ways, maybe forever, ways that confused and troubled him even as they filled him with a strange rush of exultation every time he allowed himself to remember, but that didn't mean Brylee felt the same way. By now, she might be wallowing in regret, furious not only with herself, but with him, too. Considering the way she'd behaved after they'd merely *kissed* outside the Boot Scoot, it wasn't a huge stretch to imagine her mad enough to spit nails.

"Hello, again," Landry said, evidently address-ing Nash.

Cleo finally stepped inside, closed the door, set aside her big purse and hung up her baggy gray car-digan sweater with the patches on the elbows. She glanced curiously at Zane, as though his eyes had spontaneously changed color or he'd sprouted an extra limb since she'd seen him last, but she must have picked up on the general mood, which was dicey, because she bit back whatever she'd been fix-ing to say.

"Did my dad come back?" Nash asked Landry, straight out. "Have you seen him? Heard anything from him?" The tone of the kid's voice and the sudden, rigid stillness of his skinny frame gave no indication whether he was hoping for a yes, or for a no.

Landry frowned, standing in deference to Cleo's presence and giving her a brief nod for a greeting, but Nash definitely had his full attention.

"One email," Landry said. "He needed money."

Nash's Adam's apple bounced along the length of his neck a few times, and he swallowed audibly. "Did you give it to him?" he asked, so softly that hearing him was a challenge, even in that weighted silence filling the room. "The money, I mean?"

Landry sighed. "Yeah," he said. "He's a hard man to refuse."

"Did he say anything about me?" Nash persisted, after digesting Landry's answer for a few seconds. The kid looked so wan by then that Cleo trundled over and touched his forehead with the back of one hand, checking for fever.

"No," Landry replied, with just enough hesitation to indicate that he wished he'd slipped a lie in ahead of the blunt truth. "No, he didn't mention you. But I'm sure that was just an oversight…."

Nash's face contorted in a way that was painful to see, for Zane at least. The boy didn't say anything, though. He just pushed his way past the two older brothers he barely knew and hurried in the direction of his room. A slam sounded in the distance, and Slim, who had traipsed after Nash, came back alone, his ears drooping, rebuffed.

Zane started to follow Nash's trail, but Cleo stopped him in his boot prints with a firm, "Let the boy go. He'll be fine, but he needs to be by himself right now."

Landry sighed and shoved a hand through his already-rumpled hair. Maybe he'd been asleep when Zane got back from Brylee's place, but haggard as he looked, it seemed more likely that he'd been *trying* to sleep. And failing miserably.

There was more on his brother's mind, Zane thought vaguely, than a big future in the bison-wrangling business, but he flat-out didn't have the energy to pursue the matter right then. Between Nash and the interlude with Brylee, his circuits were already on overload.

Cleo got busy setting up the coffeemaker for morning, putting away the jug of milk Landry had left on the last counter standing, and Zane bent to console the confused dog with a few words and a quick backrub.

"What was *that* all about?" Landry asked, jabbing a thumb in the direction Nash had gone.

"Three guesses," Zane answered crisply. "And the first two don't count."

"Dad?" Landry inquired blankly.

"Bingo," Cleo affirmed, sounding sad and very, very tired.

With that, everybody went their separate ways,

Cleo to her room, Zane to his, Landry to whatever corner of the house he'd chosen to crash in. They were still short one bed, so he must have bought himself a sleeping bag in town or something.

Maybe, Zane reasoned, his brother had even outfitted himself with a tent and a portable stove and plenty of other outdoor gear. Until a little while ago, he'd hoped Landry's plans included heading back to Chicago, sooner rather than later, but now it seemed that Little Brother might just be stupid enough, *stubborn* enough, to set up a camp over there on his part of the ranch and dig in, bent on cornering the bison market before winter.

Still shaking his head when he reached his room, Zane took his phone from his shirt pocket and checked the time. It was eleven forty-five—too late to call Brylee.

But he did it, anyway, because he'd *slept* with the woman, after all, and some kind of acknowledgment was definitely in order.

BRYLEE HEARD A PERSISTENT, jangly sound, tried hard to ignore it and realized she couldn't. What if someone was hurt or ill? What if Casey and the baby were stranded somewhere along the road between Parable and Three Trees?

She sat up in bed, switched on the lamp and picked up her cell phone, yawned out an inelegant, "Hello?"

"You're awake, then." The voice was Zane's.

And the sound of it jolted Brylee into full sensibility, in the span of a mere moment, something even the late-night ringing of her phone hadn't done.

"I am," she confirmed, quite unnecessarily.

Zane cleared his throat. "Tonight was—" He fell silent, and she could feel him searching for just the right words to let her down easy.

Brylee squeezed her eyes shut, waited. The man certainly hadn't wasted any time clarifying the situation, had he?

Zane began again. "Tonight was incredible, Brylee. *You* were incredible."

Tears brimmed along her lower lashes, sudden and hot. Her heart pounded so hard she could feel it on the outside of her body, and in unusual places, too, like her knees and elbows and the balls of her feet. An odd, semihysterical giggle escaped her, wouldn't be held in.

"Who is this?" she quipped, dabbing at her cheeks with the back of one hand.

Zane laughed, a quiet, thoroughly masculine sound.

Brylee pushed a lock of hair back from her forehead.

On the rug beside her bed, Snidely chased rabbits in his sleep, all four legs moving.

The silence lengthened, but it wasn't unpleasant. In fact, it was faintly electrical.

Finally, Brylee asked, "How do you define *incredible?*"

He chuckled, and that was as nice to hear as his laugh had been. "In this case," he replied gruffly,

"I'd define it as incomparable, as better than any other night of my life."

Brylee's throat thickened, and her eyes scalded with fresh tears. "You said it yourself," she said gently, cautiously. "It's too soon, Zane. We have to put on the brakes, before it's too late."

CHAPTER SIXTEEN

BRYLEE'S PRONOUNCEMENT THAT it was time to step back from each other for a while, catch their breath and get some perspective made perfect sense to Zane. After all, they'd actually been acquainted for about five minutes, a fact he'd tried to remind her—and himself—of the night before.

Before the lovemaking. The epic, apocalyptically good lovemaking that had rocked Zane to the foundations of his being, altered his worldview—hell, his view of this and any other universe that might be out there—had turned him, essentially, from one man into another.

Was this a bad thing? That seemed unlikely, if only because the whole Brylee experience had an almost sacred feel to it, but it might be a long time before the dust settled enough for either one of them to see clearly.

He sighed. There were his own words again, back to bite him in the ass. *It's too soon.*

On the other hand, how the *hell* was he supposed to do without the woman, give up everything he'd been searching for all his life? It would be easier to swear off oxygen and water.

Now that his entire psyche had just been flame-gunned and then rebuilt so completely that he'd have to get to know himself all over again, and staying away from Brylee Parrish was probably the only remedy for what ailed him.

Once the phone call was over, he'd stood there in his dark room for a long time, staring out at a shadowy, moon-washed landscape, wondering how he was going to survive this.

He didn't even attempt to sleep—it would have been futile, draining rather than restoring him—and by morning, he was like a wild man, pacing, anxious, unable to focus on anything but the shattering prospect of losing something he'd never really had in the first place.

It was crazy. *He* was crazy.

When Cleo entered the kitchen, soon after daybreak, wearing a pair of fluffy slippers and a bright purple chenille bathrobe with a few full tours of duty behind it already, given the signs of wear, she stopped at the sight of Zane, drew in an audible breath and rounded her big eyes so the whites seemed much more prominent than usual.

"What's happened?" she asked, small-voiced and clearly expecting to be told that someone near and dear had died, or at least received a sobering diagnosis.

Zane sighed and his shoulders drooped without conscious instructions from his brain; he'd never meant to worry the poor woman. He hadn't even expected to encounter her at this ungodly hour, for that matter.

"There's no tragedy unfolding," he said hoarsely. *Not for anybody but me, anyway.* "This is something personal."

Cleo, visibly relieved, steamrolled over to the coffeemaker, took a mug from the lineup on the counter beside it and poured herself a stiff dose of caffeine—the dregs of the last batch, since Zane had been swilling the stuff for hours.

While her cup steamed on the counter, she hastily built another pot of coffee, and when she turned toward him again, she looked like her normal, exasperated-with-it-all self.

"You look *awful,*" she told him, before taking a sip from her mug, making a horrified face and sluicing the contents into the sink. Since the new batch was just beginning to brew, she padded over to the card table and sank into one of the chairs to wait for it, simultaneously directing Zane to take the other one.

Still only two chairs, Zane thought, tracking no better than he had at any point since the telephone conversation with Brylee. If he didn't invest in some new furniture, and soon, they'd have to start eating meals in rotating shifts.

To say he sat down would have been an embellishment; it was more like his knees gave out and the chair seat happened to be situated in just the right place to break his fall.

Cleo regarded him in shrewd silence for some time, then stealth-bombed him with, "Is this about Brylee Parrish?"

Zane's mouth dropped open, and he'd have sworn he heard the hinges creak when he closed it again. He'd groused to her about Landry, and his dad, and even his agent, but said very little about Brylee's effect on him.

Cleo gave a rich, throaty laugh, a throwback to her torch-singer days, most likely, and shook her head. "You thought it was some big secret?" she asked. Then she waved a hand in amused dismissal. "Well, come on up to speed, Mr. Boss Man, because the whole *county* knows you fell for Brylee the first time you saw her. We ladies of a certain age discussed it at the barbecue and between every number called at bingo."

Zane didn't try to deny anything—obviously, that would have been pointless. Anyhow, he was too busy scrambling to get even a slippery grip on how such an event as falling in love could have been so evident to everybody but him.

And maybe to Brylee.

He began to feel just a little bit better, but it must not have shown on the outside.

Cleo assessed him with a sweep of her eyes. He saw fondness in her gaze, along with sympathy and no small amount of wisdom. "Well, now," she said, "I reckon most people would see something like this as a *good* thing. So why do you look as though your very best hopes and dreams are about to be repossessed, hooked up to a tow truck and hauled away, like some ole car you can't meet the payments on?"

The image she'd painted, colorful as her clothes and down-to-earth as her converted-cooler suitcase, forced a chuckle out of Zane, but it sounded like sandpaper gnawing at rusted iron. "I look that bad?" he countered, stalling.

"Worse," Cleo said. She folded her bathrobed arms in front of her and leaned on them, bent slightly forward, like a senator trying to look stern during a complicated but boring investigation into some questionable industry.

Except, of course, that Cleo really cared what he'd say next. "You gonna sidestep this all day," she challenged, "or tell me what's going on? I might be able to help, you know."

Zane sighed. Spread his hands briefly, maybe in a gesture of baffled helplessness, maybe just to buy another few seconds. "Brylee's scared," he finally replied, keeping his voice low because this was definitely not a subject he wanted to let Landry and/or Nash in on. "She didn't say as much, but I'm thinking she's getting ready to run, get as far away from Parable County—and me—as possible."

"Well," Cleo said, drawing out the word as she mused for a while, "that wouldn't be any kind of solution, of course—running away, I mean—but I can understand her concern. She's been through the ro-

mantic wringer, that girl, and it's natural that she'd
be a mite on the skittish side."

"I agree," Zane said. "I'm willing to give Brylee
all the space she needs, no problem. But at the same
time, I'm afraid I'm going to lose her for good." He
sighed, shoved a hand through his already-mussed
hair. He was still wearing yesterday's clothes, and
his whole face itched because he hadn't shaved and
the stubble crop was coming in. Little wonder Cleo
thought he looked like a long stretch of rutted road
with nothing good at the end of it—he sure as hell
felt like one. "Maybe I ought to take Nash, head for
L.A., tie up some loose ends, like selling the condo
and sorting out my stuff. Brylee's lived around here
her whole life—she has family and friends and a
thriving business to think about, while I'm the new
guy—"

Cleo rolled her eyes, but her smile was tender.
"Hold it," she said. "Before you go gallivanting off
to California, or Brylee runs off to wherever, why
don't you *talk* to the woman? You know, hammer out
some kind of a plan, agree on a course of action you
can both live with."

Zane laughed outright this time. "Why didn't I
think of that?" he teased.

"Because you've been too busy chasing your
tail, that's why," Cleo responded, with righteous
certainty. The coffeemaker had chortled through
its cycle by then, and she got up to pour some for
herself. She offered a refill to Zane by raising the

carafe, and then set it down again when he shook his head.

Privately, Zane reflected that it hadn't been his own tail he'd been chasing, but Brylee's. Well, last night he'd caught her. And he'd be a damn fool if he let her go, because it might be ten lifetimes before he met another woman like her. It might be never.

Slapping both palms down onto the surface of the card table in resolution, he scraped back his chair, stood up and headed out of the kitchen and back to his room, peeling off clothes as soon as he'd crossed the threshold, finally jarring Slim out of his deep slumber on the rug.

Never mind the dog. Right now, Zane needed a shower. He needed a shave. He needed to shape the hell up and tackle this thing like a man.

He stepped into a hot shower, soaped up, rinsed, remembered he had a horse to feed and shifted down a few gears. He'd take his time, wait for the rest of the world to open for business—and then he'd home in on Brylee Parrish like a heat-seeking missile.

THE HABIT OF going to work was so ingrained in Brylee that staying home to listen to sad music and use up facial tissue didn't even occur to her, sorrowful as she felt.

She dressed in jeans and a blue cotton shirt, brushed her hair and caught it up in a clip, forced down half a serving of fat-free yogurt standing in front of the fridge with the door hanging open, while

Snidely gobbled kibble. Soon after she'd given up on breakfast, she brushed her teeth again and set out for Décor Galore.

Snidely went with her, like always, but her loyal sidekick kept looking over at her from the passenger seat, during the brief drive, as if expecting her to do something wholly un-Brylee-like. Again.

She smiled and reached over to pat the dog's ruff. "What do you say we put Amy in charge of the company, spend some of that money we've piled up on an RV and hit the trail for a year or two, old buddy? See where the road takes us?"

Snidely gave a soft whimper at the prospect. For a dog, he could be a real stick in the mud.

Brylee felt her shoulders droop as her own enthusiasm ebbed. Leaving her business in Amy's care wasn't a problem, because she'd already scaled all those professional mountains, met every career goal, and now she desperately needed a change—a *big* one—but she wouldn't just be leaving Décor Galore, Zane Sutton and the heart-threat he represented if she took off.

She'd be leaving Walker and Casey, too. Shane and Clare and Preston and, in essence, the new niece or nephew due in six months or so.

She'd be leaving Three Trees, and Parable County, and her church, which, admittedly, she'd been attending only intermittently for the past couple of years. The people who made up the congregation mattered, though, even if some of them did still have their noses out of joint because she'd caved and agreed to hold her and Hutch's wedding in *his* hometown instead of her own.

She'd be leaving good friends, and the annual rodeo, flaking out on her promise to Casey that she'd serve on the panel charged with the responsibility of picking a queen to reign over that year's festivities.

She'd be leaving Timber Creek Ranch and her horse, Toby, and alternate Friday nights at the Boot Scoot Tavern, with Amy and the others in their close-knit group.

By the time she pulled into her parking space next to the warehouse, she was downright disenchanted with the whole idea of a lengthy road trip. Besides, she knew what Walker would say, what Casey would say, what *everybody* who mattered to her would say—that she was taking the coward's way out. She'd been burned by love once, yes, and badly. But did that mean she should let plain old, garden-variety fear dictate the course of her life?

No.

Still, what were the alternatives?

She sighed heavily, blinked back tears of frustration—and, yes, bitter sorrow—shut off the SUV and reached into the back for her purse.

She and Snidely got out of the rig and made their way to the side door, as usual, the one that opened onto the warehouse, near her office. The forklifts were running, transferring boxed merchandise from here to there. Amy was spouting orders like an army drill sergeant.

With a wan smile, Brylee ducked into her office, with Snidely, and pulled the shades on the window overlooking the main part of the warehouse, a tacit don't-bother-me gesture she rarely used. One of her most fundamental policies was, after all, accessibility to her people.

Methodical as a robot programmed to represent her normal self, Brylee put away her purse, made sure Snidely's water bowl was full and sat down decisively in front of her computer monitor.

Half an hour later, when she was mercifully embroiled in the accounting program that had been giving her fits on Friday, a knock sounded at her office door, vigorous enough to make the window blinds rattle and cause Snidely, heretofore sleeping near her feet, to lift his head and prick his ears forward.

"Go away, Amy," Brylee called, in a pleasant but firm tone. "I'm busy."

The door opened. And Zane Sutton stood in the gap, looking like three different kinds of bad news.

The echoes of last night's stellar sex marathon sparked like tiny bonfires all over Brylee's body. She opened her mouth, closed it again.

Zane stepped inside and shut the door behind him with slightly more force than necessary. "Thanks," he said acidly, "I think I *will* come in. Nice of you to ask."

Brylee's face flamed, and her throat went so tight that it hurt to swallow. Damn, but the man was hot, even in old jeans, a plain cotton shirt and barn boots.

Snidely, no longer alarmed for whatever strange reason, lowered his muzzle to his outstretched forelegs and let his eyes roll shut again.

Zane, meanwhile, stormed over to Brylee's desk, slapped both hands down hard on the surface and leaned in until their noses were nearly touching.

"What—" she managed to croak, but that was it. For the moment at least, her entire vocabulary seemed to consist of one word.

A muscle bunched in Zane's jaw, and his eyes blazed with blue heat. "I *love* you," he said.

Brylee stared at him, blinked once or twice, but since most of the English language remained just out of her reach, she said nothing. Her mind, though, was in overdrive.

Zane Sutton *loved* her? Yikes. Did she love him back? *Yes,* her soul cried out, though her tongue was still in dry dock.

"Listen up," he went on, calmer now, but his tone as matter-of-factly blunt as ever. "This is how it's going to be. We're giving this relationship six months. We'll ride horseback, go out to dinner, take in a movie once in a while—hell, we can even play miniature golf if you take the notion—but I'm not walking away from whatever's happening here, and, by God, Brylee, neither are you."

She finally found her voice, though it was little more than a squeak. "Did you just say you love me?"

His chiseled features softened almost imperceptibly, but Zane still meant business, that was just as clear. "That's what I said," he practically growled. He was still braced against her desk, his face was still a fraction of an inch, if that, away from her own. "Tell me you don't feel the same way, Brylee, that we don't have something special happening here, and I'll walk out of here and never bother you again. But that's the *only* thing that will do the trick."

Brylee stumbled over options for a moment. She couldn't tell Zane she didn't love him—because she did. She knew that, knew it with everything she was and everything she had.

This was, just as he'd said, *special*. As in, probably never-again special.

"I love you, Zane Sutton," she said. "I wish I didn't, because that would be safer and simpler, but I do."

Zane grinned then, and relief glimmered in his eyes now. "You agree to the plan, then?" he asked, after a few moments, during which the earth seemed to alter its orbit around the sun, at least for her. "Six months of getting to know each other, a normal courtship?"

Brylee swallowed, blinked back another spate of tears, happy ones this time. She nodded, managed a misty smile. "And I won't even insist on a round of miniature golf," she offered.

He threw back his head and laughed at that, and the sound was filled with joy.

"You could kiss me now," Brylee suggested.

Much to her surprise, Zane straightened his back then, eyed her solemnly and shook his head no.

"That might lead to sex," he explained gravely, and in his own sweet time.

"Well, not *instantly*," Brylee responded, in full blush, at last trusting her legs to hold her up and getting to her feet. "Not here in the office, I mean..."

When she stood facing him, a mischievous grin curling her lips at the corners, Zane took her shoulders gently but firmly into his hands.

"No sex," he repeated.

"Are you kidding?" Brylee asked, once she'd caught her breath. "Last night was—"

"Last night was all the proof either of us should need that we're good together in bed," he interrupted, serious as St. Peter guarding the pearly gates, keeping the would-be crashers at bay.

"But...this is—"

"But nothing, Brylee," Zane said. "Sex complicates things, muddies the waters. This is the most important thing that's ever happened to me, and I want to get it right."

Brylee's eyes widened. Another shift altered the terrain of her heart, which was still raw from the *last* upheaval, swapping deserts for oceans and stony canyons for green meadows.

"Okay," she said. "Okay. But it just so happens that I have a stipulation to make myself."

His grin slanted, and love danced in his eyes. "Shoot," he said, and waited to hear her terms.

She slipped both arms around his neck. "We're not sealing this deal with a handshake, mister," she informed him. Then, her lips a breath from his, she whispered a command. "Kiss me, cowboy. Right here and right now."

EPILOGUE

Six months later

THREE TREES FIRST PRESBYTERIAN church was packed with wedding guests that mid-December evening, as fat flakes of crystalline snow drifted lazily from a twilight sky.

Candles flickered, casting spells all their own, and the bridesmaids—Amy, a Madonna-pregnant Casey and Clare—wore red velvet gowns, floor-length and trimmed in white fur, with hats to match. In lieu of flowers, they carried muffs embellished with sprigs of holly, and the giant evergreen in the entryway behind Brylee and Walker perfumed the air and splashed white fairy lights over the bride's veil and white velvet gown.

Up front, with the minister and Nash and Landry, Zane looked downright elegant in his perfectly fitted tuxedo. His gaze, along with that of everyone else in the sizable church sanctuary, was riveted on Brylee, her face covered by a billowing, rhinestone-studded veil, her arm linked with Walker's.

Brylee's heart tripped into a faster beat, and happiness brimmed to overflowing within her, but she was only human, and a little trepidation, especially considering her *last* wedding, seemed natural.

The first chord of the march sounded, ringing through the familiar church.

Casey looked back, winked at Brylee and started, with remarkable grace for someone due to give birth in approximately fifteen minutes, toward the altar.

Amy followed, beaming with delight, and not just because Brylee was *finally* getting married for real. Amy had just been made acting CEO of Décor Galore, and she and Bobby were in counseling, too, with every hope of working their way back to each other.

Clare, the last to make the long, measured walk, took a moment to turn around, hug her aunt hard and whisper, "This is *it,* Brylee. *Be happy.*" With that, she, too, headed up the rose-petal-scattered aisle.

Walker looked down at Brylee, smiled and squeezed her arm. "Ready?" he asked.

Brylee drew a very deep breath, let it out slowly. "Ready," she replied.

Then it was zero hour. The moment had come.

Brylee closed her eyes briefly, offered up a silent and very fervent prayer and allowed Walker to guide her, since she was in a daze, seeing nothing but the gossamer netting of her veil and Zane, standing tall at the front of the church, waiting for her, watching her with a love she knew to be solid, true and forever.

Still, the midway point was something of a milestone, that being where Hutch had announced that he couldn't go through with the rest of the ceremony the last time around, but Zane's gaze never wavered.

He seemed to be *willing* her forward, to take her place at his side, not just for that night, but for always and always.

For Brylee, everything happened in slow motion after that.

Walker gave her away, his voice gruff with pride and love, and tears rolled down Casey's, Amy's and Clare's faces, even as the brightness of their smiles rivaled the candlelight.

Zane moved to stand beside her and subtly took her hand, gave her fingers a gentle squeeze, full of meaning. *I'm here to stay, babe. For good.*

Brylee's throat tightened and went so dry she was afraid her vows might come out as gruff croaks, but the whole ceremony went without a hitch, right down to "I now pronounce you husband and wife."

After the kiss, though, Zane broke tradition by sweeping his bride up into his arms and *carrying* her back down the aisle, while the wedding guests laughed and cried and even applauded.

The reception, over at the Somerset Inn, passed in a blur, just as the wedding had. There were photographs to pose for, and the usual, precious routine of feeding each other cake while cameras clicked all around them.

There was that first dance, with Brylee and Zane alone on the floor at first, while the band spun out the old standard "At Last," the music unfurling like bright, multicolored banners and causing more clapping, laughing and crying among the guests.

"Now can we have sex?" Brylee whispered to

Zane, a couple of hours later, when the celebration was finally beginning to wind down. Six months of close but hands-off proximity was all she could stand, and she made no secret of it, with her new husband at least.

Zane laughed. "Well, not *now*," he retorted, with a twinkle. "But the moment the door of the bridal suite closes behind us? Hold on to something, Mrs. Sutton, because I'm planning on taking you down."

Everything inside Brylee crackled at the prospect. Six months was a long, long time to abstain, but they'd managed it. Somehow.

Soon after the spicy exchange with Zane, Brylee danced with Walker, who informed her, with a sparkle in his eyes, that Casey thought she might be starting labor, so they'd be heading straight for the small hospital in Parable, in short order. Clare had her driver's license now, and she'd get herself, Shane and Preston home just fine.

Brylee said she was worried about road conditions, but Walker silenced her with a brotherly kiss on the forehead.

"This is your wedding night, sweetheart," he reminded her. "And that's all you need to think about."

The song ended, and before Walker could lead his kid sister off the dance floor, Hutch appeared in front of her, grinning. He and Kendra had a son now, in addition to their two daughters; they'd been cheek to cheek during the reception, even when the music wasn't playing. Both of them were lit from within.

Brylee smiled up into the face of the man she'd once believed she loved, and was destined to spend the rest of her life with. "Thank you," she said, very softly.

Hutch arched one eyebrow, pretending to be puzzled, but his grin was unchanged. "Told you so," he teased. "Remember?"

"I remember," Brylee confirmed, as they moved in time to the music. She was getting tired; she wanted to get out of her beautiful but cumbersome dress and especially her high heels, but this moment was almost as much a part of her wedding as the vows and the music and the flickering candlelight. "You said I'd thank you for calling it off someday, when I met the right man." She scanned the couples surrounding them, spotted Zane waltzing with Clare, his head thrown back as he laughed at something she'd said. "And you were right, Hutch. Once again, thank you."

He chuckled and kissed her forehead, much as Walker had done, and when the set was over, he squeezed her hand, grinned again and walked away.

Zane was immediately there, taking her into his arms.

"Happy?" he asked.

"Happy doesn't begin to cover it," Brylee replied, gazing up at him. "I love you, Zane Sutton."

"And I love *you,* Mrs. Sutton. Now, what do you say we sneak out of here and get started on our honeymoon?"

"Sounds like a plan to me," Brylee said, grinning.

BRYLEE WONDERED, AS Zane set her back on her feet inside the modest but beautifully decorated bridal suite, if any bride had ever gotten naked as quickly as she did.

She took a look around, saw that a cheery fire crackled on the hearth, champagne cooled in a silver bucket full of ice, fat snowflakes were falling beyond the windows, and the floor, as well as the bed, had been liberally sprinkled with all-color flower petals, bright as the pieces of a broken rainbow.

And she practically scrambled out of the magnificent dress and the heavy petticoat beneath, tore off the twinkling veil, kicked away the satin shoes that had been pinching her feet from "I do" onward and stood before her groom in silk stockings, a teddy, what was left of her summer tan, and the elegant silver cuff bracelet Zane had given her a few months before, as a sort of pre-engagement gift. The exquisitely fashioned horse-head in its center represented their shared love of animals, and, like her rings, she rarely took the piece off.

With an appreciative chuckle, Zane locked the door behind them without turning away from her. He divested her of the stockings and then the teddy, and then, hooking a finger under the knot of his string tie, he worked that loose. Pretending to remember something crucial, he snapped his fingers and said, "Damn. I forgot to bring condoms."

Brylee helped him out of the fancy tuxedo coat, the cummerbund, the snow-white shirt with its pleated front. "Good," she said, splaying her hands over his wonderful chest. "We can make a baby."

He laughed, kissed her teasingly, ran his hands over her shoulders, her breasts, the curves of her waist and hips. "That's a fine idea," he said, as though pleasantly surprised by her decision.

In truth, they'd agreed weeks ago to start their family as soon as possible, and they'd both been busy rearranging their lives, making room for each other.

Zane's house had been transformed, thanks to the amazing Cleo, probably still kicking up her flashy heels at the reception, and her devoted construction crews. Toby had already been installed in the renovated barn, along with Nash's horse, Luckdragon, and, of course, Blackjack. Nash was now Zane's legal ward, a permanent part of the family, and he seemed to love it.

Brylee, for her part, wasn't ready to sell Décor Galore outright, or to go public, but in a year, when her personal sabbatical ended, she might just do that. In the meantime, Amy was definitely rising to the challenges of running a major company, blossoming under the increased responsibility and certainly the much larger paycheck, and Brylee knew she could trust her friend not only to take care of her "baby" but cause it to thrive.

Zane kissed away every coherent thought in Brylee's head over the next few minutes and, somehow, they wound up lying on the fake-fur rug in front of the fireplace, Zane as naked as she was.

Brylee ached to be joined to him again, and she

knew Zane felt the same way, but his damnable self-control was the stuff of legends—very private ones, of course.

He still knew where to touch her, where to kiss, where to nibble or use his tongue, and in no time at all, he'd transformed her into that fitful she-wolf she'd been before, moaning and writhing with primitive need.

Finally, in complete desperation, Brylee locked her fingers in his love-tousled hair and pulled him into another kiss, this one so steamy, so commanding, that Zane was doing all the groaning.

"Inside me," she rasped, when the need for air forced them to pause. "I need you *inside me,* Zane."

He took her quickly, with a hard, deep thrust, and if she hadn't been so busy flexing with the instant climax that resulted, she might have been surprised, given the way he'd drawn things out that night after the barbecue at Hutch and Kendra's.

But the sweet violence seizing and then reseizing, in the innermost parts of her kept her fully occupied.

Finally, with a sigh, she was satisfied—only to feel yet another release building inside her, more slowly this time, and even more treacherously, deliciously powerful.

Zane, meanwhile, moved upon her, inside her, at an exquisitely slow pace. He told her he loved her, that she was beautiful, that she was *his* now, as much as she was her own.

Could love break a heart?

Yes, Brylee concluded breathlessly, moving in

rhythm with her husband, climbing, climbing, arching her back to take him deeper, not only into her body, but into her soul itself. Love was breaking *her* heart, in those glorious moments of fast-approaching ecstasy, breaking it *open,* enlarging the mysterious interior and flooding it with light, making room for Zane and for their children, and for their children's children.

With a lusty shout, Brylee gave herself to her man, completely.

And she received all of Zane Sutton in return. For keeps.

* * * * *

Read on for a sneak peek at Linda Lael Miller's
The Yankee Widow, *a richly layered, emotional novel about one woman's courage and the choices she must make in the face of a dangerous war.*

ONE

JACOB

The first minié ball ripped into Corporal Jacob Hammond's left hand, the second, his right knee, each strike leaving a ragged gash in its wake; another slashed through his right thigh an instant later, and then he lost count.

A coppery crimson mist rained down on Jacob as he bent double, then plunged, with what felt like a strange, protracted grace, toward the broken ground. On the way down, he noted the bent and broken grass, shimmering with fresh blood, the deep gouges left by cannon balls and boot heels and the lunging hooves of panicked horses.

A peculiar clarity overtook Jacob in those moments between life as he'd always known it and another way of being, already inevitable. The boundaries of his mind seemed to expand beyond skull and skin, rushing outward at a dizzying speed, hurtling in all directions, rising past the treetops, past the sky, past the far borders of the cosmos itself.

For an instant, he understood everything, every mystery, every false thing, every truth.

He felt no emotion, no joy or sorrow.

There was peace, though, and the sweet promise of oblivion.

Then, with a wrench so swift and so violent that it sickened his very soul, Jacob was back inside himself, a prisoner behind fractured bars of bone. The flash of extraordinary knowledge was gone, a fact that saddened Jacob more deeply than the likelihood of death, but some small portion of the experience remained, an ability to think without obstruction, to see his past as vividly as his present, to envision all that was around him, as if from a great height.

Blessedly, there was no pain, though he knew that would surely come, provided he remained alive long enough to receive it.

Something resembling bitter amusement overtook Jacob then; he realized that, unaccountably, he hadn't expected to be struck down on this savage battlefield or any other. Never mind the unspeakable carnage he'd witnessed since his enlistment in Mr. Lincoln's grand army; with the hubris of youth, he had believed himself invincible.

He had assumed that the men in blue fought on the side of righteousness, committed to the task of mending a sundered nation, restoring it to its former whole. For all its faults, the United States of America was the most promising nation ever to arise from the old order of kings and despots; even now, Jacob was convinced that, whatever the cost, it must not be allowed to fail.

He had been willing to pay that price, was willing still.

Why then was he shocked, nay *affronted*, to find that the bill had come due, in full, and that his own blood and breath, his very substance, was the currency required?

Because, he thought, shame washing over him, he had been willing to die only in *theory*. Out of vanity or ignorance or pure naivety, he had somehow, without being aware of it, declared himself exempt.

Well, there it was. Jacob Hammond, husband of Caroline, father of Rachel, son and grandson and great-grandson of sturdy, high-minded folk, present owner of a modest but fertile farm a few miles south of the small but industrious township of Gettysburg, Pennsylvania, was no more vital to the noble pursuit of lasting justice for all than any other man was. In any larger scheme, neither his life nor his death would truly matter.

He knew his wounds were grievous, that a quick death was the most merciful fate he could hope for, and still he wanted so much to live, to return to his beloved wife, to his child, to the modest but thriving farm that shone in his memory, fairer than heaven itself.

The sacrifice was terrible, unspeakably so.

Was it worthwhile?

Jacob pondered that question, decided that, for him, it was.

The country had splintered, bone and blood, perhaps never to be mended. It was far from the ideal set forth by those bold intellects who had gathered in Philadelphia back in '76, in a blaze of fractious brilliance.

Somehow, in the sweltering heat of a Pennsylvania summer, and yet no doubt cooler than their collective temperaments—out of dissent, out of greed and ill humor and stubbornness and all manner of other mortal failings—these remarkable men had forged a philosophy, a glorious vision of what a nation, a people, could become.

To Jacob, bleeding into the ground, in the midst of an endless war, that goal seemed more distant than ever, hopeless, even impossible.

And still, had he been able, he would have fought on, died not just once but a thousand times, not for the country as it was, but for the noble, sacred objective upon which it had been founded—liberty and justice for all.

Whatever the cost, the Union must hold together.

So much hung in the balance, so very much. Not only the hope and valor of those who had gone before, but the freedom, perhaps the very existence, of those yet to be born.

In solidarity, the *United* States could be a force for good in a hungry, desperate world. Torn asunder, it would be ineffectual, two bickering factions, bound to divide into still smaller and weaker fragments over time, too busy posturing and rattling sabers to meet the demands of a fragile future or to stand in the way of new tyrannies, certain to arise.

We hold these truths to be self-evident, that all men are created equal...

That belief, inspiring as it was, had chafed the consciences of thinking people since it flowed from the nib of Thomas Jefferson's pen, as well it should have.

Like many of his contemporaries, the great man himself had kept slaves.

The inherent contradiction could not have escaped a mind as luminous as Jefferson's, nor could the subtle difference in phrasing as he wrote those momentous words. He had not written that *some* men were created equal, but that *all* men were.

Strenuous opposition to the indefensible institution of slavery had been raised, of course, but in the end, expediency prevailed. Representatives of the Southern colonies, with their vast fields of cotton and other valuable crops, would face certain ruin without their millions of unpaid laborers. They had refused to join in the rebellion against Great Britain if slavery was outlawed.

Since the effort would surely fail without them, the concession had been made.

But what was the value of freedom if it remained the province of white men while excluding all others?

Alas, the question was too big for a man in the process of dying, alone and far from home.

There was nothing to be done, save letting go. In

the deepest recesses of his heart, in that calm place beyond fear and pain and fury, Jacob prayed that the will of God be done, in this matter of countries and wars.

Then, with that petition made, he raised another, more selfish one. *Watch over my beloved wife, our little daughter, and Enoch, our trusted friend. Keep them all safe and well.*

The request was simple, one of millions like it, no doubt, rising to the ears of the Creator on wings of desperation and sorrow, and there was no Road-to-Damascus moment for Jacob, just the ground-shaking roar of battle all around. But even in the midst of thundering cannon, the sharp reports of carbines and the fiery blast of muskets, the clanking of swords and the shrill shrieks of men and horses, he found a certain consolation.

A whisper of hope. Perhaps he'd been heard.

He began to drift then, back and forth between darkness and light, fear and oblivion. When he surfaced, the pain was waiting, like a specter hovering over him, ready to descend, settle upon him, crush him beneath its weight.

Consequently, Jacob again took refuge deep inside, where it could not yet reach.

Hours passed, perhaps days; he had no way of knowing.

Eventually, because life is persistent even in the face of hopelessness and unrelenting agony, the hiding place within became less accessible. During those intervals, pain played with him, like a cat with a mouse. Smoke burned his eyes, which he couldn't close; it climbed, stinging, into his nostrils, chafed his throat raw. He was thirsty, so thirsty. He felt as dry as last year's corn husks, imagining his life's blood seeping, however slowly, into the ravaged earth.

In order to bear his suffering, Jacob thought about home, conjured up vivid images of Caroline, quietly pretty, more prone to laughter than to tears, courageous as any man he'd ever known. She loved him, he knew that, and his heart rested safely with her. She had always accepted his attentions in the marriage bed with good-humored acquiescence, though perhaps not with a passion to equal his own, and while he told himself this was the way of a good woman, he sometimes wondered if, to Caroline, lovemaking was simply another wifely chore. Yet another duty to perform, after a day of washing and ironing, cooking and sewing, tending the vegetable garden behind the kitchen house and picking apples and pears, apricots and peaches in the orchards when the fruit ripened.

Jacob was not the sort of husband who took his wife's efforts for granted. Whenever possible, he had lent her a willing hand, little concerned with what constituted "women's work"; he hadn't been above changing a diaper, gathering eggs or hanging out the wash.

No, work was work, whether it fell to a man or a woman to do it. As a farmer, though, he'd had fields to plow and harvest, livestock to tend, tools and wagons to maintain, and even with Enoch's help, getting all that done took every scrap of daylight and, often, part of the night.

Oh, but Caroline. Caroline.

She was a pure wonder to Jacob. Her price, if one could've been set, was indeed far above rubies; she might have been the model for the woman described in the thirty-first chapter of Proverbs. She was certainly virtuous, and she looked "well to the ways of her household, and ate not of the bread of idleness." Moreover, she stretched "out her hand to the poor" and reached "out forth her hands to the needy."

Caroline not only met the many demands of marriage and motherhood, she was an active member of the local Ladies' Aid Society. These women were among her closest friends, all of them determined to serve the Union cause and to sustain and encourage the soldiers who fought for it.

She had written to him about how they gathered regularly in each other's homes, these warriors on the home front, to make quilts and shirts, mend blankets and knit stockings, bottle fruits and vegetables and other foodstuffs, write letters to lonesome souls in faraway army camps, and to plan campaigns and strategies for the future.

They ventured out into the community, too, cajoling friends, neighbors and strangers alike, willing to beg and borrow, if not steal, whatever items a soldier might find useful—headache powders and other expedient remedies from the druggists, soap and coffee beans and homemade balm for chapped lips and blistered heels from anyone who had them to give.

Gettysburg was a thriving market town, with many prosperous residents and, in the early days of the war, the donations were generous. Merchants gave goods by the crateful, flour and dried beans by the barrel. Farmers brought their bumper crops of potatoes, squash, carrots, onions and turnips to the ladies by the wagonload, often with great slabs of salt pork and crocks brimming with fresh eggs, preserved in water-glass.

He has seen for himself when he was back home on brief leave how all this bounty was carefully sorted and cataloged by the ladies of Gettysburg before being sent on, mostly via the railroads, to a distribution center in Baltimore, from which it would be dispersed to battlefronts and hospitals all over the North.

Of course, as the war dragged on, and the inevitable shortages arose, the flood of goodwill had dwindled considerably, but Jacob knew from Caroline's letters that scarcity only redoubled the determination of petticoat generals such as his wife. In her words, they simply "pushed up their sleeves and worked a little harder."

Caroline was no stranger to hardship, and neither were most of her friends.

She was accustomed to enduring trouble, disappointment and heartache, having had more than her fair portion of all those things, and she bore up with remarkable stoicism, the current state of the nation notwithstanding.

The work of farming was fraught with perils;

crops could be destroyed by hail or drought or a freak frost, wildfires and plagues of grasshoppers, or made worthless by a drop in prices.

He and Caroline had grappled with several disasters and come through, although not without struggle.

Still, life had been harder on Caroline than it was on many folks, right from the first.

She'd been only four or five years old when a fever struck, sudden and vicious, carrying off her mother, father and younger sister in the space of a single day. Caroline, too, had fallen ill, but somehow she'd pulled through.

Her paternal grandparents, Doc Prescott and his wife, Geneva, had taken her in and looked after her with all tenderness, but she'd been sickly for some time, and grieved sorely for her mama and papa and beloved little sister.

More losses followed; her grandfather had died recently, and she'd mourned at the gravesides of two of her dearest friends in as many months, both of whom had died in childbirth, along with their infants.

And then, before their precious Rachel, there had been the lostbabies, his and Caroline's, the first midway through her pregnancy, a wizened little creature, bloody and blue, carried away in a basin to be buried, the second, a boy, carried to term but stillborn.

It had been Enoch, God bless him, who had seen to those impossibly small bodies, laid both little ones to rest in the small family cemetery, said words over them, and wept as if they'd been of his own flesh. Later, he'd carved markers for them, sturdy wooden crosses, less than a foot high, with no names or dates.

Now, with his own death so close, Jacob wished Caroline hadn't tried to be so strong or worked so hard to hide her grief from him, from everyone, holding it close and guarding it like the darkest of secrets. If only he'd sought her out and taken her into his arms and held her fast, held her until they could both let go and weep out their sorrows together.

Alas, Jacob's own grief had been a sharp and frozen thing, locked inside him.

There was no going back now, and regret would only sap what little strength that remained to him.

He took sanctuary in the remembrance of happier things, finding brief shelter from the gathering storm of fresh pain. In his mind's eye, he saw little Rachel running to meet him when he came in from the fields at the end of the day, dirty and sweat-soaked and exhausted himself, while his daughter was as fresh as the wildflowers flourishing alongside the creek in summer. Clad in one of her tiny calico dresses, face and hands scrubbed, she raced toward him, laughing, her arms open wide, her fair pigtails flying, her bright blue eyes shining with delighted welcome.

Dear God, Jacob thought, what he wouldn't give to be back there, sweeping that precious child up into his arms, setting her on his shoulder or swinging her around and around until they were both dizzy.

It was then that the longing for his wife and daughter grew too great, and Jacob turned his memory to sun-splashed fields, flourishing and green, to sparkling streams thick with fish. In his imagination, he stood beside his steadfast friend Enoch, once more, both of them as close as brothers gratified by the sight of a heavy crop, by the knowledge that, this year anyway, their hard work would bring a reward.

"God has blessed our efforts," Jacob would say, quietly and with awe, for he had believed the world to be an essentially good place then. War and all its brutalities were merely tales told in books, or passed down the generations by old men.

He saw Enoch as clearly as if he'd been right there on the battlefield with him, instead of miles and miles away. He stood vivid in Jacob's recollection, the black man his father had bought, freed, then hired in his own right to work on the family farm years back, grinning as he replied, "Well, I don't see how the Good Lord ought to get *all* the credit. He might send the sunshine and the rain, but far as I can reckon, He ain't much for plowin'

Jacob invariably laughed, no matter how threadbare the joke, would have laughed now, too, if he'd had the breath for it.

He barely noticed that the terrible din of battle had faded to the feeble moans and low cries of other men, Rebels and Union men alike, fallen and left behind in the acrid urgency of combat.

He dreamed—or at least, he *thought* he was dreaming—of the heaven he'd heard about all his life, for he came from a long line of churchgoing folk.

He saw the towering gates, studded with pearls and precious gems, standing open before him.

He caught a glimpse of the fabled streets of gold, too, and although he saw no angels and no long-departed loved ones waiting to welcome him into whatever celestial realm they now occupied, he heard music, almost too beautiful to be endured. He looked up, saw a dazzling sky, not merely blue, but somehow *woven*, a shimmering tapestry of innumerable colors, each one brilliant, some familiar and some beyond his powers of description.

He hesitated, not from fear, for surely there could be no danger here, but because he knew that once he passed through this particular gateway, there would be no turning back.

Perhaps it was blasphemy, but Jacob's heart swelled with a poignant longing for a lesser heaven, another, humbler paradise, where the gates and fences were made of hand-hewn wood or plain stones gathered in fields, and the roads were winding trails of dust and dirt, rutted by wagon wheels, deep, glittering snows and heavy rain.

Had it been in his power, and he knew it wasn't, he would have traded eternity in that place of ineffable peace and beauty for a single, blessedly ordinary day at home, waking up beside Caroline in their feather bed, teasing her until she blushed, or watching, stricken by the love of her, as she made breakfast in the kitchen house on an ordinary morning.

Suddenly, the sweet visions were gone.

Jacob heard sounds, muffled but distinct. Men, horses, a few wagons.

Then nothing.

Perhaps he was imagining things. Suffering hallucinations.

He waited, listening, his eyes unblinking, dry and rigid in their sockets, stinging with sweat and grit and congealed blood.

Fear burned in his veins as those first minutes after he was wounded came back. He recalled the shock of his flesh tearing, as though it were happening all over again, a waking nightmare of friend and foe alike streaming past, shouting, shooting, bleeding, stepping over him and on him. He recalled the hooves of horses, churning up patches on the ground within inches of where he lay.

Jacob forced himself to concentrate. Although he couldn't see the sky, he knew by the light that the day was waning.

Was he alone?

The noises came again, but they were more distant now. Perhaps the party of men and horses had passed him by.

The prospect was a bleak one, filling Jacob with quiet despair. Even a band of Rebs would've been preferable to lying helplessly in his own gore, wondering when the rats and crows would come to feast on him.

An enemy bullet or the swift mercy of a bayonet would be infinitely better.

Hope stirred briefly when a Federal soldier appeared in his line of vision, as though emerging from a void. At first, Jacob wasn't sure the other man was real.

He tried to speak, or make the slightest move, indicating that he was alive and in need of help, but he could do neither.

The soldier approached, crouching beside him, and one glimpse of his filthy, beard-stubbled face, hard with cruelty, put an end to Jacob's illusions. The man rolled him roughly onto his back, with no effort to search for a pulse or any other sign of life. Instead, he began rifling through Jacob's pockets, muttering under his breath, helping himself to his watch and what little money he carried, since most of his pay went to Caroline.

Jacob felt outrage, but he was still helpless. All he could do was watch as the other man grabbed his rucksack, fumbled to lift the canvas flap and reach inside.

Finally, the bummer, as thieves and stragglers and deserters were called, gave in to frustration and dumped Jacob's belongings onto the ground, pawing through them.

Look at me, Jacob thought. *I am alive. I wear the same uniform as you do.*

The scavenger did not respond, of course. Did not allow his gaze to rest upon Jacob's face, where he might have seen awareness.

The voices, the trampling hooves, the springless wagons drew closer.

The man cursed, frantic now. He found Jacob's

battered Bible and flung it aside in disgusted haste, its thin pages fluttering as it fell, like a bird with a broken wing. The standard-issue tin cup, plate and utensils soon followed, but the thieving bastard stilled when he found the packet of letters, all from Caroline. Perhaps believing he might find something of value in one or more of them, he shoved them into his own rucksack.

Jacob grieved for those letters, but there was nothing he could do.

Except listen.

Yes, he decided. Someone was coming, a small company of riders.

The thief grew more agitated, looked over one shoulder, and then turned back to his plundering, feverish now, but too greedy to flee.

At last he settled on the one object Jacob cherished as much as Caroline's letters—a small leather case with tarnished brass hinges and a delicate clasp.

He saw wicked interest flash in the man's eyes, as he fumbled open the case and saw the tintypes inside, one of Caroline and Jacob, taken on their wedding day, looking traditionally somber in their finest garb, the other of Caroline, with an infant Rachel in her arms, the child resplendent in a tiny, lace-trimmed christening gown and matching bonnet.

No, Jacob cried inwardly, hating his helplessness.

"Well, now," the man murmured. "Ain't this a pretty little family? Maybe I'll just look them up sometime, offer my condolences."

Had he been able, Jacob would have killed the

bummer in that moment, throttled the life out of him with his bare hands, and never regretted the act. Although he struggled with all his might, trying to gather the last shreds of his strength, the effort proved useless.

It was the worst kind of agony, imagining this man reading the letters, noting the return address on each and every envelope, seeking Caroline and Rachel out, offering a pretense of sympathy.

Taking advantage.

And Jacob could do nothing to stop him, nothing to protect his wife and daughter from this monster or others like him, the renegades, the enemies of decency and innocence in all their forms.

The bummer snapped the case closed, put it and the letters inside the rucksack and grabbed it, ready to flee.

It was then that a figure loomed behind him, a gray shadow of a man, who planted the sole of one boot squarely in the center of the thief's back, and sent him sprawling across Jacob's inert frame.

The pain was instant, throbbing in every bone and muscle of Jacob's body.

"Stealing from a dead man," the shadow said, standing tall, his buttery-smooth drawl laced with contempt. "That's low, even for a Yank."

The bummer scrambled to his feet, groped for something, probably his rifle, and paled when he came up empty. Most likely, he'd dropped the weapon in his eagerness to rob one of his own men.

"I ought to run you through with this fine steel

sword of mine, Billy," the other man mused idly. He must have ridden ahead of his detachment, dismounted nearby and moved silently through the scattered bodies. "After all, this is a *war,* now, isn't it? And you are my foe, as surely as I'm yours."

Jacob's vision, unclear to begin with, blurred further, and there was a pounding in his ears, but he could make out the contours of the two men, now standing on either side of him, and he caught the faint murmur of their words.

"You don't want to kill me, Johnny," the thief reasoned, with a note of anxious congeniality in his voice, raising both palms as if in surrender. "It wouldn't be honorable, with us Union boys at a plain disadvantage." He drew in a strange, swift whistle of a breath. "Anyhow, I wasn't hurtin' nobody. Just makin' good use of things this poor fella has no need of, bein' dead and all."

By now, Jacob was aware of men and horses all around, although there was no cannon fire, no shouting, no sharp report of rifles.

"You want these men to see you murder an unarmed man?" wheedled the man addressed as Billy. "Where I come from, you'd be hanged for that. It's a war crime, ain't it?"

"We're not 'where you come from,'" answered Johnny coolly. The bayonet affixed to the barrel of his carbine glinted in the lingering smoke and the dust raised by the horses. "This is Virginia," he went on, with a note of fierce reverence. "And you are an intruder here, sir."

Billy—the universal name for all Union soldiers, as Johnny was for their Confederate counterparts—spat, foolhardy in his fear. "I reckon the rules are about the same, though, whether North or South," he ventured. Even Jacob, from his limited vantage point, saw the terror behind all that bluster. "Fancy man like you—an officer, at that—must know how it is. Even if you don't hang for killin' with no cause, you'll be court-martialed for sure, once your superiors catch wind of what you done. And that's bound to leave a stain on your high and mighty reputation as a Southern gentleman, ain't it? Just you think, *sir*, of the shame all those well-mannered folks back home on the old plantation will have to contend with, and it'll be on *your* account."

A slow, untroubled grin took shape on the Confederate captain's soot-smudged face. His gray uniform was torn and soiled, the brass of his buttons and insignia dull, and his boots were scuffed, but even Jacob, with his sight impaired, could see that his dignity was inborn, as much a part of him as the color of his eyes.

"It might be worth hanging for," he replied, almost cordially, like a man debating some minor point of military ethics at an elegant dinner party far removed from the sound and fury of war. "The pleasure of killing a latrine rat such as yourself, that is. As for these men, most of them are under my command, as it happens. Well, they've seen their friends and cousins and brothers skewered by Yankee bayonets and blown to fragments by their cannon. Just yesterday, in fact, they saw General Jackson…relieved of an arm." At this, the captain paused, swallowed once. "Most likely, they'd raise a cheer as *you* fell."

Dimly, Jacob sensed Billy Yank's nervous bravado. Under any other circumstances, he might have been amused by the fellow's demeanor, but he could feel himself retreating further and further into the darkness of approaching death, and there was no room in him for frivolous emotions.

"Now, that just ain't Christian," protested Billy, conveniently overlooking his own moral lapse.

The captain gave a raspy laugh, painful to hear, and shook his head. "A fine sentiment, coming from the likes of you." In the next moment, his face hardened, aristocratic even beneath its layers of dried sweat and dirt. He turned slightly, keeping one eye on his prisoner, and shouted a summons into the rapidly narrowing nothingness surrounding the three of them.

Several men hurried over, although they were invisible to Jacob, and the sounds they made were faint.

"Get this piece of dung out of my sight before I pierce his worthless flesh with my sword for the pure pleasure of watching him bleed," the officer ordered. "He is a disgrace, even to *that* uniform."

There were words of reply, though Jacob couldn't make them out, and Jacob sensed a scuffle as the thief resisted capture, a modern-day Judas, bleating a traitor's promises, willing to betray men who'd fought alongside him.

Jacob waited, expecting the gentleman officer to follow his men, go on about his business of overseeing the capture of wounded bluecoats, the recovery of his own troops, alive and dead.

Instead, the captain crouched, as the thief had done earlier. He took up Jacob's rucksack that Billy had been forced to leave behind, rummaged within it, produced the packet of letters and the leather case containing the likenesses of Jacob's beloved wife and daughter. He opened it, examined the images inside, smiled sadly.

Then he tucked the items inside Jacob's bloody coat, paused as though startled, and looked directly into his eyes.

"My God," he said, under his breath. "You're alive."

Jacob could not acknowledge the remark verbally, but he felt a tear trickle over his left temple, into his hair, and that, apparently, was confirmation enough for the Confederate captain.

Now, Jacob thought, he would be shot, put out of his misery like an injured horse. And he would welcome the release.

Instead, very quietly, the captain said. "Hold on, Yank. You'll be found soon." He paused, looking serious. "And if you should happen to encounter a certain Union quartermaster by the name of Rogan McBride, somewhere along your journey, I would be obliged if you'd tell him Bridger Winslow sends his best regards."

Jacob doubted he'd live long enough to get the

chance to do as Winslow asked, but he marked the names carefully in his mind, just the same.

Another voice spoke then. "This somebody you know, Captain?" a soldier asked, with concern and a measure of sympathy. It wasn't uncommon on either side, after all, to find a friend or a relative among enemy casualties, since the battle lines often cut across towns, churches and supper tables.

"No," the captain replied gruffly. "Just another dead Federal." A pause. "Get on with your business, Simms. We might have the bluecoats under our heel for the moment, but you can be sure they'll be back to bury what remains they can't gather up and haul away now. Better if we don't risk a skirmish after a day of hard fighting."

"Yes, sir," Simms replied sadly. "The men are low in spirit, now that General Jackson has been struck down."

"Yes," the captain answered. Angry sorrow flashed in his eyes. "By his own troops," he added bitterly, speaking so quietly that Jacob wondered if Simms had even heard.

Jacob sensed the other man's departure. The captain lingered, taking his canteen from his belt, loosening the cap a little with a deft motion of one hand, leaving the container within Jacob's reach. The gesture was most likely a futile one, since Jacob couldn't use his hands, but it was an act of kindness, all the same. An affirmation of the possibility, however remote, that Jacob might somehow survive.

Winslow rose to his full height, regarded Jacob solemnly, then slowly walked away.

Jacob soon lost consciousness again, waking briefly now and then, surprised to find himself not only still among the living, but unmolested by vermin. When alert, he lay looking up at the night sky, steeped in the profound silence of the dead, one more body among dozens, if not hundreds, scattered across the blood-soaked grass.

Sometime the next morning, or perhaps the morning after that, wagons came again, and grim-faced Union soldiers stacked the bodies like cordwood, one on top of another. They were fretful, these battle-weary men, anxious to complete their dismal mission and get back behind the Union lines, where there was at least a semblance of safety.

Jacob, mute and motionless, was among the last to be taken up, grasped roughly by two men in dusty blue coats.

The pain was so sudden, so excruciating that finally, *finally*, he managed a low, guttural cry.

The soldier supporting his legs, little more than a boy, with blemished skin and not even the prospect of a beard, gasped. "This fella's still with us," he said, and he looked so startled, so horrified and pale that Jacob feared the kid would swoon, letting his burden drop.

"Well," said the other man, gruffly cheerful, "I'll be a son of a bitch if Johnny didn't leave a few breathin' this time around."

The boy recovered enough to turn his head and

spit. To Jacob's relief, the boy remained upright, his grasp firm. "A few," he agreed grudgingly. "And every one of them better off dead."

The darkness returned then, enfolding Jacob like the embrace of a sea siren, pulling him under.

Don't miss The Yankee Widow
by #1 New York Times *bestselling author*
Linda Lael Miller, available now.

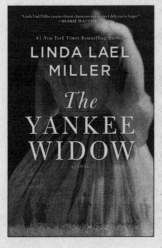

LINDA
LAEL MILLER

The daughter of a town marshal, Linda Lael Miller is a *New York Times* bestselling author of more than one hundred historical and contemporary novels. Linda's books have hit #1 on the *New York Times* bestseller list seven times. Raised in Northport, Washington, she now lives in Spokane.

The "First Lady of the West," #1 *New York Times* bestselling author Linda Lael Miller, cordially invites you to Parable, Montana— where love awaits

Wedding bells are ringing in Parable, Montana, but Brylee Parrish hasn't enjoyed the sound since being jilted at the altar by Hutch Carmody. She's over Hutch now, and running a multimillion-dollar business is challenging enough for this country gal. So she *should* avoid falling head over boot heels for A-list actor Zane Sutton. He's come home to his rodeo roots, but Hollywood lured him away once and just might again. Yet everything about him, from his easy charm to his concern for his young half brother, seems too genuine to resist...

Zane didn't come to Parable for love—but count on a spirited woman to change a jaded cowboy's mind. Problem is, Brylee's not convinced he's here to stay. Good thing he's determined to prove to her, kiss by kiss, that she's meant to be his bride.

www.LindaLaelMiller.com

$8.99 U.S./$11.99 CAN.

ISBN-13: 978-1-335-99396-0

50899

9 781335 993960

EAN

HQN™

HQNBooks.com